THE LIGHT OF THE SPELL

BOOK ONE

THE LIGHT OF THE SPELL

BOOK ONE

This book is a work of fiction. Names, characters, places, and incidents are the product of the author's imagination or are used fictitiously. Any resemblance to actual events, locales, or persons, living or dead, is coincidental.

Cover Design: Enchanted Ink Publishing
Map Design: inkarnate.com
Editing: Enchanted Ink Publishing
Book Design and Typesetting: Enchanted Ink Publishing

The text type was set in Adobe Caslon Pro

ISBN: 979-8-9914789-1-5 (E-book)
ISBN: 979-8-9914789-0-8 (Paperback)

Thank you for your support of the author's rights.

WWW.NCHARPER.COM

N
W
E
S
THE
MOUNTAIN TOWERS
ASTER
LOWER VIL
WHEATRICH
ABAGAIL
ARNICA
BLACK RIVERS
ARNICA STATION
CENTRAL STATION
LITHOPS ISLAND
MARKET RO
GREATER BAY
BAY CITY
R
C
FENNEL
CHURCH OF ALCHEMY
CLOVE
BUR
MOUN
LOSTMERE
MEADOWSWEET VALLEY
RIVER REALM
HARR
HAUNTED SWAMP
N
VALERIAN
SOUTH PORT
LESSER BAY
SOUTHERN VALERIAN

LD OF YU'E
REALM OF ICE AND SAGE
THE OTHER
BORDER PORT
ECHINACEA ISLANDS
DENDROS
SMITH TOWN
HINDLEY
NORTHMOST STATION
LAVENDER WILDLANDS
LAVENDER BAY
LAVENDER PORT
THE ISLE
SOUTHERN BRIDGE
HEATHER STATION
TOP POINT
LINCOLN
HEATHER
BRITTLEBUSH WASTELANDS

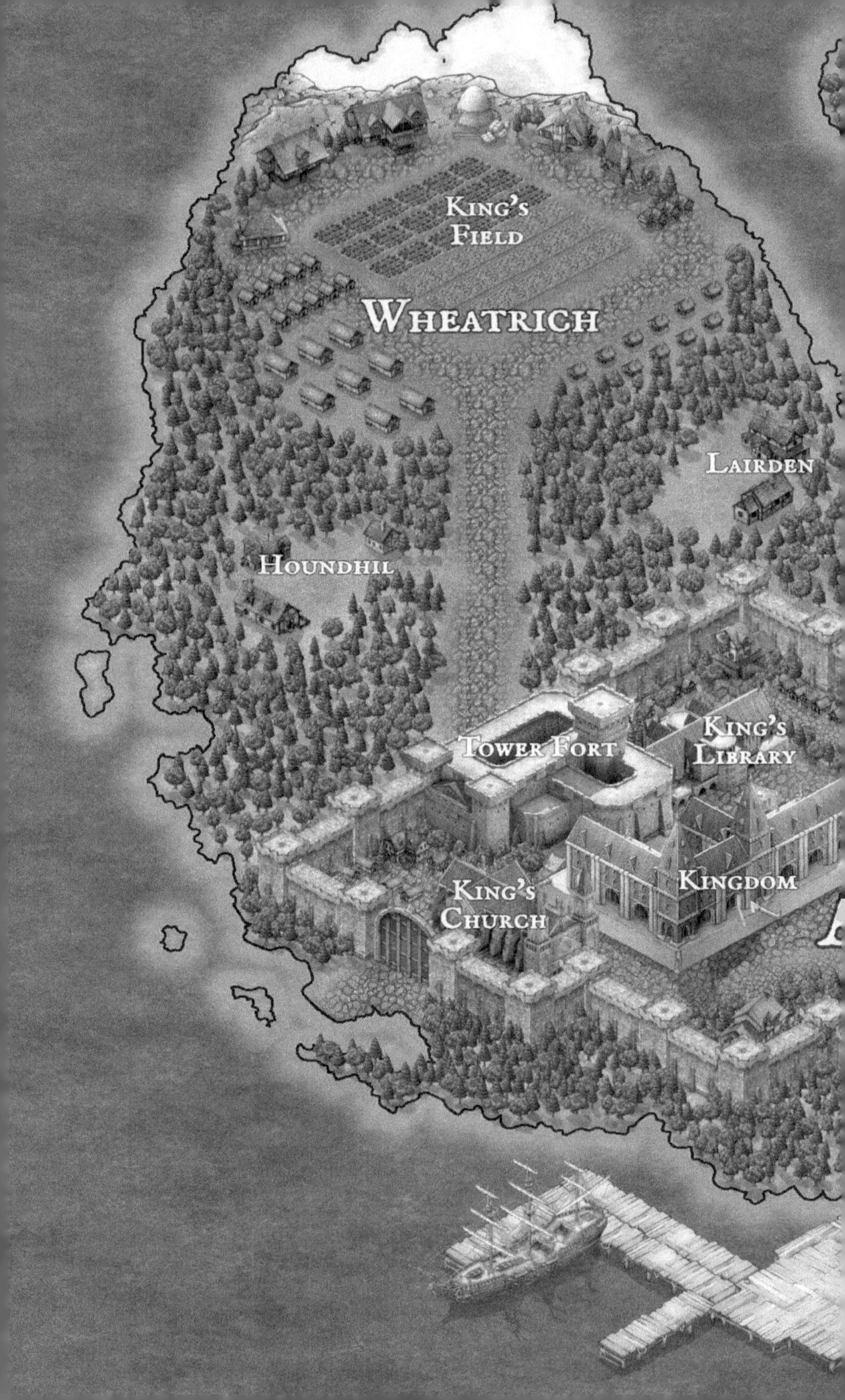

KING'S FIELD
WHEATRICH
LAIRDEN
HOUNDHIL
TOWER FORT
KING'S LIBRARY
KING'S CHURCH
KINGDOM

ABAGAIL
NICA
BLACK
RIVERS
BAY CITY

LIONEL'S HOUSE
GUARDSMAN POST
BLACK RIVERS LINHAY
SOU
KINGDOM BRIDGE
KING'S LIAISON
ARNICA

ABAGAIL
NORTHERN MARKET
LACK RIVERS
ARNICA STATION
DREG'S PUB
IAN'S BUTCHER & GROCERY
BLACK RIVERS LIBRARY
MARKET
TOWN WELL
COBBLER
TANNER HOUSE
VISITOR'S INN
TAILOR & SALON
MARKET BRIDGE
IA'S AKERY
NUWA DESIGNS
TOWN HALL

Lionel's House

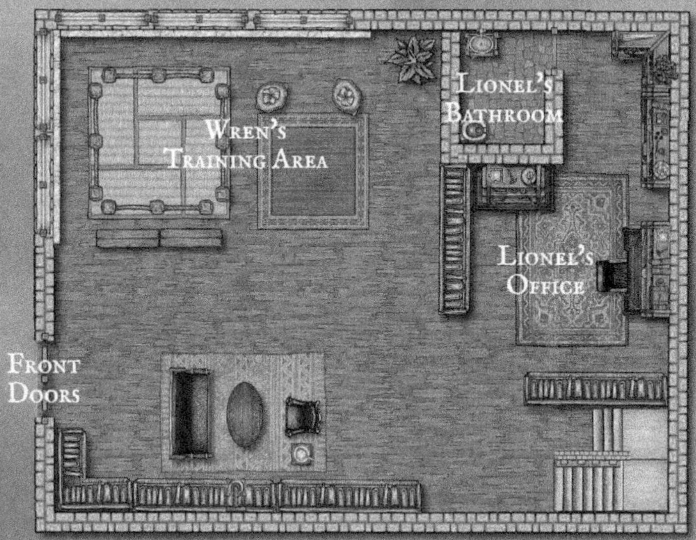

Ground Floor

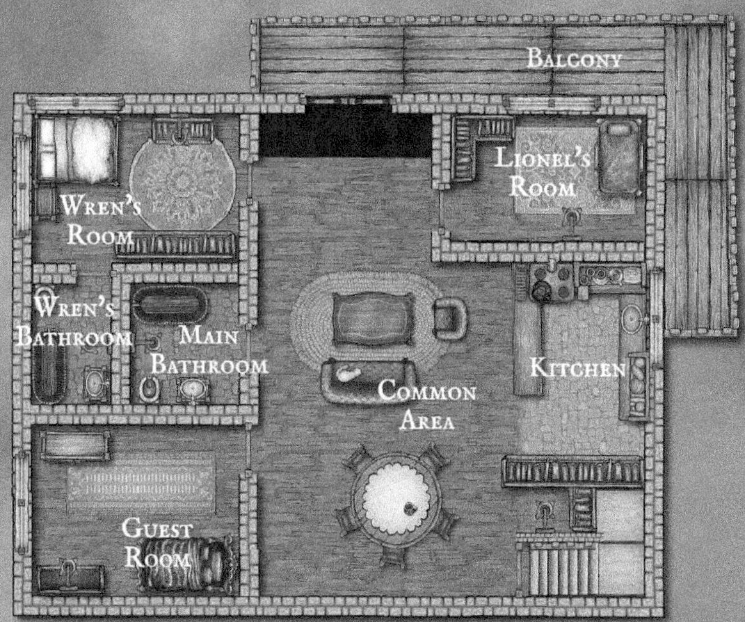

Second Floor

N.C. HARPER

THE **LIGHT** OF THE

SPELL

BOOK ONE

PROLOGUE

*"The only thing necessary for the triumph of
evil is for good men to do nothing."*

Edmund Burke

S DUSK CREPT IN, THE LAST WAVE OF BUSINESS throughout the market was in full swing. Townspeople tried to collect the last of their shopping before they headed home for the evening. Children played off their excess energy by chasing each other with sticks, pretending they were swords. Others busied themselves with some other form of mischief.

Pickpockets, grifters, and shoplifters *thrived* at dusk.

A large boar shifted on its hind legs and grunted.

"I'm tellin' ya, ther's not a better price here." He spoke gruffly.

"But it's puny!" a young woman argued. "This radish is bottom of the barrel, at best! The poor thing is emaciated."

"If ya ain't buyin', then leave, girly." His nostrils flared. "It's almost dark an' I wanna go ta the pub!"

"But—" she started but was halted.

"Juss take it!" the boar snarled loudly. "Take it an' go!"

Two hoofs pushed her away roughly.

She stumbled slightly but remained upright.

"Go get your stupid drink, Boris. You clearly had a long day." The young woman spoke sweetly, but a darkness loomed behind her eyes.

He growled in response and slammed the sliding door to his shop closed with fervor.

"Boars are notoriously short-tempered, Bianca. I don't know why you pick a fight with Boris every time you shop here."

"Well, it's all about portrayal," Bianca began. "You see this radish? Not the best-looking thing around. But it's still good to use in a stew."

"It's just a radish."

"It's the *principle* of the radish."

". . . Oh . . ."

"Just think about it for a little bit." Bianca sighed and shook her head. "It'll come to you . . . eventually."

The streets steadily fell under the shadow of the encroaching night as the pair walked in step with each other.

"I still don't get it, Bianca," the taller woman muttered softly. She risked a peek at her companion and looked immediately forward again when she had been caught.

"Torrie, if you wait until shopkeepers want to close up, they'll do anything to get rid of you. You need to start small before you can start trying for the good stuff." Bianca fiddled with the root vegetable. "But they are business owners, so they still want your money. You and me? We are cute and clever enough to use it to our advantage. Always keep that in your back pocket."

"Bee, you're vile." Torrie giggled.

"You'll pick it up. It comes with practice and time."

"I look forward to learning all that I can from you," she replied with a sinister undertone in her voice.

They passed through a narrow alley that led onto the main street. Long, gray fingers of clouds drifted across the darkening backdrop, and the crescendo of the ambient sounds of night filled the chilled atmosphere.

The moon began her march into view over the trees beyond the horizon.

Bianca pulled on her companion's sleeve and dropped her voice to a whisper.

"There." A tanned finger pointed at a pair of women that appeared to be approximately the same age.

They looked incredibly similar to each other. Siblings, without a doubt.

Four children, the oldest no more than six or seven, ran in loops around the women. Their small hands would grab at the sisters' skirts occasionally and tug at the fabric as they dashed in haphazard rings around their victims. The kids bumped into each other and squeaked with glee as they wove around them like circling vultures.

"A nice target to practice on. Those kids are the perfect cover. If you're careful, they won't feel you reach into their purses." Bianca watched the scene and continued with a brimming grin. "Just keep an eye out for the kids. Those little rats will squeal if they see you, or *they'll* try to steal it from *you*."

The pair of women casually closed the distance between them and the sisters. As they drew nearer, they were able to overhear some of the conversation.

"I just can't see why the Guard isn't doing anything about the disappearances, Gwen. Monster sightings have been happening more often. Shouldn't they be more reactionary? The attempted coup was barely two years ago. You'd think they would have learned."

"I know, Laila. There were lots of disappearances before the coup, too. I totally agr— Hey!" The woman snatched a small wrist and yanked it away from her dress. "Get out of here, you little shits! Go home!"

The oldest child shrieked with a wild grin and ran off laughing. The remaining two looked between each other before following suit.

"Let me go, lady!" The young boy tried to pull away from her but wasn't quite strong enough to do so yet.

"Leave adults alone when they are talking! You are being rude!" Gwen released the boy's wrist, and he tumbled onto his butt.

"At least I'm not ugly like you!" He stuck his tongue out at her and sneered. "See you later, uglies!" He quickly gathered himself before he sprinted off after his friends.

Gwen began to turn back to her sister but instead collided with another body.

"Oh! I am so sorry!" Torrie gripped Gwen's shoulders to steady her. She quickly dropped her hands to the other woman's sides with her palms open.

"It's fine," Gwen replied half-heartedly.

"Gwen, are you all right?" Laila called.

Gwen turned her attention to her sister to tell her that she was fine.

Unfortunately, this was the opening that Torrie was hoping for.

The last of the sunset was gone, and the light of the moon was the only light to see by, as the streetlights had yet to be visited by the lamplighter.

With the attention off of her, Torrie plunged one of her hands into the small purse at Gwen's hip. Easily fingering two coins free, she retrieved her hand without Gwen noticing.

"That's good, someone needs to— Hey! Hey! Thief!" Laila pointed at Torrie before she had a chance to pocket her spoils.

Gwen glared at Torrie and shoved her by the shoulder.

"Give me back my money!"

Bianca appeared beside her companion with an apologetic smile.

"Sorry about that, deary." Her imposing stare turned to Laila. "We are just so hungry, you see." Bianca drew the sickly radish from her bag. "This was all we could manage for the week."

Gwen glowered at them with disbelief. "Not my problem."

"That doesn't make it okay to steal," Laila added as she joined her older sister's side and folded her arms.

"Yes, yes, you're right," Bianca purred. "We weren't planning on eating tonight, but I'm having second thoughts. Could I treat you for dinner as an apology?"

Torrie could feel the shift in Bianca's energy. A welt of excitement formed in her chest, and she felt her fingers twitch at her sides.

She *was* in fact, very hungry.

The four women stood in silence before Gwen sighed. "No thanks. Just keep the money." She glanced to her sister. "Let's go home. It's getting late."

Laila nodded.

"That's a shame." Bianca's voice grew low and menacing. "We were hoping to have something to eat."

"They smell delicious," Torrie hissed, her restraint quickly waning. "No doubt *he* will pay well for whatever is left over . . ."

Before the sisters had time to process the situation, Torrie was on top of Laila.

Gwen shouted but was also quickly apprehended.

"The more you struggle, the better you taste," Bianca whispered in her ear. "Go ahead, scream if you like."

"Help! Help!" Laila cried as she tried to wrestle with Torrie. "Please, someone! Help us!"

The less seasoned grifter chuckled with a monstrous rumble. "No one is here." She brought her watering lips to Laila's jaw and grinned. "No one can hear you."

"I can."

Bianca and Torrie turned to the new voice with a start.

A lone woman stood a few yards away from the altercation with a long staff clutched in one hand. The top of the staff looked almost like a spear. It had a wide-based arrowhead of steel that came to a sharp point, but it had the addition of a hook that split away from the point halfway up. The very tip of the hook had a small curl of its own that curved suddenly in the opposite direction.

The tip of the spear was used by a lamplighter to flick open the glass hatch of the hexagonal lantern. The latch to open the door was a little over ten feet from the ground, so the staff made it possible for a person of any height to light them. The *smaller* curl was used to open the valves and bring them to life.

The woman had a medium build and a long ponytail that brushed the small of her back. A gentle breeze seemed to hover around her, causing the tendrils of hair to twist around her form as they danced.

"Hello, Wren," Bianca hissed. Her nails tightened on Gwen's shoulder and neck reflexively. "You got demoted to lamp duty, I see. Still misbehaving too much to get into the good graces of the king?"

The newcomer turned the staff over to hold it with both hands. She rolled her eyes at Bianca's comment and shook her head once. Instead of regarding the supposed insult, she bobbed the solid-wood staff up and down with one hand.

"I volunteered." She smiled and turned her attention back to the grifters.

A sudden and intensely strong current of air pushed the assailants off of Gwen and Laila with a forceful blast. The sisters scrambled to their feet and dashed down the cobblestone street in the direction of their home.

Bianca and Torrie sailed through the wind before they hit the ground fifteen or so yards away from Wren.

Before they could get up, she rushed at the pair with the hooked staff in a striking position at her side. She landed a blow squarely on

Bianca's abdomen and pivoted to hook the side of Torrie's shoulder. It caught hold and tore a large gash through the younger grifter's sleeve and flesh.

Bianca caught Wren's elbow as she struck Torrie. The more seasoned grifter lashed outward and caught the left side of Wren's face with a sharp nail. She sneered and cackled.

"Nearly got your eye there," Bianca taunted. "I won't miss next time."

Wren scoffed and swiveled on one foot to position herself between them. The long stem of the staff collided with Bianca's back and Torrie's chest with enough force to send them both careening to the ground. She pressed the length of the lamplighter's staff into their bodies and held them against the street with her weight.

"This is your second offense." Wren pressed harder. "I could arrest you both just for pickpocketing. I could have you sentenced to death for trying to *eat* two civilians."

"You can try," Bianca hissed and struggled under Wren's weight.

Torrie thrashed violently and managed to free herself. She swept her long nails at Wren's leg and caught hold of her ankle. With a sharp tug, she threw Wren off-balance enough for her to lunge forward. Torrie pinned her to the ground with a heavy slam and grinned.

Bianca quickly gathered herself and circled Wren with a sick smile painted on her face. "Feeding on you will be much more satisfying than those meek little humans." Her grin widened to expose her pointed teeth from behind her lips. "Did you know that red heads are my *favorite*, Torrie? They taste so much sweeter than the others."

Torrie grasped at the staff and quickly spun it to restrain Wren against the ground. It pressed into her ribs and locked her elbows to her sides. Torrie's weight on her chest made her gasp softly as the wind was swept from her lungs.

"Mine too." Torrie leaned forward to stare into Wren's face. She said nothing more, but her parted lips dripped saliva onto Wren's cheek. The grifter chuckled. "Look, Bee. You made her bleed."

Bianca climbed on top of Wren and clamped her wrists at her sides in a vise grip. She closed into Wren's face and sniffed once. With another sickening grin, Bianca's tongue brushed against the wound on Wren's cheek, and she smacked her lips together with content.

"Delicious."

Wren tried not to wince when the grifter's saliva burned the open flesh in an instant with white-hot pain.

Bianca shifted her weight on Wren's right wrist and pressed down.

The pressure on her wrist made small pockets inside the joint pop painfully.

Torrie laughed wickedly and tugged Wren's ring finger backward, eager to join in. The knuckle surrendered as the bones within it dislocated loudly. She cackled as her hand closed around Wren's middle finger next, and removed the joints within it from their sockets, too.

Wren cried out with one quick sound when each knuckle gave before her eyes pierced Bianca's.

Bianca licked her lips and narrowed her eyes at the helpless woman beneath her. She opened her mouth at a teasingly slow speed and hovered over Wren's throat for just a moment too long.

"I wouldn't do that, ladies."

A deep, baritone voice froze the two grifters in place.

They looked in its direction to find an ominous figure standing within reach.

His sudden closeness stunned Wren's attackers long enough for her to get her left arm free, but the staff pressing across her chest held her in place. She rocked her shoulders to one side in order to pivot at the waist in an effort to wriggle out. Wren couldn't see the source of the voice, with Bianca still inches from her neck, but she didn't quite care to know who it belonged to.

Her priority was getting free.

"Who are you?" Torrie hissed.

Wren's left hand felt around for *anything*. Trembling fingertips found the pointed hook at the end of the staff. She was able to get enough of a grasp around it to snap it off.

The motion jarred Bianca's attention back to her prey. She clutched Wren's throat in a tight grasp and bared her pointed teeth with a snarl.

Wren gasped and coughed. Her left hand tightened around the hook desperately, and her eyes narrowed.

The curl of the lamplighter's hook fit in her palm so that the six-inch point of the arrowhead poked outward, perpendicular to the curve of her hand and wrist.

Wren growled dangerously. Her eyes were locked on Bianca's, and she tried, in vain, to wordlessly warn the grifter of what was about to happen.

Bianca's dark eyes held a threat of their own as they burned into Wren's, hungry and wild.

With her final exhale, Wren plunged the pointed tip into the side of Bianca's head with every ounce of strength that she had left as her own vision faded.

Torrie's bloodcurdling scream was the last thing she heard before she succumbed to blackness.

CHAPTER ONE

"Thoughts without content are empty, intuitions without concepts are blind . . . The understanding can intuit nothing, the senses can think nothing. Only through their union can knowledge arise."

Immanuel Kant

THE ROOM WAS DARK, LIT ONLY BY THE GLOW OF THE moon reflecting off the mirrors that lined the corner and far wall to the left of the front door.

Moonlight shimmered against the glass as a figure moved methodically around a dangling sandbag that swayed like a pendulum. The room smelled of dust, sweat, and well-worn burlap mats.

A rhythmic tempo of knuckles jabbing into the sandbag echoed in the otherwise empty space.

The moon infiltrated the room through two long windows above the pair of mirrored walls. The angle of the shadows alluded to the early hour, each a long and stretching veil of black that did well to mask whatever was beneath it. Floating particles of dust seemed to glow in the pale light but would vanish completely if they drifted into shadow.

The figure grunted softly when a miscalculation smashed her sore knuckles into the canvas bag. Pain radiated up her right arm, causing it to involuntarily twitch. She shook her hand once to divert her focus from the pain and narrowed her eyes at the bag.

'Maybe it's time to give it a rest. Dislocated joints need ice after being reset.'

Lionel's words before he left lingered inside her mind, and her lips tightened. Her bright hazel eyes glared at the bag, and she sucked in a sharp breath through clenched teeth.

Wren's shoulders heaved as she threw a set of punches forward in tandem with a slow, steady exhale.

The dangling sandbag rattled the chains above it with a metallic groan. It swayed from the blows and, once she'd come to a stop, took quite a while to become still.

Strands of hair the color of a soft, orange-red sunset escaped her long braid, and clung to her high cheekbones. With another weighty sigh, she wiped the streams of sweat that beaded and trickled away from her hairline.

Hand still throbbing, Wren pivoted on one foot and lifted the other. In a quick, disciplined motion, her bandage-wrapped foot slammed into the bag.

The chains creaked again as the bag rocked back and forth. A frayed seam along the bottom of the canvas finally gave way. It didn't take long for a mountain of sand to form beneath it.

Wren watched the sand drain out with a blank expression etched into her features.

"Very impressive. If only you'd used any of those moves last night. Might have been able to defend yourself a bit better."

Wren swiveled as her eyes shot to the source of the voice.

It was a deep, oddly familiar baritone that made the small hairs on her arms and neck stand on end. She brought her balled-up fists level with her shoulders, and tucked her elbows against her ribs as she scanned the room.

The thick shadows made it difficult to make out many details of the tall figure. He loomed in the open space between the stairs that led up to the next floor and the front door to his left. He was near enough to the doorway into Lionel's office that he could easily enter the room with one wide step to the right.

"Who are you? Sneaking up on someone from behind, in their own home," Wren growled. "How cowardly."

"Cowardly?" Her jaw set firmly when he chuckled at her. "You don't even know me."

"Then, by all means, let's get acquainted. Come on out where I can see you."

The deep voice chuckled again, and she saw a pair of large hands lift in a shrug. The dismissive gesture from his broad shoulders made her temper flare.

He was easily over six feet tall and had wide shoulders. Everything about him seemed formidable. He cocked his head slightly and began a slow advance.

"How did you get in here?" She struggled to keep her voice even as she tried to suppress her temper. Or her anxiety? She didn't allow herself time to consider it. "Why *are* you here?" Wren's hands clenched tighter, and she mentally kicked herself for having made her knuckle worse when another pang shot up her arm.

The tall figure stopped when both feet reached the waterfall of moonlight through the main window just above the front door. He took another step forward into the light so that she could see him clearly.

He had a strong jaw that was dusted with dark stubble. Disheveled ebony hair brushed the tops of his ears and concealed most of his forehead. His jacket collar sat upright to ward off the chill of the late-winter night, and the tips of his collar brushed his chin as his head moved. A crimson scarf was snaked around his neck, tucked beneath the jacket's folds, and emphasized his broad shoulders.

Yet his eyes were what gleamed brightest against the darkness.

Brilliant green pools, the color of a hazy tropical morning, watched her intently. His gaze was unsettling, but she couldn't find the willpower to turn away or even *move*.

Because of her position in the room, Wren stood directly in the moon's view.

She was just over five and a half feet tall, with a medium frame, and wore old, comfortable clothes. A baggy navy tunic fluttered around her shoulders and torso. She had a gray sash wound around her waist, and simple, black trousers. Her bare feet were both tightly wrapped in cloth strips that wound up to her ankles.

She stood with the measured posture of a fighter and kept her eyes locked on the dark figure. Her hair was bound into a half-hearted braid slung over her shoulder. A few strands wisped around her face, clinging to the light brown freckles that dusted her skin.

"How did you get in here?" Wren asked again with less of an attempt to contain her anger.

He smiled handsomely and stuffed his hands into the pockets of his black jacket. He looked away from her and cleared his throat once.

"Door was unlocked," he stated amusedly.

"Liar. The front door has been locked all night."

He shrugged with a wry grin.

"I didn't say *that* door was unlocked. Besides, wouldn't a better question be *How did I get back here last night?*"

Wren gnashed her jaw shut and glared. She clenched her hands into fists at her sides and involuntarily winced. Her right hand relaxed as she let out a sharp exhale and tried not to let it show on her face.

The light of the moon, however, shone on her like a spotlight; one would have been blind to miss it.

She'd been training for hours. The bruises from the night glared against her pale biceps, and purple circles beneath her eyes gave away her exhaustion.

The man noticed the wound on the left side of her face that had been hurriedly dressed. It was a sizeable scrape atop the crest of her cheekbone that still bore angry inflammation.

"If your hand is injured, why are you training with it?" He advanced once more, black boots softly plodding on the hardwood floor.

Her eyebrows knitted together, but her eyes could not waver from his.

When he was an arm's reach from her, he stopped and extended his hand.

As much as she wanted to move away and put more space between them, she couldn't budge.

Those green eyes held her still.

Shards of golden flecks emanated from the center of his irises and struck something in her like a hammer to a bell.

She gave no response as she felt his hand touch hers, nor did she say anything when he turned her fist over so the moonlight would shine on her palm. His fingers traced her clenched ones, gently working them out of their locked position until her hand relaxed fully, and he pressed his palm against hers to splay their fingers.

"Nik."

She blinked when his deep voice snapped her from her daze. Wren ripped her hand back and shoved him, landing a well-aimed blow in the center of his chest.

He took a step back to regain his footing. A smirk played across his lips after he shook off his surprise. Nik lifted his palms upright in a show of surrender.

"What are you doing here, *Nik?*" Wren hissed his name. She folded her arms across her chest and narrowed her eyes.

Nik glanced around the room, absorbing its details through the darkness with a small smirk quirked across his lips.

There wasn't much to it.

Old mirrors lined two of the walls and met in a corner that doubled as a makeshift boxing ring. Two sandbags hung near the ring, only one of them still containing sand.

The wall to his right was an *actual* wall of books, and he was able to see into the office through the bound spines. The wall between Lionel's office and the stairs was a much longer version of the library-style shelves that gave off an air of muted openness, complimenting Lionel's gentle personality. The bookshelves were stuffed beyond capacity in some places, while left purposefully open in others. Mostly burned candles were scattered about and gathered dust between the books alongside various knickknacks that littered the shelves.

"I was invited," he stated flatly as he took in the room. "I knew how to get in because I brought you back last night."

Her face morphed from aggravated skepticism to full outrage.

"Get out," she glowered as her arms unfolded. She shifted into a defensive battle stance. "Get out *now*, or I'll throw you out."

Nik shuffled his foot slightly, as though about to step forward, yet he remained in place with a blank detachment to his expression.

Wren watched him, not willing to make the first move.

The difference in their size alone would be too great for her to be able to take him head-on. Her mind sifted through any way that she could think of to get him out, and her muscles tensed unconsciously.

All that Nik did was watch her.

"I wasn't joking," Wren warned again. "Go away, and *stay* away."

"Put your guard down, woman. I have no intention of harming you, nor of leaving." He took a small step back and purposefully looked away. Nik located a light switch and flipped it on.

The old lights sputtered to life slowly before they flooded the modest space.

Wren dropped her hands and stood back upright. She refused to take her eyes off the mysterious figure before her.

"Then what is it you want?"

His head tilted slightly, and he said nothing.

"What? Quit staring at me and say something." She turned her head to look anywhere but those captivating eyes. "Answer my question, *Nik*. Why are you here?"

"Those girls were only humans." He changed the subject. "Why do anything at all? Their fate had nearly been sealed as soon as those grifters set eyes on them."

Her face twisted in disgust as her incredulous eyes ventured back to his.

"Fate? Screw fate. Humans are still living things." Wren folded her arms. "To me, it's more questionable how you could bear witness to something like that and *not* intervene."

He ghosted around her weightlessly, and their eyes followed each other like circling tigers. Nik stopped by a bench near the hanging sandbags and fixed his gaze on the one with a mound of sand beneath it.

"They were simply in the wrong place at the wrong time. It's the circle of life . . . Cat eats mouse. It's how the balance is meant to be." Those eyes seemed to glow against the shadows cast across his face. "You were the one that inserted yourself into the situation."

"I did what was *right*. Regardless, what makes you think that I care about your opinion?"

A small smile quirked his lips, and he shook his head, dropping his eyes to his hands.

"You're right, I know you don't care what I think. I'm just surprised such an unusual creature stepped in to help two mere humans. You could have done nothing, and your pretty face would have been unscathed. You could have done nothing and kept from injuring your hand. Yet . . ." He met her eyes and pinned her in place. "Yet you chose to help. Why?"

"What do you mean *why*?" Wren held her breath for a moment before letting it out as evenly as she could manage. "It was the right thing to do. I was there, and they had no way to defend themselves against a pair of deranged grifters."

"And you can?"

She pursed her lips tightly and glared at him.

"I *did*. They got away."

Nik emphatically rolled his eyes with a half smile painted across his face.

"Right, sorry. For the record, I never said that I *wouldn't* have stepped in to help them, had you not been there."

Anger welled at the top of her stomach, and she dashed forward before she could stop herself.

Nik watched her carefully and let her close in, unmoving. When she neared the edge of his reach, his hand shot out and snatched her by the arm. He pushed her toward the nearest flat surface with an effortless shove.

Her back slapped the wall harshly. She growled and pulled at her arm to break free.

"Bad idea," he warned.

His strong hands held her against the wall by her right bicep and her left forearm bent uncomfortably over her head.

Another jolt of pain sparked when his hand tightened over the bruises encircling her arm. Wren hissed and narrowed her eyes at him. She arched her back against the wall and drew her legs upward. She then jerked her arm and shoulder free as she forced her legs against his chest like a wedge and kicked out hard.

Nik staggered backward and looked up with just enough time to catch her foot aimed directly at his head. He was mildly surprised by her strength as he struggled to keep his grip on her ankle.

Her mind raced to think of a way to break free as she kicked against his hold.

In the few seconds of her deliberation, Nik tugged her closer to him and grabbed her right hand.

She twisted at the waist, ignoring the shot of pain in her chest where her staff had held her to the ground. The moment she felt the slightest slack in his hold, she flung him away with a sharp gust of air.

His mass slammed into the wall beside the front door while she tried to maintain her balance.

Before she could turn around, an impossible force collided with her back. She crashed against the hardwood floor and cursed. Her sore ribs howled at her as they bored into the planks under his weight.

"I don't want to hurt you. I came here because I was *asked* to."

Nik loomed over her, holding her to the floor with one hand splayed across her back.

Her arms were pinned beneath her, and long billows of breath plumed across the floor under her nose.

"Just trust me when I say don't go up against a reaper, creature. If staying alive is in your best interest, it's unwise to pick a fistfight with me when you're already injured. Even in peak form, there's no way you could beat me."

"Stop calling me *creature* and get off," Wren growled and struggled to get free. "You're crushing me."

Nik allowed her up and smirked when she glared at him as she righted herself. He slumped to the side and dropped into a seated position on the floor beside her.

Although she was now free, she remained seated as well.

"Who are you, *really?*" She watched him intently, eyebrows low. "And, if you think humans aren't worth it, what gives you the right to care if *I* do?"

His green-and-gold gaze washed over her again.

They watched each other silently for what felt like hours.

Wren looked away first.

"I was on my way somewhere. I just happened to be in the area," Nik answered finally with a shrug. "*You* wandered into *my* path. I can't help my curiosity if a creature I've never seen before was involved in an unwinnable situation."

Wren's eyes narrowed.

"My name is Wren. Not *creature*. Tiny mind needs to learn manners." His look of disbelief almost made her smile. "What makes you think that I'm not human?"

"Your scent. The wind during the fight smelled *just* like you. And"—he tipped his chin down to see her better—"humans don't have eyes like yours."

"What? My eyes are entirely normal."

"They are not. They are the eyes of a hunter." When she gave no response, he turned his shoulders to face her fully. "How to ask this with these pesky manners you insist I use . . . What exactly *are* you?"

Surprise flushed her face, and she stood in a quick and fluid motion.

He was not long to follow suit and remained beside her once on his feet.

"I'm getting tired of talking to you. Why the hell are you *in* my house?" Frustration bubbled through her clenched teeth.

"I already told you. I was invited." Nik shrugged and looked away from her.

Wren folded her arms across her chest and tried to keep her growl to herself.

"You know, there is a vast difference between you and me. I did the right thing because it *was* the right thing to do. You said you're a *reaper*? That's fitting. I can't expect you to have any appreciation for the living world. You're only there to collect the loser. Is that what this is about? You're bent out of shape because I interrupted your *work*?"

A soft smirk quirked his lips.

"You're dodging my question, but I'll play along. Your assessment of me is mostly wrong, but it's fine. Allow me to correct you.

"A reaper is neither dead nor alive. What you call 'appreciation for the living world' is what I consider a product of balanced and fair reaping.

"Now, humans. Humans are so often the cause of their own misery that you'd be hard-pressed to find one that isn't. Seldom do they take responsibility for themselves, and even then, only at the very end do they beg for the *same* mercy that they neglected to show to others throughout their own lives. They manipulate, lie, steal, and murder, then have the audacity to beg for mercy. I've watched it for years. As a man and as a reaper."

Wren's eyebrows knitted together, and she shook her head.

"You're wrong. Not all humans are like that. Creatures are guilty of the very same crimes that you accuse humans of committing. I watched it. Those girls would have been *killed* by creatures. Is it because the grifters weren't *human* that it's all right to murder? As long as it's a *human?*"

Nik laughed aloud and ran his hand through his hair.

"You sound like you're a knight ready to swoop in and save the day."

Wren clicked her tongue and shook her head.

"Forget it. I can't reason with some ignorant, judgmental *bully* with a god complex, and I refuse to entertain your revolting company any longer." She pressed her hands into his chest, urging him toward the front door.

Nik planted his feet where he stood, unmoving. He allowed her to shove him a number of times before he swiftly collected both of her wrists with one hand. He kept her hands between them and leveled her with a stare.

"*Lionel* invited me here." He refused to loosen his grip when she tried to pull away.

"Let go of me," she muttered darkly. "I don't believe you." Her hands clenched into tight fists, ready to be unleashed at the first opportunity.

"Tell me what you *are*, and I'll let go," Nik countered and tilted his head, entirely unfazed by her struggling.

"Why does it concern you? What I *am* matters to me, and me alone. The only part that *does* concern you is to know that you best stay out of my affairs."

The front door opened, allowing fresh, early morning light to beam into the room behind Lionel.

"Fia had the pastries that you like, Wren. Oh, hello?"

From where he stood, the light seemed to emanate from his blond hair like a halo. Lionel was only slightly taller than Nik, and slender. Short blond curls twisted around his temples and ears, framing his handsome face neatly. He appeared to be only in his mid-to-late thirties yet had the presence of one with lifetimes of wisdom.

He had a small box tucked between his arm and abdomen; the other eased his keys back into his coat pocket with a gloved hand. His brilliant blue eyes took in the pair before him and blinked a few times.

"Ah, Nikolas! You made it! It's been so long. I didn't recognize you at first." He tipped the door shut behind him. "Did Wren let you in? I brought a splint kit and breakfast. Are you planning to join us?"

Nik hesitated to release Wren. He relaxed his hold and turned to face Lionel fully to give a polite nod.

Wren stepped away, her glare burning into his back.

"No, I hope that you don't mind. I noticed a way in when I brought her back last night. You should *really* keep the balcony door locked."

"Oh, I see. That was you." Lionel glanced between the two. "Thank you for getting her home safely."

Nik shrugged with a cheeky grin. "The empty room is upstairs?"

Lionel gave him an uneasy smile. "I wouldn't bring that up just ye— Wren! Don't—"

Lionel's attempt to intervene was a half second too late.

Wren loaded and fired a kick into Nik's side, just below his ribs.

He gasped softly as the wind was knocked from his lungs. He stumbled to his knee and shot her a mixed look of fury and reverence.

"Damnit, Wren. *Always* violence with you! *I* asked him to come here." Lionel crouched beside Nik and offered his hand. "I'm sorry, Nikolas. Though, to be fair, I *did* advise that I be present when you meet. You are both rather . . . lacking in decorum and social graces. I'm certainly not surprised that the two of you didn't get along right away."

Nik nodded once, his eyes still on Wren.

"Nah, she's charming." He glanced to Lionel's gloved hand as he regained his footing. "You still wear the gloves, huh?"

"They help with white noise."

"Yeah, I remember. Do you still get headaches?"

"Hey! Can I be clued in, here? What is going on?"

Both men turned to Wren.

She held her arms to her chest and set her jaw tightly. Her fingertips pressed into her biceps, and her eyes narrowed.

Lionel frowned at her and patted Nik's shoulder once without looking at him.

He watched him approach the furious woman calmly with guarded surprise.

Lionel paused directly in front of her. His cerulean eyes looked into her hazel ones, searching. He offered a warm smile and touched the crown of her head softly. Lionel slipped his gloves off and into the breast pocket of his coat. His bare hands tucked any loose, damp hair behind her ears. They paused over her shoulders and offered a comforting squeeze before they drifted to gently hover over her arms, right over where her fingers dug into her bruises.

Upon feeling Lionel's warmth hover over her hands, her grip stiffened painfully.

"Wren, we talked about this. You know that we need whatever help we can get. I told you that we had a guest coming to stay for a while."

She glowered at him, but the muscles in her hands gradually relaxed.

Lionel coaxed her to sit beside the makeshift boxing ring and turned his attention and his hands to hers. He knelt down before her, balanced on one knee, as he examined her knuckles.

"You need to stop training with injuries like this. You will eventually break something that I can't fix."

"You called a *reaper* for help? How is *death* supposed to be helpful?" Wren angled her chin away from Lionel and pursed her lips. "You can't be serious about him staying here. Doesn't the inn in town still have empty rooms?"

"It won't be that bad. It's foolish to write someone off without giving them a chance to show you who they really are. I've known Nikolas for a very long time. You can trust him, as I do."

She tossed a repelled look at Nik and shook her head. "I have no desire to."

"Stop being stubborn, Wren." Lionel positioned his body to block her view of Nik. He turned her hand over, sighing once. "You haven't given him a chance," he said softly after a brief pause. "He will surprise you."

She looked away with no response.

Heat radiated between Lionel's two bare hands resting over her injured knuckles.

Wren pulled both of her legs to her chest and dropped her chin to onto her knee.

Lionel's eyes slipped shut, and he drew a deep breath into his chest. The trace held the breath until a prickling sensation flooded the veins of his arms. As he exhaled slowly, billows of glittering blue haze drifted from his palms and wrapped around Wren's inflamed joints like water.

The waves of warmth that Lionel's touch exuded began to shift in texture and color, morphing from translucent blue to opaque white.

Flutters of sensation sprinkled up Wren's shoulder and through her chest. Tendrils of mist moved around her hand, lacing between her fingers and leaving trails of heat beneath her skin.

Wren pressed her eyes shut tightly and tried not to wince as the heat intensified.

Visions of two small children floated through her mind. Lionel's boyish face couldn't have been more than five years old, yet he looked the same somehow. The back of a young boy that she assumed to be Nik soon came into focus. The sounds of playing children yelping in joy reverberated and compounded her headache.

Then shadows and flames burned at the back of her throat.

The images glowed hot and red with fire, instantly melting the greens and blues into blacks and grays smeared with tears. Rain seared her skin as the images of joyous children became a grave gathering. Human silhouettes shrouded in black stood in a wide circle around mountains of bundled flowers, and pictures of a young Nik alongside two adults were propped up on white easels.

Nik's picture was of a boy who had likely *just* met his teenage years. His round face and green eyes held little in the way of expression, and, through Lionel's vision, the framed portrait felt as though it was looking directly at her.

When they locked eyes, she noticed something that flickered through the back of her mind.

No gold? Wren growled to herself and pushed the thought away.

Her palms tremored with a chill from the orchestra of mourning cries that echoed throughout raindrops. Three deep trenches in the ground drifted into the river left by the relentless rainwater and shed tears.

Lionel felt her hands tense between his.

She opened her eyes and instantly turned away from his *infuriatingly* understanding stare.

"He may be your old friend"—she hesitated and closed her eyes again—"but that doesn't make him mine."

Lionel sighed and shook his head delicately.

Wren stood abruptly, rotating her right hand and testing the joints.

"Thank you, Lionel." Without looking at either man, she turned to the stairs and vanished to the second floor.

A long silence lingered in the light of the rising sun.

"What did you show her?"

Lionel looked to Nik. His expression was as conflicted as it had been with Wren.

". . . Our childhood." He sighed as he shook his head. His hands blindly found the gloves in his breast pocket and slipped them on. He knelt down to collect the small box and tucked it back into the crook of his arm.

Nik's brows furrowed and he glared. A long-forgotten rage that the memories withdrew welled at the top of his stomach.

"All of it?" he managed calmly.

"No." Lionel paused before he let out a dismal sigh. "I only showed her your family's funeral."

CHAPTER TWO

STEAM BLOOMED FROM THE RUNNING WATER. THE TOO-hot droplets streamed through Wren's hair and saturated it to a deep shade of mahogany.

Wren didn't want to turn off the water. A constant thudding in her chest made her uneasy. Flashes of Lionel's shared vision still faded in and out of her focus. She looked down at her palms, her sight distorted by the thick steam.

A shiver suddenly rolled through her shoulders and down her spine. The memory of the trenches in the cold rain raced through the forefront of her mind, and she winced.

Wren was quick to turn up the heat of the water to rid her mind of a mourning crowd that watched on as three caskets were lowered into the ground. She rubbed her face and cupped a small handful of steam just under her nose.

She stayed like this for a short while before eventually flicking the spigot off.

The sad rain was as inescapable as the ice that it left under her skin.

Wren wrapped herself in a towel before she grabbed a second from a basket above the sink. She draped it lazily over her head and tucked her hair into its folds before she pushed open the door to step into her bedroom.

The corner of her eye caught her reflection in the mirror, and she paused. The gash on her face was still bright and angry, as were the dark purple circles beneath her eyes. Her milky skin was flushed pink from the hot water, but the base of her throat still had a few light bruises around its circumference.

Lionel did his best to heal the marks from Bianca's chokehold. The bruising, while significantly better than last night, was still able to be seen beneath a tunic without an undershirt.

Wren sighed and rubbed the towel against her scalp.

Her bedroom was sparce and unassuming. The walls were a sun-dried sage-green color, and a few paintings and framed book passages hung scattered within their empty spaces. The paintings were of landscapes, animals, and skies, all unsigned.

A few books sat neatly on two short shelves made from oak and pushed together beside her bedroom door. Her bed was tucked into the far side of the room between a dresser and a bedside table with a small lamp atop it.

The dresser, however, was claimed by a pure-white, slate-eyed cat.

He was sprawled on his back with four paws that dangled lazily at the ankles above him. His fluffy tail flicked absentmindedly, and his ears twitched when they registered Wren's footfalls.

"Lionel is insane," she muttered to herself while she dried and dressed. "There is no way this will go well. It's absolutely insane. He just invites his long-lost childhood friend, and then lets him *live* here? How does he *expect* this to go?"

Expressive eyes watched Wren pace.

"You don't get it, Jack. This guy thinks he's some cool, mysterious, all-knowing . . . arbiter of *justice*." Her emphasis was accompanied by an eyeroll. "It's infuriating even being around him! I don't foresee living with him to be anything but disastrous."

The cat rolled onto his belly and slid onto the hardwood floor. He sat down at her feet and let out a small, demanding sound.

Wren smirked and shook her head as she chuckled. She scooped him into her arms and rubbed his cheeks with the pads of her thumbs.

He purred loudly in response.

"Hi, fatso," she whispered with a sigh and rustled the whiskers poking out of his eyebrows with her thumb.

He playfully grabbed her palm with his teeth.

She smirked and gently wrapped her hand around his face.

He bit down again and wrapped his front legs around her forearm. With her arm firmly trapped in his clutches, he kicked his back feet against her arm and munched on the crook between her thumb and forefinger.

Wren laughed softly and splayed her hand just above his exposed belly.

He froze and watched her, eagerly waiting for his turn.

The standoff ended when she gripped his belly and gave it a shake.

He closed like a bear trap on her hand, chomping down repeatedly without breaking skin.

She chuckled again, caressing his cheek and whiskers.

"Sweet Jack," Wren hummed.

A soft rap at the door pulled the pair from their shared moment.

"Breakfast is out, and the coffee just finished." Lionel stepped into her room and slid the door shut behind him with a gloved hand. He wasn't surprised to find her watching him coldly. "I asked him to meet me at the train station this morning. So I could introduce you two properly. I suppose he arrived earlier than expected."

"How are you even friends? You are nothing alike." Wren walked to the dresser, which had a green pillow on its top. "Does he have something on you? Are you being blackmailed?"

Jack reluctantly allowed her to set him onto it.

"Is he really a reaper?"

"Yes." He gave her an apologetic smile. "Do you really want to get into this without any coffee?"

His attempt at a joke broke through her unamused mask.

She turned away from him, but Lionel knew what the side of her face looked like when she smiled.

"We can work this out, Wren. He is rough around the edges and takes some getting used to . . ."

As she listened silently, her smile gradually faded.

"But so are *you*, knucklehead. Give him a chance."

She folded her arms and leaned her hip against the dresser. "You already gave him the speech you're about to give me, right? Give her a chance, she's not so bad once you get to know her, yadda-yadda . . ."

Lionel tried to contain his own smile.

"Work together, play nice, get along, blah-blah." Wren glanced at him. "What?"

"No, keep going." Lionel bent his hand at the wrist and motioned for her to continue. "I like your version better. You were on a roll."

She shook her head and jabbed his shoulder lightly with her palm.

A comfortable silence wafted through the room.

Jack meandered toward Lionel. He pawed at him a few times before he received a pat on the head.

"Did he know that you are a trace when you were kids?"

"*That's* what you're curious about?"

Wren simply stared at him.

Lionel sighed heavily through his nose before he continued. "Not at first. Neither of us knew for a while. I learned of it from my parents as a child after my first . . . episode . . . As we got older, he eventually figured it out on his own. He was a regular, human kid. We've been friends as far back as I can remember. His family was . . . *mostly* kind and got along well with my own. Nikolas has survived some trying times, Wren. His life has not been easy."

"What do you mean?"

Lionel shook his head. "I won't tell his story for him. I *will* say that he and I grew closer *after* his body was buried. When he returned years later, he sought me out long after I had left Heather. He had surprised me back then with how much older he looked. This time, I nearly didn't recognize him." Lionel hesitated before he added, "Give him a chance, please. Have I given you reason to doubt me yet?"

Wren's face puckered at him, and she pushed away from her dresser to head toward the door.

He didn't need to hear her say he was right to know that it sank in.

Jack turned when she moved away and was not long to follow behind her.

Lionel had insisted that Wren take the largest bedroom when she first moved in.

Her room was in the far-left corner of the rectangular building from the top of the stairs, one floor above her training area.

There was a door to a spare bathroom a short way down the hall from Wren's room. A third door, directly across from the stairs, led to the spare bedroom.

Lionel's bedroom was across from Wren's. There was a set of double doors made of glass between their rooms that led out onto a balcony. The balcony wrapped around the exterior of Lionel's bedroom and reached down the building to the kitchen.

The space unoccupied by rooms was shared between the common area and the kitchen.

The open kitchen shared a wall with Lionel's bedroom and had full view of the rest of the common living space. Tall windows lined the brick-laid walls behind the kitchen area that gazed out over the balcony.

A round, sturdy dining table occupied most of the central common space and was encircled by five comfortable chairs. An L-shaped counter marked the border between the common space and the modest kitchen that was made up of necessities only. There was a small fridge beneath the counter to the left of the sink. The window above the sink faced the balcony, out into the snowy, still-sleeping city.

A mustard-colored armchair sat facing the balcony doors and, beside it, a faded mint-green couch large enough for two faced in the same direction.

Jack followed the pair into the kitchen, weaving effortlessly between Wren's strides.

Wren retrieved two ceramic coffee mugs from an eye-level cupboard and sighed.

"Are you having coffee today?"

Lionel grinned with a childish expression.

"Well, *I* made it. So . . . it's the best; yes. Thank you."

Wren rolled her eyes, but the corners of her lips twitched with a smirk.

He pulled a chair out to sit in, only to have it quickly stolen by the stark-white cat.

"You did that on purpose."

Jack replied with a tilt of his head and a twitch of his tail.

Lionel pulled the chair beside him away from the table and sat, eyeing the cat with a smirk.

The white cat peeked over the top of the table where a stack of pastries that were tastefully plated far out of his reach sat. This setback, however, did not stop Jack from reaching a paw outward to try to snag one.

Lionel smiled and shook his head, pulling the plate farther out of the cat's reach.

Wren poured a small amount of cream into one mug and brought both, filled to the brims with coffee, over to the table. Once she'd set them down, she gave Jack a quick chin scratch and smirked.

"Good Jack."

"So, tell me. What was so incorrigible about this morning?" Lionel took a sip of coffee but did not look away from her. "From what Nikolas told me, he was noncombative and straightforward. He even carried you home last night. Granted, he *did* break in . . . But his retelling does sound a lot like you, Wren. I'm just trying to understand."

She turned away and sat down across from him, staring into the creamy-brown coffee swirling in her mug. Wren considered the question thoroughly, opening and closing her mouth a few times without saying anything.

"He, I-I," she stammered once and clipped her teeth shut.

Lionel leaned over the table and offered her a warm smile.

Wren responded with an abject look in her eyes, and the inside tips of her brows were turned up.

"I couldn't beat those grifters alone," she whispered into her coffee, and her eyes darted away. "I can't figure out if I'm grateful that he showed up when he did or ashamed that I *even needed* his help. Plus, he's an ass."

"Wren . . ."

They shared a look at the sound of the spare bathroom shower turning off and fell silent.

She ground her teeth together and shifted in her seat, turning her back to the room.

Jack hopped out of the chair and onto Wren's lap. He curled into a ball and batted at her long, nearly dried hair.

"I'll tell you when I figure it out," she said curtly.

Lionel sighed and frowned. "Wren, I know trust is hard for you." He propped his elbows onto the tabletop. "But you know that you can always trust me, don't you?"

She said nothing, eyes downcast at the snowball in her arms. To busy herself, she doodled small web patterns in the white fur on his tummy.

Jack purred happily.

"I trust *you*, Lionel," she finally admitted. "I'm unsure about all of this, but . . ." She paused for a moment and looked up at him. "What's going on in the city is getting worse. Those grifters were trying to take two women last night. That's the third incident this week. The Guard doesn't want to do anything about it."

Jack blinked at her with his glimmering slate eyes, and Wren rubbed his cheek.

He was purring so loudly that the soft rolls of sound filled the room with a comforting aura.

"I am going to hike some today and check out the forest. Even if there's nothing out there, at least it's better than sitting around doing nothing."

"Alone?" Lionel leaned back in his seat and straightened his back. He offered Wren a slight smile before she begrudgingly nodded. "The skies will be clear today." His smile crinkled the edges of his eyes. "I believe that Elliot will arrive this evening, so I have preparations to make for her."

"Great. Nik can stay and help you," she muttered.

The bathroom door opened, and Lionel shifted in his seat to greet his friend.

"Was the shower all right?"

"Perfect, thank you." Nik didn't miss how Wren's shoulders stiffened as he entered. "Just what I needed. Coffee in the kitchen?"

"Yes, the left cupboard just above the pot. Cream and milk are in the fridge by the sink, sugar on the table here." Lionel stood from his place at the table, giving Wren a gentle smile. "I'll give you the grand tour after I feed the furry one."

Lionel hopped to his feet and made his way to Nik's side. He gave a signature grin and followed the other into the kitchen.

Jack stirred from his bliss when Lionel neared his food bowl and leapt from Wren's lap to gallop into the kitchen as well.

"You have a cat?"

"No, the *cat* has a building. He was here before I moved in, and I didn't see any reason to kick him out. He's a great mouser, and even better company."

"You haven't changed at all." Nik's returned smile was pure and genuine. It softened his features and, without the dark coat and black boots, allowed a new light to emphasize his striking appearance. His vibrant eyes met Wren's briefly before they turned back to Lionel. "You'd hold a funeral service for any animal that had to be slaughtered in our village. Insisted we commemorate their anniversaries every year, too."

When Nik's eyes had turned back to Lionel, Wren, against her better judgment, didn't look away.

His slicked-back hair reached just below the nape of his neck, and the tips were still beaded with droplets of water. A gray tunic clung to the few still-damp spots dotted around his shoulders. Even without his jacket, his height and build were imposing.

Wren wisely turned her attention to the mug of coffee between her palms. She knew better than to meet those eyes again.

His stare would drown her.

Instead, she took a long sip of coffee to shield most of her face and nodded softly.

"That sounds like exactly what I would expect from a Little Lionel."

"Well," Lionel interrupted while he clapped his hands together to rid them of crumbs, "enough about me. All right, Nikolas. The tour." He motioned to the three rooms along the edges of the building. "Wren's room, bathroom, your room. Mine's over there." He turned to point to the door beside the kitchen. "Laundry's done on the balcony. The wash basin is on the other side of the kitchen sink, and the hanging lines should already be out." His cerulean eyes glanced around the room until they found Jack, and he pointed. "Cat."

Nik chuckled and shoved Lionel's shoulder.

"I don't think I can remember all that. Can you draw me a map?"

"I'm going to get ready," Wren said abruptly as she stood from the table. "I'll let you know before I leave, Lionel." As she turned, her hand shot out to grab one of the more ornately decorated pastries.

"Where are you going?" Nik set his mug on the table and looked between the two.

Lionel smiled, and he purposefully avoided Wren's darkening glare.

"She's going to inspect the Arnican forest just north of us for any clues as to what is going on in the city. You could accompany her, Nikolas!" Lionel clapped his gloved hands together, still only looking at Nik. "You can get to know each other. You know, a fresh start? Plus, it'll put my mind at ease to know you'd have backup if your habit of finding trouble rears its ugly head." He finally turned to Wren, meeting her fuming expression with a gentle smile.

Silence fell upon the room, broken only by the white cat's crunchy breakfast.

Nik watched Wren intentionally before he answered. When he did, his lips quirked into a smirk.

"Sure. Sounds fun."

Wren rolled her eyes emphatically and slipped into her room as she muttered to herself. Her curses were muffled by the sweet, buttery pastry as she chewed with fervor.

CHAPTER THREE

"Knowledge speaks, but wisdom listens."

Jimi Hendrix

THE PAIR TRUDGED THROUGH FRESHLY FALLEN SNOW that blanketed the footpath into the forest.

For Nik, it was only about knee-deep and relatively easy for him to kick out of the way. It was still fluffy enough that it was about as taxing on him as walking through a knee-high tide.

Wren plowed her way through snow that, for *her*, reached much higher up her legs. She strode a few paces ahead of Nik and scowled at the ground. She would occasionally look up to take in their surroundings before glancing at the shadowy man that followed her.

If their eyes met, hers instantly shot back to the ground in front of her in a reflexive aversion to his.

They had already crossed through the thick lining of trees at the edge of the city and made it into the untouched area of the forest. The rest of the hike was much more bearable.

The tunnel of white trees wove together around them and stilled the air. Some had pale bark that made the trunks almost vanish against the sheets of white behind and around them. Clumps of evergreen needles and sturdy flora stood proudly amongst the ice and snow, flourishing in the lingering winter's cold.

The layers of snow gradually thinned as the tall trees grew thicker above the hidden pathway. Before long, it was merely ankle-deep with the help of the canopy overhead. The pathway was considerably easier to traverse and gave Wren's fatigued legs a much-needed break.

Small sounds began to bounce about the trees in the frozen air. Soft bird calls and mammalian chatter echoed around them as they walked in otherwise silence.

Despite his heavy black boots and large frame, the reaper strolled weightlessly.

Wren's eyes fluttered to the bones and tendons of the forest as she nibbled on her lip.

The twisted branches held secret traces of small burrows and dens in the hollows of tree trunks, beneath bushes and ferns and given away only by their tiny footprints in the snow.

The silence between them allowed her thoughts to drift, and her pace unconsciously slowed.

A bright red bird stared at them, his chest puffed and orange beak cocked to the side to get a better look at the two. He chirped courageously, but his nerve wavered as they approached. His quick wings flapped and swiftly carried him to the comfort of tangled branches.

Nothing like the forest, Wren mused to herself with a half smile.

The red bird lingered in the shadows of brush. It shifted between two unkempt limbs, watching and following the travelers curiously as they continued down the lost path.

"Lionel showed this trail to me," she said softly, angling her head toward Nik but not looking in his direction. "I knew the forests to the north of here, but not those of Black Rivers." She halted and stared into a hidden cove of branches, nestled inside of the ripples of snow and brush.

The bird rushed across the clearing of the footpath and soared back into the depths of the trees.

Nik said nothing as he came to a stop beside her.

"Lionel wants me to apologize to you." She kept her stare fixed on the trees and continued, "He wants us to be *friends*." Her eyes finally turned to him, and she pursed her lips. While she did face him, her eyes still evaded his. "But I am not a liar. I am not sorry, nor am I pleased with the way things have played out thus far. However, I respect Lionel more than anything." Wren balled her fists at her sides before she hesitantly reached out to him with her right hand. "So, at least . . . peace, I guess."

Nik's emerald eyes were fixed on her. A disbelieving smile tugged at the corner of his mouth.

"You are garbage at apologies. Has anyone ever told you that?"

"Yes. That's why I don't usually do it." Her fingers curled, and she narrowed her eyes when he didn't reciprocate the gesture. "Forget it. I suppose this makes us equally socially inept."

His hand closed around her wrist and held it captive. Before she had time to even attempt to break away, he turned her hand over in his and placed his right palm against hers.

"Hand . . . shake," he mocked, speaking slowly, and turned their joined hands around as though it was an entirely new concept to him.

Wren set her jaw and yanked her hand away.

"You aren't funny." She turned and resumed her trek along the pathway.

"Sure." Nik smirked. He waited for her to walk a reasonable distance away before he followed her. "We can have a fresh start. Try to be friends."

"Uh-huh," came her flat reply.

"Lionel mentioned that you used to live in the forest." He watched her tentatively nod. "Were you born out here?"

"I don't know. I have theories as to why anyone would ditch a kid in the actual middle of nowhere, but I think it's more likely they died. I lived in the forests east of the bridge, in the southern part of Abagail." She paused and sighed. "Even now, I remember many of the routes I used to take and the places where fresh water could be found. All of that remains, and yet I don't remember any parents."

The nonchalance in her demeanor made Nik wince internally.

"I lived in the heart of the forest. There was a little home nestled out there on the edge of the northern river. It was pretty dilapidated, and not much to it, but it worked as a shelter nonetheless. It had four walls and a roof. The water from the river beside it was fresh and plentiful, too. I had everything I needed."

"How did Lionel find you?" His boots mutely strode through the snow behind her.

"I don't know. Lionel just showed up one day. He said that he could feel my presence in the forest and wanted to offer me some sort of magical protection." Wren paused and glanced into the trees. "He told me that he was a trace . . . But I had no idea what that meant."

"Did he tell you what a trace is?"

Wren shrugged. "Eventually we got there. It took a while for us to learn to communicate, but he explained it to me. That he's a human who has abilities that let him feel and influence those around him and can perform small healing incantations. He can also foresee certain events and their potential outcomes before they happen. Through the years, I've come to believe there is a lot more that he can do but won't say out loud."

Nik nodded without a word as they continued their walk along the footpath. He strode a few paces behind her with his hands stuffed into his jacket pockets.

Wren dared a glance over her shoulder. When he caught her peeking, she quickly turned away and back to their path.

"I had a hard time understanding him until I learned he could . . . *speak* with visions through touch. When we finally had a way to communicate, he showed me what a different lifestyle would be like if I left the forest."

"And you didn't try to kill him when he touched you?"

"Oh, no, I did." She chuckled once. "I'm sure you can put together how well the first meeting went all on your own. I was a lot smaller then."

"Well, I *do* know Lionel. He's a lot stronger than he looks."

She nodded. "Yeah . . . and faster."

Nik laughed and allowed the smile to linger on his face. "So, what happened next?"

"He started to visit often. Insisted that he preferred the forest to Black Rivers." Wren pursed her lips slightly. She paused and drew a breath in through her nose. "Lionel tried to convince me to go back with him every time I'd see him . . . I refused."

"How old were you when you met?"

A conflicted expression drifted across her face. "I was probably five? Maybe six. I really don't remember. It was a long time ago."

"He was obviously able to convince you eventually. How?"

She dropped her eyes to the snowy earth and sighed. "Weeks of rainfall resulted in the floods from the mountains that eventually forced me out . . ." Wren shook her head as she recalled the memories. "There was a landslide in the mountains to the north that redirected the river beside my home. I was flooded out, and shortly after, my little house got washed away. I really had no choice. Everything that I made for myself, *by* myself, in the wildlands was just . . . gone."

"Why do you think he found you special?"

"What?" Wren recoiled and pinned him with a glare. "What kind of question is that? You know what, no. Your turn." She propped her knuckles onto her hips. "What did Lionel show me? You two as kids and a funeral?"

"What?" Nik stopped in his tracks and narrowed his eyes back at her.

"I shared about me. It's your turn, *friend*." Wren folded her arms across her chest and cocked her hip to one side.

"My turn? Are you *still* five, maybe six years old?" A swift jab into his bicep made him sigh. "Fine. It was probably the funeral that Lincoln held for me and my parents. That's not really a secret. Practically all of the southeastern nations heard about what happened."

"What happened?"

"I died in a fire." He paused briefly before sighing again. "I worked for my stepfather on his farm, just outside of Heather. The town that we lived in, Lincoln, was a good day's walk away from the main city. There weren't many of them, but the people there were good-hearted. It helped that everyone adored my stepfather, especially Lionel and his family."

"What happened to your birth father?"

Nik shrugged. "My mother never really talked about him. Any time I'd ask, she'd make a new story up on the spot. The only consistent thing in her stories was that I was a baby when he died. Eventually, I just stopped asking."

Wren looked over to him as he spoke.

He glanced down at his hands. As they walked, he turned his clasped palms over repetitiously.

"What's your mother's name?"

Nik smiled to himself. "Elaine."

Their eyes met for a brief moment, and they looked away in unison.

Nik cleared his throat. "She had a hard time of it before she met Dumont, my stepfather. Lionel and I spent more time taking care of her than she did of herself when it started to get worse. She would go days without bathing, speaking, or eating. Like she was living in a stupor no one could break through."

Wren watched him with a soft look that, admittedly, caught him off guard.

"Dumont was good friends with everyone, and before we knew it, he would show up to walk me to school and drop breakfast off for my mother. He baked fresh bread made from his own grain every day and always saved the best loaves for her. When they got married, nearly everyone in town and from nearby villages attended. My mother was happy for a good while.

"She was never really of stable mind. Her moods would hit us almost as hard as they hit her. Her beauty faded as quickly as her kindness did. My stepfather spent less and less time with her at home. He'd say he was on the farm working or in the bakery, but I'd look for him. He was never there during the times my mother would go over the edge. He'd disappear. I can't say I blame him for it."

"She'd hurt you?"

"I'd call it more . . . *lashing out* than I would call it hurting." He nodded, holding her eyes. "It never really got to me. The work I did on the farm made me strong, so it wasn't much of a beating whenever she had one of her episodes. I usually stayed at Lionel's when she got like that."

"Where did your stepfather go?"

"Don't know. Lionel and I tried to follow him a few times. I'd be lying if I said I didn't try on my own, too. But"—Nik shook his head—"he would always lose us after crossing Southern Bridge. I'm sure he knew we were onto him and did what he had to in order to keep us from knowing."

"How does all of that add up to your funeral?"

Nik laughed aloud once and looked around them before his eyes settled on a large rock with a thin layer of snow atop it. He reached into the breast pocket of his jacket as he sat with a tactless *thud*.

Wren watched curiously but said nothing.

Nik pulled a gray case from the pocket and flipped it open. He removed a white, hand-rolled cigarette out of the case and placed it between his lips. He held the open case out to her and patted his pockets with his free hand. "Want one? I'm not about to get into this without a cigarette."

She gave him a strange look before she hesitantly plucked one from the case.

Nik tucked it back into his pocket and fetched a box of matches next. He casually lit his and took a short drag before he passed the box to Wren.

She stepped beside the boulder and brushed away a small section of snow.

"Thank you."

"Mm-hmm." He nodded once.

They sat in a brief silence and stared in opposite directions.

"My mother burned down the barn," he murmured after a long stretch of quiet. Gray smoke plumed from his nostrils as he sighed. "I fell asleep in the late afternoon, after I had finished cleaning the horse stalls out. The loft was comfortable enough, and Dumont was due to be home soon." He took another lengthy drag.

Wren chewed on the inside of her cheek and stared at the cigarette in her palm as she listened.

"It was only until after I became a reaper that I learned my mother had died in the fire as well. Burned to a crisp while holding the door shut from the outside. My stepfather was found on the only road that led to the farmhouse." His eyes caught Wren's and held her with his stare. "He had been stabbed to death. Forty-three times."

"What?"

Nik looked away from her and instead into the late-morning light that glistened in the cold air.

"My mother killed him, me, then herself. Something in her became monstrous, and she decided she was done trying to fight the shadows away." He took another long drag and pressed his fingers into his forehead. "I'm glad that I was an only child."

Wren had yet to light hers as she stared at him silently.

"When I stood trial for judgment after my death, there was no bright light or cloudy staircase. It was dark and empty, and in an instant, I stood before them. I was angry, full of spite and resentment, but . . . Shown mercy. I was told that they had been watching over my family as my mother gradually lost her mind. They told me that I had the potential to be part of something world changing if I'd dedicate my regifted life to acting out their will. When I agreed, Yu'e herself gave the blessing that sent me back to the world of the living as a bringer of judgment.

"She had said, '*Children should not have to pay for the sins of their parents. They are innocent and should be protected. We will endow you with the responsibility to protect the innocents and gift you with abilities with which to do so.*'" He smirked and tapped his cigarette against the edge of the rock. "I'll never forget those words."

Wren fought down a lump in her throat.

"My mother had been possessed by something that drove her mad. My death had come unjustly, at the hands of a mother no longer in control of her faculties. I was gifted power in exchange for my service, then returned to this realm. I was made responsible for bringing justice to others and removing those who take away innocent lives from this world." A wry laugh escaped him when he noticed an unidentifiable emotion flicker behind Wren's eyes. "Hey, I got another chance to live. It's good to be *not* dead."

Wren scratched the back of her head and looked down. "Kind of an ironic thing, especially considering what you said to me this morning. About it being pointless to save humans. What's even more ironic is that you intervened to save *me*, someone you'd never met and knew nothing about, yet you'd simultaneously be perfectly fine to let two innocent girls be eaten by grifters."

He gave her a look from the corner of his eye but decided to ignore her. Nik glanced between her and the unlit cigarette in her hand. Wordlessly, he took it and the matchbox from her and placed one end between his lips and lit the other. He drew the ember in and exhaled before he held it back out to her.

She nodded once when their eyes met and took her now-burning cigarette back.

The flecks of gold that littered his emerald irises glistened in the sparce light. His eyes seemed to glow, even in the shadows of a tree.

She forced herself to look away and cursed under her breath.

Stop looking at him. She shook her head and trained her stare on the trail of smoke at the tips of her fingers.

"Your turn to share now." He crossed one ankle over his knee and shifted his shoulders to look directly at her. "What are you?"

"No, that's not how this works," she cautioned, leaning away from him slightly. "Why did *you* get to live? You asked me why *I'm* special, and here you are blessed by the *goddess* for a *world-changing* purpose?"

"I told you way more about me than you told me about you."

Wren rolled her eyes and frowned at him. "Maybe we should just go back to not talking," she stated curtly and stood to rejoin the pathway. "Thanks for the light."

They walked in silence, Nik a strict three paces behind her.

When there was no tobacco left to burn, Wren pushed the singed end into her trouser pocket.

They followed the pathway until it stopped at the edge of a small pond surrounded by a clearing. The frozen surface of the water was covered in a deep curtain of snow. Tall, thin branches and stem husks poked out from the undisturbed surface of white.

From their vantage point, they were able to make out a hallway of tangled trees at the opposite side of the clearing. The branches were woven so tightly together that the shadows they cast made it impossible to see where it led.

The clearing was eerily quiet and entirely unmoving.

As Wren's eyes ghosted around the setting, a gentle wind rushed down her collar and made the hairs on her neck quiver.

No bird calls bounced in the glassy white world. The trees stood guard like statues of stone, as there was no hint of wind to move them. No animal prints or tracks defiled the flawless surface of the snow.

"Something isn't right." Her voice fell to a whisper, and she crouched down to pull back small clusters of frosted brush. "Do you feel that?" She sniffed the air and glowered. "There's something foul in the air."

Nik nodded.

Wren's eyes scanned the clearing as she cautiously advanced toward it.

He grabbed a fistful of her green coat and tugged her away from the edge of the brush.

Wren lost her balance and wavered backward. She braced for collision with the ground, but Nik tucked his hands under her arms in time to catch her.

"I feel it too, but that doesn't mean we go charging in. Stay with me." He pulled her back to where the trees still held a semblance of warmth. "I've felt this before, but I can't remember where."

Wren allowed him to steer her away from the clearing, and she nibbled her lip as she suppressed the urge to look back.

"I think we need to get Lionel out here," she said quietly.

He nodded and took the lead, clearing a small path for her in the deeper currents of snow.

She followed closely behind him. Every few paces, she would pause to cast a lingering glance at the clearing.

Nik seemed to notice her hesitation and clipped to a stop. "Why are you stopping?" He looked at her from the corner of his eyes and shook his head. "Stay close. Something doesn't feel right here." Nik extended his hand to her, but she just stared at it. "Fine." He dropped his arm back to his side and turned away. "Just keep up."

Wren narrowed her eyes and fluffed the collar of her jacket closer to her ears. "Just go. I'll be right behind you."

CHAPTER FOUR

*"Wisdom and deep intelligence require an
honest appreciation of mystery."*

Thomas Moore

THEY RETRACED THEIR STEPS AND FOLLOWED THE PATH-
way back toward Black Rivers. The sun began to dip into
the afternoon hour by the time Nik and Wren made it
back to the treeline.

The island town within Arnica's territory was a merchant hot-
spot due to its location between the two rivers. Because of this, it
also had a high population of traders, merchants, and their families.
That, and it was one of the only on-foot routes into Arnica north of
Market Road.

Black Rivers was also home to the last train station for the railroad that ran to the north, parallel to Market Road. It connected
Arnica to the border of Dendros and was the frequent choice of
transportation for commonfolk and drifters.

The name of the town, which was rather unoriginal, came from
the two fingers of a river fed directly from the Northern Sea that

split away from each other and acted as a moat around the entire town. The land between the points where the rivers split and re-joined encircled the massive promontory upon which Black Rivers had been built.

A second stone bridge over the southern river led into the Arni-can mainland. This bridge was long and wide enough to accommo-date a high capacity for foot-traffic.

Rumors told that any poor souls who tried to enter the waters around Black Rivers would be lost into the unknown instantly, pulled in by water nymphs or sirens or serpents, depending on who was asked.

And the townspeople of Black Rivers sure did *love* their rumors.

Wren led the way through the streets. She maintained a pur-poseful ignorance toward the faces that watched them pass by.

Many of the small crowds hushed to murmurs or whispers when the pair came within earshot.

"I hate this part of town," Wren growled quietly.

"Why?"

"We are going to check the station for Elliot," she deflected with a glare. "Her train is due soon, and we can likely beat Lionel there."

Nik shook his head and turned his attention to the whispering onlookers.

Their sharp eyes followed Wren with predatory attentiveness. When they realized that she was not traveling alone, the vacant and brazen stares turned to him.

He had his answer as to why Wren was so tense.

"How far is the station from here?"

Wren shrugged and tugged her coat closer around her throat. "Fifteen minutes."

The entire duration of the walk was the same: nasty looks for seemingly no reason, voices turning to whispers until the pair had passed by, and a sea of faces dark with enmity.

They approached an elaborate train station, complete with giant columns made of pure-white marble that had been mined from the Aster Mountains.

It was crowded by hordes of people bustling through one another. The mass of bodies was a chaotic mixture of shoulders pushing others around to make their way as people shouted obscenities.

Because Arnica Station was the last stop for any passenger or cargo train traveling west from Dendros, it was always bustling. The direct path between the two nations on opposite sides of the continent turned a month's journey by foot into a three-day journey by train.

"There." Wren's voice drew Nik's attention away from the clusters of gossiping murmurs. "She's by the vendor stands."

He followed Wren's pointed finger to a young woman that stood against the exterior wall of the train station.

She had a lovely, heart-shaped face surrounded by curly brown hair that brushed across her shoulders. She was average height and slender in build with immaculate olive skin. She stood awkwardly with the handle of a large suitcase clutched in both hands. It seemed comically too big for her to have handled it on and off the train alone. She looked close to Wren in age, early to mid-twenties.

Wren made her way to the young woman with a small smile.

Nik paused and stuffed his hands into his pockets. He nudged a small rock with his boot absentmindedly as he watched her retreating form.

Elliot's eyes were a vibrant chocolate brown. When they caught sight of Wren, they lit up like a sky suddenly filled with stars. She struggled to shift her suitcase to one side so that she could move.

Wren greeted her by reaching for the luggage and pulling it away.

"I have news." Wren gestured behind her with her chin. "It's a long story, but in short, it's all Lionel's fault."

Elliot's eyes drifted to the tall man a short distance behind her friend.

His broad shoulders and dense, barrel chest made him a daunting presence. Not to mention that he was nearly as tall as Lionel.

She squinted and tilted her head.

Although he didn't look old, Elliot couldn't determine if he was in his twenties, thirties, or forties. Yet, even from this distance, she could tell that he was extremely handsome. Despite that, there was something that unsettled her about his crimson scarf and piercing green eyes, which she could make out clearly despite the distance.

Elliot furrowed her brows.

"Who is tall, dark, and handsome over there, and why is he staring at me?"

"You're giving him way more credit than he deserves. He doesn't need an ego boost."

"Ah, I see. You've already gotten to know him." Elliot's grin widened when her sarcasm drew a scowl from Wren.

"I told you that it's a long story. We can talk more when we get home."

The two women made their way back to Nik, and Elliot scrutinized him with every step.

He didn't miss the curly-haired woman sizing him up. Their eyes met, and he held her stare for the few uncomfortable moments that it took *him* to size *her* up. His emerald orbs freed her when they drifted to Wren, who outright ignored him.

Elliot's breath had caught in her chest when she and Nik locked eyes. She had halted mid-step until he looked to Wren yet kept her own gaze on the strange man. She pursed her lips when she noticed how much more intensely he seemed to watch Wren than he did her. Her brow quirked curiously, and she turned to look at her friend.

"But really," Elliot whispered, "what's his deal? Is he single?"

"Shut up, Elliot."

"Rude."

They met back up with Nik, and he offered a polite nod.

"Elliot, I presume?"

"Wren didn't tell me your name." She smirked at Wren with a gleam in her eyes.

Wren scoffed and clicked her tongue in disapproval, and Elliot wisely looked back to Nik.

"I'm Nik. It's a pleasure to meet you."

Something about their exchange made an uneasy feeling flutter in the pit of Wren's stomach.

"Let's go home. You can become formally acquainted there."

The busy street grew more difficult to navigate the closer to they got to the heart of the populace. The stone road began to widen as they made their way through a residential borough that bordered the marketplace. Piles of snow littered every corner and cover of the iced-over pathway.

A towering statue of a bearded man was chipped into a pillar of the same marble as the columns of the train station stood in the center of the main thoroughfare. The figure had a large frame and severe features that looked down his nose at the people as they went about their business.

The piercing eyes in the crowd grew more numerous, too.

Nik tucked his left hand in his coat pocket, kept his right arm at his side, and eyed the stares that followed Wren like shadows.

Regardless of where they were within the city, Wren always seemed to draw a dubious air from the townspeople.

"Oi!"

A familiar voice was followed by a shuffle of feet.

Elliot turned to see what she had been dreading approaching them through the crowd.

"Oh no," she whispered.

Nik heard her and followed the direction of her stare.

"Hiya, darlin'!"

Wren's back stiffened, and she came to a stop. The suitcase bashed into the side of her leg, but she was entirely unfazed by it.

Elliot clapped her hands on Wren's shoulders and urged her to keep walking.

"Keep going, Wren." When her friend showed no sign of moving, Elliot turned to Nik. "We need to leave," she insisted. "*Now*."

The source of the voice broke through the mass of villagers and continued to advance on them.

Nik lifted his arm in front of Elliot and put himself between the girls and the new arrival.

A bulky man with a thickly bearded face stood with his hands clenched at his sides. He had strong shoulders and a long stride that thundered toward them. He occasionally fumbled, and he stank of stale beer. The man's bloodshot eyes lay fixed on the curly-haired woman.

Although he was only slightly taller than Nik, he was far larger.

"We never got ta finish our conversation las' time, darlin'. I gotta pal that wants ta meet ya. *Real*, real bad. He saw ya las' time ya stayed with yer lil friend. He asked me ta introduce ya." His attention moved to Wren, and his grin grew more unsettling. "Hiya, birdy. I woulda brought 'er home when we was done."

"Get out of here, Brock," Elliot warned with a dark look. "Your childish crush on me needs to end. I have no idea where you've come up with the idea that I would want anything to do with you *or* your friends in *any* capacity. Your sister can spread all the nasty rumors about me that she wants to, I don't care. They are nothing more than lies."

"Naah, she don' mean no harm." His face scrunched up into what could have been a smile but was actually a sneer. He shrugged and looked her up and down. "I didn't know ya were comin' back ta town so soon. Woulda made ya a nice, comfy bed right next ta mine."

"You're mad."

His feet fumbled beneath him again as he continued to close the distance between them.

"I'm not going to stop her from beating the shit out of you this time if you don't go away *now*." Elliot's voice was firm but quivered once as she tried to avoid a seemingly unavoidable confrontation.

"Brock! Get yer drunk, deadbeat ass back into the house!"

A hefty woman with wispy, unkempt blond hair charged after him. She was tall, an easy four inches taller than Wren, and had a sinister look in her eyes. She had deep frown lines etched around her mouth and a low-set brow. Her skin was ashy and tanned from poor diet and decades spent in the sun.

"Ay, ay! I see ya, demon! Get that harlot outta here!"

The shrill voice drew Wren to turn. She dropped the suitcase and scanned the faces within the crowd.

"Rumors," Wren mumbled to herself with an angry expression.

"Shit," Elliot seethed and shook her head. She grabbed her friend's arm and tugged. "Wren, let's *go*. This is stupid." When Wren pulled her arm free, Elliot's hands clenched at her sides.

"Enough is enough, El." Wren patted Elliot's shoulder and offered her friend a small smirk. She then looked to Nik as her lips set into a thin line. "Don't let anyone near her." She hesitated briefly before adding, "Please."

Nik watched her carefully.

There was something in her eyes that shone like they had during their first formal introduction.

He drew a breath in through his nose and accepted her request with a single nod.

Wren spun and strode toward Brock, maintaining an unwavering stare that was focused on him. She ignored the murmurs of the forming crowd of curious observers as she neared him.

They stopped only a few feet from each other, eyes burning

into one another. Brock's height advantage over her was daunting, but she refused to acknowledge the gnawing feeling that urged her to walk away.

"Lemme through! Le— Ugh! Let me *through!*" The blond woman struggled through the shoulders of onlookers before she forced her large body between Wren and Brock. She slapped the back of Brock's head and glowered at him. "I swear I will beat sense into that thick head of yer's even *after* it splits open! Get back in the damned house, and don't so much as fuss on yer way back!" Her tired gray eyes turned to Wren. "Ya said ya'd keep yer nose outta here, ya demon. Going back on our deal?"

Wren's eyebrows furrowed together as she crossed her arms over her chest.

"Honorah, your backward-ass idea of the word *deal* means very little to me lately. What of the two grifters from last night? Is that part of the *deal* you are referring to? Because that would mean you neglected your end first, letting criminals roam freely in the center square and turning a blind eye to their crimes. They were behind the recent disappearances, weren't they? You knew, and yet you did nothing."

Honorah's eyes narrowed at her, but she said nothing in retort.

"Get back inside, and we will gladly continue on our way out of your shithole."

"Fine with me, demon. Keep *yer* filth in *yer* borough, else next time I won't be so generous. I'll let Brock deal with ya."

Wren smirked. "Promise?"

A wave of rage boiled within Honorah, and she instinctively drew her fist back.

Wren anticipated her easily and half-stepped to the left.

Honorah followed her with a swivel, charging into the other woman until she caught a handful of sunset hair. A firm tug brought Wren to the ground face-first.

She managed to tuck her chin in time to guard her eyes and nose, but the side of her face scraped across the ice and stone from the impact.

"Please stop this! Nik, do something!" Elliot tugged at the sleeve on his jacket, desperately trying to get him to intervene.

He shook his head without looking at her. "No," he replied plainly. "Wren isn't even fighting back. If she needed help, she would have asked."

"You obviously don't know her at all."

"Hm."

Elliot glared and tried to push by him.

Nik caught her elbow easily and pulled her to his chest. His other hand snatched her shoulder, and he held her in front of him. "Wren will be just fine."

"I'm not worried about Wren being *fine*. I'm worried abo . . ." She cut herself short and sighed. "Never mind. Will you *please* let me stop them?"

"No."

The large woman huffed with a grin and turned to circle Wren, who made no attempt to get back up.

Instead, Wren focused on breathing evenly and had her eyelids pressed together.

Honorah cackled softly, intoxicated with adrenaline and excitement. She kept circling Wren with a devilish expression, waiting for her to move.

"Still fighting dirty," Wren muttered to herself and pressed her palms against the stone. She flexed her shoulders to push herself upright and balanced her weight between her hands and knees.

Once Wren reached a crouching position, Honorah grabbed a fistful of her green coat and slammed her knee into Wren's abdomen.

Wren tumbled away from the blow and hit the ground with a hard *thud*. She shifted to sit upright and rubbed the back of her hand across her cheek.

Blood and dirt clung to her face and ear. The wound on her cheekbone began bleeding again.

"My patience is wearing thin." Wren's stare was locked on Honorah and rapidly grew severe. "If you keep antagonizing me, you're going to regret it."

Honorah laughed once and looked around to the townspeople.

A small crowd had gathered into a semicircle around the two women. It pulsated with murmurs and sneers and was sprinkled heavily with mischievous laughter.

"Ya tease me with yer mockery, even after everything that ya done to my family. Then threaten me? Get up, demon." Her voice suddenly dropped to a whisper. "I got a message from Seth. Tells us he *can't wait* to see ya again."

A sharp gust of wind tore through the empty space overhead.

Wren's eyes flashed dangerously for a split second before she squeezed them shut. Her teeth bored into her bottom lip as she struggled to keep her composure. Wren shook her head, and her hands clung to her temples as she drew deep breaths in and out through her nose.

Window shutters tremored and slapped the stone buildings to which they were attached. It ripped at loose hair, clothing, and rattled debris. Lighter shards of things were plucked into the current of air. The quick gust was so sharp that it pulled gasps of surprise from the crowd, leaving them silent.

It slowed as it drew closer to Wren and curled in on itself like a tidal wave's narrowing scope before it crashed back down.

"Wren!"

Wren's eyes moved to Elliot at the sound of her voice.

The gleam that Nik saw before was now something entirely different.

They showed fear. And fury.

No, they *radiated* fury.

Honorah advanced while jeers and taunts from the crowd encouraged her to fight in their stead.

Brock watched from the edge of the bar's doorway. He gave his sister a wild grin, cupping his fist and flexing his arm in an approving gesture.

The blond woman drew her foot back and planted a second kick square on Wren's back, just between her shoulder blades.

Wren caught herself from falling this time with her hands splayed on the ground, but her breathing became shallow and slow. She was still as stone aside from her fingers slowly curling until they became tightly clenched fists.

Honorah chuckled and crouched beside her with a daring look painted across her face.

"I know ya were the one that killed my brother, *demon*. I know *what* ya really are." She leaned in and whispered, "He told me. And I think ya know as well as I do that he ain't gone. Ya feel him too, don't ya?"

Wren's head swiveled to pin Honorah with a glare. A sudden, unidentifiable glint flashed behind her eyes when they locked with Honorah's, and her desire to engage was palpable.

Honorah paused when their eyes met and folded her arms as she stood upright. When Wren said nothing yet stared with an intensity that spoke for itself, Honorah grimaced and spit onto the ground.

Right between Wren's hands.

Wren's eyes narrowed and nostrils flared. Maintaining her composure was becoming increasingly more difficult, and her desire to do so was dwindling. Wren took a deep breath without looking away from Honorah and clenched her jaw.

The hazel color of Wren's eyes gradually began to lighten as they stared, locked on the woman. As the saturation of her irises reduced, the contrast against the whites of her eyes somehow seemed to become more pronounced.

Honorah's own gray eyes widened when she noticed them change.

"Break it up! Someone separate them!"

Everyone turned to see Lionel hurrying toward them.

At the sound of his voice, Wren's eyes slammed shut, and she turned her head away. A pounding feeling thudded in her ears, and her knuckles ached. She shifted her weight back and allowed herself to sit. She brought her knees to her chest and dropped her forehead onto them. Her hair pooled around her face and cloaked it behind a ginger curtain.

Members of the crowd hustled over each other to clear a path to Wren and Honorah.

The blond woman scoffed when she felt someone touch her arm to coax her away from Wren. Honorah jerked her arm away from them and narrowed her eyes at Lionel.

Elliot took advantage of the situation to break free from Nik and sprinted over to Wren.

"Try to relax, Wren. I'm here; it's all right." Her firm grip found Wren's shoulders and squeezed hard. "Just focus on your breathing."

Honorah pursed her lips and looked to Nik. "They're dangerous, ya know. Both of 'em."

He arched a brow in response.

She scowled and gestured to Elliot and Wren.

"That *creature* and her harlot friend." Honorah's husky voice practically hissed her words. "She's a demon, ya know." She looked Nik over once and offered a wink and a smirk. "If yer new here and got any wits about ya, I say stay away. Nothin' but trouble fer poor Lionel, and he just puts up with that one." She looked to Wren. "Absolute terrors, both of 'em. *I* can show ya around."

Elliot bristled and looked over to Honorah.

"Bite your tongue, you horrible woman! You have no grounds to make such accusations aside from making up bored gossip and spreading *blatantly* untrue rumors!"

"Ladies, please." Lionel hastily made his way to Elliot and Wren. A settling calm that emanated from him filtered into the crowd and trickled warmly through the whipping wind. The gale slowed as the opposing warmth dissolved the dying storm.

"What is the petty squabble regarding this time, hm? Honorah?" He looked to the large woman standing beside Nik and shook his head. "Just because Black Rivers is annexed from the kingdom doesn't at all mean you can brawl in the streets. You can still be brought into custody under the kingdom's law for instigating a fight with a guard."

"Hmph," Honorah replied and crossed her arms.

Lionel turned to Elliot, and his eyes softened when they met hers.

"I tried to stop it, Lionel. I even asked *him* to help, but he just stood there! Like an oaf!" Elliot glared at Nik from where she hovered beside Wren. Her slender hand held her friend's shoulder and gently rubbed her back. "Honorah, you should be ashamed of yourself! You kick and taunt her when you know she won't fight back. Just as vile and hideous as always."

Lionel gave Nik an apologetic smile before he looked back to Elliot.

"It is all okay now, my dear. You did a fine job, even without Nikolas's help."

His honey-sweet voice soothed her temper slightly, but anger still lingered in her eyes.

Lionel knelt down and touched the crook of Wren's neck.

"Wren," he hummed quietly.

She remained still and unresponsive with her arms wrapped around her legs and eyes shut tight.

"Let's leave now, all right? We will all go back home." He motioned to Nik with a tilt of his head.

Lionel and Elliot looped their arms through Wren's and heaved her to stand.

Elliot moved in front of Wren and attempted to get her attention with a few soft smacks to her cheek. She frowned when her friend's eyes did not open. Elliot brushed a lock of her hair back and winced at the blood slowly draining from the crest of her cheek and the top of her ear.

"Oh, Wren," she whispered.

"I'll carry her, El, don't worry." Lionel tucked his arm the rest of the way around Wren's back and lifted her from the ground. "I will be back, Honorah. We will be having a very long discussion. It would be wise of you to find a way to convince me to not report this incident."

The large woman laughed aloud. "Says *ya*. I ain't stayin' around just to get an earful from ya." She huffed and smiled, yellow and cracked teeth poking from behind her lips.

"I'll take them back, Lionel." Nik stared at Honorah before he turned to his friend. "Just bring Elliot's suitcase back with you when you're done here."

Lionel blinked once before he nodded. "Thank you, Nikolas. I won't be far behind." Lionel shifted Wren's form into Nik's arms.

Nik cradled her knees and adjusted her to rest in a crescent shape against his chest. Although he had carried her to Lionel's home last night, Nik still found himself surprised by how light she was.

"Show me the way back, Elliot."

CHAPTER FIVE

"The measure of a man is what he does with power."

Plato

Over here." Elliot beckoned Nik to the small couch in front of the balcony door. The couch faced the view, allowing the rising moon to flood the room in its white light.

Nik obliged and placed Wren onto the soft cushions, carefully easing her head to rest on the arm.

Her freckled face was pallid, and the outline of her lips was kissed with a hint of blue. Her hands twitched at her sides, fingers clenched and unclenched, never fully uncurling, like she couldn't relax. Her eyes were still shut tight.

Nik took a seat in the armchair beside the couch to watch her closely.

Elliot veered into the kitchen in order to retrieve a cloth from one of the cabinets. She flicked the light switch on before turning to the sink and dampening the white rag.

The sound of the faucet running filled the quiet just as the low, orange light filled the room.

Elliot wrung the towel out tightly until it was nearly desaturated and made her way around the counter to Wren's side.

"She's not a demon," Elliot murmured as she brushed a thin lock of hair away from the bridge of Wren's nose. She pressed the warm cloth against her wounds to wipe them clean. When Nik neglected to provide a response, she peered at him from the corner of her eyes. "Honorah hates Wren because she killed her older brother. She had to, though. He was pure evil . . . A tyrant willing to burn Arnica to the ground along with anyone who would not follow him in order to take it for himself."

"Honorah's brother?"

"Seth," she nearly hissed. "Seth Tanner. He and his cult overthrew the Southern Boroughs two years ago, then made an attempt at the throne. His stronghold was right here in Black Rivers. Most of his men lived in or around the marketplace that we just came from. They pillaged their way through most of the southern region of the kingdom, making way for Bay City."

Nik's eyebrow arched curiously.

Elliot frowned at him. "You don't talk very much, do you?"

Nik replied with a quick smirk that creased his cheek but remained silent.

She shook her head and rolled her eyes. "I've got the notion that you and Wren didn't get off on the right foot."

"Oh?"

"The silent treatment is *her* game." Elliot shrugged. "I can't imagine that she'd take well to someone like you, who plays it too."

"I'm not playing games," Nik said firmly. "I listen. I wait for the right time to say what I think. When I do, I choose my words carefully."

"Hm, then there's no doubt about it." She giggled softly. "I bet that got right under her skin."

Nik smirked again and glanced at the subject of their conversation.

Her face was a bit more relaxed now, and the wrinkle between her eyebrows was beginning to soften.

"Tell me more about Seth. What was his plan with Bay City?"

"I assume it had something to do with the fact that it's Arnica's port city to Greater Bay. It's the largest port on the western coastline, and the main entry by sea to the kingdom . . . And it has a generous population of people that hate King Reed and his sanctions. The people there were ready to light the powder keg as soon as they learned of Seth's plan to take the throne for himself.

"Not to mention that he and his men could control imports from Market Road through Black Rivers, effectively cutting off resources to the citizens of Arnica." Her heart-shaped face turned back to Wren. She brushed her friend's forehead with the cloth and dabbed away any blood that had yet to dry.

A soft murmur escaped Wren's lips when the cloth grazed the wound on her cheek.

"He killed lots of people. He used the promise of power and property to brainwash creatures to do most of his dirty work. Those that didn't want a part in his army were either killed on the spot or taken as a prisoner. Trolls, snatchers, vampires, and fae of nearly every variety . . . The humans were often too stunned or scared to fight back. Not that a man would stand much of a chance against a troll, and fae can outwit most humans easily," she muttered darkly.

Nik opened his mouth to reply but fell silent when Wren stirred.

She inched her way to a more comfortable sitting position and groaned softly at the burning pain in her ribs. She rubbed at the scrape along her cheek and temple with a scuffed palm. Still bleeding. A deep frown darkened her face as her eyes rolled into focus. They flicked from Elliot to Nik in deliberation. She drew a steadying breath and settled on Nik, still refusing to meet that gold-and-green stare.

"Where is Lionel?"

He didn't answer right away. Instead, he stared at Wren as though he was perplexed by something. When he opened his mouth to speak, he was interrupted by Elliot.

"He's on his way back, Wren," she chimed with a bright smile, any inkling of her earlier foul mood gone. "I'll grab you some water." She rose from behind the couch and drifted into the kitchen.

Wren groaned again as she swung her feet to the floor. Her hand massaged the back of her neck and focused mainly on the throbbing spot on her scalp. Her fingertip brushed the torn helix of her ear, and she gasped softly when it stung.

"Fantastic," She growled and dropped her eyes and hands to her lap with a sigh. She turned them over a few times to examine the angry red skin.

"Why didn't you fight back?"

Wren laughed a single, breathy laugh before she looked up at him. "It's complicated." She pushed her palms into the cushion to stand but was halted by Nik's outstretched hand, a hard and frustrated look etched on his face.

He stood before she had a chance to and eased her back into a sitting position on the couch by her shoulder.

"Uncomplicate it." Nik watched her closely to make sure she didn't try to stand again. "If I'm to help, I don't think leaving things out because they are *complicated* is the best way to start." He looked to Elliot, still in the kitchen and staring shamelessly.

"Help how? What could *you* do?" The curly-haired woman crossed the room and leaned over the couch to hand Wren a glass of water. "Also, who *are* you?"

"I already told you my name." He shrugged his jacket off. "Lionel and I grew up together. We've been friends for a long time." He folded the shoulders of his jacket together, then neatly in half, and set the garment on the back of the mustard-colored armchair.

"Aw! That's sweet!" Wren rolled her eyes as Elliot gushed. "What was Lionel like as a kid? I bet he was as handsome and kind then as he is now! Does he really not know how to ride a bicycle?"

"Elliot."

"What? Lionel never talks about his childhood, and now we have someone else to ask! I know he hates bicycles. Now we can find out why!"

Wren drew a sharp breath in through her nose and stood despite Nik's cautioning stare. "Lionel asked him here. For what, I don't know yet. So far, the only thing either of them will say is that he's here to help."

Jack rounded the side of the couch and mewed at Wren happily. She plucked the white cat from the ground and turned him over in her arms as his slate eyes lidded contently.

"Well, I actually needed to talk to you, Wren . . . Something strange happened."

Three sets of eyes turned to Elliot in an instant.

She rubbed the back of her neck as she searched for her words. "I heard about what happened last night while I was at the train station. Most people said it was a mugging gone wrong or an animal attack . . . But one of the women they found had been absolutely shredded, the other stabbed in the side of the head." Her shoulders tremored unconsciously. "Brutal."

Wren and Nik shared an uneasy look but remained silent.

"If you ask me, that doesn't sound like a mugging . . ."

"Is that the strange thing?"

Elliot's eyes met Wren's questioning ones, and she shook her head.

"No, the strange part is that I overheard two Guardsmen talking about it at the station gate. One of them said that it was a sign of worse things to come. The other . . . well, the other guard seemed rather pleased. He said that he's looking forward to something that's going to happen during the festival." Elliot shook her head again. "I couldn't hear their whole conversation because the train was getting ready to depart, and we were going in opposite directions."

"That isn't that peculiar, El." Wren caressed Jack's cheek and ruffled his whiskers with her thumb. "More than half of the guards on the king's payroll are corrupt. I'm not surprised they are letting things get worse for some cheap thrill or because of a bribe. There are always rumors that something will happen at any festival within Arnica."

"What about the attack? The way the two women died? That isn't peculiar to you? I mean, come on. The *timing*?" Elliot's eyes narrowed, and she crossed her arms. "I heard that one was literally in pieces! Come on, Wren. You and I both know that isn't a mugging or an animal attack!"

Wren sighed and deposited Jack onto the couch's cushions. "I already know what happened last night, and it's not what you're thinking." She rubbed her temples and winced when the injured side throbbed beneath her fingertips.

"What happened, then?"

Wren shot her friend a stern look. "I was there. It was me, all right? I killed one of those women. They tried to take Gwen and Laila Michair last night, and I had to stop them."

"Tried to take them? They weren't human, then? I heard that the two women were human." Something in Elliot's voice gave away a sudden waver of nervousness.

"They were grifters. I don't know what drove them to do something like that, but they did. Who knows how long they've been at it and just hadn't been caught. Something had to be done." Wren folded her arms and looked out the glass doors.

The moon was in full view through the panes. A cloudless sky allowed for it to glow proudly against the twinkling, velvet backdrop.

"They were out for blood, El. You might even remember them. Bianca and Torrie?" The sudden stillness from Elliot was all she needed as confirmation. "If that's all you have to be worried about, forget it. The situation has already been handled."

"You shredded one of them to bits? I'm not joking about this, Wren. You're sworn to protect people as a guardsman, not to kill! If the king finds out, he can have you stripped and banished!" Elliot frowned and folded her arms. "You really did that?"

The hiccup of genuine fear in Elliot's question made Wren's heart hurt.

"Wren killed the grifter with the head wound in self-defense. As for the shredded one, I did that bit."

Elliot's eyes shot to Nik, wide and disbelieving.

Wren tilted her chin down and sighed with inexplicable relief.

"You? How can you do that to a person?"

Nik set his lips in a tight line and met her stare. He stuffed his hands into the pockets of his pants and shrugged. "You've clearly never met a starving grifter before."

Elliot gasped and glared at him. "I don't see how that devalues their li—"

"They don't value anything but themselves. Grifters are a deeply narcissistic subspecies of vampire that think blood tastes better when their victim is literally scared to death. Adrenaline is the salt on their feast." His cautioning stare stifled any argument out of Elliot. "They will say or do anything to feed. The pair last night were starving. They wouldn't have stopped after killing those girls."

"Did you recognize either of the guards at the station?"

Nik and Elliot turned to Wren, whose eyes were locked on the world outside.

"I— ah, I don't know their names, but I've seen one of them before."

"Can you describe him?"

Elliot nodded as she reached for one of her curls and twisted it around her finger absentmindedly. "A bit large around the waist, dark skin, and a big gray mustache."

Wren sighed and finally looked back into the room. She settled on Elliot with an apologetic smile. "That sounds like Sir Charles."

Elliot's blood went cold and her back went rigid. "Yes! That nasty bastard." She tapped her chin and shook her head. "I knew I recognized him."

"Just hope he didn't recognize you," Wren uttered darkly.

Elliot went quiet and looked away. She spotted Jack, content on the couch, and curled her arms around him and brought him to her chest. "I'm going to take a shower," Elliot said softly. "I'll get Jack's dinner ready, too. I assume we'll be splitting your room?"

Wren nodded mutely.

Elliot didn't need to see her to know the answer. Her back was to the pair in the room, and she was already halfway into Wren's room. "See you in there, then." Elliot turned to flash a grin before she clipped the door shut.

Wren shook her head and fished through the pockets of her trousers. She plucked a partially smoked cigarette from it and made for the glass doors.

Nik hesitated before he followed her outside.

Wren sighed into the late-winter air, a plume of white cascading from her nose and mouth. She placed the rolled paper between her lips and patted herself down for a matchbook.

The sudden flare of a lit match turned her attention to Nik.

He already had a fresh cigarette in his mouth and held it to the flame. When the tobacco began to ember and burn, he shook the match out with a few flicks of his wrist.

Wren watched him do this without moving. She felt a sudden lump form in her chest when the amber glow of the lit match cast a new light against his features. It emphasized his strong cheekbones and stubble-dusted jaw and made the gold in his eyes shine.

"How long have you and Lionel lived here for?"

She jumped when his sudden question startled her from her thoughts. Wren looked to his outstretched hand that presented her with the freshly lit cigarette. "Lionel's been here some twenty or so years, I'm not entirely sure." She shrugged and accepted the offering.

"And you?"

"I've been here about eighteen years." Wren paused and took a short drag. The corners of her lips drew into a pensive frown. Her eyes slipped shut, and she clenched her hand at her side. "Long enough for practically the entire kingdom to hate me," she murmured to herself.

Nik sighed before he tucked the tips of his fingers under her chin. A gentle tug brought her face back upright. Before she had a chance to respond, he gave her a soft smile.

Caught off guard, Wren blinked. She hastily collected herself and shoved his hand away, eyebrows low.

His eyes narrowed slightly at her, yet he put his hands up, palms facing out in surrender.

"You keep hiding your face when you talk to me," Nik defended. "So, you're one of these guards? From what you said in there, you know them pretty well."

Wren gave no response as she silently took another drag and exhaled.

"If you're sworn to protect them, why do they hate you?"

"They don't necessarily see what I do as protection. Many think that I am the reason the kingdom seems to be filling with creatures that have no intention of cohabitation. Anything strange happening in Black Rivers is somehow my fault and my problem. Honorah's rumors don't help, either."

Nik watched her intently.

She shrugged and sighed. "And yes. I, unfortunately, hold status in the kingdom as a member of the King's Guard."

"Why unfortunately? Shouldn't that be a good thing?"

She pursed her lips and looked away. "Lionel says it is, but I hate it." Wren's tongue raked over her teeth and rippled under her tightened lips. "It's done nothing but label me as some pariah. People look at me like I have some ulterior motive to be suspicious of. You saw it firsthand in the marketplace today." Her teeth clapped together, jaw clenched tight. "They pick fights with me because they know I won't fight back."

"She started it," he pressed. "You can defend yourself, can't you?"

"Nope." Her eyes closed, and her chin tipped back down. "The logic there is that humans couldn't possibly hurt me if I can single-handedly fend off a golem. '*People will be people, but you've faced worse, so just endure it*' was the exact verbiage, if I remember correctly." Wren's hair swayed around her downcast face as she shook her head.

"How *is* it that you can fend off a golem?" Nik took a small step toward her. He procured the space beside her so that they were shoulder to shoulder. He waited for her to look at him before he emphasized their height difference with his arm. "You aren't very . . . big. Or heavy."

Wren shook her head again as a smile cracked into a wide grin. Soft laughter rumbled in her chest, but she groaned when it stirred the anguish in her ribs. Her hand instinctively hovered to her side to apply pressure on what was absolutely going to leave a bruise.

"I'm well aware of my size." She drew in an even breath and hesitated. "It's *what* I am. That's what the Guard cares about. If I was *only* human, I'd simply be arrested or banished after the first few incidents. But instead, if I am to live within the city, I am sentenced to protect citizens that hate me."

"Then what *are* you?"

"A tempest."

Nik turned to face her directly, lowering his shoulders so that they were eye to eye. "You're lying."

Silence drifted between them.

Wren watched Nik carefully from the corner of her eye, pretending to not look at him.

He leaned away and settled against the exterior wall beside her with his arms folded. "You can trust me, Wren."

"So you say," she muttered, "but I'm not convinced."

Nik shook his head and sighed.

"Wren, I told you about my mother. My stepfather. What happened to me after I died. I will answer any questions that you have honestly. I do not intend to deceive you in any way." His voice was soft, but there was an earnestness to it that caught her off guard. "But I need you to trust me if I'm to do that."

She rolled her eyes as she shook her head, purposefully turning her attention elsewhere. Wren held the cigarette out to him and waited for him to take it. She kept her face angled away from him and drew in a sharp breath. "I'm a spell."

Nik's eyes shot open wide, and his chest pulled in an unconscious gasp.

"A spell? That's not possible," he growled. He was at her side in an instant and gave her a sideways look. "Don't joke, I'm serious."

His fixed stare penetrated her, and she stood frozen in place.

"I'm *being* serious."

"There are no spells. They've been extinct f—"

"Nearly a century, yeah. I know."

The door at the top of the stairs swung open, and Lionel stepped into the apartment. He drifted into the main sitting area and slumped into his favorite, mustard-yellow chair. His eyes fluttered shut, and he pressed his gloved fingers into his brow in exhaustion.

"That woman is incorrigible," Lionel muttered softly. He glanced to Nik and Wren, and a knowing smile crept onto his lips.

Lionel's entry helped Wren to free herself from Nik's pinning stare. She drew in a shallow breath and moved away from him. Her knees wavered slightly as she crossed the threshold into the apartment.

He watched her, still in disbelief. He dropped the cigarette into the snow and followed her in like a shadow.

"That's impossible." Nik quickly snatched her forearm and tugged her backward. "Lionel, you knew this and did not tell me?" He turned his attention to Lionel with an incredulous expression painted on his face.

Lionel rubbed his forehead and eye sockets in exasperation and rolled his head against the back of the chair. "Timing, my friend." He poked one eye open and smiled at Nik. "Plus, you'd be just as upset learning this through a messenger." He slinked his arm over his face and turned to look at them. "Who could I trust to deliver that sort of news to you and no one else?"

"But for *eighteen years?*" Nik ground his teeth and looked back to Wren. "This is why you wouldn't tell me."

She pursed her lips and nodded.

"Do the townspeople know too? The king?"

"No," Lionel supplied instantly. "They think that she is a tempest. Only Elliot, myself, and three other villagers know, and now you."

Wren freed her arm roughly and scowled. She reached around Nik to yank the glass door shut with purposeful force.

"What right do *you* have to be upset about this?" Wren leveled him with a glare.

Nik glared right back. His ebony eyebrows were set low and hands were clenched at his sides.

"I don't like being left in the dark about something this important. Especially by my oldest friend."

"I knew you would act like this," she said in a quiet voice before she took a step away from him. "I'd be lying if I said I was surprised."

"There's no use quarreling, you two," Lionel chimed in to break their staring match. "The cat is out of the bag now, so we can move on together, or get stuck being upset about things we cannot change."

"So, what *do* I need to know, Lionel?" Nik reluctantly pried his eyes away from Wren and over to Lionel. "If there is anything else you two aren't telling me, now would be a great time to fill me in."

"Nikolas." Lionel sat up from his armchair to peer at his friend. His voice was so soft and warm that it lulled a wave of ease into the room. "We can talk about it all now if you would like to."

"Great," he growled tersely. "Let's start with her. How do you know she's really a spell? How can you be so sure? You understand how impossible that is, right?"

Wren narrowed her eyes and folded her arms. It took all of her strength to remain quiet.

The trace smiled at Nik apologetically. "In order to explain that, there are things you must first understand." Lionel sighed and motioned for them to take a seat.

Wren took the hint and selected one of the five chairs at the circular table, eyes still locked on Nik.

Nik remained in place, searching his friend with a conflicted look of suspicion and disbelief. He eventually complied and sank into the end of the couch beside the armrest.

Lionel gave them both a gentle smile that brightened the murky ambience of the room. He took their silence as his cue to begin.

"Spells are, by far, the rarest creature known to exist in all of Yu'e." He propped his elbows on his knees as he leaned forward. "They were supposedly the perfect predator. Authors and scribes claimed that, of the two that have ever been, the sky was their domain. They fight by use of strong winds, intense fire storms, and, in at least one instance, a hurricane of lightning and thunder . . . There is no way to verify if it's true or not, unfortunately. The only two that have ever been recorded in history were depicted as powerful but volatile creatures capable of great feats. In fact, the most well-known spell is Eurynome."

Wren's face twisted with disgust at the name, and she looked away from the two men.

Nik shifted in his seat so he could lean his elbow on the armrest. He peered at Wren through the corner of his eye to gauge her body language as Lionel spoke.

She caught his glance and glared.

Lionel noticed the exchange but, wisely, chose to ignore it.

"Wren is able to disrupt air currents and manipulate them, right?" It wasn't a question. "She is also incredibly fast when she has to be." Lionel gave her a warm smile. It went unrequited. "These abilities, even in her adolescence, in conjunction with her ability to shift—"

"Lionel!" Wren's eyes burned into him.

He could only frown back. "It's better this way," he said gently. "Nikolas is right. Keeping him uninformed makes his being here pointless."

"Good. I'm glad to know you're still deciding what's best for me."

"Wren," Lionel replied with a sigh. "You know as well as I do that there is something looming in the very near future. You need to trust me that requesting Nikolas's presence *is* in your best interest."

Wren scoffed. "We wouldn't even be in this mess if you would have let me leave after Seth's attempt on the kingdom. I had to reveal myself in order to stop him; there was no other way." She set her jaw tightly and held Lionel's eyes with intent. "The townspeople have made it clear that I'm not welcome here, and I'm not waiting anymore, Lionel. It's time that I leave."

"Why would you leave?"

All eyes turned to Elliot, who had emerged from Wren's room.

Jack followed closely behind her before breaking off to jump onto the counter. He hopped from the surface onto the table and seated himself proudly beside Wren.

No one spoke while Elliot took in their expressions.

"She isn't leaving, my dear." Lionel smiled. "We are only discussing the current situation."

"It would be better for everyone if I did," Wren persisted. "Elliot would be safer if she isn't seen with me anymore. She could live here with you, and you guys wouldn't have me to babysit . . . And all in the Kingdom of Arnica will rejoice." She gave Jack a loving stroke and ruffled his ears. "I can't keep living like this."

"You don't mean that, Wren." Elliot dashed to her friend's side and took her hand from Jack's head. "You're only feeling off now because of what happened at the market! You kept yourself together, and that in itself is a win!" Her heart-shaped face gleamed a bright smile. "Jack and I are here to help! I made him a cat fortress on your bed, I call it his *cat*-stle. He has a lookout tower and everything! I used your tabletop lamp as a base . . . Don't worry, I covered it. I came out to get more pillows from Lionel's room . . . We didn't have enough for the moat."

Wren stared at Elliot blankly, and the rest of the room was silent.

Elliot's wide smile refused to fade, and Wren finally gave in.

"Why would he need a moat if the fortress is already on top of my bed?"

Elliot's face lit up, and she pulled her friend into her room by the arm. "Come see!"

Wren reluctantly allowed herself to be dragged along and pursed her lips. She turned to Lionel and Nik with narrowed eyes before she disappeared into her bedroom.

Nik gnashed his teeth together and turned his full attention to Lionel.

"You need to fill me in. Why did you keep this from me for so long?" His rugged features wrinkled in frustration.

"I had to be sure. I knew you would be angry with me, and, for that, I am sorry. Wren is very rough around the edges, but she has incredible determination, and a gentle nature . . . Once you get to know her. When I found her in the forest, she was practically feral."

"She told me all about that."

"Really? That's very surprising." Lionel cocked his head to the side and placed his hand to his chin in deliberation. "Even Elliot knows better than to ask her about that. She's not usually in the mood to remember those times." He gave his friend a wide grin. "I'd say that's a good sign."

Nik's face slowly relaxed as he settled into the long-missed presence of his childhood friend.

"All right, tell me the whole truth this time. Don't leave shit out if you think it'll make me mad; that's the shit I need to know." Nik met Lionel's endlessly blue eyes and smirked.

"All right." He nodded.

The two men settled into seats across from each other and took care to get comfortable.

"Wren and I both feel as though something bad is going to happen at this year's festival. She is correct in that incidents like last night have become a normal occurrence over the past few weeks." Lionel drew in a weighty sigh.

"The pair of grifters?"

"Yes." Lionel nodded slowly. "And it gets worse." He sat back in his chair and pressed his pants flat in an attempt to busy his idle hands. "King Reed has dispatched only a scant number of guardsmen to help the citizens, keeping Wren and the vast majority to himself. As things have worsened, the king chose to allow only the more experienced guardsmen and Wren to intercept any attacks."

"Some king."

"Yeah." Lionel nodded again as he rolled his eyes. "There was a report of a peryton about a week ago in Wheatrich, north of the kingdom. Once Wren's unit arrived at the farming town, it was on them within minutes. It went through many of the guardsmen until it saw Wren. As soon as that thing knew she was there, nothing could tear its eyes off of her. It went for her, and only her."

Nik pursed his lips and hummed softly. "The peryton was there to find her?"

"Indeed. It was the scout, I imagine. It terrorized them all for hours. I tailed her unit as they traveled to Wheatrich . . ." He hesitated and sighed. "Call it paternal instinct. I couldn't let her go alone. I had to follow her . . . Thinking back, perhaps I shouldn't have." He rubbed his eyes with his thumb and forefinger. "It was my being there that prevented her from killing the beast. Who knows where it went once it managed to get away."

"It happened the way that it was supposed to, Lionel. Our response to those instincts is what determines our fate. Your instinct compelled you to accompany her. What happened afterward is what was meant to be."

Lionel scrunched his face in playful disgust. "You sound like a true arbiter when you talk like that."

"I am, you idiot."

"It was a joke, Mr. Grumpy. Lighten up."

"Hilarious. Now keep going. What else?"

"In the end, Wren had a choice to make: kill the peryton and face judgment for the crime, or let it live and release it, even though it now had her scent. If she killed it, the king would have her imprisoned for breaching the contract she made when she became a guard. When she saw me there . . ." He hesitated for a moment before trying again. "She originally planned on killing it until she saw me."

"What contract would demand such a thing?"

"There is a very one-sided treaty that king Reed made with certain creature clans in the surrounding area. They protect his borders; he gives them free reign of his kingdoms' outermost streets. Guardsmen cannot kill creatures of any kind, for fear that it may be an ally to any of the king's various thugs. Lawbreaking creatures are to be apprehended in the same manner as lawbreaking humans are. The catch is that the guardsmen have been incentivized by the king to do nothing if they see a creature breaking the law. They're always let go after a few hours."

"So, if Wren killed the peryton, she would have been thrown in jail?"

"Or worse."

"Death?"

Lionel shook his head. "If my foresight is correct, I believe the king wants to imprison her within his castle and keep her at his side. His obsession with her is stomach-turning."

"Why would he treat her differently than the other guardsmen?"

"For one, she is the only female guardsman. The other reason being, ever since the attempt at his throne two years ago, the king has demanded that she stay under his watch. He felt the best way to do it was to insert her into his forces to gain control over her movements."

Nik remained silent for a long time. He digested Lionel's words with deep consideration. What felt like hours passed before he leaned forward and looked directly at Lionel.

"All right, next question. How did you find Wren?"

CHAPTER SIX

*"Let us be grateful to people who make us
happy, they are the charming gardeners
who make our souls blossom."*

Marcel Proust

Lionel's cerulean eyes flicked to Wren's closed door
before returning to Nik.

"A man came to see me in a panic. He told me that
something had happened to his mother on her return trip
home. She and her family lived just north of Market Road. She had
taken the trail to Market Bridge, as she had every day. When she
noticed a commotion in the forest, she decided to investigate it. Her
son was hardly able to provide any useful information, as his mother
had been hysterical. He begged me to see her myself.

"When I saw her memories . . ." Lionel seemed hesitant to allow his next words to escape him. "I knew the time had come." He
was silent for a while. His eyes were focused elsewhere, and a small
frown tugged at his practiced smile.

Nik took the silence as an opportunity to get up and casually made for the kitchen. He filled a cup with water and returned to the sitting area. He set the cup on the table and offered a quick smile.

"Thank you, Nikolas." Lionel's eyes brightened. He took a short drink and nodded.

"Sure," Nik replied as he sank back into the couch. "What did she tell you?"

"Although her voice was still thin, she said that she had stumbled right into a fight between a goblin and another, unidentifiable creature. According to her, as soon as the creature noticed her, it ran right at her like a rabid beast. She turned and fled but didn't make it far before the creature tackled her to the ground from behind. She fell directly into thick brush and passed out."

Nik crossed his arms over his chest and turned his eyes to Wren's door as Lionel spoke. Something in the back of his mind stirred uncomfortably.

"Her description of the event was adequate, but her mind's *depiction* of it was more than enough for me." Lionel glanced out the glass doors and perched his chin on his palm by balancing his elbow on his knee. "The goblin did frighten the woman, but it was the creature that truly terrified her. I pressed her to give me more details, but the woman was pretty rattled and had very little to say."

"So, you watched her memories? You saw *precisely* what she saw?"

"Indeed," Lionel said through a cough. "As you already know, when I read a memory, I am planted *into* it. I see the scene as an objective party as it unfolds before me, like a ghost in a dream. I saw the creature firsthand.

"It had silver eyes that shone like the stars, and four long limbs. Something about its face was so human-looking, but its body was covered in scales and feathers. It stood with a hunched back, like a defensive cat. Four bones protruded from its back, and they seemed to flex and shift like limbs as it moved.

"As soon as it noticed the woman, its eyes went wide. The goblin hardly regarded her, yet the creature made its move.

"It happened so quickly that her eyes couldn't keep up with it, which made it more difficult for me to keep up with her range of emotions. When she was struck from behind, her memory began to get hazy. But . . ." He paused and followed Nik's eyes to Wren's room. "I saw fragments that I don't believe *she* remembers." Lionel took a deep breath and gave Nik a serious look. "After it fought off the goblin, it carried her back to the main road where she would be found. She never told anyone that bit.

"Many people were present while I helped unfold the memory. I tried to get them to leave so she and I could be alone, but I'm unable to do two things at once." Lionel folded his hands across his stomach and shook his head. "A group of kids had overheard this and wanted to go find this creature. Unfortunately, they did. None of them were gravely injured, but it was startling to see what damage it could inflict. They were covered in lacerations from what was likely its claws, and tufts of hair were missing that had been burned off . . . One of the older boys involved was left with rather nasty gashes on his back and neck, like he had almost been torn open from behind.

"The people in the village panicked and did as humans tend to: act out of fear. Much of the forest that bordered the northern river was burned down in search of the creature, but everyone turned up empty-handed . . . If they turned up at all.

"I found her before they did. I first saw her in a dream." A sad smile vanished as suddenly as it had appeared. "I had to be careful every time I went to see her, lest someone follow me and find where she lived. I had to visit a lot . . ." He rolled his eyes and smiled with exasperation. "If you think she is difficult to reason with *now* . . . I was worried that if she knew there was a search going on, she would run or attack . . . The flood was unfortunate, but it brought her to where I could keep her safe. A blessing in disguise, if you will."

"But how can you be sure that she is a spell? There's no way one could just pop into existence from nothing."

"Well . . . No one knows that for certain. There's never been an account of a spell actually being born, nor any mention of parents, so there's no way to rule out how they come to be. I know that she is because I have seen her shift. It's . . . petrifying." Lionel shook his head. "But it only happened once. It was when she had to . . ."

"When she had to kill Seth?"

Lionel's eyebrows shot up. "Wren told you that?"

"No, Elliot did," he replied stiffly. "When we got back. Wren was still out of it."

"Ah." Lionel nodded and glanced out at the moon. "Then she probably told you why she had to do it?"

"More or less. That he was a tyrant using the creatures that live around Arnica as his tools to gain power."

"Hm, sort of . . . mostly." He paused, sparing another quick look at the closed bedroom door. "Seth built himself an army of pirates and mercenaries living within coastal settlements all around Greater Bay by promising them riches and land once he took the crown. He even ventured to the surrounding lands, rallying anyone who had a problem with the king or simply a hunger for blood to join him. Many did. He campaigned for years, garnering the support of numerous powerful and resourceful criminals.

"They invaded Arnica's southern coast in a single night. Organized groups of these madmen must have lain in wait for weeks. Each town fell to them so easily . . . It was as though they had been poised and ready to attack for some time. It was planned and executed meticulously.

"The villages they selected were all gone before the sun rose. By morning, they held Bay City. By the end of the week, they held all of the Arnican-owned coastlines and seaside towns along the southern half of the kingdom.

"Those who managed to flee all of this spilled into the heart of the kingdom and brought with them their unrest. The King's Guard patrolled for weeks to keep the people at peace, but the only things that remained consistent were the disappearances and the night raids by any of Seth's men that made their way behind the walls.

"After a few days . . . creatures started showing up too. The guardsmen were too afraid to interfere. When they did, they didn't win. Citizens seldom left their homes, and those who ventured out alone usually vanished.

"The king grew paranoid of even his allies outside his walls and increasingly suspicious of those within them. He decided to pull the guardsmen out of the cities and away from his people completely. There was no one to hold back Seth and his men anymore, and all hell broke loose." Lionel dropped his head into his hands and shook it once. His eyes met Nik's. Within them, the tumultuous agony that only a broken-hearted father could feel swirled in the cerulean depths. He offered a brief smile, but it didn't reach his eyes. "Wren, still a civilian at this point, threw herself into the havoc when it reached our doorstep. She picked a fight with a mountain troll and got beat down pretty badly . . . She recovered quickly and trained downstairs all day and, often, all night. She has a gentle nature, a kindness that she hides behind that thick shell . . ."

Nik listened silently. He could feel a strange sensation crawling up his back and along his shoulders. Deep within him, an unshakeable notion that something terrible was being left unsaid lingered.

"I didn't want her to get involved," Lionel continued. "I was concerned she would be found out as the creature in the forest, or worse . . . But I couldn't stop her. It was the right thing to do; the citizens were suffering, and the king knowingly allowed it to happen.

"She witnessed firsthand what this legion was doing when she met Elliot. The poor girl was being pulled outside by pirates, and one of them was holding her by the ankles, trying to get under her skirt. Her parents had both been killed by the heathens only moments before, and she'd watched it happen . . . She narrowly escaped the same fate." Lionel cleared his throat and purposefully trained his eyes into the nothingness of the cloudless night sky through the pane of the glass door. "Wren happened upon them and . . . She killed all five of them with a metal pipe that she'd found earlier in the night. To this day, she insists that she was able to do it without the use of her abilities." Lionel chuckled and smiled. "I've always thought that it was a strange thing to be proud of, but . . . It was *something* that she was proud of."

Nik had to stop himself from smirking. He unconsciously itched the top of his lip with his knuckle in order to distract himself.

"She's tried to convince me that killing had no effect on her. But it did . . . It *does*. It's distorted her focus and hardened her heart."

"It sounded like those ones needed killing, though."

Lionel sighed and looked at his gloved hands folded in his lap. "I know, Nikolas. And I agree. But it was hard on her and on Elliot. Killing evil bears an evil of its own. You understand that." He leaned back in his seat. "If the situation demanded it, I would not hesitate to take a life in order to protect my family."

The air filled with a comfortable silence while Nik processed the information. His jaw was set firmly, and his furrowed eyebrows wrinkled the skin between them.

"I know that it's a lot, my friend," Lionel said softly. "I am sorry that I didn't call for you sooner. To be fair, my messenger *did* have some trouble finding you."

Nik grinned dimly and looked out the glass doors. "It's good that you waited, I admit. I was caught up in Valerian for some time. There were many insidious things lurking within the cities. I stayed out there for years and still would be there had you not sent word. I'm glad that another reaper was able to take my position so soon."

"I didn't realize Valerian had become so perilous." Lionel blinked in thought before he continued, "What of the southern nation?"

"They're perfectly fine. The higher classes left Valerian, making the island to the southwest their new homes. Over the last few years, all of the elites moved into Southern Valerian and in their absence, it has only been getting worse. Similar to your king cowering behind his walls, those at the top of the social circles have a very loose interpretation of the term *government* and care little for those that they deem beneath them. I should be thanking you, actually."

Lionel smiled and stood. He clapped his palm on Nik's shoulder casually as he strode by.

"I'm going to turn in, my friend. I'll answer whatever lingering questions you may have in the morning."

Nik nodded once and waved him off. Before he could stop himself, his emerald eyes found themselves once again locked on the closed bedroom door of the only living spell.

THE DAMNED BEAM OF LIGHT AIMED *STRAIGHT* FOR HIS EYES.

Nik groaned and reluctantly sat up from the soft pillows.

The murmurs that had aided the light in drawing him from slumber moved around in shadows beneath his closed door. The warm smell of coffee and strong tobacco helped to convince him to leave the folds of the blankets. His bare feet met the cold surface of the hardwood floor with an alarming jolt. He groaned again and stood fully to make his way toward the door.

It opened with a soft creak that inadvertently announced his presence.

Elliot lounged in Lionel's mustard-yellow chair with a large mug of coffee cupped neatly in one hand, and the other balanced a thick book on her thigh.

Jack was splayed out on the coffee table that her feet were propped upon. She would wiggle her toes inside thick brown socks, and he'd swipe at them playfully.

Wren rolled tobacco into a slip of paper in the kitchen. Her hair, unrestrained and mussed from slumber, reached well below the center of her back and drifted around her with every movement.

She acknowledged him with a tired nod as he filtered into the room.

"Good morning," Elliot chimed happily. "There's coffee in the kitchen if you're a coffee drinker."

Nik stifled a yawn and made his way to the kitchen with a polite dip of his chin in response. He paused briefly to glance at Lionel's still-closed bedroom door.

"He won't be up for a while," Elliot said with a wide grin. "I heard him tossing and turning when I went for a midnight snack, so I camped out here to keep an ear out for him. He barely slept all night. If he was having a vision, he likely won't wake up until suppertime." She set her mug on the table beside Jack and scratched his ears. She eyed Wren without a word as she watched her seal the now-tobacco-filled paper.

"What?"

"You haven't eaten anything yet. You aren't going to have that before breakfast, are you?"

Wren smirked at her friend, nonchalantly sipping from her coffee mug. Wren licked her lips and wiped them with her knuckles to disguise her amusement.

The brief silence that followed kind of spoke for itself.

"I ate before you woke up."

"Before I woke up? I've been on the couch. I would have heard you."

"Nah." Wren couldn't hold back the gradually widening smile. "You were still sleeping. I ate quietly."

"Yeah, right. What'd you have?"

Wren averted her eyes by glancing to her coffee. "Coffee."

"Damnit, Wren!" Elliot sat forward in her chair with narrowed eyes. "That's not breakfast! What did you eat yesterday? *Did* you eat yesterday?"

"I think so. Oh wait, yes. I had a strawberry pastry."

Nik passed behind Wren to reach for the coffeepot as the two had their exchange. He poured himself a mug, wearing a smirk of his own.

"Cream and sugar." Wren turned slightly to meet his eyes as she pointed to the refrigerator and table.

He stared at her as he took a large swig of his coffee. Nik didn't look away after he'd lowered it from his lips, caught by something glowing in the morning light.

Her eyes housed a subtle ring of silver that glittered around the perimeter of her irises. The creases from her usual scowl etched around the corners of her eyes were lighter, and her ginger brows sat relaxed and natural.

The silver ring even drew attention away from the wounds across her cheek and on her ear.

"*What?*"

"Your eyes are different."

Wren looked immediately to Elliot with disbelief clear on her face.

The human bit her lip and shrugged.

"Barely! They *barely* changed. Telling you wouldn't have made it go away any faster . . . I didn't think he'd notice. He didn't say anything about it yesterday, so I figured it wasn't worth mentioning." Elliot's lips fell into a frown, and her attention shifted to Nik. "It happens whe—"

"It means nothing," Wren interrupted, then sighed and turned her face to the countertop. "Want one?" She held up the freshly rolled cigarette, refusing to meet his eyes.

A second, previously rolled one lay beside her other palm on the counter.

Wren was careful to keep her eyes trained away from him in an effort to veil how insecure his stare made her.

Nik accepted it before he took a small step closer to her. His hand abandoned the hot mug to brush a lock of her hair behind her ear. His thumb ghosted over the length of the gash on her cheek as he tucked the strands away.

The contact made her jump, and she reflexively shoved him away. Wren stared at him with a mixture of surprise, anger, and confusion.

Elliot gaped at them. "This is highly unsettling. Look, even Jack is uncomfortable." She pointed to the white cat, his perch unchanged, and his tail flicked, entirely uninterested. "Not helping," she whispered to Jack tersely.

"Do I unsettle you?" Nik begrudgingly looked away from Wren. His eyes landed on Elliot, and she folded her arms.

"Yes. Definitely yes. And you've got Wren acting weird, too."

"I'm *not* acting weird." Wren snatched the cigarette and walked around the edge of the countertop. She kept her chin low until she reached the cold glass door that led to temporary freedom. She balanced the cigarette between her lips as she pulled on a pair of old brown boots, not meeting any of the eyes in the room.

She could feel Elliot's disapproving stare jabbing her in the back.

Wren turned to face her as she tossed her faded green coat over her shoulders and slid her arms into the sleeves. She patted down the jacket pockets until she felt the familiar rectangle of her matchbook.

"I'll be right back."

Elliot huffed dejectedly.

Wren pushed the door open and retreated into the winter morning.

"Impossible." Elliot snorted with a shake of her head. Her eyes wandered to Nik and narrowed. "Well?"

"Well what?" He had reclaimed his mug of coffee and took a careful sip.

"Wasn't that a secret signal to talk in private?"

The corner of Nik's mouth twitched up into a feeble smile. He set the mug down and stepped into his boots and jacket before he gave Elliot a small nod.

She rolled her eyes and fell back into the mustard chair.

"They're both idiots," she muttered to Jack and propped the book up in front of her face. "And you." Elliot gave the cat a soft poke in the stomach. "Next time I need you to back me up, at least put in an effort. I won't get you any whitefish when we go to the market if you leave me hanging. Uncool."

Jack tilted his head to the side and meowed.

"Yeah, uh-huh." She peeked at him from behind the book cover and smirked. Her hand reached out to give his head an affectionate rub. "Apology accepted."

CHAPTER SEVEN

"Keep your face always toward the sunshine
– and shadows will fall behind you."

Walt Whitman

FRESH SNOW COVERED EVERY FLAT SURFACE AND CLUNG to nearly every vertical ledge. Mounds of fat snowflakes had collected on the railing around the balcony during the night. Three snow-covered chairs surrounded a snow-covered table.

The snow was ankle-deep and heavy enough that any forgotten plants in pots would be done for. The balcony curved around the corner of the house and was spacious enough for a small gathering, but Wren preferred it empty.

She trudged through the blanket of fresh snow until she reached the end of the balcony. Wren pressed her elbows into the railing and leaned forward. Her hair framed her face as she looked down to stare blankly at the street.

Small decorations adorned windowpanes and doorways. Wooden flowers that were scattered everywhere poked out of snowy mounds, and various folded paper birds and hand-made figurines occupied the storefront windows.

The Seasons Festival began in two days.

Wren drew in a slow, steadying breath.

Elliot is sure to go to the flower show. Not to mention the vendor stands . . . Ugh. And her alleyway shortcuts, she thought bitterly. *She doesn't understand how dangerous things have become since her last visit . . . But I don't want to scare her. Or worse . . .*

The glass door opened and closed behind her, and as the footfalls approached, her shoulders stiffened under her coat.

"Was that a secret signal for me to follow you?"

Wren turned her face away from Nik when he leaned against the railing beside her.

"Not intentionally." Her voice was quiet. "Just returning the favor." Wren idly rolled her unlit cigarette between her index finger and thumb. Her downcast eyes stared at the paper, but her focus was elsewhere.

Silence settled into the atmosphere for a short while before it was broken by a soft, feminine chuckle.

"Most times I come out here, I don't even light it," she murmured. "Sometimes I just need to be alone for a little while, you know? I love them both, but . . ." She pulled in a deep breath of frigid air through her nose. "Sometimes I wish I still lived in the forest. Away from all of this . . . But I think it'd break their hearts if I ever said it to them."

Nik listened mutely and drew his matchbox from his coat pocket.

Wren sighed and fell quiet.

He struck a match against the box and puffed the end of his cigarette. He plucked it from his lips and exhaled as he offered it to Wren.

She stared at the ember for a moment before she took it.

"Thank you," she mumbled and held her unlit one out to him in exchange.

"Do I unsettle you too?" He kept his eyes set on the street as he took it from her hand.

She chewed the inside of her cheek and hesitantly turned to face him. "My eyes change when things like yesterday happen." Wren dodged his question. "I don't really know why. It happens when I start to los—" She stopped herself short and looked away.

Nik glanced at her from the corner of his eye for a moment but did not move his head.

Wren took a short drag and shook her head. "I can't trust myself with altercations like that. It doesn't help that Honorah knows exactly how to get under my skin. She and Brock know that I'm not a tempest. They know what . . . happened to Seth. They just can't *prove* it."

Nik remained silent, keeping his gaze trained on anything but her.

She seemed to open up more when he didn't look at her.

"I think they are trying to provoke me into snapping again, only publicly. I'm sure she's convinced the Guard to cooperate. They hate me so much." She scowled. "It's probably the only chance they have of convincing the king that I should be banished. Although, I don't think that her goal is for me to be *banished*. Lionel disagrees with me, but I can feel it," Wren muttered darkly. "She wants me dead."

"Are you really going to leave?"

Wren sighed and shook her head. "Elliot would never forgive me if I left; she knows that I'd never come back. But everything in me is telling me to just . . . go." She turned to the glass door, and she frowned. "And Elliot would be . . ."

"Just fine, I'd wager. She has Lionel."

"And Jack." Wren chuckled inaudibly. Her face adopted a conflicted expression, and she shook her head. "I don't even know where I would go if I left Arnica," she hummed after a short while. She took another gentle drag and dared a glance at Nik.

He angled his chin to look at her over his shoulder. Nik's strik-ing green eyes were partially veiled by the ebony strands of sleep-mussed hair that swept across his face. Dusky stubble accentuated the curves of his cheeks and softened his square jaw.

"I think I know why Lionel asked you here, but it's just a theory. He likes to be purposefully, frustratingly, ambiguous." Wren shook her head of untamed hair and rolled her eyes.

"He always has," Nik added.

Wren smirked and looked back to the city around them. She moved to the corner of the patio out of view of the apartment's interior and stretched to grab the bottom rung of an iron ladder mounted on the wall.

The old mechanism hesitated and groaned before it was able to drop the ladder down for use.

She brushed the snow off of the footholds and pinched the em-ber out of her half-burned cigarette. Wren tucked it into her front coat pocket and placed her hand on the ladder.

"The view is better from the roof." She motioned with her chin. "Also, Elliot is pretending to read. She changed seats to see us better."

He glanced to the room behind the glass.

As he did, the curly head poked behind the book she held. Elliot reached for her mug and averted Nik's stare.

He followed Wren up the ladder and onto the rooftop, his own cigarette secured between his lips as they ascended. He shouldn't have been surprised to see a single, ancient-looking chair perched on the rooftop of the rectangular building.

"I wouldn't recommend sitting on it. I'm not sure if it can hold you. It can't hold me without making horrible sounds. I've been meaning to replace it."

"I see what you meant now," he said offhandedly.

Wren furrowed her brow in confusion. "What? About the view?"

"The night we met, when you defended the case for humans." He idly pushed a heap of snow with his foot. "Elliot is rather entertaining."

"She is my friend," Wren said roughly.

Nik held up his hands and smiled. "I didn't mean anything by it. I like her. She is very lovely. She clearly cares for you deeply."

Wren sighed and looked out over the still-sleeping city. "There's a festival in two days." She reached into her coat pocket. "It's a big deal in this town . . . in pretty much all of Arnica. Elliot hasn't missed a single one, and I know she'll sneak away to go by herself. She always does. It's not too simple for me to walk through crowds, so I suppose I understand why she goes alone."

Wren held her palm out to him as she brought the partially burned cigarette back to her lips.

Nik retrieved the matchbook and set it in her hand. He watched her light it and arched his eyebrow.

The way that she closed her eyes when taking a breath in and the sigh that escaped in the smoke made the crease above the bridge of her nose soften. Something in her demeanor relaxed, if only for the moment that she took to breathe out.

Wren noticed Nik staring and glared at him. "What?"

He shrugged and looked away.

"Out with it."

"I think there's more to you smoking than wanting time alone."

"Tha—"

"When you inhale, your face relaxes. As soon as you exhale, it goes back to your usual, surly expression."

"*Surly?*" she asked indignantly. When he smirked, her lip curled and eyes narrowed. She growled and turned to stare at the horizon.

A silence fell between them, both knowing that Nik wasn't wrong, but one party more reluctant to admit it. The quiet quickly grew unbearable, and Wren couldn't take it any longer.

"It gets the taste of blood out of my mouth," she murmured.

"Hm?"

Wren pursed her lips and finally met his eyes again. "When I . . . When I start to change, it's like my mouth fills with blood. There isn't any there, though. Just the taste. It's nauseating." She stared at the burning cigarette between her fingers. "This helps. They don't taste great, but it's better than blood." Wren turned to give him a serious look. "Don't tell Elliot. It will only make her worry more when it happens. Or Lionel, for that matter."

Nik drew a deep breath in through his nose and nodded once. "Sure."

Wren turned away from him and shook her head as she took another delicate drag.

"With the strange things happening"—she opted to change the subject—"like those grifters, I'm convinced there will be some incident at the festival. I obviously don't want that to happen at all, but even more so if Elliot is there when it does. Everyone knows her association with me, even when I'm not with her. The citizens have been growing more hostile toward me in the last few months, and I don't like when she is on her own."

"So, you want me to babysit her?"

"What? No." She held his matches back out to him. "I will be with her as much as possible. Lionel is probably going to ask you to be an additional set of eyes during the festival. No one here really knows you, nor do they know that you aren't a human . . . anymore. If you keep a low profile, it'll be easy for you to move around on your own since you can fend for yourself."

"What is it that I would be looking for?"

"Anything suspicious. You know about as much as I do now." She pensively tapped ash away. "You know of the disappearances already, but I doubt that Bianca and Torrie were the only two contributing to the vanishing of the townspeople. My intuition is telling me that something . . . bigger is coming."

Nik had to remind himself to look elsewhere. Lionel seemed to be the only one unbothered by his eye contact.

"The Guard is in on it, Nik. I'm *in* the Guard." Wren clicked her tongue against her teeth and crossed her arms. "Lionel doesn't listen. He still believes there is hope here."

Nik sighed and dropped his palm onto her shoulder gently. "Lionel knows what's going on," he began. "I've known him for a long time, Wren. From what I gather, he is aware that you are looking for a way out. He's neither blind nor stupid. You don't give him enough credit."

"I know." Her averted eyes glared at her boots.

His hand on her shoulder was warm and heavy.

"You just have really bad timing." Wren sighed and tilted her face to the sky.

The storm from the night lingered in the dense, gray sky. Walls and heaves of clouds drifted through the icy atmosphere like a slow-moving, overhead stream.

More snowfall was a significant possibility.

"This Seasons Festival is the Arrival of Spring." The tone of her voice softened. She stared blankly at the clouds. "In two days, this street is going to be packed with townspeople, guests, and vagabonds."

Nik remained silent and offered her shoulder a reassuring squeeze.

Wren, realizing his hand was still there, shrugged him away.

"We should go back inside," she muttered and started toward the ladder. The spot on her shoulder felt suddenly cold, but she pushed the thought from her mind and descended.

When they reached the balcony, Wren made for the railing and pressed the barely smoked cigarette into the snow. She glanced at Nik and motioned for the door.

He did the same and reentered the apartment first.

Wren slid the door shut behind them. They deposited their boots onto the stone floor without looking at each other.

Wren's boots slipped off easily. She fluffed the chill off of her jacket and held her hand out to Nik.

He blinked and handed her his own jacket.

Wren tipped her feet into a pair of leather slippers and hung up their coats.

"You were out there a looong time . . . I bet your coffee's cold," Elliot said.

"Well, I *apparently* gave him the secret signal to follow." Wren's eyes narrowed at Elliot.

The human blushed angrily and stood from her seat.

Wren walked into the kitchen to retrieve her coffee. She stopped where Jack sat on the countertop and smiled warmly at the white feline. Her pale hand ruffled his cheek and ear tenderly.

"I hate this. I hate being left out of what's going on," Elliot pressed. "It's bad enough that I can only spend spring and summer here, so I'm always a step behind. And more importantly, unless you two are going off and talking about how pretty the other one is, what is so secret that it can't be said in front of me?"

"Pretty?" Nik asked, perplexed.

There was a pregnant pause in the room. Neither woman regarded his question, instead caught in a staring match.

Elliot's eyes, narrowed and firm, bored into Wren's conflicted ones. She stood with folded arms, an uncharacteristically irritated frown painted on her heart-shaped face.

Wren rubbed the back of her neck and sighed. Her head slumped downward, and she cupped the mug in her palms.

It *was* cold.

Wren sighed again and looked to Elliot's defiant form.

"Elliot, you are right." She offered an apologetic smile. "It hasn't been fair to you." She looked over to Nik and half smiled.

"I'm worried about the festival. I know that you want to see it all and enjoy it, but I don't think that it's safe for you to go by yourself."

Elliot scowled directly at Wren, leaning against the opposite side of the counter to level their eyes.

"Oh, is that all? You are worried every year," she challenged. "I can take care of myself, Wren. Warden, can I please see the air balloons?"

"It's *may I*." Wren's lips ticked into a smirk when Elliot boiled over. Before her friend had a chance to erupt, she continued. "You know that's not what it is. You remember what happened yesterday. That was in the *market*. In broad daylight. Not to mention the grifters. The festival will have even more people crowding around, and someone like Honorah or Brock could be in it anywhere. Waiting for you to be alone.

"Additionally, the reports of creatures in the area should rightfully raise some serious concern for you. Clove hasn't been dealing with Arnica's internal conflict. It's not safe here. *And* I care about what happens to you." Wren paused a long moment before she released a breath that she hadn't realized she was holding. "Elliot, in a forest of tigers and bears, a pack of wolves can only do so much to protect their own."

Elliot's hands pressed into the counter until the tips of her fingers went white. "Wren, I am a grown woman. I know how to take care of myself," she repeated through clenched teeth.

Wren bit back the comment on the tip of her tongue and looked away. "I'm not saying that you can't," she defended, straining to keep her growing agitation out of her voice. "Is it so unfair of me? I am *one of* them, Elliot. You know that I am. Just because I choose to contain . . . what I can do doesn't mean the same can be said for other creatures. *Stronger* creatures."

Elliot glared but gave no verbal retort.

"What if Lionel stays with her?"

They turned to Nik, who stood behind Wren in the kitchen, as he sipped at his coffee and watched them argue.

"Lionel is far too busy to spend as much of his time with me at the festival as I want to spend there," Elliot countered as a soft dusting of pink crept across her cheeks.

"Royal commerce is closed during the festival. Lionel has no classes. Plus, I'm sure he'd love to go with you." Wren smiled knowingly at her friend. "I would be sincerely stunned if he turned down a day at a festival with you, let alone three. There *is* a lot to do."

Elliot shook her head fervently.

"Try asking him," Nik suggested.

Elliot's blush spread to the tips of her ears, and she tucked her chin to her chest.

"Good morning, everyone! Are you discussing the festival?"

Everyone turned to Lionel.

He stood in the entryway of his bedroom and tousled the hair on the back of his head.

Elliot's eyes widened, and she quickly shot a warning glare at Nik and Wren before she turned back to the trace.

"No, we were just talking about the wea—"

"Yes, Elliot is upset with Wren because she doesn't want her to go to the festival alone. Wren's upset with Elliot for not taking the danger seriously," Nik replied around another swig of coffee. His emerald eyes danced between the two women looking at him with a matching shade of incredulity.

"Well, I can completely understand her concern. The current state of affairs has Black Rivers more treacherous for its citizens than ever. However"—Lionel saw Wren set her jaw tightly as he continued—"Elliot is a perfectly capable woman. Has her training with you not proved satisfactory, Wren?"

Wren drew in a tight breath and closed her eyes. "She's done wonderfully." The syncopation of her words belied the reluctance beneath them.

Lionel beamed at the quarreling women in time to see the curly-haired human stick her tongue out at the sunset-haired spell.

"I think it would be wise for me to accompany you, then. I've loved the Seasons Festival from the moment I moved here, and you have a good eye for the best vendors."

"No, Lionel, it's okay. It'd be selfish of me—"

"Nonsense. I would love to, Elliot."

Her eyes widened, and she forced herself to look away.

"Well—" Wren mercifully changed the subject but not before she smirked to herself. "I'm going to get ready for the day. I need to go to Abagail so I can pick up my armor."

"How far is Abagail?" Nik asked.

"About a three-hour ride. Maybe a bit longer with the snow." Wren plucked the coffeepot from the stove and topped off her mug. As she carried it out of the kitchen toward her bedroom, she paused at Elliot's side. Her free hand slipped to Elliot's shoulder, and she leaned in close.

"Told you so," Wren whispered into her ear with a mocking tone.

Elliot shoved Wren away from her, spilling lukewarm coffee everywhere.

CHAPTER EIGHT

"Look closely. The beautiful may be small."

Immanuel Kant

THERE WAS A MODEST STABLE ABOUT A TEN-MINUTE walk from Lionel's home, in the opposite direction of the market. It had a sturdy oak frame that was taller at the entryway than it was at the back. A single stall was tucked into the cozy shelter curtained by the overgrowth of the surrounding trees, and the cobwebs stretched into the shadows above. There were no fences in or around the stable, and a half-empty trough rested against the back wall.

Aside from the mice and wild birds that pecked at the food, the stall was empty.

Wren trudged through the deep snow. She followed a snowed-in footpath headed right for the stable that she knew by heart. The snow over the path was significantly less deep than the covering around its edges, but that didn't make it *shallow*.

The blankets reached just below her knees and were, unfortunately, just deeper than her boots were tall.

She tried to ignore the feeling of snow that had already started to compact around her legs inside of her boots. It gradually became more difficult to push out of her mind when the snow began to melt and soak through her tucked-in trousers and, finally, her socks.

Wren tugged her fatigued green coat closer around her body and glowered. The many shoddy repairs on the arms and chest hinted at the indefinite battles it had lived through, but the garment still moved with her effortlessly.

As though the repairs that had been made to it were the reason that the coat fit her so perfectly.

"Where is your horse? You *do* have a horse, right?" Nik's inquiry made Wren scowl. He squinted at the stable as they grew closer to it. "Don't tell me it lives in that hut . . ."

Wren paused to lean against the trunk of a tree, breath faintly labored and eyes focused on the stable.

Too much snow, she thought bitterly and tried to pry bits of packed snow out of her boots with her fingers.

The only indication that Nik accompanied her was the faint *crunch* of the snow beneath his footfalls.

"She'll be here. You didn't *have* to come with me, you know." She mimicked the inflection of his question.

Nik's longer legs moved more easily through the heaves of snow than hers could. He closed the distance between them and held his hand out to her.

"Do you want me to carry you?"

Her eyes narrowed, and she pushed him away. Wren took a moment to adjust the heel of her boot before she continued down the narrow pathway.

Nik followed her along the single-file route with a smirk.

When they reached the stable, Wren shifted her feet out of her boots, one at a time, to shake out the snow and brush it away from her trousers. Even with the snow now gone, the wet fabric clung to her skin and left her with an unshakeable chill.

He chuckled as he watched her clean the snow out of her boots.

"You should have let me carry you."

"I'm fine," she said automatically, purposefully looking away from him. "It's just snow."

"Ah, well."

Wren didn't have to see him to hear that annoyingly charming smirk of his.

"I hope that you brought spare socks."

Wren took a deep breath and tried to ignore him completely. She turned her back to him and approached an old wooden box with a leather strap buckled around it.

It was well hidden in the far corner of the structure, underneath the trough, and held shut with a simple pin tumbler lock.

She retrieved a key from the breast pocket of her coat and angled the box so that the lock faced her as she opened it. Wren picked up a twisted white object. It was pale as bone and con- torted into an imperfect spiral shape. She looked directly at Nik and waved the item in the air above her with a *charming* smirk of her own.

"What is that?" He followed her into the stable.

The interior of the *hut*, as he called it, was rather spacious and surprisingly warm.

"A calling horn."

"Your horse is wild?"

Wren closed the box and pressed the lock back together. When she stood upright, she placed the trinket between her lips and ex- haled, sounding the horn four times.

No audible noise emanated from the calling horn, yet Nik still felt a sudden and sharp pressure between his ears with every bellow.

Silence filled the small clearing that the stable resided in. No birds dared to chirp, nor critters to patter.

Nik stared at Wren, taken aback by the quiet. Even he wouldn't break the silence. The pressure in the air still pounded his ears in reverberating waves.

A tremor rustled the branches around them and flowed into the clearing like a brook. It moved through the trunks of the trees and through the earth like trickling water as it traveled through the limbs blanketed by snow.

"She isn't my *horse*." Wren sniffled once from the cold air and covered the tip of her nose with her elbow. "She is an arion. And she is my *friend*."

Nik rubbed his temple and narrowed his eyes at her. "You could have warned me," he said in a low voice.

Wren chuckled at him and shrugged. "I could have, yes." She tucked the palm-sized horn into her pocket and continued, "But giving you a headache seemed so much more fun. Tit for tat."

He gave her a look of pure disbelief. "And what, exactly, did I do to warrant that?"

"You called her stable a hut," she said plainly as she walked by him and into the snowy clearing.

"It *is* a hut."

Heavy thuds echoed in the trees around them. An approaching storm of earth-pounding hoofs plowing through the powder rolled toward them steadily.

"It's *not* a hut," Wren muttered quietly. "I worked really hard on it."

Before Nik could reply, the footfalls were upon them, and a blond mare emerged from the shadows of the trees. Her withers were at level with the top of Wren's head and were elongated and curved with strong muscles. A golden mane swirled around her light ears and shining coat, and she had bright honey-golden eyes.

Wren approached the mare and held her arms out wide.

Without breaking stride, the arion tucked her broad neck into the shallow crook of Wren's shoulder and head. The arion nosed the wounds on her face with a soft nicker. She sighed through large nostrils before she regarded Nik. She eyed him for a moment before she blew another heavy breath out through her nose.

"I'm all right, Rain. And . . . you get used to him." She stroked the arion's neck tenderly. "He's Lionel's friend."

The mare sighed again and took one step backward to face Wren directly.

"I am headed to Abagail today. Would you like to accompany me?"

She snorted once and stomped her heavy hoof.

Wren glanced to Nik and quickly looked away when their eyes met.

"Don't worry, I called for two."

A handsome stallion emerged from the shadows of the trees and trotted to a stop a few paces behind the golden mare. He was dusky-gray with a few white pits of color along his neck and belly. Although he was as large as the mare, he was still clearly a young arion stallion.

"Great," Nik said dryly.

"Nik, this is Rain." Wren spoke the name with deep admiration.

The mare nickered softly and shook her head once.

"That is Diamo. He's never had a passenger before."

"*Great*," Nik repeated, exasperation thick in his voice.

ELLIOT PACED CEASELESSLY.

Jack's slate-blue eyes watched the slender girl as she walked the same pattern around the apartment: around the circular dining table, glance at the door to the stairs as she passed by the kitchen, check the balcony, check Wren's room, and then pause. She stared at the door to Nik's room without moving for a few moments longer than she had the others. Her features were twisted into a frustrated frown, and her arms were folded over her chest.

"I can't believe her sometimes, Jack."

The cat blinked at her.

She spoke in a low voice, even though Lionel was in the spare bathroom showering. Elliot doubted that he could hear her, but she wasn't willing to take the risk.

"She knows that I can't be alone with Lionel . . . I can't! He's so . . . *intimidating.*"

Jack stood and yawned wide. His white hind and tail stretched upward as the whiskers on his cheeks trembled at the action.

"You're not helping me. She knows how I feel about him. It's going to be *so* awkward!" Elliot rubbed her nose into her hands and groaned.

The cat jumped from his perch on the kitchen countertop and began to make his way toward Wren's open bedroom door. He leapt onto her bed and curled himself into a midmorning nap.

"Fine," she murmured harshly. "I can take a hint."

Elliot huffed into Wren's bathroom and began her own morning routine.

She let loose her shoulder-length hair and turned the water spigot to the left. A rush of water coursed out of the pipe that snaked up the wall and out of the head of the shower like a gentle waterfall.

Elliot continued muttering to herself as she showered and dressed. The tunic and pants she selected hugged her slender frame fittingly. She dried her curls quickly and clipped a small portion of it behind her ear with a pin that she'd given to Wren as a gift. She walked out of the room only to see that Lionel still had yet to emerge from his. She nibbled her lip and stared at his closed door when a jolt of sound startled her.

Elliot clutched at her chest and sighed.

Just the doorbell.

Her gaze lingered on Lionel's door.

Over and over, Wren instructed her to *never* answer the door if she or Lionel were absent. She frowned inwardly.

I don't need babysitters, Elliot thought as she strode toward the stairs.

After the landing, the right-hand side of the wall was another library-style bookshelf that allowed one to see directly into Lionel's office on the other side. Though it was a challenge to find enough space between the books to look through.

Many of the spines were dried out and aged, frayed by time. The newer, more recent books were brightly colored in comparison to the palette of muted brown, red, green, and black.

Elliot passed through, habitually looking at her favorite title: *Market Road Leads to Dendros.*

The book was palm-sized and a faded gray color with chipped, black lettering. It was not a lengthy book, but the pages were filled with poems and songs and artworks of creatives recounting their travels that never ceased to enthrall and tickle her.

The doorbell rang a second time, and again, Elliot jumped.

She took her time making her way to the door while she tried to make out the silhouette in the door's frosted window. Elliot finally recognized the shape of a helmet of the Guard. Her breath caught in her chest, and she paused mid-step, hand hesitating over the doorknob.

"Excuse me, dear." Lionel appeared behind her and eased her to the side with a light grip on her shoulders. He opened the door with a friendly wave to the man behind it and purposefully positioned his body to hide Elliot from view.

A broad-shouldered man stood attentively. His sharp, red jacket was crossed over the right shoulder by a wide black strap. A rapier dangled on his left hip, a pistol on his right. His thick arms were folded over his chest, and a black-booted foot tapped impatiently.

"Sir Charles, it's good to see you again!" Lionel offered a cheerful smile. "Forgive my delay in answering the door; I was dressing after a shower. Can I help you this morning?"

"I hope that you can, lad." Sir Charles unfolded his arms and revealed a small notebook. "I was tasked with looking into the incident at the market yesterday."

"Pardon?"

His gray mustache shifted on his face.

"A report was filed to look into what happened, since a high-ranking member of the Guard was involved." He flipped the book open and rustled through the pages. "Ah, here." He stopped as he spoke and read what was written aloud. "A member of the Guard, reportedly Lady Wren, instigated an altercation with one Honorah Tanner after threatening her brother, Brock Tanner."

Elliot clenched her fists at her sides. "That's not true," she whispered.

Lionel let out a soft sigh and shrugged. "Sir Charles, you misunderstand the circumstances of the event."

"Were you there to witness these circumstances?"

Lionel smiled again. "I was not. However, Lady Wren and Miss Elliot were both there. I also had a long conversation with Honorah as soon as I broke it up. You should also bear in mind my abilities." He tapped his forehead as he smiled, despite the surge of panic that emanated from Elliot. "I have taken their statements. I would be happy to bring you copies of them."

"I would much prefer to speak with them myself." His mustache bristled from the last syllable he uttered. "Are they in?"

Lionel shook his head. "I'm sorry, no. Miss Elliot is out on an errand, as is Lady Wren."

Sir Charles narrowed his gray eyes. "When do you expect them back?"

Lionel's smile never wavered, even as Elliot fussed behind him.

"I'm not quite sure, sir. I will gladly send word for you when they are back so that you may conclude your report."

His polite demeanor finally cracked through Sir Charles's gruffness.

Elliot couldn't help but feel the air around Lionel gradually warm and arched a brow.

The guardsman's cheeks pillowed with a smile, and he nodded.

"Good, yes. That would be very good, lad."

They shook hands briefly. Lionel's white gloves were a stark contrast against the roughened black leather ones that Sir Charles wore. With a nod, the mustachioed member of the Guard turned around and left.

Lionel slid the door shut and turned his attention to Elliot.

"It's all right, my dear." He smiled at her. "You won't have to talk to Sir Charles about what happened in the market. I'm willing to bet that Wren already has a plan. She knows that you don't like having to talk to them."

"Yeah," she muttered.

Lionel placed his palm on her shoulder. His smile creased the edges of his eyes. "Don't worry." His thumb massaged where her collarbone merged with her shoulder. "No one will believe Honorah. Everyone there saw her antagonize Wren. Not to mention, she's an infamous troublemaker . . . just like her brothers."

"Wren did nothing wrong." Elliot clenched her jaw. "You know that the Guard has been itching to find a reason to throw her in prison." She choked back a sudden pang of guilt that made her shoulders tremor. "They all hate her because of me, Lionel."

He frowned as he felt her resolve slowly crumbling. "What happened wasn't your fault Elli—"

"Lionel." She spoke over him forcefully. "You *know* that it was my fault. No one can convince me otherwise."

Lionel's smile didn't hinder her well of emotions.

"She was laying low . . . No one really knew that she existed . . . When Seth invaded the city . . . When his henchmen killed my parents . . . Seth was *there* when she killed those men. She's had a target on her back since that day."

Lionel smiled sadly and placed both of his hands onto her shoulders. He leaned in to plant a soft kiss on her forehead. "You can't carry that burden, my dear. Not a thing worth carrying, thoughts such as those," his gentle voice hummed. "Wren does not hold you responsible for what happened. Not at all. You're too wonderful of a person to be incriminating yourself for how others behaved."

Elliot sighed and met Lionel's gaze. "I don't want to be dead weight to her. She has been talking more and more about leaving Arnica. It would be selfish of me to try and stop her, wouldn't it?"

"Not at all. You're en—"

"It would, Lionel," Elliot interrupted. "Wren has been abused here ever since Seth's insurrection."

"Elliot, you aren't listening to me." He sighed through his nose and rubbed her shoulders with his thumbs. "The actions of others are not yours to be held accountable for," he repeated. "Seth's aftermath split Arnica. The politics in this country had been polarized long before Seth Tanner existed, and she is in a difficult position. I don't blame her for wanting to leave, either."

"Then . . . why have you been discouraging her from going?"

Lionel's cerulean stare shifted toward the front door. "I worry what trouble will find her all on its own . . . For what she is . . . Without either of us to help her remain balanced, there's no telling what could happen . . ." His words lingered as though he had more to say.

Elliot remained quiet, polite, but also impatient.

"Wren is very powerful. So much that I question her ability to contain it." Lionel looked back to her and brushed her cheek with his gloved palm. "If she decides to leave, ultimately, we won't be able to stop her."

"We could go with her, right?"

Lionel's expression dropped. "I'm not sure." He glanced at the door again. "If I know Wren, she will leave without saying a word. In the middle of the night, even. We'd probably never have a chance to find out."

Elliot chewed on her lower lip. "I don't think she would leave without a goodbye . . ."

"I hope that you are right, my dear."

She drew a deep breath in and turned to face Lionel head on. "Is Nik here because you saw something? Do you already know that she is going to run?"

Lionel's face went blank, and he tightened his lips. "We both know that her departure from this kingdom is inevitable," he said softly. "I don't know that we would be able to keep up with her when she does finally go. Once she is out there . . . she could go anywhere."

"And Nik *can*?" Elliot tried to veil the hint of disbelief in her voice but wasn't quite sure how well she did.

"Nikolas is a reaper. Once they catch the scent, nothing can hide from or outrun a reaper." Lionel smiled again and ruffled her still-damp hair. "Not even Wren."

"What do you mean?"

"Well, reapers have a rather unique ability to track. They are similar to a bloodhound in that, once they have the *scent*, so to speak, they can track anything anywhere. His position and abilities were granted to him by the gods themselves. He may very well be just as powerful as Wren."

"I hadn't thought of that," Elliot considered aloud. "I wonder if *she* knows that." She crossed her arms and sighed through her nose. "I suppose . . . if . . . *when* Wren does bolt, we'll find out, won't we?"

He chuckled once and smiled tenderly. "Indeed."

"Lionel," Elliot posed, "what did you mean by *scent*?"

He quirked a brow at her. Without realizing it, his smile had widened. "They don't steal souls, as some may claim. They bind themselves to someone, and once the connection has been made, it becomes unbreakable." Lionel motioned to the stairs with a tilt of his head. "Reapers, the common kind, bind to those they will take into the afterlife. They track down their assigned wrongdoers and bring them in like soldiers. A *penitent* reaper on the other hand, they have a more important duty."

"And what duty is that?"

His eyes seemed to glow as he extended his gloved hand to her.

She timidly accepted it and allowed him to draw her close enough to tuck her hand into the inside crook of his elbow. A blush bloomed on her face when his arm hugged hers tighter against his chest as they walked in step.

"A penitent reaper is more like a bodyguard. Instead of making a bond to their prey, they can make an unbreakable bond with the one they will protect. One meant for a greater cause." His tone was nonchalant, but there was an apprehension beneath it that Elliot picked up on. "Unlike the common reaper's bond, who will make it regardless of how its prey feels about it, a penitent bond must be agreed upon by both parties before it can be made. If he can make that connection with Wren . . . If he can get *through* to her . . . I don't think I will be as worried for her when she leaves."

"I don't know." Elliot chewed the inside of her cheek and unconsciously winced. "If they *do* develop feelings for each other . . . I think I'd be more worried for her."

Lionel gave her a curious look from the corner of his eyes but let the comfortable silence between them fill the empty space around them as they made their way back upstairs.

CHAPTER NINE

> *"Don't walk behind me; I may not lead. Don't
> walk in front of me; I may not follow. Just
> walk beside me and be my friend."*
>
> *Albert Camus*

THE MOUNTAINOUS PATH THE GROUP FOLLOWED HAD a steep drop-off at its edge.

Very steep.

The other side of the crevasse was imperceptible behind the dense fog and cutting precipitation.

As a heavy storm distorted the surrounding area, gray-black clouds towered overhead, shifting with the tumultuous current above. The wind whipped around Nik and Wren as they trudged along the narrow, snowed-in pathway.

The pair of arions carried them resiliently through the onslaught, steady and seemingly unaffected. Arions were notorious for their memory and ability to navigate in conditions that many cannot. Once they had taken a path, they would not forget a single footfall. This allowed them to travel at night and, in this case, minimal-visibility conditions.

They gradually made their way toward an old bridge that connected to the other side of the valley.

The path they traversed was on the literal edge of a mountain. The valley between it and the neighboring mountain was as dark as it was sharp. Harsh winds constantly tormented the sides of the mountains into lifeless and frozen shards of rock.

The frigid wind pulled at everything: branches and limbs from the bushes and trees, Wren's hood and jacket, Nik's crimson scarf and black collar. All were violently ripped in every direction by the furious gale.

Wren caressed Rain's broad neck, idly picking loose ice from her mane.

The mare's pace slowed to allow Diamo to close the short distance behind her.

He, too, was covered in the heavy snow that sifted in the wind. The pits of white in his otherwise smoky-gray coat concealed him well in the storm.

The giveaway was the ebony-haired reaper that he carried.

Nik's clothing was plastered in frozen lumps of snow. His scarf shielded his face against the winds the best it could, but his skin beneath it was frozen regardless. The bloodred fabric shone like a beacon in the biting storm, rivaled only by his green eyes that penetrated the haze to meet Wren's.

She looked away from him instantly and gestured with her chin.

"There is a bridge ahead," Wren shouted over the wind. "We're almost there."

"You've been saying we are almost there for a while, Wren." A quirked smile perched on his lips widened once they were side by side. "I'm beginning to question your ability to gauge distance. Either that or you've been leading me on this whole time and got us lost in the snow."

She scowled and shot a glare at him. "Arion don't get *lost*."

The next few paces brought them to the bridge, only halfway visible in the white flurry. Rain eyed the stallion knowingly before she started across the bridge.

It was surprisingly stronger than it looked, albeit wobbly in the storm. Though the bridge was old, its construction was sturdy.

The arions followed along single file until it let out onto a heavily wooded flat with no visible path onward. The mare's particular familiarity with her herd's territory made it effortless for her to navigate in the blinding whites and grays.

Wren ruffled the snow away from Rain's mane and ears again before she leaned back and pulled the collar of her jacket up to pat her face.

"Once we get through that pass"—she gestured to a tunnel of tree limbs braided together—"we will be fifteen minutes from Abagail."

"Good." Nik brushed a large snowflake from his eye. "The trees will stop the snow from reaching us, too."

Wren nodded.

The tunnel did, indeed, shield them from the fury of the snowstorm. The twisting branches embraced any existing warmth in the crisp atmosphere and cradled it close.

As they neared the end of the wooded tunnel, Rain slowed. With a soft nicker, she and Diamo clipped to a stop.

"We go on our own from here," Wren said softly. "Arions stay clear of people." She reached forward to stroke the shoulders and strong chest of the mare. "Thank you, my friend," she whispered and slid from her back to land smoothly beside Rain.

Nik dismounted and rubbed Diamo's chin. He was thanked by a wet snort that slapped him in the face.

". . . Thank you for the ride." His voice was deliberately even and monotonous.

Wren snickered softly. She ducked her face behind Rain's head when she noticed his glare had moved to her. She caressed the arion's face and ears with confliction in her eyes but a smile on her lips.

Rain bobbed her head and nudged Wren affectionately. With a last scratch behind her golden ears, the pair of arions departed and disappeared into the trees.

Wren looked to Nik.

He had pulled his scarf from his shoulders so that he could use one end to wipe his face.

She couldn't hold back her own snort of laughter.

"Rather uncalled for," he grumbled.

"I think it was cute." Wren shielded the persistent smile with the back of her hand and brushed the small collections of snow from her coat and pants. Her palms and cheeks were bright red from the long, cold ride.

That was what she told herself.

"Shall we, then?" Nik looked away from her and down the clear pathway into town.

Plumes of gray smoke contrasted the hazy winter storm, rising from chimneys behind the tree line. As the pair grew closer to Abagail, the small town revealed itself to be derelict. Many of the buildings were missing chunks of their walls, had chipped bricks and splintered wooden windows and doorframes, or both.

A handful of people moved about the streets. Most of them paid Nik and Wren no mind. One passerby who made eye contact with them offered a sorrowful smile. He had sunken-in yet kind eyes. The remaining few regarded them with a nod, or not at all. Their faces were not unfriendly; they all seemed uninterested, but there was a collective sadness that they shared.

A sign for the Abagail Athenaeum caught Nik's attention, and he reached for Wren's shoulder.

"I'm going to check out the library."

She paused to follow his gaze before nodding. "Sure, I can meet you there once I'm finished at the armorer."

Nik broke away from her with a short nod and turned to leave.

WREN MADE HER WAY TO A CORNER SHOP AT THE END OF THE road. The light inside was dim through the windows and only slightly better once inside. A slender stream of smoke flowed from the structure's narrow chimney and into the gloomy atmosphere.

A small bell chimed when she pushed the door open and sounded a second time as the door shut behind her.

The man behind the counter looked up over a pair of small lenses balanced neatly at the tip of his nose. He squinted dark eyes and angled his chin upward before his cheeks perked up with a smile. He had thin gray hair that swirled around his head, and dark skin that held years of wrinkles. Despite the wrinkles, his posture and overall energy still retained his youthful strength.

"Ah, good. You received word that your armor is ready. This way." He set a golden pocket watch down on the counter and motioned her to follow.

The armorer led her through a curtained doorway. His tools and materials were scattered about the makeshift workspace that clearly doubled as his living quarters. There was a partition near the back of the room where the foot of a bed could be seen.

"Your measurements made it rather difficult to properly lace the plates to move with you." He brought her to a mannequin and adjusted the shoulders of the armor. "But I believe to have done your request justice."

The black armor hugged the chest of the dummy. The light shone from its surface as if it had been made with dragon scales. Black studs of metal secured the movable parts of the armor tastefully.

"It's *incredible*, William. Is it as light as it looks?"

"Try it on. You tell me, dear."

His callused and scarred hands unclasped the straps on both sides of the chest piece and expertly slid it off of the mannequin.

"It's a work of art." Wren smiled at him. "I almost don't want to wear it."

"It's one of a kind, my dear." William laughed heartily and handed it to her. As he leaned in, he placed a genial kiss on her cheek. "Just like you."

Wren's eyes softened, and she placed a soft kiss of her own on his scruffy cheek.

"You are far too kind, William. I have your payment." Her eyes shone with a smile. "Plus, there's a little extra for the rush order and the trouble."

"No trouble at all."

"Well, keep it anyway. You earned every bit of it."

Nik found a reclusive spot in the corner of the great Athenaeum Hall with a large dusty book splayed on the table before him. He skimmed the faded text with intense focus and tightened eyes.

> Records maintained of the spell are few in number yet are detailed in their own respect.
>
> From Sire Peters's account, a spell is a monstrous and unpredictable scourge that feels only rage . . . . The Great Terror of Echinacea Islands was not a gryphon, dragon, nor phoenix, but a spell driven mad.
>
> In a night known as Echinacea's End, the spell named Eurynome Draven burned the largest town of the island,

Hindley, down in a storm of fire and lightning.

Sire Peters was king of the nation of Echinacea when his fury rained down. As soon as he learned of the event, he enacted a royal order that any spell found amongst them be killed on the spot. Any citizens suspected of harboring one would meet the same end.

Statements were taken by all who took refuge within the city walls, and a unanimous recount of the event depicted Eurynome as the aggressor. The perpetrator. His rage had surprised everyone, and his destruction had been absolute. He intended to wipe the town off the map.

Many townspeople did not survive. They burned alongside the tinder and rubble instead. Those who made it to safety were haunted by the screams of their brothers and sisters and the sound of his relentless thunder.

All who survived were petrified of thunderstorms until their final days.

It is said the true suffering came from Eurynome's betrayal. He was one of them. Before he became a monster, he, at first, was a friend. How could he have deceived them all so effortlessly? . . . So thoroughly?

A true monster if ever one existed . . .

He grew into such a towering creature. From a man to a four-winged beast in an instant, and a scream . . . a feathered, scaled, and nameless terror that craved fire and death.

His power was unimaginable. The clouds overhead, black as a moonless, starless night . . . lit only by flashes of light within them, all of which were followed by mountainous thunder that rattled bones. When he struck, hot bolts of lightning lit fire to anything his breath did not.

The only question that no one had an answer to was why . . . Why did he do this?

Footsteps brought Nik from the pages he'd already reread numerous times and to the approaching attendant.

"I found the reference that you requested, sir. *Unusual Beasts* by Ebner Breve." An imp, no taller than Nik's hip, set a thick book on the table. "It was not easy to locate, as it has never been requested." His forced smile puckered his ash-white face. "Very difficult, indeed . . ."

"Of course." Nik rolled his eyes and reached into his pocket. He dropped a copper coin into the imp's outstretched palm with his own terse smile.

"Should you need anything else, I shall be near, sir."

"Thanks." Nik turned his attention to the new book.

Its cover depicted an ancient dialect of symbols, long lost with time. The aged pages were hardly legible, and most were written in extinct languages, but its illustrations were clear.

There was one passage that already had a handwritten translation scratched within the margins of the ancient letters. On the page to the right of the text, a picture of a great beast with four wings, surrounded by a towering storm cloud, was expertly sketched onto the parchment.

Dear Mr. Breve,

Thank you for reaching out to my father. I regret to inform you that he has passed. However, I am happy to contribute to your book in his stead. How shall I begin . . .

I know that everyone hates spells. Any story that can be found only tells of Eurynome. But they are not all like him. They can also be peaceful and shy. I have yet to see one good line written of a spell . . .

So, I give this to you: my detailed, and first-hand account of knowing a spell in the flesh for posterity. A truthful contradiction to the many that are sick with fear of the unknown and outright animosity drawn from only one single occurrence . . . Should you choose to publish this.

Eurynome has no power, unless provided by the willing . . . He is gone. We cannot, in good conscience, paint an entire species with the single brush handed to us by the first of its kind that we have encountered. History must be recorded by all sides, by all kinds.

A glen nearby my village was home to one of these creatures.

In the picture, the distinction between scale and feather was nearly impossible. The eyes of the creature were the only features of the inked sketch that were clearly distinguishable. The two pairs of wings were drawn in a way that made the shadow seemingly float off of the page.

Her name was Acela Inar. She was reclusive yet kind. She kept to herself for the most part, but we would see her at a festival on occasion. She had a wonderful family of five, all full of love and compassion for each other and those around them.

Her two sons, Caleb and Othaniel, were courageous and outgoing, just like their father. They clearly adored him and wanted only to emulate the best parts of his personality.

Ren was a gentle giant that was a regular in town. He used to sell the vegetables grown in his garden and the eggs his chickens laid. Although he towered over all of us and had severe features, his nature was unbelievably generous. He sold his goods for next to nothing; any children that approached him paid nothing.

Caleb and Othaniel would often come into town with him. I caught my brother, along with the other village boys, wrapped up in their world of make-be-

lieve adventures so many times that I simply stopped counting.

Her only daughter, Renata, often stayed home with Acela. They stuck to each other like honey on your hands on a hot summer's day. Although she had been named after her father, her mother was the clear favorite . . . Her mother was the strongest woman I've ever met or will meet.

Acela rescued my father's flock from a pack of werewolves. They had killed four of our sheep, and we would have lost my father, too, had Acela not shown.

From what he had told me, her transformed body was massive. She had feathers rigid enough to lift her four powerful wings. She was covered in shimmering scales so hard that the claws and teeth of the werewolves did nothing against her armor.

The whole ordeal probably lasted only a few seconds, but, to him, time slowed . . . and he was frozen along with it.

Her movements were calculated and swift. She was being careful to injure, not kill. She only wanted them to leave my father alone and chased them off into the woods without a single casualty. Well, other than the poor sheep.

My father was certain the creature that had saved him was Acela. He said that, without a doubt, he could feel her presence emanating from the beast. He swore that it was her voice that came from the creature when it told him to run.

A direct quote from my father: "Her eyes were a different color, but when they met mine, I heard Acela's voice in my mind. I know it was her. I'm certain of it."

> *My father tried to thank her for it what must have become hundreds of times. But she'd deny knowing what he was thanking her for. She refused to acknowledge what he saw, even if it was only to thank her for saving his life and what was left of his flock.*
>
> *Acela was taken along with the other women when Adrean's men showed up. My brother and I tried to find her family, to try and help them . . . But I wish that we hadn't. Her home was still smoldering when we finally got there. Her family was still inside . . .*
>
> *When my village searched the wreckage, they only found her husband and her sons. They searched for her daughter for weeks, but there was never any sign of her.*
>
> *I hope that Renata made it out alive. I hope that she—*

"What are you reading?"

Wren drew his attention from the pages with a start.

She chuckled once and sat beside him. "Did I scare you?"

"No," he replied quietly. "I'm researching."

"Oh, goody." Wren's brow furrowed, and she looked at the first book that Nik had discarded. Her eye caught the name Eurynome on the open page, and her breath stilled.

The rope that held the bag for her armor slipped from her hands, and it met the ground with a loud clatter. A few eyes glanced up from the surrounding space at the sound, but they didn't linger before returning to their own business.

Wren growled softly and slammed the book shut. "I'm ready to leave Abagail," she murmured darkly and stared at the book's cover.

The black lettering on the cover was still a vibrant shade, as well as most of the cover. The top quarter of the book was sun-bleached from having been filed away beside a shorter book for so long and within eyeline of sunlight. The text spelled out the title with an over-complicated choice of calligraphy. *A Collection of Beastly Encounters*, a book with no named author.

Nik narrowed his eyes at the now-closed book and let a heavy breath out through his nose.

"I hadn't finished reading that."

She bit back an aggravated retort and, instead of letting it out, gnashed her teeth together. "Your obsession with this is disturbing, you know," Wren whispered and pursed her lips. Begrudgingly, she flipped the book back open to search for his lost pages.

"To you, it might be an obsession. However, *you* don't consider the fact that others know nothing about what you are and might want to learn more. I wouldn't necessarily consider two books an obsession." He turned to face her fully, straddling the bench-style seat. "We are allowed to be curious, Wren. Even you know that. Do you really want to spend your life lying to everyone about what you are? Why does it matter so much that no one knows?" When she gave no response, he tightened his lips and tried again. "What are you so afraid of?"

His last question made her eyes narrow. Her hands clenched, and she stared fiercely at the book on the table.

"I'm not trying to upset you, Wren." He brought his hand closer to hers, his palm hovering above her tight fists.

Just before his hand was near enough to touch hers, she recoiled. "I know you aren't *trying* to upset me, but this is a topic I won't talk about." She took a deep breath and leaned away from him. "Especially not *here*."

Nik glared at her. "Grow up," he said in a low voice. "Just because *you* don't want to talk about it doesn't mean *I* can't learn about it on my own. I know that you want it to stay a secret for some reason, and that's fine, I will respect that." He hesitated, to gauge her body language.

She was pissed, but . . . still.

"But I find it too fascinating to ignore." He tilted his head slightly, his ebony bangs brushing across his long eyelashes as he did so.

She shook her head and met his eyes steadily.

"Stories of them still exist . . . Well, rather stories of *one* still exist. Should people find out that there is another one living amongst them? They'd kill me before they'd run me out of town. Elliot and Lionel would be in danger, too. Harboring a monster comes with charges of its own . . ."

Nik watched her emotions wane with his own stoic expression masking his thoughts.

"It would be better for everyone if I left Arnica," she muttered. The sting of tears itched the corners of her eyes, and she dipped her chin. She could feel his eyes on her and couldn't bring herself to meet them.

"Wren," he tried softly. "Talk to me."

Wren jerked away from him and stood in order to gather her armor. "There's an inn three streets down if you want to keep researching." Her ability to suppress the frustration welling in her chest chipped away with each taken breath. "I'm heading back to Black Rivers. See ya."

Nik reached for her arm and held her in place. "You are insane if you think I'm going to let you go back to Lionel's on your own, at night."

Wren pulled away and took a long step backward. "I've made the trip before on my own plenty of times. I don't need your help to get back."

He stood and faced her fully. Nik seized both of her arms and refused to let her pull free this time. "Stop running away from everything and just listen. It's *infuriating*."

Her cheeks flushed pink, and her eyebrows went low. Wren opened her mouth to respond, glowering, but Nik cut her off.

"You aren't anything like Eurynome." His voice was just above a whisper. "Just because he went mad doesn't mean that you will, too. The only thing that we can do is to learn more. Find out *why* it happened."

She flinched visibly and tried, in vain, to pull free.

"Elliot and Lionel would be devastated if you run away on them. Don't you at least want to give them the chance to help you?"

Wren froze, and her eyes slipped shut. Her lips pulled into a deep frown as she angled her chin away from him. "Let me go," she managed roughly.

Nik glanced around the library briefly before he eased her back down to sit.

She cooperated but kept her eyes shut tight.

He let her arms go as he sighed. "I will talk to the attendant about the books, and we can head ba—"

"It feels like the only option," Wren whispered in a dejected tone. "Running away . . . At least I'm good at *that*."

Nik drew his coat from the table and slipped it on. He looked to Wren, conflicted, before he wrapped his crimson scarf around her neck. The wounds on her face and ear still glared at him boldly, and his eyebrows twitched unconsciously.

Her glassy eyes snapped open and finally met his, instantly giving her away.

He let a heavy breath out through his nose and cupped his palm against her face. "Don't cry," he whispered. His thumb brushed across the crest of her cheek when her eyelashes failed to catch a tear she could no longer hold back. Their eyes remained locked for a short while before he broke the silence. "Let's go."

Wren looked away but nodded.

He adjusted the scarf around her neck with a small smile. He lifted her armor satchel to his shoulder, then gathered the two books into one hand.

Wren moved toward the massive doors lethargically, eyes downcast and jaw clenched.

Nik's free hand hovered over the small of her back as he followed a half step behind, urging her forward without ever touching her.

"Ehm, sir, the books . . ." The imp attendant approached them. "They are not to leave the athenaeum."

Nik stopped and leveled him with a withering stare. "You said yourself they've never been requested. Why does it matter if I take them? How much are they worth to you?"

"Sir, I am not allowed to accept bribes." His creeping smile belied his words. The imp's round eyes grew bright with interest. "But, if you are insistent, I . . ." He cut himself off and tapped the tips of his long fingers against his palms. "I d-doubt the bookkeepers here would even notice if they were to be . . . lost . . ."

Nik folded his arms and remained silent with a dark look on his face.

The black eyes of the imp flicked between Nik and Wren, settling on her for an uncomfortable duration of time. "Their worth, eh?" His tongue flitted across his teeth and smiled wider. "What is *her* worth to *you*?"

Nik stepped into his eyeline, obscuring the imp's view of Wren. "You cross the line, imp." His eyes narrowed. "I will give you two silver coins. One for each book. Take them and let us leave in peace."

The imp sneered. "Tsk." His black eyes met Nik's piercing ones, and he swallowed hard. "Yes, sir. Two . . . two silver coins. Very good."

Nik placed the coins in the imp's palm forcefully and glared one last time at the seedy creature before he and Wren left the athenaeum. His hand lingered over the small of her back as they stepped outside.

"Are we going to be returning the same way that we came?"

Nik's question hung in the air for a moment before Wren replied.

"Unfortunately, no. The arion won't travel with passengers at night. The forest is too dangerous, and having passengers would put them in a very vulnerable position. Not to mention that it's end of hibernation season for many creatures that like to eat meat."

The pair stepped on to the street and was met by the icy slap of the late-winter twilight.

Wren shuddered abruptly at the cold. She hastily adjusted her jacket and scarf to tuck around her ears and under her chin. She took a deep breath of the air and, subsequently, a deep waft of Nik's earthy, cedar scent. She blushed as she hooked her finger into the crimson fabric to tug it a bit farther away from her nose.

"It's colder than I thought it'd get," Wren murmured and tucked her chin.

Nik smirked, pretending to not notice and fixed his gaze in front of them.

The evening light had all but faded. The doors of shops were shut tight, most sparse with light. Even the windows in the floors above the shops were dark, only a few emitting the faint orange glow of reading light.

"I'd feel rather silly if I were you, Wren." Nik chuckled when he felt her sharp glare. "You said that you'd go back . . . on foot." He glanced at her from the corner of his eye. "At night." She pursed her lips when he pointedly paused. "At the end of hibernation season. Alone."

"So what?" Wren scowled and shrugged. "I *have* done it before. I *lived* out there. There's nothing to it." Her tight eyes dared a glance at him without turning her head.

Those golden-green eyes met her stare with a perceptive quirk to that *stupid* smirk of his.

"Three streets, you said?"

Wren dropped her eyes to the ground and scowled. She shook her head and faced forward as she folded her arms around her torso.

"Yeah," she grumbled as she took a few purposeful steps ahead. "This way."

Nik stuffed his hands into his jacket pockets and followed a short distance behind her.

The quiet in the street only amplified the silence between her footsteps.

"I can't get used to how quietly you walk. It's creepy." Wren paused so that he was beside her and pushed him forward. "I'll follow you."

"Well, I *am* a reaper." He purposefully caught her stare. "Walking quietly and being creepy are part of the gig. And you're the one who knows where we are going."

She looked away and pushed his back forward. "Keep going that way. You can't miss it."

CHAPTER TEN

"For a friend with an understanding
heart is worth no less than a brother."

Homer

JACK PACED THE FLOOR OF THE COMMON ROOM. HIS WHITE paws padded back and forth, and his slate-gray eyes periodically flickered to the door.

"Lionel, even Jack is concerned. They should have returned by now." Elliot pulled the curtain around the balcony open. "Something bad must have happened!"

The warm weight of Lionel's palm fell onto her slender shoulder.

"It's all right, Elliot." His gentle voice seemed to catch Jack's attention as well. "It has been snowing on and off here. Abagail *is* on the foothills of the Aster Mountains. I imagine they were likely snowed in."

She turned to Lionel, eyes wide. "That's not better!"

He furrowed his brow and tilted his chin slightly. "Do you not trust Nikolas?"

"No! I—" Elliot stopped short.

The room grew notably warmer and the air softer in a single breath. A calm swept through her body and made her lashes feel heavier. She nibbled on her lip and looked outside at the snow.

He's trying to help me relax . . .

Jack came to a stop at her feet and stared up at her inquisitively. He took a few steps closer until his front paws rested on her toes.

"I just don't know him, I guess. He doesn't know enough about Wren to be able to help if something . . ." She sighed out her nose and slid into the mustard-yellow chair.

Jack seized the opportunity to jump into her lap. He forced his white head roughly into Elliot's hands with a pushy meow.

"I don't trust him to keep her safe. They *just* met."

Lionel laughed softly as he made his way to the kitchen. "Nikolas is very capable, my dear." He paused to select two mugs and a clean saucer from the cabinet above the sink. "You aren't giving him much credit."

"Well, you said that his powers are granted by the gods?"

Lionel smiled as he poured hot water from the kettle into the two mugs. "Yes. Reapers are commonly made up of individuals whose lives ended unjustly. They are given back their mortal lives in exchange for their service to the gods in stopping more reapers from being created." Lionel retrieved a glass jar filled with milk from the fridge. "That is the balance." He smiled sadly as he poured a small amount in both mugs, as well as the saucer on the counter bedside them.

"So, what does he do?"

"Reapers act out the will of the Court of Balance, as well as maintain order to the extent to which they are capable. I've heard them called the swords of the Court, but I feel the term is rather dismissive."

"Just like Wren does for the Guard."

"Very similar, yes." He wrapped one hand around a mug and clasped the saucer with the other. Lionel delivered the mug to Elliot and set the saucer on the knee-high table in front of the mustard chair. "When his life was returned to him in exchange for his service, he was entrusted with very powerful abilities to defend himself and others."

Jack eagerly leapt from her lap and to the offering.

"The Court of Balance selects souls of the departed that meet a certain, uh . . . certain criteria."

"What do you mean? What is the Court of Balance?" She curled her fingers in the air mockingly. "And what criteria?"

Lionel's cerulean eyes softened when they met hers.

Her chocolate-brown eyes shone with the ambient light, amplifying it somehow. The tight rings of chestnut hair draped around her heart-shaped face. The soft light behind her made it seem as though she was shrouded in a soft glow.

Elliot frowned and waved a hand at him. "Lionel?"

He smiled to himself and cloaked it behind a sip from his mug. "I'm sorry, my dear. I lost myself in thought for a moment. I do apologize." He crossed his legs loosely and balanced the mug on his thigh before he continued. "The Court is something most humans know about, yet little of. Many that do know of the Court have built temples and communities of disciples that worship or despise the gods.

"It is a place where souls might be given things such as a second chance at life or peaceful and eternal rest. It is also a place where souls might be damned to punishment or sentenced to atone for sins committed during life."

Elliot unconsciously glanced to Jack, watching him lap up milk from the saucer. She drew in a heavy breath and dipped her chin to her chest. "I see." She hesitated, to formulate her words. "So, what are the criteria? What gives them the power to decide such things?"

"Both of those are good questions." Lionel looked to Jack as well. "Many have asked them, too. The ambiguity of the Court is frustratingly profound, so much so that there are those who do not believe the Court is real at all.

"To my understanding, the Court of Balance is a source of meaning and judgment during and after life. It is overseen by Mia'el, the god of life and death; Aeon, the god of time; and Yu'e, the goddess of the moon and earth.

"Mia'el is said to be in charge of the Court, as he will have the final word when casting judgment. He evaluates one's life and determines where they will be . . . placed. Punishments are said to be severe, while virtue is well-rewarded.

"Those who return to this realm have claimed that Yu'e's word greatly influences Mia'el. She is the force of empathy to which souls like Nikolas are given life again.

"Aeon cares not for the deliberation between Mia'el and Yu'e. He is the one that watches over those like Nikolas, who have been returned to the world of the living. He will intervene if responsibilities are not upheld and bring them back to Mia'el and Yu'e for a second judgment." He paused to shake his head. "I've never heard of one being returned to life twice.

"Reapers are what help to ensure the balance is maintained. The more innocents that perish unjustly, the more reapers there will be. With more reapers, fewer innocents will perish. That is why some call them the swords of the Court.

"Nikolas died at a young age. He stood before the Court, as everyone does, and received his judgment. Becoming a penitent reaper was the role that he was offered." He paused and tapped his chin once with his index finger. "It is very rare that such a young boy was to become a high level grim, so it's debatable on whether he was gifted or cursed."

Elliot pursed her lips and bit back her questions regarding the circumstances of Nik's death. "Strange," she murmured instead and looked out the window at the twirling snow. "I still don't understand why you are so insistent that he can protect her. Have you seen his abilities? Have you seen these so-called godly powers?"

"Nikolas is here solely to protect her . . . Elliot." His voice was melodic and soothing. "It has been growing increasingly uncomfortable living in Arnica. I'm not sure what is going on, but I can't shake the feeling that something is coming. Something . . . something bad."

"What do you mean?" Elliot asked, staring at Lionel. "Wren said the same thing."

"Would you like me to show you? In order to explain, there are things you will first need to know."

Elliot chewed on the inside of her cheek for a few moments before she nodded.

He removed his hands from her shoulders and tugged off both of his gloves. He took a small step away from her and, with a deep breath, pressed his palms together in front of his chest. His eyes slipped shut, and his chest expanded as his lungs filled to capacity.

A warm aura filled the room, and the air turned sweet in both aroma and taste.

Lionel closed the small distance he put between them and embraced her.

Elliot's eyes widened and her mouth hung open, but she was too stunned to speak.

The bare palms of Lionel's hands began to glow softly against the fabric that covered her shoulders and back. The sweet warmth emanated once more and grew in strength.

Elliot's eyes fluttered shut as shadows of images crept into her vision like a dream.

Wren couldn't have been older than thirteen. She stood inside of the boxing ring with her arms folded across

her chest, and dark red splotches littered her face and body.

She was small in size and rail thin, but the look in her eyes was the same.

"I'm not going to lose next time, Lionel! I know I can beat him one on one, but he fights dirty!"

"Violence won't defeat dishonesty, Wren. He's twice your age." He frowned and held a clean towel out to her.

"He was hurting people, Lionel! Seth and his goons were terrorizing the people in the market. I had to do something!" Wren's breath heaved once, and she roughly grabbed the towel from Lionel. She stepped down from the ring and pressed the fabric against her face. "I didn't shift or anything. I just . . . leveled the playing field."

Lionel gave her an unimpressed look that she could feel through the veil of the towel.

"So, what did you do?"

Her hands stilled momentarily before she lowered it just enough for her to peek at him. "I used the wind to dump old planter water on them . . . I didn't intend for one of the planters to fall, too." She smirked behind the towel. "It landing on a goon's head was just a happy coincidence."

"Wren." His eyebrows furrowed, and a deep frown etched onto his lips. "You could have been found out! Did anyone see you?"

"No, I was behind the flower cart, and no one was around. They saw me after the fact and assumed it had been me." Wren flopped onto the bench beside the ring and let the towel flutter to her lap, still clutching one end lightly with her fingers. She stared at her hands. "I couldn't outrun them, though. I need to get stronger and faster."

"You shouldn't push yourself like this, Wren. Training your body under such duress isn't going to help you keep control. It will only exhaust you. You need to focus on training *your mind. That's the only way that you can control yourself. Your mind is what controls your body. Focus on that."*

She narrowed her eyes at him and stood up swiftly. Wren shoved the towel into his chest and turned back to the ring.

"Thanks for the towel."

"YOU SHOULDN'T HAVE BROUGHT HER TO BLACK RIVERS, *Gibbs."* Ian the butcher stared at Lionel with unreserved disapproval. He shifted his weight and adjusted his belt with clawed hands. "I know you mean well, I do, boy. But"—his black eyes glanced up the stairs—"that girl isn't a tempest. We both know that."

"Yes," Lionel admitted reluctantly. "That is true."

"She is too young to know how to control herself. What happened with Seth was unfortunate. I'm glad that she wasn't hurt too badly." Ian smirked and laughed softly. "She is a tough little shit. I'll give her that. Such a shame to know that the whole thing was over a planter. But . . . she isn't safe here. I'm sure that you have already seen what will happen."

Lionel smiled at the kind kappa. "I know, Ian. But what else am I to do? Where could I have sent her safely? She's . . . I was entrusted to have her in my care. You already know that. Where else are we to go?"

The butcher pursed his lips. His reptilian eyes glanced up the stairs a second time. His tail flicked absentmindedly behind him, and he adjusted his belt again. "I don't know, my boy. I understand your position." He clapped a three-fingered claw onto Lionel's shoulder. "I know it's against your nature to send her away. But the townspeople . . . members of the Guard . . . Lionel, I hear all of their whispers." His black nail tapped against the side of his head. "They forget that I have *better hearing than them since they can't see my ears. I hear them all whisper about her." His frown deepened. "They're catching on to her."*

"I hear them too, Ian." Lionel took a deep breath before he smiled at the butcher. "The day will come when we leave Arnica. I don't know when it'll be, but . . ." He caught himself glancing up the stairs. "I just want her to have a fair chance of being part of a community. She was alone in the forest, starved." He looked back to the kappa. "She is such a gentle creature, Ian. It breaks my heart that no one else can see that."

The kappa sighed and nodded. "I am not telling you what to do, Gibbs. I only mean to help my friends."

"I know, Ian." Lionel smiled. "Thank you."

Flames licked at the disintegrating strips of wood. Anything flammable was fair game as the raging fire advanced through the streets of Arnica. The spreading inferno followed a demon made of fire, hungry to watch everything burn, barreling toward the gates of the kingdom.

Townspeople screamed, frantic, and rushed in every direction. The crowds disoriented everyone within them with blind terror.

Bandits, human and creature alike, followed the flame beast and picked off anyone they could snatch.

A broad-chested man sat upright on the back of a pure-white horse. His tanned skin was taut atop strictly trained muscles itching for a fight. His armor was mostly black with decorations etched in gold and was stained with fresh blood. The steed upon which he sat wore armor to match, blood spatter and all.

The cluster of bandits around the man on the horse was the nastiest of the horde. They pulled screaming women from their homes by their hair and into the abyss of chaos, returning shortly thereafter with a sickening look of pleasure on their faces and clothing drenched with blood.

Seth rode a few paces behind the fire demon. The stallion stopped abruptly with loud protest when the demon incased in the inferno paused before him.

A dark, four-legged creature stood between Seth's army and the kingdom's gates. A heavy pressure emanated from it and made it difficult for them to draw in a deep breath. It stood in such darkness that only the fluttering silhouette and glowing silver eyes were able to be made out from the plumes of smoke.

"Master?" A nine-foot-tall ogre beside Seth's horse spoke gruffly.

"Finally." A grinning sneer darkened his face and he kicked the belly of his steed. The stallion obediently strode forward before it halted beside the fire demon. "What are you waiting for, demon? Burn that thing down."

The inferno blazed into an intense shade of super-hot white. It lurched toward the silver-eyed shadow at an alarming speed.

The creature dodged the flames easily and perched on the top of a nearby building. The demon followed closely behind, constantly rolling at and missing the creature. This dance went on for what felt like hours but was only seconds.

"Demon!" Seth called out angrily as he drew his sword from the hilt on his hip. "Finish it now or get out of my way!"

The fire demon ignored Seth, desperately trying to catch the beast.

The silver eyes watched Seth carefully as he approached. In a moment of hesitation, the fire demon caught the beast and exploded into a furious ball of white. The ball's diameter continuously changed in size, pulsating, while it twisted like molten clouds in a tight, flowing formation.

Seth stopped in his advance with a wild and wicked smile on his face.

A terrible howl split the air in a piercing scream, and the cloud of blinding light intensified.

"Fire will cleanse this corrupted kingdom. A new ruler will change the course of Arnica's destiny forever! Nothing shall escape my cleansing flames!" Seth's booming voice was amplified in his deep chest, tight with excitement.

His battle cry drew a cacophonous roar of approval from the army behind him. They followed him closely as they drew nearer to the gates. Many even took the chance and broke ahead, eager to draw more blood and clear the way for Seth Tanner.

The fireball flickered briefly before dissipating in a towering swirl of smoke.

The four-legged beast remained standing, and its jaw held the remains of the fire demon. The humanoid limbs of the demon dangled from sharp, backward-pointed teeth.

Seth and his men stood frozen as they watched the beast spit out the lifeless body of their comrade.

A sudden gust of wind sliced through the street, suffocating many of the nearby brush fires that consumed the town. It circled around the four-legged beast like a current. In the brief moments of Seth's inaction, a massive pair of wings unfolded from its back and thrust into the whirlpool of wind to propel the beast forward at alarming velocity.

Seth broke his men from their trance with an infuriated cry. His steed tore into a sprint at the shadow, sword outstretched.

The army followed.

A rumble of what could have been laughter drummed from the silver-eyed creature before, with a mighty flap of its unusual wings, it shot swiftly above the horde. Just out of reach.

The beast soared above them, coming into full view from the light of the burning city.

Its long body was similar to that of a dragon but was feathered along the top of its neck, shoulders, and back. Its wings were also dragon-like, but instead of a membrane between each finger, the wings were made up of a glorious set of sunset-colored feathers in a variety of sizes that gleamed in the flickering firelight, revealing their bladelike edges. Its long tail was covered with a myriad of black scales and sunset feathers that gradually scattered down its length. At the very tip was another pair of wings, much smaller than those on her back but otherwise identical.

Flames burned behind its bleach-white teeth, ready to explode outward. Its legs were tucked against its armored belly, and its curved talons were clenched into fists. The tightly packed scales covering its body gave no weak points. Even the feathers that emerged from the shimmering black scales looked as though they were sharp enough to draw blood.

Silver eyes watched the army of humans and creatures circle below it.

A second pair of identical wings unfolded from against its back and from the tip of its tail. The four wings flapped in an effortless pattern that kept it hovering.

"Archers!" Seth called loudly.

Spears of iron rocketed toward the beast, most falling short or missing entirely. The few that made contact bounced off its reinforced body.

"Bring that monster down! Get the Giant now!"

The four-winged beast circled above, waiting.

LIONEL'S HOME CAME BACK INTO HAZY VIEW AS THE SHAPES AND shadows of his vision dissipated.

"Was that . . . Was that thing Wren?" Elliot's voice was soft and uncharacteristically shaken.

Lionel held her a moment longer. He caressed the back of her head tenderly and sighed. "Yes. After she found you and brought you here that night . . . Seth drew her back out. He pushed farther into the city and made it to the gates. Wren . . . made a decision and followed through on it."

The room was quiet. Elliot absentmindedly looked to Jack, asleep on the mustard chair.

"The townspeople have no idea that she is capable of transforming to such a thing. Revealing herself would have only ensured her execution."

"What! Why? She was protecting the kingdom from Seth!" Elliot pushed away from Lionel so roughly that the pure white cat stirred and looked to her. "Why would people just automatically kill a spell if it didn't do anything wrong?"

Lionel frowned and shook his head. "Fear is an overwhelming thing, my dear. Mankind is more vulnerable to it than creatures or fae tend to be. I have watched fear infect men and women like a poisonous fog. Once Seth had fallen, it was easy for the king to twist the narrative to turn Wren into a third-party aggressor in order to make himself the hero. Humans are very . . . susceptible to suggestion. Malevolent men like Seth and the king use fear as a weapon in the form of misinformation and hatred in order to fuel his men's lust for violence and vengeance."

"What do you mean?"

"Well." He gently took Elliot's wrist and led her to the couch. He sat down before he tugged her beside him, positioned close enough to his chest to turn Elliot's cheeks a bright shade of pink. Lionel wound his arm around her shoulders and rested his palm on the crown of her curls. "There used to be a library in the kingdom that had extensive documentation on creatures such as fae and undead. Mythical creatures were harder to find, but any books that had information on them were well documented. I was fortunate enough to have been able to read many of them before . . ."

His hesitation made Elliot's warm eyes turn to him expectantly.

He sighed and tucked a loose curl behind her ear.

"About a month before Seth's attempt to overthrow the king, a fire destroyed not only the library but many of the rooms that the families of the Guardsmen lived in. In a panic, they moved everyone who survived inside of the castle to take refuge.

"Seth himself set fire to the library. I have seen it in the memories of others as clearly as I see you now. I can only theorize as to his rationale, but I think he intended to destroy the knowledge and history of the kingdom, while simultaneously making his first attempt at the crown . . .

"He snuck in one of his agents, impersonating a soldier, and made an attempt on the king's life the night after the fire. The agent was apprehended and sentenced, but Seth was never found out. With so many unanswered questions, guardsmen grew more and more paranoid."

Elliot nestled herself into the crook of Lionel's arm, pressing against him as she listened.

He smiled and placed a soft kiss on the top of her head. "Before you knew her, Wren had a much harder time controlling her temper enough to not rouse suspicion. Not to mention that she and Seth never got along. Seth had somehow convinced the king that Wren, an outsider, should be the prime suspect of the fire." His fingers distractedly wound through her curls. "When she became a member of the Guard, it was not by choice. She was an unknown. The king didn't trust her, and he wanted to keep her somewhere that he could watch her. Closely.

"To this day, the remaining Tanners hold the same grudge against Wren as their late brother. That is why Honorah antagonizes her and you. She knows that picking on you will instantly make Wren bristle."

"That's bullshit," Elliot growled.

Lionel laughed and squeezed her shoulders affectionately. "It is absolutely bullshit."

Elliot chewed on the inside of her cheek as she pondered whether or not to ask her next question.

"Go ahead, dear." Lionel chuckled. "I can feel that you have more to say."

"Well, um." She sat up to meet his eyeline straight on. "How did you have such a clear vision of what happened?"

The trace smiled sadly and shook his head. "I read it from Wren when she let me treat her wounds. You may not remember much, but she had been put through the gauntlet that night. Returning to her human form is a painful ordeal, and she had nearly lost her arm."

Elliot shivered and flinched. "I'd rather not think about that scar," she whispered.

Lionel nodded. "Indeed. Truth be told, I showed you all that I know of that night. She refuses to tell me how it happened." He crossed one leg over the other and folded his arms in his lap. "Simple mind readers can only manage seeing one-dimensionally, and they cannot transfer what they see to others. When a trace does it, we *experience* it. I can see and relay a memory as clearly as though I stood within it. When I treated Wren that night . . . that memory was the only memory that I could read. Over and over."

"Wow." Elliot glanced out the glass doors and frowned. "But . . . how does that tie in with Nik being able to protect her? If anything . . . now I feel even more uneasy about all of this."

Lionel lifted one hand to run it through his curls and sighed through his nose. "I have been seeing the memory of that night in my dreams for weeks. If it is a premonition, I will feel much better knowing that someone with power drawn from the gods stands behind her. Especially someone that I would trust with my own life."

Elliot frowned and shook her head. "I guess . . ."

CHAPTER ELEVEN

*"Courage is not the absence of fear, but rather the judgment
that something else is more important than fear."*

Ambrose Redmoon

WREN PEERED INTO THE RENTED ROOM FROM THE
doorway.

The overused hardwood floor was covered by tattered, trampled carpets. A medium sized dresser sat pressed against an off-white and cracked wall by the entryway. A window on the far end of the room overlooked the streetlights, glowing dimly outside from behind frayed curtains.

The wall perpendicular to the only window had a modest fireplace with a generous heap of wood beside it. A pair of wooden chairs were positioned a few feet away from the fireplace.

Her eyes then landed on the main problem with the room.

"One bed, eh?" Nik gently pushed her into the room when he grew tired of her blocking the doorway. "That won't be so bad." He tipped the door closed as he shook his head.

"I'll take the chairs and the blanket," Wren countered. She pulled off her snow-caked boots and placed them on the small portion of stone flooring around the hearth. She knelt down to inspect the chimney before lighting a fire. Wren stacked three logs of firewood into a pyramid and stuffed the provided kindling into the gap beneath them.

Her pale fingers found the box of matches on the mantel in the same moment that Nik's did. She recoiled so quickly that the box tumbled to the floor, littering the stone and wood with matches.

"Don't do that!" She glared and knelt down to collect the matches, looking anywhere but at him. Wren growled at herself when she felt the heat of pink bloom across her face and pursed her lips. She brushed a lock of loose hair behind her ear and took a deep, silent breath as an excuse to conceal her face.

Strong hands closed around her wrists to draw her upright.

"Do what?"

The mocking smirk on his face turned Wren bright red as her temper flared. She pulled herself free and stepped back.

"Appearing out of nowhere. You're so quiet that you need to wear bells or something. It's like you do it on purpose."

"We've already discussed this. I can't really help it." Nik gathered up the matches and box with a smirk still painted on his face. He struck the head of a match against the rough patch on the side of the box and waited for it to ignite before he tossed it into the kindling below the stack of firewood.

"Whatever." Wren retrieved the blanket from the bed. She slid out of her jacket as she sighed and unraveled Nik's scarf from around her neck. She slung them over the back of the chair and dragged it closer to the fire by the backrest. She angled the pair of chairs so that she could rest her legs on one while she slept on the other. Refusing to meet his eyes, she wrapped the thick blanket around her body and sat down.

"You're serious about sleeping in the chair?"

"Uh, *yeah.*"

Nik shook his head and, in one quick motion, tucked his arms under Wren's legs and behind her back. He lifted her from the chair effortlessly and dumped her out onto the bed that was only two short steps away.

"I'll take the chairs and the pillow." He grabbed the pillow from the headboard and made for the chairs. "You can have the bed and the blanket."

Wren blinked, dazed slightly. "Hey!" She fumbled to get free from the blanket and sat up to glare at him. "Why would you do that? I was perfectly fine to sleep in the chair."

Nik gave a small snort as he kicked his legs onto the other chair. "Because I'm a nice guy."

Wren rolled her eyes and turned over to pull the blanket under her chin. "Whatever you need to tell yourself. Good night."

Nik smiled at her back, trying to ignore the smallest pang in his chest.

"Good night," he hummed as he settled in beside the growing fire.

WREN'S EYES SHOT OPEN. IT TOOK A FEW MOMENTS FOR HER TO focus on the light from the tiny fire. She drew a deep breath in as she sat upright and glanced over toward the hearth.

Nik slept, covered by his coat and his crimson scarf wound around his neck. The rhythm of his breathing was audible in the silence. It occasionally quivered, likely in response to the chill in the room.

The fire was dying out.

Wren flipped her legs over the edge of the bed. Her hands clutched the corner of the mattress and supported her slumped figure with locked elbows. The curtain of her hair moved like a stream every time her head shifted even slightly.

What the hell was that dream . . . Her right hand gripped her forehead. She pressed her palm into her eyes and shifted her weight to her left arm. A silent sigh escaped her.

A soft *pop* from the fireplace echoed in the sparce room, sounding larger than it had been.

Wren stood and made her way toward it. She eyed the pile of firewood and plucked a log from the top. She added it to the fading flame slowly to allow the lick of fire to engulf a small selection first to prevent it from being snuffed out.

The hollow *thunk* of the tossed log reverberated in a whisper throughout the room. Flies of ember sprang from the already smoldered wood inside of the hearth.

She sighed again before deciding to sit on the floor in front of the fireplace. Wren wrapped her arms around her knees and stared into the twisting flames. Hazel eyes reflected the fire like a mirror as they stared into something far away.

Figures shimmered in fleeting glimpses within the depths of the orange, yellow, red, and white.

Wren stared, fixated on what must have been a trick of the eyes.

A silhouette formed and faded in the frantic flames, clearly human and running. Smaller figures began circling around it in a chaotic manner before they leapt onto the humanoid shape and engulfed it. The shapes remained for only a few moments longer before being swept up with smoke in the form of a terrible and winged creature.

Wren blinked and leaned forward slightly, adjusting one of her legs to support herself.

"Elliot?" she whispered to herself softly, horrified and motionless as she stared into the fire.

"Can't sleep?"

The warmth of another body appeared beside her, and she averted her eyes. "It was cold." Wren rested her chin on the top of her knee. "Sorry if I woke you."

"I don't mind."

A comfortable silence drifted between them, broken only by the fresh wood crackling in the fireplace.

"You were muttering in your sleep." Nik chuckled as he leaned his weight on his hands at his sides.

"Muttering? About what?"

He shrugged. "Nothing you said made much sense."

"Oh." She clicked her tongue on the back of her teeth.

He remained quiet and kept his eyeline trained on the flames.

Something in her voice made it seem like there was more she wanted to say.

He glanced at her from the corner of his eye, so as to not move his head, and was taken aback by the sadness in her expression. Nik decided to say nothing of it. For now.

"I have these dreams sometimes," Wren started quietly. "They feel so real, but I can hardly remember them once I wake up. But . . . I feel like they are trying to tell me something important." She tucked her chin so that her forehead tapped her kneecap and snapped her eyes shut tightly. "It's maddening."

"Does Lionel know about your dreams? Has he analyzed them for you?"

"I don't know. I haven't told him, but there's no telling if he already knows somehow. He can be so cryptic about things he doesn't want to discuss. Always deciding what I do and do not need to know."

Nik tilted his head to the side. "Why not? He could probably help you understand it more than you want to admit."

"No." Wren finally lifted her head and met his eyes directly. "There are things I don't tell Lionel or Elliot, and for good reason."

She looked back to the fire with a scowl. "Everyone has things they won't say."

"What sort of things?"

Wren ran her tongue over her teeth behind tight lips and glared into the burning logs. There was a pause between them as she tried to collect her thoughts and restrain her temper.

"Things I don't want to talk about," she said flatly and shifted to stand.

"You're doing it again, you know."

"Doing what?"

He watched her intently, still seated on the floor by the fire. "Running away."

She inhaled sharply through her nose and whirled around to face him. The warmth of the refreshed fire had yet to thaw the chill on her skin. Tired and cold, she couldn't stop herself from giving in to her frustration.

"Of course I run away," Wren snarled without thinking. She closed the distance between them and pushed sharply at his shoulders. She loomed over him, eyes dark and brows low. "I put everyone around me in constant danger, not to mention that I'm a social pariah. *Of course* I run away! We've been over this!"

Nik's eyes widened at her when she moved. He was locked into a reclined position and had to balance on his elbows to keep himself somewhat upright. His legs were outstretched with Wren leering over him.

In her rage, she hadn't considered the position they might end up in from her rushing at him. When she realized that his legs were on either side of her and that her face was only inches from his, she withdrew so forcefully that she stumbled backward. Her back slapped the hardwood floor with a hard *thud*.

Idiot.

Wren laughed once as she draped the crook of her arm across her eyes.

Nik shook his head and sighed. He was on his feet in an instant and wrapped his arms around her in order to hoist her from the floor to the bed. He sat them both onto the mattress and held her tight, with her arms pinned to her sides, as she tried to squirm away.

"Let go of me!"

"Relax," he argued and squeezed her tighter. "I'm not going to do anything."

Wren growled but gradually allowed herself to.

"There," he hummed with an unseen smile. "It's not so awful, is it?"

She gave no reply. Instead, she ducked her chin against her chest and frowned.

"I won't hurt you, Wren. I'm not going to tell Lionel something you don't want him to know, either. If you want me to keep a secret, say the word."

"Yeah, you would. You've been friends for decades. Why wouldn't you tell him? Not only that, but he *is* a trace. Any slip of thought, and he'd find out anyway." Wren craned her head to meet Nik's eyes. "Let me go," she tried again.

Nik sighed heavily through his nose. "I can't. My arms are broken like this now."

"Stop trying to be funny, Nik. I mean it," she warned.

He shifted on the bed and moved her to sit beside him. "Fine. We can stay like this if you would quit running away. I just want to talk." He tipped his head back to rest against the headboard and folded his arms over his chest. His eyes slipped shut with a sigh.

"Why do you even care?"

The reticence in her voice made him peek at her through parted eyelashes.

She sat beside him on the bed with her legs pulled to her chest and stared at the fire blankly. Her unrestrained hair poured over her shoulders and nearly reached the top of the mattress. The ends were frayed somewhat, and small tangles were braided into the strands.

"About me," she murmured against her knees. "Why do you care about me? The entire time you've been here, it's like you follow me everywhere. Are you stalking me because of what I am?"

Nik didn't reply right away. He watched her silently tug at a loose thread at the hem of her sleeve before considering her question.

"I feel that we are more similar than we are different, and I think that you know it, too." His eyes reclaimed hers. "And no, I'm not *stalking* you." Nik paused and contemplated his words while his hand idly found hers. When she didn't pull away, he took the opportunity to lace their fingers together. "I think that *you* are fascinating, so I'd say I follow you around because I want to know more about *you*. Is that so wrong?"

Wren drew away from him with a skeptical look on her face. "I don't know if it's wrong . . . but it *is* creepy."

He smiled at her and tucked a loose strand of hair behind her ear.

In the next moment, a burst of wind exploded from the window. The force shattered the glass before the panes even had the chance to hit the wall. It sliced through the air overhead like a blade and consumed the modest fire in one gulp.

A rattling hiss followed closely behind.

A shadow with yellow eyes slinked into the room. Its long and spindly limbs crawled into the small sliver of moonlight that remained.

Eight hair-covered legs stepped over one of the chairs by the fireplace. Its scaled, serpentlike tail smashed into the chair closest to it with one powerful swing, sending shards of hardwood outward and propelled itself into the ceiling corner by the shattered window. Eight eyes encapsulated its arrow-shaped head in a ring, pointed in every direction and all-seeing.

"It's an omen," Nik whispered. The reaper positioned Wren securely behind him without taking his eyes off of it.

The creature was about as tall as the arions but considerably longer. Its arachnoid limbs splayed into a crouch, nestled into the corner that it claimed. The thick tail rattled in the air between it and them. A massive gland with a long, hooked stinger lay folded against the protective scales. It had a pair of venom pouches between its two front legs. The shortest pair of legs hungrily folded over each other, and the inky fangs clacked and scraped against each other. Each yellow eye had a vertical pupil, and all eight seemed vacant and primal. Its scaled, viperlike head twitched this way and that as it mapped the room from every angle.

Wren tried to even her breathing, but her heart raced defiantly.

"N-Nik?" Her voice trembled as she placed her palm against his back.

Rapid clicks suddenly began to emanate from the creature. Its hind legs shuffled across the walls and ceiling as it tagged ends of impossibly sticky silk against them. The clicks intensified as its web grew larger, more intricate, and opaque.

Nik could feel her shaking against his back. The hairs against his shoulders and neck stood on end as the clicking grew increasingly louder and rapid.

"Hide, Wren. Don't run." Nik waited a moment for her to move on her own, and when she didn't, he shoved her off the far side of the bed from the omen.

Her shoulder hit the floor roughly. She scrambled onto her hands and knees, jostled from her stupor, and tucked herself under the bed.

The omen danced eagerly upon the shimmering webs. It tilted its head to the side as it looked Nik up and down once before it opened its four-cornered mouth to release a shriek. The toothed jaws unfolded like a deadly snapping flower, each lined by rows upon rows of teeth. It threw one of its rear legs forward to cast a rope of silk at him.

Nik ducked to the side and rolled off the bed. He remained in a crouch and extended his hand behind him with his fingers splayed out wide. His hand and fingers began to turn pallid and colorless and, gradually, into nothing more than bone. The flesh and nails fluttered off like ash and dispersed into nothing.

Hair-thin tendrils of purple whisps began to form beneath his outstretched palm. They grew thicker and bolder as they twisted into a whirlpool of smoke that obscured his entire hand.

The omen lurched at Nik with the jaws between its legs bared and its rattle clattering.

His hand tightly clasped the familiar snath of a pitch-black scythe as it materialized in his hand in an instant. He raised it just in time for the creature to be within his strike range.

Nik predicted that the mandibles on its chest would be the first to move close enough, and he automatically heaved the giant blade in front of him. The toe of the scythe sliced clean through the omen's left venom sack and severed the dripping appendage from the monster.

It screeched sharply, rearing back before it slammed its horned tail into the floor four times in a circle around him. The wood shattered from the force of each impact, and tiny bubbles of neon-green venom dotted the places where the stinger had landed.

Nik rolled in the direction of Wren, tucking his scythe close to his torso, and pitched forward. He jumped to his feet and whirled the scythe in the air above him to force the creature back, determined to keep himself between them.

It withdrew with a nasty hiss, inky black blood spewing from the fresh wound. The tail aimed at Nik, stinger drawn, and shot at him like an arrow let loose.

Nik's left hand ghosted over the length of his scythe, toward the curve of its blade. A cloud of purple smoke gathered beneath his palm as it moved, growing larger as he neared the point of the blade. He rolled away to avoid the tail as it slammed to the ground where he had just been. Nik remained near enough to the omen's tail to thrust the orb of purple smoke against the shining exoskeleton with as much force as he could gather within a split second.

The orb dissipated into strands fine enough to force their way around and between its armored body in the same manor that water would flow around each stone as a new stream is born.

The omen cried out furiously as it withdrew in such haste that it tripped over two of its eight legs and tumbled to the floor. It writhed and shrieked as it righted itself and shook its head to regain its bearings.

Nik growled, and his hand tightened on the long snath of his scythe.

The serpentine eyes of the omen landed on Wren, still hidden under the bed. It moved as though new life erupted from within as it spun fresh tendrils of silk and hurled them at Nik, its eyes never wavering from the petrified spell.

He dodged them easily and followed its eyeline with a clenched jaw. He slammed the blunt end of his scythe into the floor repeatedly in an attempt to get the creature's attention back on him.

It ignored him completely and barreled toward Wren.

Nik dashed after it while he collected another orb of purple smoke in his palm. Silently and impossibly fast, he lunged between the gaping four-pointed mouth and Wren.

She scrambled away from the bed a heartbeat before it was crushed beneath the weight of the omen's body.

Nik reached her as the creature lifted itself from the ruined bunk. Without breaking stride, he grabbed Wren's shoulder and tossed her behind him to obstruct any clear shot at her. He leapt and drove the second orb into the omen, this time in the back of the omen's throat. He then twisted his torso so that he could ram the blunt end of his scythe into the orb in order to force it deeper into its mouth.

When the base of his scythe made contact, the orb swelled to twice its size and shattered, sending needle-sharp fragments in every direction. The bottom of the omen's mouth began to sizzle and crack before its flesh started to melt away.

Any of the shattered remains of the orb that touched Nik simply dissipated without effect. His large frame shielded Wren, who had curled into a tight ball behind him.

The omen reeled back and howled in pain. It brought up one of its legs and kicked Nik in his abdomen. As he staggered backward, it quickly spun to slam its broad tail into him. There was enough force behind it to send him across the room and into the wall beside the closed door.

The omen's entire body began to audibly simmer and steam. The scales silvered and slowly turned transparent like leaves in autumn. They then began to flutter, as though paper thin, and large sections of its armor began to disintegrate into dust.

Wren's eyes were wide as she tried to inch away from the beast, her heart racing so fast that she thought it may stop beating at any moment.

The omen continued to cry out as it thrashed on the floor. Its limbs whipped around in every direction while its rapid clicking reverberated in the empty air.

Purple smoke hissed as it traveled along every inch of the omen's body, flooding every pocket and streaming between each plate of its armor. It raged like a brush fire until it engulfed the omen entirely. Still fixated on Wren, the creature started to crawl toward her, fumbling and slow.

The clicks were rapid and loud, loud enough to shoot jolts of paralyzing fear down her spine.

Her wide eyes were locked on the encroaching omen. Her tremoring ankles and knees kept her from standing as her teeth chattered painfully. Despite how desperately she urged herself to run, she was too stunned to move.

Nik pushed himself up, ignoring the throbbing in his side, and forced himself to his feet. He looked between Wren and the omen and dashed forward.

When the omen was only a few paces from Wren, it drew back for one last reach at her.

In the same moment, Nik's scythe sliced clean through the omen's withering tail.

The appendage fell soundlessly and turned to dust upon impact with the floor.

He forced himself between Wren and the omen once more, curling his arm around her shoulders as he hoisted her to stand. Once she was upright, his hand tightened on the ball of her shoulder, and he pulled her against his chest protectively.

When his warmth registered, Wren felt herself grip his tunic as she hid her face against his chest, her eyes shut tight.

Nik watched it keel back with no expression and crumple, before it, too, reduced to dust.

The broken panes of the still-open window tapped against the wall in the cold breeze.

Wren glanced to the pile of ash and watched silently as it dispersed across the hardwood floor. Her eyes were stuck on whisps that curled at the crest of the pile in the gently invading nighttime wind.

Although the creature was dead, its rattles and clicks still echoed between her ears like angry bees inside their hive. Her knee quivered unconsciously and, before she had time to process that it had, gave. Wren fumbled against Nik's chest and slipped out of his hold. She caught herself on the floor with an outstretched palm, and the impact sent a jolt of pain from her wrist to her shoulder.

"Wren!" Nik released the scythe from his grip as he dropped beside her. It disappeared in a subtle puff of purple dust as soon as he let go. As the dust dissipated into the atmosphere, his hand returned to its usual, skin-covered state. He grumbled to himself as he eased her into a sitting position. "Wren? Look at me." The side of his index finger lifted her chin so that he could see her eyes.

She pushed his hand away and groaned.

Nik frowned and recaptured her chin, this time with his thumb and forefinger.

"Are you hurt?" He could hardly hear her quiet attempt to find words. "Wren, talk to me. It's all right. You're safe now." He sighed when she still didn't answer and lifted her from the floor.

Wren's hands returned to his tunic, gathering fistfuls of it as they tightened.

Nik brought her to the overturned but intact chair and righted it with his foot. He placed Wren into the seat and gripped both arm rests, ensuring she couldn't run away.

"Please." He spoke softly and brushed a lock of hair away from her downcast eyes.

The action made her flinch, and she turned away from him reflexively. Wren's chest shuddered slightly as she took multiple heavy breaths. Saliva pooled in her mouth, and she struggled to swallow it.

"M-my dr-dre . . ." she stuttered before she clicked her jaw shut. Wren closed her eyes and tried to ignore how violently she must have been shaking. Her fists clenched and unclenched on her lap.

Nik waited with his palm cupped against her left cheek. His thumb ghosted over the healing gash across her cheekbone, and he felt himself frown.

"I think . . . I saw t-the o-om-men in a dr-ream," Wren managed. "I could-dn't rememb-ber when I w-woke . . ." She shook her head and grabbed at her hair around her ears.

Nik leaned back but refused to surrender his grip on the arm of the chair. Her helpless expression made something in his chest ache.

"I couldn't remember much of it when I woke up." Her voice still trembled, and she spoke slowly to keep from stuttering. "This always happens if I have a dream I can't remember. And when whatever I *did* dream happens, the dream floods back in and sweeps me away. I can't—" She stopped herself short and set her jaw.

"What do you mean by *always*?"

Wren finally met his gaze.

He watched a mixture of anger, frustration, confusion, and fear stir behind her eyes. Nik felt like he could see straight through her yet found no answers.

Wren pressed her back into the chair when their proximity registered and drew her legs to her chest. Her palms then pushed against him to force more space between them.

"Give me room to breathe." She looked to the singed logs in the fireplace in order to evade his eyes. "You're too close." Her shaken voice warned half-heartedly.

"I'm fine where I am, thank you." His lips were quirked with a smug grin. "Now answer my question. What do you mean by always?"

"I don't have to tell you anything! Gods," she growled and narrowed her eyes at him. "I don't care to share intimate details of my thoughts and dreams to anyone, least of all someone I barely know." Wren ground her teeth and lowered her voice. "Nik, you *need* to understand that trust is . . . It's impossible for me."

"Bullshit." Nik shook his head. "I see you with Elliot and Lionel. You trust *them*."

"That's not what I mean," she muttered before she could stop herself. Wren nibbled on her lip and, finally, sighed. "It's impossible to trust myself to be close to someone. I trust Elliot and Lionel, yes. But I will never completely trust *myself* around them."

"Why? That doesn't make any sense, Wren."

"I'm a monster, Nik. A *real* monster. Elliot has no idea just how horrible I can be, and I don't think that Lionel will ever forget what I did to him."

"What did you do?"

Wren dropped her face into her hands.

"Wren." He spoke her name softly. "I have seen malevolence. I told you about my mother. I've seen plenty of it since I became a reaper, too." He released the arms of the chair and placed his hands on either side of her face to hold her still. "I have seen monsters. And I see you." Nik paused and brushed his thumb across her damp cheek. "Lionel is a trace, yes . . . But *I* am a penitent reaper. It is my duty to deliver judgment unto *monsters* who inflict harm on others, human and creature alike. Just because you are misunderstood doesn't mean that you're a monster, too."

Wren pressed her eyes closed and tried to tug his hands away from her.

"Stop, Wren." He collected her wrists easily, and he glared at her. "Help me to understand so that I can help you. Lionel loves you, that is obvious to anyone. He asked me here to help you. He wouldn't have done that if he didn't care for you deeply."

She froze and stared at him. Fury and disbelief welled behind her eyes, but he continued before she could interject.

"He is my dearest friend, and I know him well. You are dear to him. From what I have seen, he recognizes that you struggle every day. I can confidently say that I know he does not want you to live this way." Nik pursed his lips and looked away.

Wren glared darkly and pushed against his chest with tightly clenched fists. "Get off!"

"Grow up." Nik harshly gripped her shoulders and met her glare with his own. "*You* are what is holding you back from figuring out just how much you are capable of doing!" He sighed through his nostrils and relaxed his knuckles slightly. Nik clenched and relaxed his jaw twice. "You are a chained dog in Black Rivers, Wren. Do you even know what you can do as a spell?"

Wren parted her lips to reply but was interrupted.

"What did you do that Lionel won't forget?"

Her jaw clapped shut, and she drew a deep breath into her chest. "When Seth's legion made their attempt on the kingdom . . . Lionel begged me to stay. He didn't want me to reveal myself because he *knew* what would happen. He knew it was a trap."

Nik watched her sad yet beautiful face churn through painful expressions as she spoke.

"I didn't listen. I couldn't stand to watch people's homes burn down. Innocent people suffered because I didn't follow my instincts sooner. Even Elliot was nearly . . . killed that night . . . I should have faced Seth. Before he gained power. I . . . I didn't want to admit it, but I was too afraid." She sighed and shook her head with closed eyes. "I said horrible things to him. I tried everything in the book to make him let me go and face Seth. When words didn't work, I . . ." Her words caught in her throat.

Nik watched her, his stare unwavering.

"I . . . I betrayed him." Wren's voice quivered. "I attacked him and ran away."

CHAPTER TWELVE

*"If you cannot do great things,
do small things in a great way."*

Napoleon Hill

SHARP RAYS OF MORNING LIGHT SHONE THROUGH THE
single window in Wren's bedroom.

Elliot's eyes were dim and clouded by two dark circles perched on the tops of her cheeks.

Relentless thoughts had deprived her of sleep all night. Every time she started to drift off, the image of the circling four-winged beast startled her into waking again, and again, and again.

An unsettling feeling lingered in the back of her mind like the foul aftertaste of bitter coffee.

The silhouette of Wren's other form echoed from Lionel's transfer and directly into her dreams. The creature that took on Seth's legion and *won* . . .

Of Wren, fighting with everything she had for an ungrateful society.

Elliot turned over and sighed. Even awake, she felt strange.

Even after sleepless hours of meditation on the matter, she had yet to decide just how she felt. The ache in her head and chest deliberated between incapacitating fear toward Wren's monstrous form, and absolute fury on Wren's behalf for the treatment she received after all she'd done.

They still aren't back . . . she thought as she pursed her lips and swung her legs over the edge of the bed with a sigh.

Jack stirred slightly from the disruption, but he remained curled in place and mostly asleep.

Her mess of curls hung in tangled ringlets around her exhausted face. If she listened closely, she could hear Lionel's steps in the common room.

If I didn't know better, I'd say he's pacing . . .

The pure white cat peeked a single slate eye at her.

"What? I bet you're worried too. You won't admit it either, just like Lionel. Stubborn men." Elliot stood and made her way out of Wren's bedroom.

"Ah, good morning, my dear." The warmth in Lionel's voice made something suddenly churn inside her stomach.

She exhaled and slumped against the doorframe. Her hand pressed into her head in an attempt to steady its spinning.

"Elliot?" Lionel set his tea on the counter and hurried to her side. He placed the back of his gloved hand against her forehead and frowned.

"You feel very warm, Elliot. Did you sleep?"

"No." She rubbed her bicep absentmindedly. "Not at all, actually."

"What's wrong?"

Her eyes turned to Lionel's, whose were also devoid of their usual lightness.

"Nothing new," she muttered. "I'm worried that Wren isn't back yet."

He watched her skeptically.

She couldn't help fidgeting slightly as her palms started to get clammy.

"That's not all, though," he pressed.

"I can't get the image of that thin—of Wren out of my head." Elliot took a small step back from Lionel and wrapped her arms around herself. "I've always felt like a fool, not knowing so many things about her . . . And your history together goes back so far, and it holds such a unique place for both of you, I feel like even wanting to *know* about it is being intrusive . . . I've always tried to keep myself from prying." Her eyes shut tight, and she tucked her chin to her chest. "I had no idea that she . . . I . . ." Her voice was lost in a sob that she couldn't hold back. "I can see why she didn't want me to kno—"

Lionel cut her off when he suddenly embraced her.

"Shh," he soothed. He slid his white gloves from his hands, one at a time to keep hold of Elliot as he did so, and pocketed them. He placed his hand on the top of her curls and tucked her forehead against his chest. His other hand pressed into her back as it radiated with an intense warmth.

Elliot blushed when he suddenly embraced her, and tried to seem unaffected, yet her fluttering heart betrayed her.

"Wren would never hurt you, Elliot." He closed his eyes and focused on honing his enchantment. "She was only trying to hide that side of herself because she doesn't want you to see her like that. She doesn't want you to be afraid of her."

A soft white light hummed beneath his hand. It glowed through tangled strands against her head with a warm aura. A calming babble of cool energy rushed through her as though it followed the trails of her blood vessels and directly toward his other palm on her back.

Elliot felt her shoulders relax slowly. Very slowly.

"That wasn't Wren. The way it moved, how it looked *through* everything . . . It was like watching a predator hunt." She clenched her teeth and held back a sigh. "What happened? I have to know now."

Lionel frowned, though she could not see it.

It took him a long time to move. The warmth between his palms gradually worked out a few of the knotted muscles in Elliot's shoulders as he deliberated on how to respond.

She didn't want to notice how close they were, yet her face flushed a bright pink.

When Lionel finally moved, he held her gently by the shoulders and leveled her to face him directly.

"I need to make sure that you know what you are asking of me. If you know everything that led up to what I showed you last night . . ." His frown darkened. "Are you sure that you are well enough for this now? Last night was a lot to take in, not to mention that you didn't sleep. It can wait—"

Elliot cut him off this time.

"I want to know *now*. I'm fine." Elliot almost laughed at how much she sounded like Wren.

"Let's at least sit down, my dear." Lionel led her to his mustard-yellow chair and seated himself across from her.

Elliot glanced over her shoulder and out the glass door to the balcony. Her imagination carried her farther than she would have liked when the silhouette of the creature appeared then vanished within the same second.

Lionel grimaced and shook his head. "For the record," he murmured, "I am against this."

"Really, Lionel. I need to know. I can't stand to be in the dark anymore."

"Oh, all right." He resigned with a groan. "Seth was in the Guard before the coup was even an idea. He claimed to be nothing more than a human, and for what it's worth, I still believe that to be the case." Lionel shifted in his seat on the couch and followed her line of sight out the balcony door.

It was snowing again.

"The Tanner family was notorious for being troublesome. There were so many of them, all unsupervised and mischievous. I believe there were nine siblings total. The Guard isn't very selective about who they recruit. They hire pretty much anyone that can swing a sword or cast an arrow and hit their target." Lionel chuckled softly. "You'd only really be turned away if you were under fifteen. Or a woman."

"Yeah, I know that already." Elliot couldn't restrain her impatience. Lionel's surprised expression made her blush. "Sorry, I didn't mean to snap," she said in a soft voice.

He offered a gentle smile in response. "It's all right, my dear. I can see that you aren't yourself right now."

She nibbled her lip and looked away from his knowing, cerulean eyes.

"Seth had it out for Wren as soon as she came to live here. He and his goons followed her if she went into town without me. They tried to take her quite a few times, but she always managed to fend them off or slip away. Seth hated that Wren, *the outsider*, wasn't intimidated by him. He wanted to make an example of her." He crossed his legs and tightened his lips. "The king did nothing about Seth Tanner. At the time, Seth was one of his closest knights, so in his eyes, Seth could do no wrong."

"What?"

Lionel closed his eyes and nodded. "The night before he struck, Seth came to see us. He told us that this was the last chance for Wren to escape his wrath and join his army. When she refused, he swore that we would not live to see his new world."

Lionel and Elliot both looked to the kitchen when a clatter filled the brief silence.

Jack had jumped onto the counter beside Lionel's abandoned tea. He watched them for a moment before dropping his hind to the countertop and blinked. His pure-white tail flicked at the tip, and he let out a quiet meow.

"When I brought her here, she remained inside for a few years while I tried to help her learn how to interact with others. Ian, the butcher, and Kora both visited during that time to help her socialize. She struggled and never had much patience with herself. Training her in the gym was most helpful in draining her of frustration. Learning to control herself physically helped her in learning to control her abilities. And believe it or not, her temper."

Elliot's lips cracked into a half-hearted smile.

I believe it, she thought without hesitation.

"After Seth failed to pin the fire on Wren, he began to insist to the king that she was not a tempest." Lionel hesitated and rubbed the back of his hand with his thumb. "I have a hunch that Seth suspected that she was a spell long before he made an attempt at the crown. *How*, I do not know. I can only hypothesize." He paused and shrugged. "I believe that he had connections in the darkest places with powerful people that provided both resources and intelligence to him. He was probably tipped off."

"So, why did Seth try to overthrow the king if they were so close?"

"The temptation of power will do terrible things to a weak-minded man." Lionel nodded as he replied softly.

". . . I suppose." Elliot watched Jack as she listened.

"Seth sold out King Reed by promising those that followed him absolute control. He betrayed the king so that he would have an opportunity to take the throne. Rumors, whispers, and memories have told me that he sought out an alchemist, others that he sold his soul in order to have the flame demon at his command. Some told that he made a deal with a pirate king to help in his invasion."

"What do you think is true?"

Lionel stared at his hands as he worked to find the right words. "I wouldn't be surprised if all were true simultaneously. He was incredibly intelligent yet allowed himself to be driven truly mad by the prospect of power. The Church of Alchemy is just across Greater Bay."

"Oh . . . Right. I hadn't considered that."

Lionel nodded. "A journey there and back would only take a few weeks by foot. Maybe one on horseback. By sea, four days maybe. It's a feasible theory that Seth made friends in the church. Alchemy is said to be able to sidestep the natural bound law of the Balance. By using glyphs or spells for things like transmutation, invisibility, mind bending, and other nefarious doings. The power that an alchemist has could plausibly summon a demon of theoretically any kind. With the right sacrifice.

"When Seth made his move on Arnica, I forbade her from leaving this house. It was a trick that he was trying to pull so that he could draw her out. Unfortunately, it worked.

"Chaos arrived on this street before the fire did. I couldn't possibly stay inside; their screams killed me. I desperately wanted to help them." He stood abruptly and rubbed his temples. He sighed as he slipped his gloves back onto his hands. "We had an awful fight."

"A fight? *You?*"

"Yes," he murmured as he made for the kitchen. He paused to give Jack a soft pat on the head. "You know how she is," he started without taking his eyes off of the mug on the counter. "She regularly speaks without thinking and without any attempt to mince her words. If she sets her mind to something, there really isn't any talking her out of it.

"I warned her that it was a trap, that Seth was trying to burn her out of hiding. She and I both knew this. When I tried to calm her through touch, she . . ."

She could feel a pang of guilt thud in her chest.

Should I have left this alone?

Lionel fell silent for a long while before he lifted his gaze to Elliot. "Are you sure that you want to know all of this?"

She straightened her back and folded her hands on her lap. *Too late to chicken out now.*

"What happened?" she murmured against her better judgment.

The silence that followed her question was painful. It lasted for what felt like hours.

"She wasn't able to keep herself from shifting. Her anger was so intense that she . . . She just couldn't maintain control. The chaos just outside our front door didn't help, either. My touch catalyzed something else within her that took over.

"It was not a full shift at first. I could tell that she was trying to fight that form . . . That, I imagine, came after she got out and before she made it to the castle wall. I consider myself lucky that it had only been a partial shift when I was around her." His shoulders shuddered. "That form is almost more unsettling than when she's fully turned."

Elliot's eyes widened in disbelief. She found herself unable to find words.

"The fight didn't last very long. I am physically strong, but she was something far stronger. She was dreadfully fast, and before I knew it, I . . ."

"Before you *what*?" A mixture of exasperation and anger forced the exclamation from her. "You're stalling because you don't want to tell me!"

Lionel's eyes gave her a pained look. "My dear"—his voice seemed small—"I don't want to tell you these things because Wren doesn't want you to hate her. After this, you may feel differently about your proximity to her. Especially with how careful she must be with her temper." He hesitated again. "She told me that directly. Wren has so few friends, she couldn't bear to alienate you with the whole truth."

"Tell me." Elliot spoke through clenched teeth. Lionel's stalling only made not knowing all the more infuriating.

He left the kitchen and walked to her with purpose. In his approach, he removed the glove from his right hand. His lips were tight and brow furrowed, yet the contact he made with Elliot's forehead was gentle and comforting.

"I will show you."

"Stop!" Lionel scolded with a groan. "If you leave, you will be killed! Do you understand? Killed, Wren!" His bare hands clutched her shoulders tightly. He couldn't stop himself from shaking her when she refused to meet his eyes. "You will be more helpful if you stay here and don't cause any trouble. The woman you brought back needs our help. Please, just listen to me for once!"

"I'm sorry, I can't do that, Lionel. I can't just sit here and watch them suffer and die because of me! If you honestly think that's a reasonable thing to ask of me, then you don't know anything about me at all!" Wren shoved at his chest sharply.

He reluctantly relinquished his grip on her. "You're being childish, Wren! You have a responsibility to self-preservation, and under no circumstances is anyone to know what you are."

"What I am?" Wren's temper boiled at the base of her throat. "What am I?" Her voice amplified as it took on a primal growl. She took a step back from Lionel and clenched her aching hands at her sides. "I am a monster, Lionel! I've read the stories. I know all about Eurynome. I know the rumors. I know, I know, I know! That doesn't matter. They won't beat

me. Seth can't beat me! I am the greater monster, and they must be stopped!"

"That's not tr—"

"Of course it's true! Why else would you keep me locked away? Why am I a secret? It's because I am dangerous. If I weren't, I would be able to control myself, control my rage. Angels don't have the thoughts that I do, Lionel. Monsters do. Trying to convince me otherwise is pointless."

Wren encroached on him with her hands clenched at her sides.

It took every ounce of effort that he had to refrain from taking a step back.

"It's why I was left in the woods to die. I am a monster that no one wants in the slightest! Isn't defending innocent people with a life no one wants in the first place a good thing? It's a win-fucking-win!"

That's when he noticed her eyes.

Her beautiful hazel irises were gone. The whites were slowly turning gray, and the pupils sharpened into cat-like points. Her irises had become silver spotlights that saw straight through prey.

Her back was hunched and shoulders were jutted forward. Hard and bone-like structures forced their way through the skin on her back, just below her shoulder blades.

"Wren," Lionel tried softly. He reached for her with a bare hand and brushed his fingers against her arm.

His attempt to quell her fury only incited it further.

Her hands warped into long black talons, and her pale skin grew dark and leathery. The knobs on her back were pure black and smeared with hot, red blood. Her head reeled back, and she howled in pain when they continued pushing through her back.

"Get away!"

Wren's shriek was swallowed by another cry of pain. Her voice lasted for only a moment before it was overcome by the hoarse cry of a rabid animal.

There wasn't enough time for him to process her warning in order to react in time.

Her eyes became pits of black and silver. They pierced through him with a glint that only those out for blood were capable of. Her dark claws clenched and unclenched while a deep growl reverberated between her ribs.

The spell charged at him at an alarming pace and smashed into him before he was able to evade. They slammed into the hard ground, Wren perched on top of him.

Sharp talons gripped Lionel's throat and squeezed. The pressure they exuded against his bare skin seared through his muscles and bones like acid. This pressure surrounded her entire form and overloaded his senses.

Lionel was blind and internally on fire, like his head was inside of a ringing bell set ablaze.

He gasped and pulled at her wrists, growing increasingly desperate to pry her off of his airway. His limbs flailed frantically when the grip didn't lessen.

"Wren," he barely choked out.

The breathless sound of her name snapped her out of whatever trance she had been locked in.

She gaped at Lionel's position on the ground and the streams of blood from nasty gash marks across his neck. Wren took a bumbling step backward, her eyes wide and frightened, infuriated and confused.

Lionel tried to sit up, but he coughed roughly enough for his shoulder to give, and he stumbled back to the floor.

Without a word, Wren smashed out of the glass window and vanished into the burning night.

Elliot's eyes were clamped shut tightly.

"Elliot?" Lionel's voice was warm and welcoming. Like honey that soothed the wounds left from the vision.

She didn't respond right away, eyes still shut and mind still reeling.

"I shouldn't have shown you . . ." Lionel sounded small. "I'm so sorry, Elliot. Please, forgive me."

Elliot eventually opened her chocolate-brown eyes and looked at him. She opened her mouth to speak, but only breath escaped.

Lionel wrapped his arms around her and hugged her shoulders with his palms. The bare skin of his hands pressed into her cloth shirt until her head was close enough to cradle with one hand.

"How are you feeling, my dear? Are you all right?"

She shrugged before she took a deep breath with a frown etched on her face. "I felt it. I felt the strength of her grip on your neck, the terror that you felt." She nibbled on her lip and shook her head. "I think you're right."

Lionel quirked an eyebrow and leaned away to see her face better. "Oh?"

Elliot hesitantly met his eyes with a determined expression. "I think it's best if she doesn't know that you showed me anything."

He allowed a sad smile to lighten his features. "Consider it our little secret."

She nodded once and drew in a deep breath through her nose. Her arms unconsciously folded across her chest, and she gave him a conflicted look.

"So," she started in a small voice, "that's why she disassociates when situations like Honorah crop up?" Elliot hummed quietly, and her arms dropped to her sides. "It makes sense that is her method of control."

"Complete control, she calls it." He nodded. "It's not my favorite technique, but it has proved helpful to her. I never enjoy pulling her out of . . . wherever it is that she goes in order to keep control of herself."

"I hate that she's burdened by this. I hate that no one else sees her value or that she is kindhearted. I *hate* that she has to meditate into another world in order to keep from changing into that . . ." Elliot couldn't find the right word and left the statement hanging.

"Yes." He looped his arm around her shoulders and gave her an affectionate squeeze. "Remember that there *are* a few people that see her value. Many of the shopkeepers that have done business with her like her enough to not make a fuss."

"Like Ian and Kora?"

He nodded and kissed the top of her head. "Precisely. They treat her kindly and do not listen to rumors about her that others like to start. We can't expect them to risk their businesses or livelihoods to make a stance against the remaining Tanners or the Guard. Even Nikolas sees her value. I just . . . I need her to be able to get along with him."

Elliot pursed her lips and tilted her chin upward to meet Lionel's eyes. "Nik seems to like her. He watches her like an eagle," she added. When he nodded, her eyes narrowed. "He'd better not hurt her. I don't think I'd beat him in a fight, but I'd get a few good hits in at the very least. I know that he's your friend, but Wren is mine, and I won't let him get away if he breaks her heart."

Lionel laughed aloud and gave her a wide smile. "I'm hoping that they can at least become friends. If they were to become more than that . . . then . . ." He chuckled and nodded. "Indeed. If he hurts her, I'll hold him still for you to get in as many hits as you like."

"Deal." Elliot's face, for the first time that morning, glowed with a genuine smile.

"Just know, my dear, that sort of thing is not in his nature. While Nikolas is rather intimidating, and he doesn't say much . . . his heart is just as big, and his kindness is just as quiet. You can rest assured that he would never intentionally hurt her."

"If you say so." She shrugged, sounding unconvinced. "You know him better than I do. I just hope that he's still that same childhood friend that you trust."

CHAPTER THIRTEEN

*"Every heart sings a song, incomplete, until another
heart whispers back. Those who sing always find a
song. At the touch of a lover, everyone becomes a poet."*

Plato

AT LEAST THE SNOW'S LET UP."

Nik's observation went unacknowledged by Wren while she packed up their things.

She adjusted the waist of her new armor under her tunic before she stuffed Nik's books into the large rucksack that her armor had been in. She lifted the strap to her shoulder and stood, her eyes on him yet refusing to meet his.

"It wouldn't matter, anyway," she finally said. "I'm sure that Elliot is already losing her mind because we didn't make it back yesterday. We're leaving today, regardless of the weather."

The name left a strange taste in Wren's mouth. A gnawing feeling that she couldn't ignore ate away at the base of her throat, and the small hairs on the back of her neck bristled unconsciously. The omen's rattle still echoed in the back of her mind, and she had to stifle a shiver.

"Is it even safe to go back?" she heard herself whisper aloud.

Nik slipped the strap of the bag off of her shoulder with an unreadable expression on his face. "What do you mean?"

Wren looked away and took a deep breath. "Until we find out where that omen came from, what's to say we won't run into another one? *Or* be tailed back to Black Rivers? How did it know that we were here?" She chewed at her lip as she stared at the shattered glass from the window. "More importantly, what did it want? Whatever the answers are could put both of them in danger."

"So"—he gathered her coat in his hands and held it open for her—"where would we go?"

We?

There was something in the casual way that Nik said the word that sent off a twinge in her chest.

Wren stared at him without blinking and swallowed hard. She finally shook her head and shrugged.

"I don't know," she admitted before turning away from him and sliding into the sleeves of her coat.

His arms closed around her from behind, fastening the jacket shut with large, nimble hands.

Her ears burned red, and she hurriedly pushed his hands away. "I can do it myself."

Nik held her fast, keeping her against his chest easily. He waited for her shoulders to relax before he placed his palm on the top of her head.

"I never said that you couldn't," he hummed in a mocking tone. "Just take a deep breath and really *think* about what you should do. What do *you* think is the right call?"

"You sound like Lionel," Wren growled.

"Sure, that's fine." He rolled his eyes. "But that isn't what you should be focusing on."

"I don't know anywhere but Black Rivers and the forests around it," she eventually murmured.

Nik's lips quirked into a smile, and he caressed her hair. "Then let's go back. We can figure it out when we are all back together." He tucked his chin and pressed his nose into her hair. "Plus, even if we are followed . . . If we are with them, we can protect them, right?"

ELLIOT AND LIONEL STRODE THROUGH THE STREETS OF THE market.

Voices called out to them from every direction, merchants eager for their attention and, hopefully, their business. The Seasons Festival decorations filled each shop front and cart in the form of wooden flowers painted in every pastel color there was.

The hustled pace of the market forced the pair to walk closely together.

Lionel's arm delicately curled around Elliot's shoulders to help her keep up with his wider steps. He glanced at one of the vendors as they passed by. He inadvertently made eye contact with the merchant behind a cart, a large mammalian creature, and smiled.

There was a thick gray coat of fur covering his body and short tail. Each silver strand glimmered in the gentle daylight when they shifted with the breeze. He had tall ears that lay flat against the back of his head, tucked down by an old, worn cap. He stared at Lionel with empty, catlike eyes.

He did not smile back.

Lionel sighed to himself and rubbed his forehead with a gloved hand. A headache began to thud behind his eyes, and his shoulders were starting to feel knitted and tight. His attempts to cast the fatigue away through touch was in vain; his gloves inhibited the contact enough to prevent any impactful improvement.

Taking his gloves off now would be a mistake.

The bitterly cold air pressed into the exposed pores of his face and bristled at the tips of his ears.

Lionel adjusted the bag of groceries over his shoulder in order to pull his scarf closer to his face. Both ends of it were neatly tucked into the neck of his dusty-gray coat that fit his slender frame handsomely.

Elliot wore a red cloak that reached her ankles and did well to fend off the majority of the early spring morning. Her hood was drawn up, and a white scarf was wound around her neck.

"Here we are." She turned to face a stone building nestled into a patch of trees near the edge of the marketplace.

Lionel held the door open for her as they entered the boutique.

A small bell chimed as the door opened and closed.

"I'll be right out, yes." A half-hearted call greeted the pair from the far end of the room.

Luxurious fabric was strewn thoughtfully around the room. The palette of expensive-looking material was predominantly composed of neutral shades of white with splashes of soft lavender, blushed rose, pale green, and cloudy blue. Stitched patterns formed intricate, flowing designs in golden and silver threads that were somehow cohesive and chaotic simultaneously.

"Welcome, welcome," the feminine voice called again as she approached. "Can I help you, yes?"

A tall woman with scarlet skin rounded the counter to greet them.

She held a small book in one three-fingered hand and a pencil in the other. Two small horns poked through the rough-looking skin over her eyes and temples. A second pair of horns ran along her high cheekbones. They were only a few inches long and curled smoothly backward, parallel to the angular curves of her skull and temples. She had a long neck that was absolutely covered with glittering jewelry.

Her humanoid torso was adorned with an ornate dress that fluttered to the ground in blankets of gold. A long scarlet tail followed beneath her skirt as she moved across the room.

"Hello, Kora," Elliot called as she approached her. "You redecorated your shop; it looks wonderful!"

"Ahh, Miss Joy, welcome back! As always, you have great timing, yes." Kora's narrow shoulders jerked back in excitement. She unintentionally hissed each word that ended with *s*. "I was going for a spring feel," she hummed sweetly. "I'm pleased you like it, yes!"

"Good morning, Kora. I'm sure you've been busy with the festival coming up." Lionel acknowledged her pleasantly.

"Oh yes, oh yes." Kora returned his smile. "Never too much work for an old nuwa, no. Won't complain one bit, I won't. Everyone is hurting for business these days, so I'll take all that I can get, yes." She set her book and pencil on a table and clapped her palms together. "I think that you will be more than pleased with your order, Miss Joy."

Elliot beamed at the shopkeeper and blushed. "Kora, please don't be so formal with me. You've known me for years."

The nuwa flapped her hand in Elliot's direction with a wide smile, exposing a bright wall of pointed teeth. "Your mum was my best customer. She said the same thing, but no can do, oh no. If it weren't for her selling my dresses in Clove, I would have never been able to afford this shop, yes." Her eyes softened, and she offered a sweet smile. "Your parents were both generous people, yes. I will be forever indebted to them." Kora clicked her forked tongue and shuffled toward the curtain behind her. "Stay right here, yes? I'm going to bring them out before we wrap them up so that you can see how they came out. I can make any small alterations, if necessary, yes?"

"Thank you, Kora."

The seamstress's long, scaley tail whipped around beneath her skirt, dragging softly against the floor in a serpentine ripple as she vanished behind a golden curtain.

"Them?" Lionel furrowed his brow. "You ordered more than one dress?"

Elliot looked at him with such seriousness that it caught him off guard.

He coughed against the back of his wrist and looked away from her briefly.

"I ordered them right after last festival's fiasco, before I went back to Clove. I thought that a new dress would give her the confidence to beat them at their own game. Kora is bar-none the best seamstress in the north. A dress made by her would upstage any snobby elite and shut them the hell up." Elliot nibbled her cheek as Lionel watched her speak. She held a finger over her lips and dropped her voice to a whisper, "It's a surprise, so don't ruin it, okay?"

He nodded and smiled his signature smile. "I promise."

"She never wears anything but dark pants and old tunics that are way too big for her. Besides, that plain blue dress she wore last time is the only one that she owns. Kora and I thought she could use something more"—Elliot tapped her chin, searching for the right word—"feminine."

Lionel grinned at her. He placed his palm on her shoulder and squeezed it gently. "I think that was a wonderfully thoughtful thing to do." His eyes brightened.

Elliot blushed and turned to the doorway Kora had disappeared into. A thought burst into her mind, and she couldn't stop the gasp that escaped. She chuckled through her nose and smirked.

"What?"

"I wonder what Nik will think when he sees her in it!"

Lionel laughed abruptly and shook his head. "What do you mean by that?" Though he already knew her answer, he couldn't resist asking.

"Uh-huh," she replied flippantly. "You know *exactly* what I mean. There is obviously chemistry between them. He follows her around like a shadow with those dumb smiles of his. Any idiot can see that she fancies him, too. Whether *she* realizes it or not." Elliot hummed once and nodded. "I bet that his jaw will hit the floor."

"Miss Joy." Kora bustled through the golden curtain with both arms full of dresses. "I would love to see how you look in yours if it's not too much trouble, yes." The nuwa hung both dresses on a tall bar with a hook secured to the table.

Elliot blushed and fumbled for her words. "Eh, I mean I—" she stuttered softly and paused. "Of course I will. It's only right for you to be the first to see it worn."

"Wonderful!" Kora plucked one of the dresses from the hook and handed it to Elliot. "I took the liberty of adding some touches to them; no extra charges, of course. Not for my best customer." Her toothy smile gleamed. "I hope you like them, yes." Kora handed the dress to Elliot and reached to draw back the curtain that led to the other room.

"Use my workshop to change, Miss Joy. Holler if you need help, yes?"

"Of course," Elliot said softly and stepped into the next room. She startled when the curtain fluttered shut behind her.

Her sudden onset nervousness stemmed from Lionel being there for the first time she tried it on.

Elliot's mind raced through thoughts of the dress fitting poorly or it being hideous on her. She had to remind herself that Kora had never made *anything* hideous.

With a sigh, she stripped hastily and held the dress directly in front of her to examine it.

It was a muted turquoise fabric, a combination of blue and green so flawless it was impossible to tell which was the dominant hue. A satin skirt was hidden under a veil of pluming blue-green tulle. It was identical in color yet so sheer it almost looked white against the bodice and skirt.

The tulle continued upward from her waist in a chaotic braid to form the bust of the dress. Each strap cupped her chest and was littered with embroidered flowers and leaves. They were all hand-stitched with such artistry that they looked real.

She slipped into the dress and turned to glance in the mirror.

The mess of flowers and leaves followed the straps of tulle to her shoulders and spilled over to pour down her sleeves. The sleeves cascaded down to her wrists and were also made of the almost-white tulle. Her olive arms were visible under the veil that billowed around a ribbon of satin that gave the sleeves their structure. The ribbon wrapped around her wrists and followed the bottom of her arms up to the shoulders. Embroidered flowers dotted the ribbons with the impression of natural randomness.

She could only stare at the reflection of the dress until Kora called from behind the curtain.

"Do you need help, Miss Joy?" The seamstress's excitement was palpable in her voice.

"Uh, sorry! No, I have it on," Elliot replied quietly. Apprehension stung her chest at the thought of Lionel just a curtain away. "I'll be right out," she called before Kora could answer. "I'm still taking it in. Kora, you outdid yourself." She drew a deep breath in through her nose and forced her bare feet to move.

Kora pulled the curtain back and, to Elliot's relief, was positioned between Lionel and her, blocking his view.

"Oh!" Kora hummed with a smile so wide that her eyes gleamed. "Oh, Miss Joy, tell me that you like it, yes!" She leaned closer to Elliot and whispered, "Do you want him to see you in it yet?"

Elliot blushed and looked down.

"He'll see it sooner or later," she said with a sigh as she tried to ignore her shaking hands.

"Atta girl." Kora clicked her forked tongue against the back of her teeth. She winked and moved to the side.

Elliot couldn't bring herself to look up.

Lionel had been rustling around as they talked, politely not listening to their conversation. Once Kora had shifted out of the way and the sound of movement ceased, the shop was silent.

Elliot mustered the courage to lift her gaze to him.

Lionel was in complete shock. His eyes were wide and full of emotion, and his mouth clapped shut. Even his breathing stilled for a few very uncomfortable seconds.

"Say something, yes," Kora encouraged, breaking the silence.

Lionel stammered softly and cleared his throat. He couldn't tear his gaze from her. When he finally met Elliot's eyes, he swallowed hard.

"I think that . . . I think that the dress is almost as beautiful as you are." Lionel addressed Kora. "Elliot is right. You outdid yourself, Kora. A true work of art."

An array of expressions behind his eyes churned as they stared unwaveringly into hers and had her questioning if he was referring to the dress or to her.

No way. Definitely the dress, she insisted internally.

Kora's grinning face peeked to Lionel from over Elliot's shoulder.

"Shall I just wrap up the other one, yes?"

THE WALK THROUGH THE FOREST HAD BEEN ARDUOUS IN THE PAST when Wren had made the journey alone. The arions wouldn't meet up with them until they reached the tunnel to the canyon bridge. That was still nearly half an hour's walk with the fresh snow. At least.

The depth of the snow made the trek feel that much longer.

Nik carried the rucksack over one shoulder and strode a few paces behind her. His vigilant green gaze watched as Wren's restless mannerisms gave away her unspoken agitation.

She walked slower than normal, and her eyes darted around their surroundings whenever they weren't cast downward. Her reactions to ambient sounds within the depths of the trees were abrupt and riddled with paranoia. Her shoulders sloped low, though she blamed it on the new armor when he had asked about it.

He didn't buy it.

"The walk isn't so bad," Nik tried. "The sun feels nice."

Wren nodded mutely after a short moment of detached hesitation without looking up.

He released an exasperated breath through his nose and reached for her arm. His grip tightened, and he gently pulled her to a stop.

"Wren," he said gruffly. "What is going on with you?"

She turned her head to hide her face. "I really don't want to talk about it."

"Come on. You can talk to me. I'm here to h—"

"Help, yeah. I know." She interrupted and glowered at the snow. "I get it."

He took hold of her shoulders and squeezed them until she met his eyeline.

"I don't know how you can help, Nik. Honestly . . . I don't," she finally admitted with a choked-back sob. "Gods, I don't even know how *I* can help." Her breath hitched, and she shook her head. Wren shoved his hands away and turned her back to him. "I don't know what to do . . . I feel . . . trapped." She spoke barely above a whisper. "Not exactly something you can help with."

Her small voice made his chest ache terribly.

Nik advanced and touched the small of her back. The strap of the rucksack slipped from his shoulder and into the snow with a *thump* as he bent at the waist to tuck his other arm behind her knees.

In one easy motion, he gathered her into his arms and held her securely against his chest. He wordlessly walked to the base of a sturdy tree that kept the boulders below its branches mostly free from snow. Without brushing away the thin blanket of white atop a large rock, Nik dropped down and leaned his back against the dense trunk. He said nothing as his arms gently tightened around her, offering her whatever comfort he could.

As the silence stretched on, Wren's resolve to hold back her tears of frustration gradually eroded. They pooled at the corners of her tightly shut eyes and seeped through the cracks between her skin. Before long, a constant stream flowed and was unable to be stopped.

Finally at her limit, she openly wept.

Nik tucked her hair behind her ear and caressed the healing scab along the crest of her cheekbone with the pad of his thumb. He forced himself to look away from her and busied himself with rubbing comforting circles on her back. Yet, despite his best efforts, his eyes found the abrasion again.

The wound on the helix of her ear from the altercation with Honorah still glared red against her fair skin, and the knuckles on her right hand still seemed to be inflamed. The sight of her lingering wounds made an unknown spark of rage kindle in his chest.

A hitch in her breathing drew his attention back to her face.

Nik reached for her chin and tilted it upward.

She squeezed her eyes shut tighter the moment she felt the side of his finger beneath her chin.

"Don't cry anymore," he whispered softly. "I know that you're frustrated and confused . . . I would be, too." He tried again to soothe her and ran his hand down the length of her hair. "Really. But you aren't trapped, and you are *not* alone."

Wren's glassy eyes finally opened and glanced up at him. "I can't figure it out," she murmured.

"Figure what out?"

"You." She sniffed once and rubbed her face with the heel of her palm. Wren pushed his hands away and used her sleeves to pat her cheeks dry. "Whether or not I can trust you. What your intentions are . . ."

"Oh?" His response was half-hearted. Nik's eyes were stuck on her lips as she spoke. He finally met her stare when she didn't reply. "What can I do to earn your trust?"

Wren scoffed and looked away. She had no answer.

Nik touched her cheek and turned her face back to his.

A bright shade of pink lit the skin beneath her freckles when his eyes gravitated back to her lips.

With his arm around her, he could feel her pulse quicken and her shoulders tighten. After a moment of deliberation, he tilted her head back slightly and leaned in.

She froze from the breath that escaped his full lips, hovering just above hers. The heat they exuded beckoned her, but her subconscious was screaming at her to run away.

The hand against her back pulled her closer, and his other drifted to the hollow of her neck. His thumb idly caressed the base of her throat as he tried to steady his own breathing.

Wren's lips trembled before they were overwhelmed by his. Her eyes fluttered shut, and her breath stilled in her chest. Without realizing it, the building tension in her shoulders had washed out of her in unison with the gasp that escaped from her lungs in an instant.

Nik's kiss was cautious at first. When his lips parted hers, it sent a sharp pang down her spine that made her shiver. She leaned away to find her breath, but his hand against her back refused to let her go.

She made a small sound that gave him pause, and he begrudgingly forced himself to separate their lips.

When they parted, her eyes blinked open, swirling with a storm of emotions and clouded over with a conflicted haze. She swallowed hard, unable to look away from him. Her lips parted and closed again and again, as though trying to form words, yet none came.

He smirked and pulled her against his chest. Before she could overthink it, he kissed her again. The small hairs on his neck and arms bristled when he felt her hands timidly creep across his shoulders.

Her fingers grasped at the fabric over his back and clutched it tightly.

He deepened their kiss and gripped her even tighter. A soft groan escaped him when her fingers laced into the ebony strands at the crown of his head. Nik didn't let her move away when she gasped a second time. He kept her lips against his, sharing their air.

"Nik," she whispered breathlessly.

The tenor of her voice shattered his resolve, and he turned her to face him fully.

He held her hips against his abdomen with her legs positioned on either side of him. His other hand secured her shoulders against him, large fingers easily covering most of her back.

Wren clenched his shoulders, and her breathing shuddered once. Her palms were barely touching the curves of his shoulders, yet her fingertips were all pressed tightly against him.

He said nothing as his lips drifted down her neck to the small spot of skin on her chest that her tunic failed to cover. Nik grazed her skin with his lips a few times before he let out a loud sigh. His nose brushed the hollow of her throat as he lifted his gaze to hers.

Wren watched him with wide eyes but remained still. She nibbled on her lower lip, and her eyebrows slowly began to knit together.

His right hand drifted to her side and clamped around her ribs. It only took a fraction of a second for his left hand to do the same.

Wren moved her hands to his chest and sighed through her nose.

"Nik," she tried again. "Let me go. We need to keep moving."

Nik lowered his lips to her collarbone, noting how the pressure behind her palms started to wane. He brushed aside the clothing that concealed the small patch of skin with his nose and teeth and placed feather-light kisses on every inch of the flushed surface that he could find.

The sensation electrified her nerves. She grabbed at his jaw to tilt his head back.

"I c-can't," Wren stammered before she clacked her teeth shut and, with an unsteady voice, tried again. "*We* can't do this now. I—" Her hand on the side of his face was hot.

His golden-green eyes were fixed on her, clouded and wild. Somehow, the shimmer of golden flecks in his eyes was amplified by the early morning light that made it through the scattered tree limbs overhead. His emerald irises became the backdrop to the captivating flickers of golden stars that made it nearly impossible to look away.

Wren couldn't concentrate.

"I don't . . ." she whispered yet involuntarily trailed her thumb across his lower lip as she searched for words. "The timing couldn't be worse, and we couldn't possibly . . ."

"I don't care about timing," he murmured, the motion causing his lips to brush her fingertip. He also didn't miss how it made her blush deepen. "I think that if you try to look at it that way, you'll always have an excuse as to why *not*."

Wren furrowed her brows and pouted. She had to force herself to look away from his mouth and, instead, tucked her chin.

"Timing is *everything*, Nik. I—" She shook her head as a pained expression spread across her features. "I have too many things on my plate already, and I've never . . ." She left her statement hanging, entirely unwilling to verbalize the rest of her thought.

"Then let me help you. Share your burdens with me, and I promise, they will all become easier to carry."

Her eyes shot to his, and her mouth hung open. She stammered a few times but never formed any words.

In her deliberation, Nik took hold of her hand and pressed his lips into her knuckles, kissing each digit individually. He slowly laced their fingers together and turned them over so that her pale wrist was exposed. His intoxicated gaze moved to revel in the myriad of fluctuating expressions across Wren's face.

The flush of pink made her skin seem like it was glowing. Her unsteady breath huffed quietly through barely parted lips, and the few mussed strands of sunset hair almost looked like a halo around her head.

Nik's eyes maintained their gravitational pull on hers as he brought her wrist against his cheek. He closed in on the crook of her shoulder and drew in a haggard breath.

"You taste sweeter than I imagined," he whispered into a handful of her hair. "Like how a flower smells," he said in a husky murmur.

"Nik," she managed. "We can't . . ." Her voice trailed off, and she squeezed her eyes shut. "Not now."

He shifted to graze her jaw with his nose, longing to engulf himself in her scent. When she didn't shove him away, he pressed his lips against the skin just below the curve of her jaw. The tips of his teeth gently clamped down before he could stop himself.

The pain from his bite jolted another soft sound from her. She blushed a bright scarlet and clapped her hand against her neck.

When his hazed eyes met her stunned ones, he smirked.

"Sorry." His cheeky grin creased the skin around his eyes. "I couldn't help it."

CHAPTER FOURTEEN

"Love is the desire to see
unnecessary suffering ameliorated."
Dr. Jordan B. Peterson

ELLIOT KNELT OVER A MOUND OF SNOW SHE HAD ROLLED into a large ball that reached to the top of her waist when she stood upright. She poised her hands on her hips to take in her handiwork.

Jack padded through the deep snow with childlike enthusiasm. He sought out larger clumps of snow to watch them glisten in the late afternoon light. The stark-white cat's ear twitched to the side, and he instinctively swiveled his head to locate where the soft crunch of snow had come from.

A robin hopped across the surface with cautious agility. Its attention was on whatever insect it found and not the calculating feline.

Jack crouched low, tail flicking excitedly. His adjustment, however, made the snow beneath his stable paws crunch loudly under his weight.

Before he had time to pounce, the bird scuttled away from an entirely different sound.

Wren rounded the corner and into view with Nik beside her. They were heatedly discussing something, and from the expression on her face, it was not something pleasant. As soon as the pair noticed the curly-haired human watching them, they fell quiet.

"Wren! Gods, what took so long?" Elliot hurried to her friend's side as they entered the snow-covered garden. She examined Wren's arms and hands before turning her attention to her face. Elliot touched the scab on her cheekbone softly and scowled. "Did you hurt yourself anywhere new?"

"No, El." Wren sighed with an exaggerated shake of her head.

Elliot's hand clasped Wren's chin and jerked her head to the side.

"Then what is *that?*"

Realization flushed over Wren's face in a vivid shade of red. Her eyes shot to Nik with a withering glare.

He shrugged once and angled his face away, failing to conceal his self-satisfied smirk.

"I don't know what you're talking about," she replied stubbornly. "Elliot, your hands are freezing. How long have you been outside?"

"Don't change the subject, Wren. It looks like you were bitten by something." The curly-haired woman leaned around her friend to get another look at the mark in question.

Wren glared at her and clapped a palm over her neck.

"Or some*one?*"

A teasing voice brought everyone's attention to Lionel. He emerged from the house with a mug of what could only be hot chocolate. "Welcome back, you two. Was your journey fruitful?" He handed the mug to Elliot and looked between the pair with an infuriatingly innocent smile.

"Oh, yes. Very much so." Nik's casual tone earned another glare from Wren, but he ignored it. He took the few steps to pass by her and kept walking toward Lionel. "I'd like to think that she and I are on better terms now." He could feel her eyes burning into the back of his head, so he ignored that too and tapped the bag at his side. "I think some of our questions might be answered. I found two books that have some specific information on them."

"Fantastic! Well, let's go inside and take a look!" Lionel patted Nik's shoulder with a gloved palm. "I have more hot chocolate ready inside if you two would like to warm up."

The childhood friends made their way inside eagerly, sharing in a quiet discussion.

Wren turned her attention back to Elliot.

She blew over the steaming mug a few times as she brought it closer. She kept her eyes locked on Wren as she took a purposeful but cautious sip. Elliot smacked her lips together to suck cold air into her mouth from the too-hot hot chocolate.

Worth it, the petite human thought as she suppressed any visible reaction to her now-burned tongue.

"Elliot, let it go. I'm fine, it was nothing. Move on."

"It doesn't look like *nothing*." Her matter-of-fact tone obstinately drove home her point.

Wren narrowed her eyes. "Then what does it look like?"

Elliot's face turned upright into a knowing smile.

Shit. Wren kicked herself mentally and pursed her lips.

Elliot always knew exactly how to get under her skin. "It *looks* like a hickey."

NIK NODDED A THANK-YOU AT LIONEL AS HE CRADLED THE WARM mug in his hands tightly.

Jack paced the floor, watching the doorway to the stairs vigilantly.

Lionel watched the girls talking outside through the window. He could tell that Elliot was glad to see her friend, even though she appeared so agitated.

"Wren seems different," he stated casually and turned to Nik. He watched the green-eyed reaper for a few moments and glanced to his mug nestled between gloved hands. When Nik gave no response, he turned his attention back upward with a serious look in his eyes. "Did something happen while you two were out there?"

"Eh, kind of." Nik turned away from Lionel. He selected a spot on the table to place his mug and reached into the satchel. He searched for words as his fingertips grazed the books' covers, and he brought them to the table. "I don't know how to explain it. Emotions were high, and she . . ." He trailed off as he scratched the back of his head.

"Nikolas?"

He furrowed his brow and leveled his friend with an even stare. "I don't know if she wants me to say anything." His voice fell to a near whisper. "But I know you'll find out anyway, so keep it to yourself. At least for now. Okay?"

Nik didn't need to see Lionel's nod to know he agreed.

"I sort of . . . kissed her?" He made a conflicted expression, torn between pride and guilt.

"Ah," Lionel replied and gestured to his neck. "So, that thing? That truly was you?"

"It's barely noticeable." Nik shook his head and leaned back in his seat in order to cross his arms over his chest. "Elliot must have elf eyes or something. You can hardly see it."

Lionel smirked. "Elliot is very protective of Wren, Nikolas. Possibly more so than Wren is of Elliot, truthfully. Something like that never stood a chance at being missed."

Nik flipped the book closest to him open and busied himself with searching for the right pages.

Lionel took the seat across from him and set his mug on the table. "And?"

"And, what?"

"Did you enjoy it?"

Nik sat up abruptly with wide eyes and dropped his hands so his palms were flat on the table. He opened his mouth to answer but was cut short by voices climbing the stairs. His lips set into a terse line.

With the girls now in earshot, Nik gave a silent response.

He nodded once.

The smile that spread across Lionel's face made Nik's ears burn. He forced himself to keep his attention trained on the open book as Elliot and Wren entered the room, still engrossed in their own hushed argument.

Lionel snuck a knowing glance at Nik.

"Elliot, come sit by me," he called and patted the chair to his right. "Have a look at what Nikolas found."

Nik clenched his fists on the table and gave Lionel a dark glare.

Lionel smiled sweetly and mouthed a single phrase: *"You're welcome."*

As young boys, they often played tricks and pranks on each other. Nik shouldn't have been surprised that he'd retained at least some of his adolescent *mis*behavior. The times he felt the urge to punch Lionel in the face were seldom, but they did happen.

This was beginning to feel like one of those times.

Elliot slid into the chair beside Lionel as Wren poured herself a generous cup of coffee.

"Oh? Curious!" She folded her legs beneath her on the seat and leaned forward so that she could read the book without needing to move it. "Where did you find these?"

"The Abagail Athenaeum. I bribed an imp to let me take them." Nik purposely ignored the sound of Wren shuffling into the chair beside him. "I didn't have much of a chance to read them, but three more sets of eyes couldn't hurt."

"So, what else did you do? I mean, since you two didn't come home last night, and Wren shows up with a hickey . . . There are some things that require answers." Elliot snickered as she looked between them. "I at least have to ask."

"Elliot, I swear," Wren warned quietly.

"*What?*"

"Wren, were you able to collect your new armor?"

"Hm?" Her eyes flickered to Lionel, then dropped to her coffee. "Yes, I am wearing it now under my tunic. It's surprisingly light."

Elliot clicked her burned tongue against the back of her teeth and folded her arms. She narrowed her eyes and stuck her tongue out at Wren, who childishly returned the gesture. She knew better than to further press the issue.

At least for now.

"What is this book called?" Elliot plucked the still-closed book from the table and turned it over to examine it. "What language is this?"

Lionel leaned over for a glance and cocked his head to the side.

"The one you have is *Unusual Beasts* by Ebner Breve," Nik offered. He tapped the one in front of him with one finger. "This one is *A Collection of Beastly Encounters*. Each passage in it is a different author."

Lionel leaned around Elliot to get a better look at the cover. He reached outward and turned the cover over so that the front page within was now exposed.

Neatly scrolled handwriting listed what must have been two hundred names onto the first few pages. Some of the names were written in languages that he understood, some were little more than hieroglyphs or scrolling lines, and a few were the single footprint of various animals.

"I believe this is mostly old elfish." He flipped a few pages forward and a few backward, scanning the text on them. He caught a glimpse of a single word and flipped back to the pages in question. Lionel ran his gloved fingertip across the ink and sighed before clapping the book shut and setting it on the table. "Breve mainly wrote in old elfish if I remember correctly. Can you read it, Nikolas?"

Nik's vigilant eyes noticed his friend's odd gesture but chose not to address it.

"Some of the passages, yes. Not all of it, unfortunately. But most of the text inside has been translated." He shifted the book on the table to face him. "I'll find the pages we are interested in."

"What's wrong, Wren?"

Elliot's question made Nik and Lionel look between the two women.

"Nothing worth mentioning," she murmured through tight lips. Wren crossed her legs and folded her arms over her chest. "Let's just get this over with, okay? I don't want to be here all night."

"Places to go? Things to do?" A harsh tone dug into Elliot's words. She couldn't stop her frustration from burning the back of her throat, much like her hot chocolate.

Knowing the depths and origins of Wren's personality issues, and the petty fights she'd seen in Lionel's visions, ignited something within her that she didn't understand.

Through the duration of their friendship, Elliot had stood up for Wren without fully knowing the full reason for her reputation. A well-earned reputation that a troublemaking, stubborn, and volatile person better left alone would have.

What annoyed her the most was that, even knowing what she did now about Wren's history and what she had endured that night . . . even knowing how soulless those silver eyes were, she refused to believe that Wren wasn't somewhere in them. Her position beside her friend would still not waver.

Elliot felt slighted that Wren was too hardheaded to recognize her loyalty. If she did, it was seldom out loud. The unpleasant thoughts she couldn't escape began to rally her temper.

"We finally have a chance to find out more about you so that we can help, and all you can do is act like it's beneath you. What about us? Aren't we allowed to be curious? Wren, we have to know more if we are going to be able to help you."

Wren scowled into her coffee and set her jaw.

Elliot leaned forward on the table, and her face tightened as she took in Wren's body language.

Wren sat with her arms and legs still crossed, and a dark look had crept into her eyes. It was clear that she was struggling with holding back her own temper as well.

Her refusal to speak finally broke the dam to Elliot's self-control, and she couldn't stop herself.

"You're so wrapped up in your own personal hell that you don't even see how much Lionel and I do for you. How badly we want to help you out of this pit you think you're in. I'm not saying you're ungrateful, but you sure as shit don't show it! You *still* haven't let us in!"

Wren's hands tensed on her arms, and her lips pursed together firmly. "*You're* more than welcome to find out more," she muttered in clipped speech. "*I* would prefer to take a shower and go to bed."

"See! There you go again! Always *you*, huh?"

"Ladies," Lionel soothed and placed a hand on each of theirs. "Let us be thankful that they made it back unharmed, Elliot. Yes? Let's all have a good night's sleep before you say something you don't mean."

Elliot jutted her lower lip out and leaned back into her seat. "Yeah," she scoffed. "Unharmed aside from the hickey on her neck that she refuses to talk about."

"Enough!" Wren shouted loudly. She slapped her palms onto the table and stood in an instant. The mug of coffee teetered between her hands from the force yet did not topple over. Her eyes were locked on Elliot, brows knitted and low. Her pale hands clenched tightly, and her arms were tense and trembling.

Elliot did her best to return the look, but guilt was already inching into the back of her mind.

Wren whipped around and made for her room without a word.

Lionel called to her even after the door to her bedroom slammed shut.

Elliot rose from her chair to follow but was stopped by a gloved hand on her shoulder.

"I'll talk to her."

Elliot huffed as she looked out the glass door and onto the balcony.

Lionel made his way to her room and lightly rapped against the door with the crook of his knuckle.

There was no reply, so he gingerly pushed the door open.

Wren was face down across her bed with her arms folded underneath a pillow. Her shoulders were trembling, and Lionel didn't miss the occasional sniffle muffled beneath the folds of the pillow.

She didn't regard him as he sat beside her.

"What's going on, Wren?"

Wren balled her fists into the white sheets and turned away from him. "Elliot doesn't have a clue about what is going on. She just got into town. She doesn't understand how much has changed since her last visit here . . . How much danger she's in . . ."

"Not that, little bird." He reached out to stroke the length of her hair. "Tell me what's really going on."

She took a deep breath through the pillow and groaned. "We were attacked by an omen last night. Or this morning? I don't know. It was a blur that lasted forever. Nik fought it off . . ." Wren's voice was muffled through the comfortable folds. "I'd never seen an omen before . . . I was useless, Lionel. Utterly useless. Nik did everything while I . . . I was too scared to even move.”

Lionel frowned and removed a glove from his hand. He rested it atop the crown of her head and closed his eyes.

When he said nothing, she continued.

“It showed up in the middle of the night, I think. I’d . . .” She sighed. Her conversation by the fireplace with Nik swirled in her mind, and she shook her head to try to rid her thoughts of him. “I awoke from a nightmare, which woke him up, too. We were attacked not long after. I doubt it would have turned out the way it did if we weren’t already awake.”

As Lionel listened to her silently, a smile cracked at the corner of his mouth as her shoulders gradually relaxed.

“Nik was amazing. I shouldn’t have doubted him,” Wren said softly and sat up. Her conflicted eyes flicked to Lionel, and she quickly added, “Don’t tell him I said that. He’s still an ass with an inflated ego.”

Lionel chuckled and pretended to zip his lips together.

Wren offered a small smile in return and slid the boots from her feet. “I had no idea he had that sort of power. The whole ordeal was . . . terrifying.”

A lull of quiet fell between them.

Lionel eventually broke it. “I was half thinking you’d run off.”

“Yeah,” she muttered. “I was half thinking about it.”

“I’m glad that you didn’t. Elliot would have driven herself mad looking for you.”

Wren snorted.

“Wren, you have to understand this from her perspective.” He paused for any sort of response.

None came.

“Just as you have, she has also been suspicious of Nikolas since he arrived.” He didn’t miss the way her shoulders stiffened at the name. “You two were gone a while. She was expecting you back last night and began to worry when you hadn't returned. Her mind went everywhere, wondering what happened. How would you have felt if Elliot hadn't come home?"

Wren sighed. "I know," she finally admitted. "A *lot* happened."

"Oh?" Lionel, not wanting to give Nik's confession away, played along. "Aside from the omen?"

Wren stared at a painted canvas across the room to avert her gaze as a light pink bloomed on her face. Without thinking, her hand gravitated to her neck.

To the spot just below her jaw.

"I—" She tried to cough away the lump in her throat. "I can't tell you."

Lionel smiled and patted the top of her head affectionately. "Why don't we head back into the other room and make peace?" His smile widened when Wren pursed her lips into a defiant pout. "I'm sure Elliot doesn't want to go to bed angry, either."

Wren drew a quick breath in through her nose. "Whatever. That's fine."

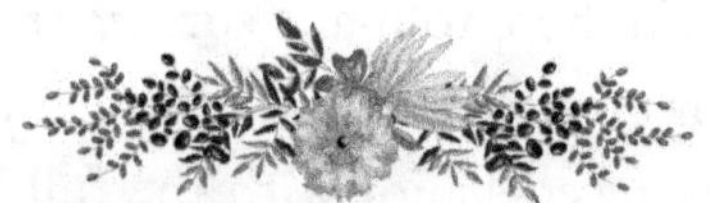

"So." Elliot's monotone voice gathered Nik's attention from the letters scrolled across the pages. "That *is* a hickey, isn't it? Any idea where she got that?"

Nik stared at her blankly, giving no indication that he intended to answer.

"Nothing to say, eh? What, Jack got your tongue?"

He couldn't fight back the smirk that crept onto his face.

Elliot, in response, tapped her toes against the floor and met his gaze.

"Yes," he said finally. "I know where she got that." He left his reply hanging in the air.

She scoffed and shook her head. "No wonder you two started to get along. You're the same frustrating person. Getting information out of either of you is like trying to push a boulder up a hill."

Nik chuckled and gave her a wry grin. "I gave it to her," he admitted as he cast a glance at Wren's bedroom door.

Elliot followed his eyes and pursed her lips. She turned back to Nik with a completely different expression than before. Her eyes lingered for a long while before she gathered her mug and stood.

"Don't hurt her." She spoke softly. "She isn't prepared for that sort of pain. And it would be cruel to put her through that on top of what she has already endured."

"I'm not here to hurt her."

Elliot turned to face him from the middle of the room. "It's still not clear why you *are* here," she muttered and felt a pang of guilt in her chest. The talk she had with Lionel the night before still seemed like it should be kept secret, and her half-lie left an unpleasant taste on her abused tongue.

But she wanted to hear it from the reaper himself.

"Really? I thought it would be obvious by now." He turned his attention to Elliot. "I'm here to make sure *no one* hurts her. It's clear why Lionel called for me when he did. It's clear to me why she is the way that she is." Nik faced Elliot with the full force of seriousness in his eyes. "She is an important presence that will make a huge impact. To Arnica . . . Hell, to all of Yu'e."

"She isn't your social project, *reaper*. Nor is she a charity case." Elliot grilled him with folded arms. "She won't be your puppet."

"Wren isn't anyone's puppet. Wren is . . ." His boldness waned, and he sighed, suddenly unsure of his words. "She's something precious that must be cherished. Protected. Here, let me put it this way." He adjusted his posture to sit more comfortably before he met her eyes again. "Penitent reapers are intended to protect ones that have a larger purpose. A destiny to fulfill. However, penitent reapers also remove *impediments* to the fulfillment of a larger purpose. I am here to make sure no one gets in her way."

Elliot sighed and shook her head. "If what you say is true, then you need to understand something." She pressed her hands into the counter and glanced at Wren's room. "Lionel and I are both protective of her. She's never acted like this . . . Like she does when you're around. Like she's something more than anxious. I don't know if I'm more happy or worried for her. She seems"—she tapped her chin in deliberation, searching for the right word—"different. I'm allowed to be worried." Her heart-shaped face tightened, and Elliot glowered. "But she clearly cares." She hesitated before begrudgingly adding, "For you."

"Yes, I know."

"And?" Her tone was identical to Lionel's when he'd posed the same question earlier.

"And what?"

Elliot rolled her eyes and groaned. "Like pushing a gods-damned boulder! Do *you* care? For her?"

Nik blinked and furrowed his brow. "I do," he replied. "And, so we are clear, I already knew everything that you just said. I understand your intentions. You care for her, too. We all want the same thing . . . For her to be happy and free from any chains. Including her own."

Elliot folded her arms and pursed her lips. "Can you do that?" Her pointed question caught him off guard. "Can you make her happy?"

He looked to the open pages of the book before him and took a deep breath. "I don't know," Nik finally replied. "But I plan to do everything in my power to ensure both her safety and her happiness."

"Hm." Her tone was flat and unconvinced. "Make sure that you do."

CHAPTER FIFTEEN

*"Confront the dark parts of yourself, and work to banish
them with illumination and forgiveness. Your willingness
to wrestle with your demons will cause your angels to sing."*

August Wilson

WREN LEANED AGAINST THE BALCONY RAILING WITH her green jacket wrapped over her loose-fitting pajamas. One arm held it closed and steadied the shiver in her chest. Hazel eyes watched the sky as the remnants of stars twinkled before they were lost in the gradient of breaking sunlight.

A sliver of smoke rose from a hand-rolled cigarette that had been neglected while its holder had been lost in thought. The suffocated ember glowed a dim orange against the still, cold dawn.

Wren's breath plumed before her with every exhale of pure night air. She sighed and drooped her head between her shoulders. The chill bit through her thin trousers and shirt. Even with her jacket on, the cold penetrated beneath her clothing and straight to her core.

What a mess, she thought with another, angry sigh.

Her focus tried to remain on the situation with Elliot, the fact that today was the first day of the festival, the creature attacks, the disappearances, the omen and wherever it came from, the strange aura from the woods . . .

Despite her best efforts, thoughts of Nik's lips against her skin washed all of the rest out. The memory caused the spot below her jaw to tingle, and she unconsciously cupped her hand to her neck.

"Shit," she growled when the motion caused the ember to fall, and it kissed the edge of her finger. She caught sight of the pile of unsmoked tobacco ash that had collected as she numbly gathered a small handful of fresh snow for the burn.

"The sun isn't even up yet, and you've already hurt yourself?"

That baritone voice startled her, and she spun to see Nik. Wren furrowed her brow and averted her eyes.

"I was distracted." Her chin reflexively angled away from him. "I'm fine." She took a silent, deep breath and managed to face him. "Why are you up so early?"

He moved in to stand beside her against the railing, mindful to leave a polite space between them. "I had a feeling you'd be awake. The festival starts today, doesn't it?"

"Mm-hm," she replied plainly. "I have the *honor* of reporting for duty." She rolled her eyes and let them wander back to the street.

"What does that mean?" He cleared his throat and glanced at her from the corner of his eyes. "You'll be gone all day?"

"No, tonight." Wren failed to keep the bitterness from her voice. "There is a banquet in the evening to set off the rest of the festival, then a grand ball afterward. They claim it's a celebration to be able to gather with neighboring nobility to discuss sociopolitical matters, but it's really just an excuse for the elite to get drunk and bed each other." She looked down at her hands and focused on the small blister forming. "They get all dressed up to flaunt their wealth and do absolutely nothing to address matters of any relevance. They claim they are acting as representatives of their people but do nothing of the sort. I have been to enough of these to know that they are nothing but bottomless-pocketed, narcissistic inbreds."

Nik took in her rant with a small smirk quirked at the corner of his lips, on the side of his mouth that she couldn't see. "And you play chaperone?"

Wren pursed her lips tightly and shook her head. "I *get to* go as the king's guest. It's the same for every festival banquet since the coup." She cursed under her breath. "I have to sit next to the creepy king and play nice while everyone gawks and gossips about me. They don't care if I hear them, either. They think of me as beneath them. A servant in a ballgown." She paused. "And no doubt Elliot has some insane getup planned that won't suit me at all. She hid my dress from the last banquet and won't tell me where it is."

Nik listened silently and let his eyes slip shut.

"She showed me the dress that Kora, the seamstress, made for her last night." Wren sighed and brought her hands to her face, ignoring the icy dampness from the melted snow against her cheeks and forehead. "It's beautiful, don't get me wrong. Kora is the best there is in, arguably, all of Arnica. It's just . . . not my style, I suppose."

"Wren." Nik spoke her name in a monotone voice. "Your *style* is dark pants, plain tunics, and that ratty old green coat."

She snorted with a small smile. "That's fair. I like to be comfortable."

"I'm sure the dress she ordered for you will be beautiful, too," he hummed quietly, then hesitated. "Lionel told me that the banquet is open to everyone. If the three of us go too, you won't be alone. It wouldn't be so bad."

Wren chuckled as she shook her head. "I mean . . . You can go if you want to. Elliot avoids the kingdom, so I doubt you could convince her to go. And Lionel will be with her whenever I'm not, so he wouldn't go either."

"So, it'll just be me. That's fine."

Wren turned to him with a disapproving look. "Nik, you don't have to follow me everywhere. I can take care of myself. I have for years. I've played this part enough times to not need backup. Why don't you find something fun to do and actually enjoy the festival?"

He let a brief silence drift between them. "Do you not want me to go?"

Her face morphed with shock, and she stammered. "N-no, it's not that." Wren cleared her throat and turned away from him. "You'll likely be irritated with the attendees the entire time. The king is really, *really* creepy and insufferable. The guests can get unruly, too. It's a lot to deal with. I figured you shouldn't walk into it blind."

"I can deal with you." He smirked.

She shoved his shoulder with a glare. "Well, you're irritating too, so you might just fit right in."

His smirk turned to a genuine smile, and his eyes captured hers.

The breaking morning light made the golden flecks within them shimmer brilliantly. The way they shone made it impossible to tell if they were moving in the sea of green or if they were just so many in number that each glittered in a rippling synchronization.

She tightened her arms around her chest and looked away. "I'm going back inside." Her voice was soft.

Nik said nothing in reply. Instead, he motioned for her to lead the way with his hands.

"This festival is going to be different, Wren. You'll be the best-looking one there. No one would dare reproach you! Your dress is going to blow everyone else's out of the water." Elliot's hands worked at fluffing the contents of the box around again. "In a good way," she added with a nervous laugh.

"That's not it, El. I'd rather not be seen at all."

Elliot put her hand on her hip and pointed a stern finger at Wren. "I don't want your downer attitude this year," she warned. "I'm still mad at you, but I'm trying to move past it because I love you."

Wren let out a heavy sigh and rolled her eyes. "I don't care if you guys read those stupid books. *Really.*" She shook her head. "I merely want nothing to do with them. I know the story. All of Yu'e remembers the story. I already know what I am. I have no interest in looking into different accounts of the same story." Wren pursed her lips. "I'm not trying to pick a fight, Elliot. I really, *really* don't want to go to this stupid banquet."

Elliot frowned, and her eyes softened. "I know, Wren." She placed her hand on her friend's shoulder. "Let's just move on. Here." She passed the box to Wren while adjusting the lid one last time. "I've been dying for you to see it, and I don't want the mood to ruin it's grand unveiling."

Wren smirked and nodded as she accepted the box. Before she moved away from Elliot, she leaned forward and placed a soft kiss on her temple. "I love you, too," she whispered and sat down on her bed. As she lifted the lid, despite her earlier apprehension, her eyes widened.

The lavender bust was entangled by beaded tendrils of glittering flowers and leaves. The thread that secured them to the tulle was a blush-pink hue, and the glittering stones shone like stars.

As Wren pulled more of the folded dress from the box, a knot of guilt pulled at her chest.

It *was* beautiful.

The waist of the dress was nearly covered by the shimmering weaves of flowers and leaves. At the bell of the dress, the threaded embellishments continued down its length. They dispersed as they neared the bottom, but the bright stones still held the eye. The blush thread outlined every petal, and it had a shimmer of its very own.

Lavender tulle covered the entire dress. The neckline was made up of densely packed embellishments in various flower shapes that clustered tightly over the cups of the modest bust. Beneath the flora was a silk fabric in the same lavender shade, and it was softer than Wren ever thought possible.

She stood with the garment clutched in her hands, and the box tumbled from her lap to the floor.

With the full length of the dress now free, it moved effortlessly with every turn of her hands. A silk skirt was veiled by the tulle and was so weightless that it flowed like purple ripples of water. She held the shoulders of the gown to her own and looked down for a full view.

Matching silk continued upward to form the shallow shoulders of the dress that became the sleeves. The satin sleeves reached down to her wrists and were a deep shade of violet. There was a single woven loop at each end for her to hook around her central fingers.

"What do you think?!" Elliot failed to keep her apprehension from her voice. "Try it on, try it on!"

Wren looked to her friend with an unreadable expression. She hesitated for a brief moment before turning her eyes back to the dress. "I can't wait to see what it looks like on," she half lied and chewed on the inside of her cheek. "I think it's beautiful."

"Good!" Elliot clapped both hands on her friend's shoulders. "I want to see it on you before you decide that you hate it, okay?"

Wren laughed once and nodded. "Deal."

With that, Elliot grinned and took her leave.

Wren turned to the mirror in her room with the dress still held up against her.

Her brows furrowed unconsciously, and she frowned. A heavy sigh escaped her, and she stripped to change into the dress.

It slid onto her body seamlessly. The clasps for the waist and bust trailed up the ribs on her side, each one a glittering stone wrapped tightly in rose-gold thread. She secured them with trembling hands, not daring to look back to the mirror.

Why am I shaking?

Her question was instantly answered by the conversation on the other side of her bedroom door.

"Wren said she liked it! I can't wait to see it on her. I think Kora made her best dress yet!"

"Yours is lovely, Elliot." Lionel's gentle voice was barely audible through the dense wooden door. "Don't sell it short."

"Lionel, what time do the shops open? If I'm going, I need to get some nicer clothes." Nik's voice in the common area made her heart race.

"In about an hour or so. Most shops will open a little later because of the festival."

Wren clenched her hands tightly, trying to force out the swimming feeling from her mind.

It's just a dress. It doesn't mean anything, she reasoned to herself. *Just get it over with.*

Her hazel gaze finally floated to the mirror.

The shoulders of the sleeves covered most of her collarbone and came to a point in the center of her chest. Their length hugged her arms perfectly, and the ringlet at the ends fit her fingers exactly. The embellished petals had been placed so meticulously that each one of them was the focal point of the bodice of the dress. The tangle of flowers and leaves at the bust was dense enough that the soft lavender silk beneath was barely visible. The silk slip brushed against her legs with every motion, and the embroidered stones rippled atop the tulle veil so naturally that the petals looked as though they were blown by a nonexistent breeze.

Wren took a deep breath and absentmindedly adjusted the sleeve over her left shoulder with a frown. She closed her eyes and shook her head before she made for the door. Her hand hesitated over the knob. Her eyes were locked on her shaking fingers while she fought to find the will to open it.

"Wreeeeeeen." Elliot's impatience grew palpable. "It shouldn't take this long to put on! It's only five buttons!"

"Fine," she resigned.

Wren turned the knob and pushed the door open. She shouldn't have been surprised to see every pair of eyes transfixed on her, but she was.

"Damn!" Elliot clapped her hands together and hurried to Wren's side. "It looks so much better on you than it did on the hanger! Do you like it?" Her hands flitted around the dress's bodice, making small adjustments of the tulle and silk. "Kora told me when I placed the order that she found a fabric in Fennel that instantly made her think of you! Isn't that cool?"

Wren managed a half-hearted hum in reply as she focused on keeping her stare away from their faces.

"She's right, Wren." Lionel closed the space between them. He put his gloved hand on her shoulder and smiled wide. "You look stunning. No one will be able to outshine you."

"That's what I said, too!" Elliot folded her arms across her chest and let out a knowing grin. "I told you so."

Wren's brows furrowed again, and she looked to her feet hidden beneath the dress.

"What do you think, Nik?" Elliot's question sent a jolt through Wren's chest. She became firmly committed to keeping her gaze locked on the floor.

He didn't answer for a few agonizing moments. He finally cleared his throat and looked away. "I like the color."

"*What?* That's the best you can come up with?" Elliot shot a dark look at him. "She comes out looking like *this*, and you only like the *color*? Gods, you're hopeless."

His emerald eyes glanced back to her and flicked over the dress again. "It's a really nice color."

THE STREETS WERE MOBBED BY TOWNSPEOPLE AND THEIR GUESTS, despite the early hour.

Lionel and Nik walked side by side as they made their way to one of the only open clothing shops.

The trace was already dressed in his festival garb.

His tunic was a soft shade of blue that made his cerulean eyes gleam. The sleeves were laced with golden strips of ribbon that braided down to the cuffs. The rigid cuffs were the same soft blue as the tunic but were dotted with small flecks of gold.

He wore a dark, royal-blue jacket that was tailored specifically to his chest. The fit of the shoulders and cut of the lapels made him appear even taller than he already was. His trousers were off-white and rather plain. Long, chocolate-brown boots covered most of his lower legs, and their heels clipped softly against the snowy cobblestone with every step.

"I would have let you borrow something of mine, but nothing would have fit you." Lionel gave a hearty laugh before he added, "Your shoulders are much wider, and I worry your arms would burst the seams."

Nik offered an earnest laugh of his own. "Don't worry about it. I know you would have if we were closer in build."

"I can't help it that you're a giant guy."

"I can't help it that you're a string bean."

"Rude."

They both laughed again and paused before a shop, having quickly reached their destination due to the length of each step that their long legs allowed for.

Lionel led the way in.

Tunics and dress shirts of every color imaginable littered almost every inch of the already-crowded store. Many of townspeople were rummaging for last-minute finds of their own.

Nik wandered to a relatively vacant corner. It had deep shades of royal colors organized across the walls in every direction. They hung neatly in rich shades of blue, green, red, violet, gold, and gray. Many of them were plain, though purposely positioned near collections of ornate jackets in matching and complementary colors.

He browsed the myriad of tops carefully before he found something that gave him pause.

It was such a deep violet color that it looked black at first. The tunic had delicate strands of dark gray threads swirling neatly across the chest. Thick, ribbed fabric encased the entire garment except for the arms. It had wide shoulders that were tipped by a twisting cord at the end of each shoulder.

"Interesting," Lionel mused, mostly to himself. He smiled at Nik. "Try it on. Here." He ducked into a different aisle of neatly folded clothing and reappeared with a pair of trousers. "These would go well with that shirt."

Nik lifted a brow at him before plucking the top from its place on the wooden hanger and accepting the pants from Lionel. He wordlessly made his way to a small room concealed by a red velvet curtain. Nik quickly slipped the violet tunic on and tugged at the hems to straighten it out. Once satisfied, he looked down his chest.

The single body-length mirror reflected the top that hugged him handsomely. The dress shirt reached just above his hip and fit the curve of his waist all of the way up to his arms. It hugged his chest well and was loose enough that he could comfortably wear another layer beneath it if necessary.

He slipped into the trousers and fastened the waist. They were a tad too big, but he already had a belt that would fix that. They were a plain black but moved comfortably with him and, like the top, complemented his well-trained frame.

Nik stepped out from behind the curtain to Lionel's waiting attention.

In his hand was a black waistcoat with silver buttons. Up close, it was embossed with a subtle leafy pattern in thread exactly the same color as the garment itself that only glimmered at certain angles.

"Put this on," Lionel encouraged.

Nik complied and slid his arms through the holes.

The cord along his shoulders fit nicely out from below the waistcoat, and as he fastened it, the length of the waistcoat complemented his height as it curved just above his hips.

Lionel then handed him a plain black jacket whose only embellishment was the understated sheen of the wool fabric's finish.

"Excellent." He smiled. "You will fit right in."

"Yeah? Is that a good thing?"

Lionel laughed and nodded. "Yes, you look inconspicuous but well-dressed enough to possibly pass as a long-lost noble, if you so choose to. If that's what you're going for." His elbow poked Nik's ribs in jest.

"Lionel, I'm a reaper. I don't intend to look like nobility. I intend to blend in and observe."

He nodded in response. "I understand." He clapped his gloved palm onto Nik's shoulder and smiled. "Let's get them and head back. The girls will probably be done getting ready by the time we get home."

Nik changed back into his own clothes and rejoined Lionel with his selection slung over his forearm.

The clerk eyed them when they approached, and Nik handed them over.

He had dense yellow-green skin that folded over his neck and shoulders. A wide, big-eyed head and face sized up the two. He had a long mouth that split most of his face. Two small nostril holes between his oversized eyes sniffed inquisitively, and he squinted tightly.

Nik had encountered bulltoads numerous times. They were common in busy marketplaces and were, by nature, standoffish. Because of that, they made great salesmen.

It took him a few moments before he recognized Lionel.

"Ah, last-minnit needs, Gibbs?" the bulltoad asked monotonously. His jet-black eyes moved to Nik. "A visitor? Come ta see the festival, eh?"

"Yes," he answered in a semi-friendly manor. "This is the first Arnican festival I've been to."

"Aye," the bulltoad said. "Spring's the best one. Ya got good timin'." He folded the dress shirt, waistcoat, trousers, and jacket as he jotted numbers into a book beside him. "Nine coppa, one silva."

"That's rather steep, Morgan." Lionel's gentle opposition made the bulltoad bristle.

"Holiday pricin', Gibbs. People that ferget ta get clothes help clean out the shop." Morgan's tone was cautioning. "Times're tough. It don't help that the missus spendin' too much on food an' wine. Ma kids need ta eat."

"I understand, Morgan." Lionel shook his head and sighed.

Nik shook his head as he dug into his pocket.

"Yer the man from the market," the bulltoad squinted at Nik dubiously. He croaked out a rough laugh. "Heard Honorah was eyein' ya. She fancies anythin' new. Shame the fight got broke up tho'. Gibbs's little one puts up a helluva ennertainin' bout." The shopkeeper winked at Lionel. "Seen 'er take down three men b'fore!"

Nik pressed the coins roughly into the bulltoad's webbed palm. "Keep the change. Consider it my contribution to your wife's alcoholism."

"Thanks fer the business." Morgan's eyes belied the pleasantness of his words as they narrowed. "Be careful with the red-haired one, lad. Gibbs did 'er fine an' all. But she's unperdiccable. Don't say I didn't warn ya."

"Morgan," Lionel cautioned firmly.

The black eyes turned to Lionel with a challenging look.

"The dissperances ain't goin' away, Gibbs. She ain't doin' her job so good." The bulltoad folded his arms and leaned back. "Ya can't pertect her forever. Shit's happenin', and no one knows what's goin' on. *She's* the outsider, an' people talk."

Nik gruffly plucked the clothes from the counter and glared sharply. "Thanks for the advice, Morgan." Nik turned to Lionel with a dark look. "Let's go."

WREN SAT PRIMLY IN THE ARMCHAIR ELLIOT CONFINED HER TO.

Elliot drifted around her as she fussed with her hair. Countless pins and stems had been poked and woven through the strands tastefully. Small pink and purple flowers were tucked into her hair with tiny clasps that secured them in place.

The majority of Wren's hair was gathered into a large bun on the crown of her head. Curled whisps of sunset strands brushed over her shoulders and framed her pale face.

The flowers nearly matched the blush of the dress's threading and embellishments. Elliot had successfully braided four bunches of flowers that followed the curve of her head and were scattered throughout the bun.

"You look great. I don't get why you seem so nervous."

"I'm always nervous," Wren countered. She fidgeted with the left sleeve of her dress and glanced to the floor.

"Not like this." Elliot's voice was suddenly close when she knelt down so they would be eye level with each other. "Don't worry," she whispered and flattened the fabric over Wren's shoulder. "It hides it."

She offered Elliot a small smile before she drew in a deep breath. "I have to know . . . What did you do with my other dress?"

Elliot flashed a mischievous grin and winked. "I gave it to Kora so she had your sizing. She probably threw it away when she was done with it."

"Great," Wren muttered.

Elliot took a step back and held her hand out to Wren.

The blue-green dress hugged the slim woman's frame like it had been sewn shut while she wore it. Her curly hair was down, with the exception of two sections of hair that were pulled from her temples to the back of her head. White and gold flowers covered the two portions of hair until they joined behind her head like a floral halo.

"You look great, too, El." Wren took her hand and stood. "Thank you for helping me get ready. And for the dress. Sorry I couldn't help you with your hair or makeup." She chuckled. "Not really my thing." She reached to the side of Elliot's face and tucked a rebellious chocolate curl behind her ear before she shifted awkwardly.

Her shoes were already uncomfortable.

They were lace-covered and propped her heels up at least two inches from the ground. They were a similar color to her dress but a few shades darker.

"Can't I just wear my boots?"

"No, your dress will drag on the ground in your boots. They aren't tall enough."

"Why wouldn't she just make the dress shorter so I could have worn them? Is that too far out of an idea?"

"Quit being stubborn."

"I hate this."

"I know." Elliot couldn't cover her smirk in time. "You're being stubborn."

The door downstairs shut loudly.

They looked at each other in a cocktail of surprise and apprehension.

"I didn't think they'd be back so soon," Elliot whispered.

"I hate *this* more," Wren muttered and nibbled on her fingernail.

The pair listened to the men converse downstairs in muffled murmurs.

"You really *do* have a thing for him." Elliot's eyes watched her friend. "For Nik."

It wasn't a question.

Wren didn't answer, but her eyes fell to her feet, and a subtle shade of red stained the tips of her ears.

"Was that your first kiss?" Elliot tried again with a slight smirk.

Wren remained silent, refusing to admit it aloud.

Lionel's voice grew more prominent as they ascended the stairs.

The top step creaked under his foot, and the two men entered.

Lionel had been mid-sentence as they walked in. One look at the women silenced him instantly. He froze in place and stared, which forced Nik to have to step around him.

When Nik's eyes found them, he did the exact same as Lionel: stopped and stared in absolute silence.

A pregnant pause hung in the room, and the girls shared another uneasy look.

Lionel's cerulean eyes shifted from Elliot to Wren a number of times before they settled on Elliot.

She looked even better than she had in Kora's shop. With her hair done so beautifully, she didn't seem human. Instead, she was more enchanting than an ethereal spirit, and he could have sworn that her shy smile emanated light. He couldn't look away from her.

Nik's emerald stare was transfixed on Wren, eyes opened wide and unblinking. His lips hung slightly ajar as he took her in. The lump in his chest prevented him from thinking, let alone speaking.

Wren's eyes were snared in his. She felt her hands tremor and heat flood her face. The healing wound on her ear's helix stung slightly and caused her to wince.

"You both look absolutely lovely." Lionel finally shattered the silence and approached them. "Nikolas, you'll need to get ready quickly. Many of the events will be starting soon, and they get crowded fast."

The sound of his name broke him from his stupor, and he was finally able to look away from Wren.

"Yeah." His voice rasped, and he cleared his throat. Without another word, he strode by the girls and into the room he'd taken up residence in. Nik closed the door behind him and shook his head. A heavy sigh escaped him as he leaned his back against the other side of it. His eyes slipped shut, and he rubbed at them roughly.

He stayed like that until his racing pulse steadied. Once calm, he took a deep breath and changed quickly enough for the group to leave by late morning.

ELLIOT AND WREN WALKED BESIDE EACH OTHER, WHILE LIONEL and Nik followed a few paces behind.

Elliot had a warm shawl carefully wrapped around her shoulders. It was a creamy-gray color that looked almost blue against her dress and thick enough to keep her perfectly warm.

Wren's shoulder wrap was a thicker, muted sage fabric that was even softer than it looked. It covered her arms and gathered around her chin like a scarf.

Wren drew a deep breath in as they approached the busier streets.

People turned curious eyes to them uncomfortably as they continued. Biting whispers were just audible over the sound of music that seemed to come from every direction.

Elliot nestled her arm into the crook of Wren's elbow and leaned in close.

"What do you think that was about?" she whispered. "He barely said anything."

"Yeah. I was there, Elliot."

"Sorry." She pursed her lips. "I just don't get it. He follows you around everywhere like a ghost, then has nothing to say when you look so pretty?"

Wren gave Elliot a playful sideways look. "Are you saying I'm not pretty unless I'm all dressed up?"

"No!" Elliot's exclamation caught the attention of Nik and Lionel. She felt their eyes on them but pretended not to notice. Her voice dropped low again. "What I *meant* was that he's never seen you so dressed up. You only wear that drab coat."

"Hey, that coat's been through a lot with me. You be nice to coatey."

"*Coatey?*"

"Yeah." Wren chuckled.

"Oooh, you mean Cody the coat." Elliot snorted.

"The coat that once was."

"The code of the indestructible coat."

"Coat of mystery."

"Coat mink stole."

"A coat for a goat on a moat."

"Coat of mysterious stains and shoddy repairs," a deeper voice chimed in from right behind them. Lionel flashed a charming smirk at them when they both spun around.

"Heh-heh . . ." Elliot laughed nervously. "How long have you guys been so close behind?"

"We just caught up to you. Why do you ask?"

"We were just playing a game," Wren said. Her eyes met Elliot's, and they shared a look of disbelief.

"Actually, I was going to see if Elliot would like to check out the flower show before they open judging."

"Oh! Yes, I didn't realize how long we've been here. Nik? Wren? Are you guys coming too?"

Wren nodded and followed Lionel and Elliot as they led the way down the street.

A strong hand closed around her wrist and spun her around. She collided with something solid and warm.

Nik stood before her with an indiscernible expression on his face. He wasn't looking at her but past her. "Can I talk to you?"

Wren tugged her arm free and glared at him. "Not here," she said through clenched teeth. "I can already hear people whispering. I would really rather not talk in a place where prying ears are everywhere." Wren turned her back to him and continued after Lionel and Elliot.

The only indication of Nik behind her was the purposeful click of his boots against the frozen stones.

CHAPTER SIXTEEN

*"You cannot swim for new horizons until you
have the courage to lose sight of the shore."*

William Faulkner

IGHT ENCROACHED QUICKLY, BREATHING A NEW BREED
of life into the streets. Orange lamp lights filled the
space with a glowing aura, and laughter and music
persisted well through dusk. The smell of alcohol was
strong enough to taste in the chilled air.

Street vendors called out to members of the crowd, beckoning
them with well-cooked meats and brightly colored dishes. Restaurant owners stood at their doorways with platters of food that they
handed to any passersby, aiming to steer the crowds into their respective eateries.

The number of families with children began to dwindle, and
the energy of the crowd grew increasingly excitable, raucous, and
inebriated.

"The banquet is that way." Elliot pointed to the castle just visible
in the distance. "Wren will probably be there already. If you stick

to the edges of the room, you should blend right in. The guests are especially unobservant after dinner."

Nik eyed her when she nudged him with her elbow. He folded his arms over his chest and looked in the direction she had indicated.

"I'll head over when Lionel comes back."

Elliot sighed and shook her head. "I don't know how many times I need to tell you all that I don't need a babysitter. Plus, you might not get a seat at the table if you take too long." She hummed softly. "Gods know what she's enduring right now. I know for a fact she'd prefer to be at home, pretending her sandbags are the very people she's with right now."

"Probably." Nik chuckled.

"She has a good gambling face, but she's actually very sensitive." Elliot touched her chest for a brief moment. "I just hope that she is okay. Being around the king makes her bristle."

"Why's that?"

"He's a creep," she replied plainly. "He's the type to make decisions on what is best for *him*. He doesn't seem to care much about his people and their strife. And he's entirely obsessed with Wren." She twirled a curl on her shoulder subconsciously. "He's been watching her for years . . . since Seth's attempt at the crown. The Winter Festival ended up with her getting into a fight with one of the other guardsmen. She spent the rest of that night in the castle dungeon for making trouble."

The crowd behind them suddenly burst with noise when they let out a synchronized cheer. The voices of two men arguing loudly was followed by the sound of fists landing on bodies, each blow followed closely by pained grunts.

Elliot and Nik peered over their shoulders at the scene.

A circle of people had gathered outside of a pub down the street. The shapes of the two men grappling were difficult to make out through the densely packed crowd of onlookers.

"She does too much for this ungrateful place. It shouldn't come as a shock when she lashes out, but everyone seems to be fine with pretending she's the provocateur." Elliot scrunched her nose in disgust. "She gets blamed for everything because of some shared delusion."

Nik hesitated before he looked back to her. "Did Wren tell you what happened the night she and I met?"

". . . No," came Elliot's cautious response.

"I found her while she was fighting those two grifters. The ones found dead . . ." Nik grimaced when Elliot's expression began to drop. He turned to face her directly. "She was defending two women from the grifters. I saw the entire thing."

Elliot turned to face him as well. The look behind her eyes was indiscernible.

"She fought valiantly . . . They just had the advantage of desperate hunger."

"What do you mean?"

"They had her pinned. One held her down while the other moved in."

Elliot frowned and shook her head. She said nothing for a long while.

"Elliot?"

"She didn't shift, did she?"

"What? No." He unfolded his arms and tilted his head. "The wind picked up a bit, but that's about it. She kept herself in control throughout the whole fight."

"Figures," Elliot muttered angrily. "She will shift for the sake of the kingdom but not to save her own life."

Nik's eyes widened, and he watched her closely.

She was shuffling her feet in place and nibbling on her lips as though they were holding something back. Her arms were crossed over her chest, and her eyes looked away from his.

"Lionel showed me everything. I even saw what happened the night of Seth's uprising. The night she turned into . . . into that thing." Elliot frowned. "Wren was so scared then; I saw it. I *felt* it. Now, she's so headstrong that she refuses to feel *anything*."

"Ah." He nodded and looked back to the castle.

A comfortable silence fell between them before it was suddenly broken by Elliot.

"You really kissed her, huh?"

Nik couldn't hide his surprise at her sudden question. "Eh, yeah. I did."

"Did you like it?"

He cleared his throat and adjusted his new jacket.

Elliot smiled to herself and chuckled aloud once. Her eyes slipped a sideways glance at Nik, and she tapped a spot on her neck, just below her jaw.

"It took quite a bit of doing to cover *that* up while she was getting ready."

Nik failed to conceal a smirk of self-satisfaction.

"I've never seen her like that," she murmured to herself.

"Like what?"

Elliot shook her head with her own prideful grin. "Can't." She tapped a finger over her lips. "Girl code."

WREN SCANNED THE ROOM FROM BEHIND AN ORNATE GOLDEN curtain.

The tall ceiling towered over the expansive room, and a shining golden-and-white marble covered the floor with a glorious sheen. Luxurious tapestries were strewn on nearly every wall that wasn't already decorated by images in stained glass and boldly painted murals.

The ballroom had been outfitted with any- and everything to do with spring. Every vase in the castle was stuffed to bursting with long-stemmed flowers and lush-green leaf blades.

Two sets of short stairs designated where the ballroom ended and the grand dining hall began.

Enormous wooden tables filled the substantial dining hall. It easily seated the elites and nobility with a few leftover spots for the first few townspeople who'd already been waiting in line for hours.

"Are you quite finished gawking?"

Wren turned to see a palace footman standing behind her. She pursed her lips and looked to his extended hand.

"The king is hungry. He sent for you right away." His stilted speech gave away his distaste of her.

"Just show me where he is."

He eagerly withdrew his hand and turned his back to her in order to lead the way.

Her feet ached with every click of her heels against the marble floor.

They approached a large, open room with bright golden walls and a large animal pelt rug.

Wren suppressed her growl at the sight of the rug, posed to seem intimidating. To her, it only looked heartbreaking.

"Ah, stunning as always, my dear."

A tall man with gray eyes and hair sat in an overstuffed and oversized throne. He had a long beard that came to a point along his chest in a neat braid. His hair was equally long and gray. He wore a glimmering crown so large that its golden face covered most of his forehead. It was cluttered with sparkling gems in various colors that lined the circumference of the crown.

"Come here." A long, decrepit finger gestured at her to obey. "Let me get a good look at you with these old eyes."

The hairs on the back of her neck bristled. She hesitantly complied and strode toward him. She clicked to a stop more than an arm's length from him and, begrudgingly, curtsied.

"Closer, dear. I want to get a good look at this lovely little dress of yours."

Bile curdled at the top of her stomach, and she took a few small steps forward.

King Reed reached for her arm and tugged her to stand beside him. He fingered the tulle of her skirt, rolling one of the embroidered stones directly over her hipbone between his thumb and forefinger.

He hummed and chuckled. The old man's hand drifted from her hip to rest across the small of her back.

Wren struggled to stifle the rage inside of her chest when his thumb caressed the curve of her spine, just above the back of her waist.

"Fits you nicely, dear. It really shows off your delightful figure." His yellowed teeth poked from behind a deceptive smile. "I look forward to dancing with you in this. Everyone will stare and wonder if you are the same troublemaker from the last festival. My dear"—King Reed let out a dry laugh—"you will have them all fooled. Hopefully this time, you'll behave."

Wren took a step away, purposely moving away from his touch.

"I was told you were hungry, Highness."

He narrowed his eyes at her for a moment, then clapped his hands against the armrests of his chair as he stood.

"Yes." He looked to his shoe, then to the attendant beside his throne. "Finish up so I can eat."

The maid jumped and hurried to secure the laces of his boot. She rushed to tie a knot and moved from his path. Her amber eyes met Wren's for a moment, and her lips tightened into a barely no-ticeable smile.

Unlike the footman, the maid's eyes had a sort of compassion in them that seemed to empathize with the gravity of Wren's position.

For only that moment, the two women connected and commiserated.

The king stepped beside Wren and held out the crook of his left arm.

Wren took a deep, silent breath in through her nose. Reluctantly, she placed her arm inside of his and allowed herself to be led toward the dining hall.

As they grew near, the king paused so that the porter had a chance to properly announce his arrival.

"Presenting His Highness, King Randon Reed, and Miss Wren, Lady of the Guard."

As King Reed had predicted, as well as Elliot and Lionel, every single set of eyes was locked on her. Their judging stares bored into her like knives.

The king led Wren to the head of the largest table within the hall and pulled out the chair to the left-hand side of his.

Wren took her seat and tried to ignore how his hand had lingered on her shoulder after he'd pushed her chair in. She could still feel the room's eyes on her, so she busied herself with unraveling her napkin and placing it neatly on her lap.

"Who else is hungry?" The king coaxed a reaction from his public. "Let us celebrate the end of winter and the beginning of spring! May all here tonight make it a prosperous season!" He looked to his attendants and snapped his fingers. "Serve the feast now."

At his command, servants flooded into the room with platters piled high with food. Some carried empty plates that were methodically placed in front of every diner. Many carried goblets full of wine and pitchers for refills, expertly weaving through the chaos.

The distraction of food brought reprieve from their stares enough for Wren to confidently look up and survey the room. She identified the royals that she recognized, as well as catalogued a few new faces.

As she scanned every seat, she couldn't help but feel a pang of disappointment.

Guess he didn't make it in time.

Wren pushed the thought from her mind with a shake of her head and chewed on her cheek. She'd successfully endured countless banquets on her own.

This would be no different, with or without Nik.

After the Winter Festival, she had to behave like they expected her to. She had to play their pointless and manipulative games in order to maintain a low profile and especially keep from getting thrown into the dungeon again.

Or worse.

The dining hall was a cacophony of overlapping voices that conversed excitedly, even with mouths full of food and wine. They argued loudly over politics, borders, religion, and whatever else they could come up with to disagree on. Each voice tried to one-up the others around them, stubbornly refusing to be silenced by any counter arguments.

Wren pushed her dinner around the plate with a fork, pretending to ignore them.

"Eat," King Reed spoke softly, leaning in close to her. His breath reeked of booze and rot. "I don't want you to go hungry. Women are rather temperamental and unpredictable when they aren't properly fed. Am I to expect another incident? You're looking rather thin."

"No, Highness."

She reluctantly poked a small slice of roasted pork into her mouth.

The king kept his eyes locked on her until she swallowed. He reached out and collected her hand with a tight grip. He brought her knuckles to his lips with a dubious quirk to his smile.

"Good girl."

It took everything inside of Wren to stop herself from inflicting severe harm on him. She instead took a deep breath and pointed her chin to the armrest on her chair, away from his eyes.

The remainder of the banquet dragged on. Endless drinks were poured, and the guests grew more restless after each one. Those not involved in the bickering began to shift in their seats uncomfortably.

The king grinned and stood. "Let us begin the ball!"

With his permission, the guests hurried to their feet and made their way to the ballroom.

Wren remained seated until the king appeared beside her chair. "Stand up."

Although she knew he was there, his voice made her jump. She unenthusiastically complied with a scowl.

He purposefully stood too close and hooked his arm around her hips once she was upright. The king took a wide step toward the ballroom and tugged her with him forcefully.

The size of the crowd inside of the room was tremendous. With the larger, more expansive space, many more townspeople were able to join the nobility. Hordes of royals, high-ranking knights and soldiers, and upper-class citizens filtered into the crowd from the banquet.

King Reed paused at the top of the small staircase.

The same footman that had taken her to this terrible man upon her arrival stood beside them and glanced at Wren with a disapproving scowl. He turned back to the room and gestured to the king.

"Presenting King Randon Reed and his escort."

The crowd's reactions were similar, if not identical, to the one she had received from the footman.

Duplicitous whispers and unabashed stares were all aimed directly at her, openly expressing a unanimous condemnation.

King Reed glanced at Wren from the corner of his wrinkled eye as he smirked. His hand on her hip tightened, and he leaned in.

"You in that dress makes me wish *I* was the only one allowed to see you in it," he whispered. When she gave no response, he chuckled and straightened. "Though I can have that arranged."

Wren's stomach lurched, and she struggled to keep her dinner down. As they made their way to the center of the ballroom, she caught sight of something in her peripheral.

In the shadow of a pillar on the far side of the room stood a large, familiar silhouette.

Nik?

Another pang shot through her. She wished he wasn't there to see the perverted king use dancing as an excuse to touch her wherever he wanted to. Wren numbly allowed herself to be brought to a stop by the king in the center of the room.

Reed's gray eyes leveled hers as his bony hand clamped against the small of her back. He gathered her right hand to hold between them as the music began. He held her uncomfortably close as he whisked her around the room.

They were the only pair on the floor, per the tradition that the first dance belonged to the king.

The attendees watched with narrowed eyes, the women half-heartedly concealing their loathsome expressions with paper fans to match their gowns, and men chuckling amongst themselves with unpleasant smiles.

"I'm rather envious that you are stealing all of the attention from me," he murmured. The king leaned in so closely to her that the tips of his lips brushed against her wounded ear. "Showing up, looking like this." He let out a sigh that sent a shiver down her spine. "It's like you *want* everyone to see how good you look at my side."

"I have no intention of being wed, Highness."

He gave a wry laugh. "Nor I."

". . . Sire," Wren replied softly. "My time is committed to my duties as a member of the Guard."

A smirk crept across his thin lips, revealing the tips of his yellow teeth. "You've been under a lot of pressure, I'm told. Perhaps I should reallocate your time."

"I have no more pressure than I can handle, sire."

"Are you sure about that? I've heard what happened with the grifters. Your commander confirmed that you were the one on lighting duty in that part of the market. I was also told that there was a broken lamplighter hook found wedged into one of their heads."

Wren's eyes widened, and she visibly flinched.

King Reed's gray eyes narrowed as his smirk grew sinister. He reached out and grazed the mostly hidden wound across her cheekbone.

"They even scratched your lovely face. Unforgivable."

The music dropped to a slower, mellow rhythm.

The pause it left was filled with absolute silence. The attention of the guests remained locked on the two of them, alone on the dance floor.

"You are carrying a lot, my dear. I am considering changing up your responsibilities."

There was something malevolent in his voice. His eyes were locked on hers and held them with the hungry ferocity of a predator set on injured prey.

"Highness?"

"I'd like *you* to consider moving into the castle. Here"—his grip on her tightened—"with me. That way, I can make sure you aren't overworked. I can keep a closer eye on you. I can't allow my only Lady of the Guard to be treated in such ways that I've heard you have been. Additionally, the investigation into the two deaths is currently being conducted. It will be favorable to me if you are more easily accessible."

Wren chewed on her lip and looked away from him.

"It is your choice, however."

It took everything within her to meet his gaze once more.

"I'm not so cruel a king that I would force my lady to move in right away. I want you to think about it. Think *very* seriously." His hand drifted up her back, grazing each vertebra with the ghost of a touch. "Poor Lionel has to clean up the messes that you make when you get into these altercations." He pressed his nose into her hair and took a deep breath in. "I know that you will eventually make the right decision."

The song drew to a close, and they gradually came to a stop.

The hand on her waist remained locked in place as the other waved the guests to join them on the dance floor.

"Think about it, my dear. The sooner you decide, the better." The king leaned close to her ear so that only she could hear. "I expect you to have a response once the festival guests have all left. I think that is more than enough time to collect your things and say your goodbyes."

"Sire," Wren replied and tried to take a step away. "You speak for me as though I have already agreed."

His expression darkened, and he refused to let her move. "Things will only worsen if you stay idle and improperly used in Black Rivers. For you *and* Lionel. And the young lady from out of country. Ellen? You can prevent anything bad from happening to them."

Wren couldn't disguise her shock. A creeping feeling made its way up her back slowly, seemingly following the exact same pattern as the king's unwelcome hand.

"Sire," she started softly and took a shallow breath, "are you threatening me?"

Something within the pallid, gray depths glimmered. "Heavens no, my love." He brushed his fingers over the small portion of her exposed collarbone. "I am encouraging you. A push in the right direction may be just what you need to make the right choice." His index finger stilled over the top of her sternum, and Wren could feel his seedy stare drifting lower. His hand at her waist stroked the embroidered flowers over her ribs with his thumb, and his hand on her chest started to move again as though a target had been set on the skin beneath her dress.

Wren tried to ignore the itching sensation that his fingers left behind and felt her hands clench into fists.

"Excuse me, my lord."

The familiar voice made her heart leap.

They both turned to see Nik. The king glared at him, instantly put off by the interruption, and Wren stood statue-still with wide eyes.

Nik's hair had been slicked back since she'd last seen him. The shadow of his stubble had also been shaved away, allowing his flawless features to gleam in the ambient light.

"I would be honored if you allowed me to dance with this stunning woman."

"And *you* are?"

"Nikolas Briar, Your Highness. I am new to your wonderful kingdom and have heard that your festivals are second to none. I'm eager to experience as much of it as possible." He glanced to a silent Wren and waited until their eyes met before he continued. "Hopefully . . . that includes a dance with the most beautiful woman that I've ever seen."

Wren's face went so hot that she had to look away.

"Rather bold of you to interrupt a king's dance with his maiden, boy. However . . ." Reed hesitated and gripped Wren's waist possessively. After a moment of deliberation, he released her and nodded. "You make a good point. Arnica *is* renowned for our extravagant parties and beautiful women . . . I suppose I shouldn't keep her from entertaining a guest. Bad manners and all."

"Thank you, sire."

Relief flooded into Wren's veins like a tidal wave once the king's hands had vanished from her body and made the tips of her fingers tingle.

Nik held his hand out to her and led her to a more secluded spot at the edge of the ballroom. He brought her to a stop at a portion of the dance floor that was still mostly vacant and lifted her hand to rest on his shoulder. His other hand gently cupped the small of her back and brought her a step and a half closer to him.

Although he held her in the manor that the king had . . . Nik's touch didn't leave her skin crawling.

It did, however, leave it electrified.

"Good cover." She finally broke the quiet, filled by the music, quiet murmurs of conversations, and the sound of her heels against the marble. "I didn't think you made it in . . . Didn't see you at the banquet." She tried to laugh, but it didn't sound quite right. "I told you that seats fill up fast."

"Cover?"

"Uhm, yeah. Just now with the king. To get me away from him?" She mistakenly met his golden-green eyes and involuntarily gulped.

He watched her without a word as he whisked her around in perfect synchronization with the music. "That wasn't a cover," he finally replied. "I meant it."

Wren opened her mouth to speak, but no words came out. She tore her eyes from his to hide her spreading blush and instead fixed her stare on his waistcoat.

"I wanted to say it earlier," he admitted. "I didn't have the right words . . . Or any, for that matter."

"Ah," she said flatly. "When you said that you like the *color*."

"It *is* a beautiful color." Nik hesitated with a smile. "Especially on you."

Wren's blush deepened, and she tucked her chin slightly.

The song continued to move the bodies inside of the ballroom with a melodious current that made the silence between them less obvious.

She glanced around the room to see most attendees finally busy with their own matters and far fewer gawking eyes than before. Wren sighed and hesitantly turned her attention back to Nik.

"You shaved your face," she said cautiously. "I never would have thought you'd be handsome under all that scruff."

He smirked at her. "Careful. I think that was almost a compliment."

"If that's how you want to take it." Wren shrugged. After a short pause, she softly cleared her throat and added, "You look nice."

"Thank you. A barber offered to clean me up after I broke up a fight. It had started at the bar across the street but ended up on his doorstep."

"Ah," she replied quietly.

As the music continued, she began to notice the details on his clothes and tilted her head to one side. Without thinking, Wren slid her hand from his shoulder to the lapel of the waistcoat tucked beneath his jacket. She started to trace the leafy patterns that shone in the soft golden light with a feather-light touch.

"Do you want to go outside?"

His question rumbled in his chest, just beneath her fingertip and startled her.

Wren quickly withdrew her hand and looked away. "S-sure. I just need to get my shawl."

"Don't worry about it." He released her waist but kept her hand securely in his. He led her to a tall doorway that opened onto an empty veranda and motioned for her to go first.

As they stepped into the cold, Nik removed his jacket and laid it across Wren's shoulders. His hands gently gripped her upper arms and steered her toward the banister as far from the door as possible. He released her once she touched the railing and settled beside her.

Wren balanced her weight on her palms so that she could look up at the velvet night sky. Her eyelids fluttered shut as she took in a deep breath of frigid air. The natural tones of bark and soil that radiated from Nik's jacket filled her nose with his, *admittedly*, comforting scent. She pulled the collar closer to her neck and drew in another deep breath.

Just like his scarf . . .

The thought suddenly brought back the memory of the omen in Abagail, and her back stiffened. The clicking sounds, although only in her mind, still made her shudder. Wren snapped her eyes shut tightly and fought the poisonous feeling away as best she could.

"Wren?"

"Nothing," she dismissed. "It's just cold."

Two hands appeared on either side of her to grip the railing. Nik's warmth hovered over her back as he shielded her from the chill with his body.

"Better?"

His voice buzzed in her ear, and she felt her cheeks ignite.

"Yeah," she whispered. "Thanks."

Murmurs and music drifted from the ballroom into the night-time air. They were difficult to ignore, which made it more difficult to appreciate the beauty of the blankets of untouched snow that covered the courtyard.

Without considering why she wanted to, Wren tilted her head back to rest it against Nik's chest.

He responded by dipping his head so that he could take in the scent of her hair, laced with the aroma of the flowers woven within it.

"I don't want to go back in there," she breathed.

"Then don't." Nik lifted a hand to touch one of the loose curls dangling over her shoulder. He twirled the strands of hair around with his thumb and forefinger.

Wren turned to face him, inadvertently pulling the lock of hair from his hold, and gave him a flat look. "I have to."

Nik frowned and re-collected the sunset curl. As he ran his thumb down the strands, his gaze floated over her dress. They paused at her collarbone, where the king's hand had been, before meeting hers once more. He tried to ignore the sudden flare of anger that burned at the base of his throat from seeing that sad excuse for a king touch her like that.

"Why? What would happen if you left?"

Wren brushed his hand away from her hair and scowled at him. "If I don't behave as he expects me to, he will arrest me . . . again." Her face twisted with disgust. She struggled to decide if it was a good idea to tell him about the king's threat or not.

'Let me help you.' Nik's words from when they had kissed echoed in the back of her mind. *'Share your burdens with me, and I promise, they will all become easier to carry.'*

Wren shook her head and tried to take a steadying breath.

"The king intends for me to move into the castle. He said that it is ultimately up to me, yet in the same breath threatened Lionel and Elliot if I choose not to. If I get arrested tonight, that will practically seal my fate."

"Why do you put up with that?"

The bluntness of his question drew a confused expression across her face.

"What?"

"Why are you giving in to them if all they do is ostracize and take advantage of you?" He pursed his lips and hesitated. "Why didn't you shift when you were fighting those grifters?"

Wren tried to hide her surprise but failed miserably. "I-I," she stuttered and looked anywhere but him. "If I had shifted, I would have destroyed the entire street. The storefronts are how people survive here. I can't justify that amount of risk over two grifters."

"What happens to the people here isn't your responsibility. I know that you think it is, but there is no reason for you to put yourself in danger to protect a community that doesn't want you here. They treat you like you don't belong, but that could mean that you do belong somewhere else. Somewhere better than this." Nik gently grabbed her shoulders. He leveled her with a serious look and gave a reassuring squeeze. "You are free to make your own decisions. Your duty isn't to *them*. It's to *you*."

She stared at him silently, conflict coloring every facet of her expression.

"Elliot has Lionel. He won't let anything happen to her, and deep down, they just want you to be safe and happy."

"Safe and happy?" She furrowed her brow.

Nik touched the back of his hand to her cheek, tracing the scab with his knuckle. "Leave. Stay. Do what *you* want to do."

She'd heard a similar speech from Lionel and Elliot, though they would be unintentionally trying to convince her to stay. But something in the way Nik said it strummed in the pit of her stomach.

Doubt?

"We've had this conversation before, Nik." She looked away and muttered softly. "It won't end well."

"You're convinced that you're alone, Wren. You aren't." Nik watched her purposefully. When she didn't meet his eyes, he gently took her chin in his hand.

She allowed him to turn her face to his, but she didn't lift her gaze.

"I could take you across Yu'e. Anywhere you want to go. There's so much more out there. Space for you to be free. The world outside of these walls is nothing like the one within them."

"I-I can't." She clamped her eyes shut and jerked away. "Elliot would never forgive me."

"I think she would. She knows that your hands are tied in Arnica. Under the thumb of the Guard. Under that pervert king." His fingers unconsciously tightened into a fist at his side when the image of the king's hand drifting down her chest flashed in his mind again. "There are entirely different realms with entirely different creatures that you can see and meet. There are villages in the wildlands that are home to some of the most wonderful souls. I can show you. All of it."

Wren laughed once and shook her head as she finally met his eyes. "Are you literally asking me to run away with you?"

Nik's intense gaze watched as her expression shifted from amusement to disbelief before he answered. "Yes."

Wren stared at him with wide eyes. His reply caught her so off guard that she took a step backward. Her back collided with the banister, and she gasped in surprise.

Nik followed her retreat and let his hand gravitate to her side. When she looked away, he gently grasped her chin and turned her face back to his.

"I will take you anywhere you want to go," he whispered as his hand drifted from her chin, up her jaw, and brushed the mussed curl aside. "I will protect you."

"Nik," she said breathlessly and pushed against his chest. "We can't just go—"

"Why not?" He placed his palms on her hips and watched her with an unidentifiable mixture of emotions behind his eyes. "Let me *help* you. Let me take you away."

Wren chewed on her lower lip and looked away from him.

When she gave no reply, he moved one of his hands against her back while the other remained on her hip. The hand on her back eased her closer to him as the pressure behind her palms waned. Nik tilted his chin to the side and lowered his face toward hers.

Wren watched him with conflicted eyes.

But she didn't push him away.

Instead, she let him tilt her chin up and met his stare. Wren glanced away for half a second before squeezing her eyes shut.

"Nik." When Wren murmured his name, it sent a chill down his spine. "I don't know what to say."

He smiled at her and chuckled once. "Then don't say anything."

With that, he closed the space between their lips and tightened his arms around her. He felt her hands move shyly across his chest and stifled a shudder. One found his waist, and the other hesitantly knotted into his slicked-back hair.

In that moment, Wren allowed Nik to try to convince her with his kiss.

The way his lips moved against hers felt natural, harmonious.

The way his arms surrounded her made her feel safe, not smothered.

The way he whispered her name against her lips made her shiver, and she finally let herself get lost within his depths.

CHAPTER SEVENTEEN

*"You're not necessarily supposed to believe
it. You're just supposed to believe in it."*

Daniel Wallace

NIK FOLLOWED WREN BACK INTO THE BALLROOM, HIS jacket still draped over her shoulders.

The king's footman approached them from the hallway between the veranda and the ballroom. He looked between the pair disapprovingly before turning to Wren.

"The king is waiting for you. He has returned to his throne room."

With an internal groan, she handed Nik his jacket. She gave him a conflicted look in the few seconds they watched each other. She nodded once without a word and allowed the footman to lead the way.

Wren could feel Nik's eyes on her back as she left him in the corridor.

"Ah, there you are, my darling. Come here." The king beckoned her with one hand when she entered the throne room. "Join me."

His other hand held a large goblet filled to the brim with wine as red as blood. He turned to the maid behind his throne and snapped his fingers. "Bring my lady a drink."

The woman bowed and hastily dashed from the room.

Wren silently closed the distance but stopped short a few paces away from him.

His gray eyes flicked over her a few times before narrowing. "That Nikolas fellow," he started, carefully watching her for any tells. "Is there something between you two?"

"What do you mean, Highness?"

He stood and approached her slowly. "I've just been informed that he has been seen with you. Frequently. In the marketplace, around town . . . I heard that he even followed you onto the veranda just now. You were out there, alone with him."

Wren suppressed the urge to take a deep breath and nodded. "I have met him before tonight."

"So, you *are* familiar." The king stopped before her, less than a step away. He looked larger in his fluffy golden cloak. King Reed lifted the mussed curl of hair from her shoulder and examined it closely.

"What do you know about him?" He twirled the bundle of sunset strands between his fingers. "What kind of man is he?"

The uncomfortable pause between his questions made Wren's heart race. She blinked at the question, searching for a neutral response. "He is an honest man, Highness. He is very curious about the kingdom and is intrigued by Arnica's culture, so I have seen it as my duty to show him as much as possible."

"Mm." He released the lock of hair and turned his attention to the healing wounds on her cheek and ear. He noticed a small dark spot beneath her jaw and roughly grabbed her chin.

Wren's eyes shot open wide, and her mask faltered.

The king's gaze took in the small bruise with penetrating scrutiny.

"As much as possible, hm?" He pressed a finger into the spot and glared. "You didn't allow him to *touch* you, right? That would transgress against me directly. Only with my permission is anyone allowed to touch what is mine."

The way his words dripped from his dry lips made Wren excruciatingly uncomfortable.

When she gave no response, he jerked her chin back to face him and leaned in close. His fingers bored into her jaw painfully.

"Curious men make me suspicious. Especially the honest ones." He released her chin and leveled her with a dark look. "I recommend you cease your interaction with that man. If he is responsible for blemishing my property, I will have him jailed. Tell me." He hummed as his thin fingers curled around the balls of her shoulders. "Did he do that to you?"

"No, sire," she answered quickly. "It happened when I fought the pair of grifters. They held me down by my neck. It is still healing. I covered it so that you would not be concerned."

"Hm," came his skeptical reply. "If that is the case, it's all the more reason for me to keep a closer eye on you, dear."

Wren shivered and looked away as the king returned to his throne.

The maid reentered the throne room with another goblet for Wren and a platter of finger food. The woman set the platter beside the king's throne and turned around to face Wren. With her back to the king, the maid gave her a desperate look and glanced at the wine in her hand. The maid reluctantly handed it to her and held her gaze.

Her amber eyes said it all.

"Don't drink this."

"Isabelle, fetch the commander and my advisors. I have a matter I would like to discuss."

She bowed to the king and hurried out of the room.

Reed turned to Wren with a dark look. He took a long swig of his wine, bloodred liquid dripping from the corners of his mouth, and slammed the goblet onto the table. With his eyes trained on her, he picked up a few pieces of food from the platter and took slow, agonizing steps toward her. He plucked the goblet from her hands and set it aside.

"Sit."

Wren tried to steady her erratic heart and hurried to find a seat.

The position the king stood in had forced her to make only one selection: his throne.

The tall arms of the seat were level with her shoulders, and the king's encroaching form edged her further into his trap.

He popped a morsel of food into his mouth and held the second out to Wren.

"Eat up." He licked his lips as he spoke. "It's delicious."

Wren held her hands up and looked away. "No, sire. I'm not feeling well." She wasn't lying. "Please, enjoy it yourself."

After a long moment of deliberation, the king ate the second piece.

A knock at the door brought relief from his penetrating eyes, but that relief was quickly replaced with dread as she recognized the men who entered the room.

The commander was an immensely large individual, easily over ten feet tall. He wore jet-black armor with a matching cape fastened to the pivot points of his shoulders. He had dark hair long enough to be braided behind his head. Woven throughout the black tendrils were strands of stark-white hair. His face was covered by a short beard, trimmed neatly to frame his large face and also dotted with white. It did well to hide the many scars that littered his square jaw.

The two other men that entered behind the commander were identical to each other. They each had pin-straight blond hair that covered half of their face. The only visible difference between them was the direction their hair was parted in. The capes they wore were white and billowed behind them as they moved like clouds. Each wore a long golden chain around their neck, from which hung a small box with a pale pink orb inside.

Wren knew none of their names, but she knew their faces well. And they knew hers.

The twin men regarded Wren with a shared look of disapproval and ghosted by her without a word. They rounded a large table and took their seats in two identical chairs on either side of a much larger, more intricate seat.

The commander also gave Wren a look as he passed by her, but his was one of quiet curiosity. Just as the twins had, he said nothing to her as he found his place behind the large chair. He stood with his arms at his sides and his long back straight and tall.

"What's this matter to discuss, my king?" one twin asked.

"Are you not enjoying the celebration?" asked the other.

Reed greeted the pair of blond men with a disdainful look and scowled. "I need information."

"On what, my king? Your wish is our command," the twins chimed in unison.

The king looked to Wren before answering. And when he finally did answer, he did not look away from her.

"A man. One Nikolas Briar."

Her eyes went wide, despite her best efforts to maintain a mask of apathy, and the king grinned in response.

"My king?" the twins inquired together.

"He is a vagabond visiting my kingdom. I would like to know all there is about strange men who enter my country. Especially the ones that go sniffing after what is mine." His knowing eyes watched Wren closely. "This is standard procedure, my dear." His hand reached out to brush her curl aside, and he glared at the bruise beneath her jaw. "Don't take it personally."

The commander watched their exchange without reaction. His stoic face scrutinized her the entire time the king had antagonized her, catching each time her mask slipped and each time panic lit up behind her eyes. He let a heavy breath out through his nose and folded his arms across his chest as he dipped his chin.

"You may leave, dear." King Reed's sneering grin made Wren's blood go cold. "Enjoy your evening. We will conclude this meeting on our own."

An unseasonable and bitter cold had set in overnight, chilling any flowers that had been left outside. The crowds moved more lethargically than yesterday. Luckily, the second day of the festival was usually much more casual and uneventful.

Most of the people strolling about were well-insulated by thick jackets, warm hats, and cozy gloves.

Lionel watched the early morning commotion from behind the balcony doors. He clutched a mug of steaming coffee in one gloved hand, the other tucked into his trouser pocket.

A door closing softly pulled his attention to the interior of the apartment.

Nik glanced to Lionel as he scratched the back of his mussed, ebony hair. He offered a silent nod as a greeting.

The trace sensed a change the moment their eyes met. The air around Nik seemed different than it had the last time they'd seen each other. He couldn't determine what the change was, however.

"Good morning, Nikolas." His voice was just above a whisper. "The girls are not awake yet."

"Morning, Lionel," he replied quietly. "How did you sleep?"

"Just fine, thank you. And yourself?" Lionel offered a mug and motioned to the fresh coffee.

"All right, I guess." Nik nodded and helped himself.

"Did anything happen last night?"

"Hm? Nothing really. I got to meet the king."

Lionel laughed breathlessly.

"That's not *nothing*, Nikolas." He gave another quiet but hearty laugh. "Anything else?"

Nik hesitated. "No, just what I've spent the past few days doing. Keeping an eye on Wren." His chuckle sounded as forced as it was. "She was stuck with him most of the night. That *pervert* hardly let go of her."

Lionel pursed his lips, and disapproval flashed in his eyes. "Yes, that man makes her extremely uncomfortable. Understandably so."

Nik nodded and took a careful sip from his steaming mug. He made his way to the couch and, as he passed by Wren's bedroom door, let his eyes linger on it until he sat down.

"He was watching me. I could feel it."

Lionel scoffed and shook his head. "You are likely *already* being watched, my friend. He is a very twisted yet intelligent man. Even more than that, he is very possessive of Wren."

"Yeah," Nik scoffed. "I got that impression, too."

"What about in Abagail? You only ever showed us the books, but you both had a strange aura about you when you arrived home."

"Well"—he smirked behind his coffee smugly—"our kiss probably had something to do with that."

"No." Lionel topped off his own mug and joined Nik in the more comfortable seating. "It wasn't anything like that. It was more . . ." His cerulean eyes went distant as he contemplated. "Ominous."

"Ah." Nik sat up and placed his coffee mug on the low table between them. "We were attacked by an omen."

"Why didn't you say anything?" Lionel feigned surprise. "Keeping secrets? What could you be hiding from *me*?"

"It has nothing to do with keeping secrets, Lionel. Believe me. I have been trying to help Wren figure out what she should do. I'm not sworn to secrecy." Nik offered a genuine smile. "It's out respect for her that I say nothing."

Lionel knitted his brows together and looked away. "I understand." He glanced at his oldest friend. "I'm just worried for her. She doesn't talk to me like she used to, and I have been having visions of something bad happening. But they've been so fragmented that they make no sense . . . I just hope you're not talking her into doing something reckless."

"What do you mean by reckless?"

Lionel blinked at him. "I've shown you what is coming, Nikolas. At least . . . what I know. You gave me your word that you would keep her safe."

"I have no intention of breaking my word, Lionel." Nik glanced at Wren's bedroom door again. "No matter what happens."

Lionel's shoulders relaxed enough for him to realize they had been tensed. A wave of what could only be described as tentative relief washed over him, and he nodded.

"I know, Nikolas." Lionel let out a soft laugh. "I will say, I'm surprised how quickly she took to you. Although"—he cleared his throat—"things can quickly become complicated when feelings of a certain nature get involved."

Nik's eyes narrowed. "Are you giving me *the speech*? Because, if so, don't bother. Elliot has done supremely well on that front already." Nik's lips quirked into a smirk. "I may have only met Wren a short time ago, but there is a connection. It's difficult to explain, but it isn't something fleeting . . ." He unintentionally hesitated and murmured his thoughts aloud without fully considering them. "It's a connection engrained in my soul now." He waited for Lionel to nod before continuing. "Remember why you called me here. You know her well enough to have known what would happen when she and I met."

Lionel heaved a sigh and scratched the back of his head. "You may be right, but I suppose I don't want to admit it. You are right about one thing," his tone and eyes grew serious, "she is like a daughter to me. I would hate to, but there isn't a thing I wouldn't do to protect her."

Nik stood and made his way to Lionel's side.

"I know that you love her, Lionel." He slung his arm across Lionel's shoulders and gave him a quick grin. "I will protect her, trust me."

Lionel sighed and ruffled Nik's already-messy hair.

"Tell me more about this omen."

"Wow, he really said that you're the *most* beautiful woman he'd ever seen?" Elliot sat upright with a very drowsy Jack curled into a ball on her lap.

"Yeah, it was really weird. I didn't know what to say. I thought it had been a cover for him to get me away from the king."

"No wonder he was so indifferent when he saw you in that dress for the first time. You stunned him into silence!" She hesitated and nibbled on her lip before adding, "To be fair, it's not like he's a talkative guy."

Wren shrugged. "He said that, too."

Elliot rubbed her chin as she scrunched her nose in thought. "Do you believe him?"

Wren squirmed against the headboard she had propped her back against. She adjusted the pillow behind her and tried to relax into it. "I *want* to . . ." she groaned and threw her head back. The feeling of those strong hands on her as they had kissed on the starlit veranda still lingered in her mind, buzzing under her skin. "I hate this."

Elliot playfully dumped Jack from her lap and leaned in toward Wren. "You hate that you like him?"

Wren grasped for a free pillow and pulled it up to her chin

with a scowl. "I don't want to talk about this anymore. Tell me about your night."

"Wren." The perceptive tone in Elliot's voice drew even Jack's attention. "Are you in love with him?"

"*What?* Absolutely not!" Wren's instant response gave her away. "I just met him. I-I barely know him. Not to mention he's certainly capable of being unbearable. He's an ass, and he's annoyingly persistent about trivial things . . . Not to mention you can't hear him walking half the time, so you can never tell if he's there or not. It's like he enjoys scaring me. It's infuriating."

Elliot's eyebrow quirked, and a wicked little grin began to creep across her lips. "Well . . . That may be true. But he's also tall, handsome, strong," she defended, "and honest. Plus, those green eyes aren't too bad to get lost in, either."

"Hm." Wren pursed her lips. "They unnerve me. I've never seen gold in someone's eyes like that before. Makes me feel like he sees *through* me . . . and it's almost impossible to look away." She shuddered. "Unnerving."

"Wait, gold?"

Wren looked to Elliot with a furrowed brow.

"Yeah . . . the little gold flecks in his eyes?"

"I have no idea what you're talking about. They're just green."

"I feel like you're bullshitting me . . ."

Elliot moved closer to her friend and reached out to clutch her shoulders. "Wren, I swear to you, I am not bullshitting you. His eyes don't have any gold in them." That cunning smirk found its way back onto her features. "Maybe that's just the magic between you two. Maybe he sees gold in *your* eyes, too. Perhaps you two are . . . *fated*."

"I'm going to get coffee," Wren muttered and slapped away Elliot's hands.

"Uh-huh."

"What? Do you want one? Am I to bring you breakfast in bed as well?"

Elliot blinked her adorable chocolate eyes and shook her head. "No, but I could go for a hot chocolate."

Wren groaned loudly and headed for the door. She opened it to see Lionel and Nik deep in conversation.

Both men turned to her when she entered the common area.

She dropped her eyes to her feet and scratched the back of her head.

"Good morning, Wren. Did you sleep well?" Lionel's voice was chipper, but there was something off about it. He sensed Wren's discomfort when she averted her eyes but pretended like he didn't notice.

"Good morning to you." She folded her arms across her chest.

"Is Elliot awake as well?"

"Yeah." Wren snorted as she made her way to the kitchen. She took a pair of mugs out from the cabinet and placed them on the countertop. "Is the coffee fresh?"

"Should be," Nik answered, looking over his shoulder at her. "And good morning."

Wren narrowed her eyes and fixed her gaze on her hands.

Damnit, Elliot . . . I can't even look *at him now . . .*

"Good morning," she mumbled back and quickly assembled a mug of creamy coffee and a mug of piping hot chocolate. Wren picked up the hot chocolate and made her way back into her room with a scowl. "I'll be right back."

Lionel smiled and brought his attention back to Nik. They resumed discussing the encounter with the omen in low voices.

When Wren reemerged from her room, Nik was describing when it had finally turned to dust. "I've never seen an omen like it before. It was like a chimera but somehow worse. Maybe not a chimera but similar enough in that it had been different creatures spliced together. *Three* creatures. The only time I've ever heard of something like that, it was a splice done by an alchemist."

Wren wordlessly collected her mug of coffee and leaned against the kitchen counter with her back to them.

"Interesting theory. It makes sense that a more powerful being could fuse so many creatures into one. If it is the work of sorcery or magic, it is the work of someone highly skilled. Likely a mage."

"Right. It's possible." Nik took a sip of his coffee and leaned back on the small couch. "If there is an alchemist or mage in the area, it could start to explain the disappearances, too."

Lionel hummed as he exhaled a heavy breath. "It's sickening to think that they must collect body parts in order to perform their sorcery. I think your theory is plausible. What do you think, Wren?"

Lionel's question brought her from her own thoughts, and she shrugged. She glanced at him over her shoulder before turning to face him.

"I can only guess. I'd never heard of an omen before, so I'd have nothing to compare it to." She settled into a wooden chair by the dining table. An involuntary shiver racked her shoulders at the thought of the slithering, eight-legged creature. The sound of its rattle still lingered in her mind. "Whatever it was, it was horrible."

"Where do you suppose it came from? Who knew that you were in Abagail?"

Wren took a sip of her coffee. "The armorer, innkeeper, and that imp." She paused and stared at Lionel for a moment. Something in her mind clicked, and she pursed her lips. "I wouldn't have put it past that nauseating imp to have said something about us being there. Not to mention the books that you had him find." Her eyes fluttered to Nik's general direction, then instantly away. "That clearing, the one that had no life in it, it is on the far side of the island . . . No one lives out there."

"Interesting," Lionel replied. "It's all very interesting. Too well timed to be coincidental, I think."

"I'm going to skip the second day of the festival."

Lionel and Nik looked to Wren's sudden proclamation with curious surprise.

"Aren't you on duty?"

"Yes, and I still will be. Just"—she hesitated and tightened her lips—"somewhere I can be more useful."

"What do you mean?"

"I'm going back into the clearing today. I agree that this all has to be connected. It's also an excuse to wear my new armor. I feel that my decision takes a higher priority than the *duty* of walking up and down the street all day to separate drunks and catch shoplifters and pickpockets."

Lionel nodded as he turned to Nik. "Nikolas, would you mind staying in town while Wren and I check out this aura? There are still many events that Elliot will want to see, and I would very much like to feel this aura for myself."

Nik folded his arms and looked between his friend and Wren, who seemed to be adamant to ignore him. He sighed and, finally, nodded. "Sure."

"It seems that you and Nik are really beginning to get closer."

They had made it nearly the entire journey to the clearing without Lionel bringing up the subject.

These *talks* were getting old.

"I guess so. He isn't as awful as I initially thought, so I'll give you that."

"I'm glad."

"Lionel." Wren spoke his name softly and hesitated. "I have a strange question for you."

"Oh? My favorite kind of question," he replied with a broad smile.

She nibbled on her lip before she mustered the nerve to ask it. "What color are Nik's eyes?"

Lionel paused mid-step to face her fully. "They are green. Why do you ask?"

She shook her head and looked away. "Never mind. It's stupid."

"Wren." Lionel gently collected her wrist and turned her around so he could level his eyes with hers. "Why do you ask? What color do *you* think they are?"

"They *are* green . . . But they . . . They're also g-gold." Her voice was small and quiet. "It's like there's glittering fragments of sunlight mixed in with the green."

A bittersweet smile broke onto Lionel's face, and he pulled her into an embrace. "You have no idea how relieved I am to hear that," he murmured into her hair.

"Why? What does it mean?"

"It is a good sign." Lionel nodded. "We will talk about it once we are safely home. Right now, we need to refocus on what we are doing out here. After that, I will answer all of your questions on the matter."

Wren nodded with a pout but knew that he was right.

Their conversation lulled when Wren motioned ahead of them.

"Take the footpath under the trees. The clearing is on the other side." Her voice was just above a whisper, and her pace slowed.

"I can sense it. The air is too still." Lionel strode in step, with caution to match.

"What could that mean?"

Lionel didn't want to answer.

It meant that Nik's theory was probably right.

"I'd wager it's deception sorcery."

Wren stepped behind him and followed closely.

The pair reached the point that she and Nik had stopped at.

Lionel continued without hesitation while Wren felt her nerve waver.

Something ominous was definitely here, too.

Despite the voice in her head telling her to do otherwise, Wren hurried quietly to catch up.

They walked in silence and with barely audible footfalls. As the trees grew sparce overhead, they also grew sickly in appearance. Eventually, the path they followed was surrounded on all sides by black tree carcasses that had shriveled away long ago.

Wren drew closer to Lionel and absentmindedly reached for his gloved hand.

He curled his fingers around hers tightly the moment her touch registered.

"You need to conceal your fear, Wren." His cerulean eyes dared to flicker from their path to her. He gave her hand an affectionate squeeze. "I can feel it through my glove."

She took in a heavy breath and nodded. "You're right." With a light squeeze of her own, she let go of his hand.

The air itself seemed to darken as they continued on. Although the sun was visible through withered limbs, the world beneath them was frozen in an eerie twilight.

They were both surprised when the toe of Lionel's boot kicked something.

It was a loose stone that had wandered from the edge of a pathway. The stones grew more tightly packed as the trail became a clear walkway that continued before them.

They shared a silent look, then turned back down the path with matching apprehension.

"Nikolas's instinct may be right," Lionel whispered.

Wren had to strain to hear him.

"I remember hearing about a cottage in the woods. It's been empty for years, even before I came to Black Rivers. As far as I know, most people don't even know it's out here anymore."

"What does that have to do with Nik's instincts?"

Lionel pursed his lips. "We might be dealing with sorcery after all."

The rest of their journey to the cottage was as silent as it was unsettling. Every ambient sound sent a shiver down her spine, and it took every ounce of self-control to keep her expression neutral.

Lionel led the way around a final curve of the path that opened into a flat span of stone and dirt.

A one-story structure made of cold, gray stone was nestled into the center of the area. The walls were caked in moss and littered with speckles of mushrooms in sickly shades of red, yellow, and black.

The air didn't move in the clearing. The dead trees surrounding them prevented any wind from penetrating the tangle of limbs. The pressure that the atmosphere exuded was enough to deter any trespasser alone.

Lionel's arm shot out to stop Wren mid-step.

She caught herself on his shoulder and shot him a glare.

He didn't look away from the cottage.

When Wren finally followed his eyeline, she immediately understood.

A pillar of orange smoke billowed from the chimney.

"This isn't good. We should have brought backup," Lionel's voice was uneasy.

"What's so scary about sorcery?"

"That's not just sorcery . . ." He pursed his lips and frowned. "That smoke? That's an alchemist's experiment underway no doubt. Smell the air and burn it into your mind. This is what dark sorcery smells like."

"It smells like death."

Lionel gave no response.

A piercing cry sliced the air with sharp waves of sound. Strong gusts of wind swirled around the clearing ferociously.

". . . Wren?"

"It's not me," came her shallow response.

The wind intensified as they noticed a shadow closing in on them from above. They both turned instantly to see a massive bird-like creature watching them only a few meters away.

Its large head was that of a bird, as well as its wings, but its body was long and scaled like a drake, with long talons to match. A black tail trembled violently, filling the empty air with a rattling hiss.

"A chimera," Lionel breathed.

"A personal best, if I do say so myself."

The pair was startled by a silhouette that appeared behind them.

The chimera situated itself beside the source of the voice with a few final bursts of wind from its wings as it landed. It also landed between them and the way out, blocking any route for escape.

The voice may have sounded human, but the source was not.

At least, not anymore.

His shoulders were hulking masses of stone with arms like boulders. His chest and neck were cloaked with a thick coat of tan fur. However, the man's face was his most striking feature.

A long seam that was stitched across his nose outlined a large patch of leather that covered nearly half of his face. One all-black eye watched them, the other obscured by the leather. Below the stitched lines, a human jawline came to a point at his chin, and gray, rotted teeth gleamed in the sparce light.

"Forgive the intrusion." Lionel cleared his throat and turned to face the man fully. "My name is Lionel Gibbs. I—"

"I know why you are here, boy. I know who you are." His venomous voice hissed. "What I am curious about is her."

Wren unconsciously took a step back and straight into something solid.

A colossal hand closed around her before she had time to turn around, trapping her arms against her body.

The hand was attached to a stone golem. Its body was a collection of gray-and-brown boulders held together by thick, sticky moss. It had no eyes, but a perfectly circular ring was situated mid-way between its hulking shoulders. The perfectly round hole went completely through the widest part of its body. A single stone floated in the center of the void and shifted in place in the same way that an eye would in its socket.

"Hey! Let me go!" Wren struggled hopelessly to get free. Her eyes looked to Lionel desperately. "Lionel!"

The golem lifted her from the ground and brought her to the half-faced man. It lowered her just enough for the tips of her toes to brush the frozen earth.

The alchemist grinned and cackled as he hobbled toward her. He leaned in close to take her in with his single eye. While within close vicinity, he took a long, exaggerated sniff of her hair.

"Splendid." His smile made Wren's stomach turn. "I wasn't expecting you so soon, girl. My preparations aren't quite ready. But I can keep you until I'm ready to use you." He roughly patted her cheek with a hard palm. His eye turned to Lionel with an insidious grin. "I would offer to pay you for delivering her to me, but I have no intention of letting you live."

Wren fervently struggled in the golem's hold. She tried to think of any way to get free, but only one answer came into her mind. She quickly looked between Lionel and the alchemist before squeezing her eyes shut tightly.

I have seen monsters. And I see you.

She forced herself to ignore the salty stinging behind her eyes.

You are what is holding you back from figuring out just how much you are capable of doing!

The reaper's baritone voice echoed in her mind and welled inside of her chest.

You are a chained dog in Black Rivers. Do you even know what you can do as a spell?

The still wind suddenly howled with a petrifyingly cold fervor. It twisted in tight rings around the clearing, picking up any loose stones and clumps of ice from up off of the ground. They were quickly joined by larger tree limbs and ice sheets in the growing vortex.

The chimera stirred and shuffled its wings to sidestep a sizable trunk that had lifted from the ground behind it.

"Wren, no," Lionel felt himself whisper.

The air suddenly went still, but any objects it had kicked up remained suspended.

Wren's eyes were still clamped shut tightly. Her brows were furrowed and lips pursed when she drew in a loud, sharp breath. In the next instant, her eyes shot open.

The full fury of the wind erupted tenfold. Any debris it had collected pelted into the golem's back, aimed directly for the circular void in its center.

After an unrelenting onslaught of stones, snow, ice, and frozen tree limbs had irritated it enough, the hand released her in order to shield its eye.

Wren hit the ground with a heavy *thud* and scrambled to her feet.

The alchemist was watching her closely with a wide grin beneath that hideous seam.

The chimera spread its wings out and lifted from the ground in a single beat.

Wren turned to face the beast circling above her and narrowed her eyes.

The once-hazel irises were now a piercing silver. The whites of her eyes had begun to darken and gray, making the growing rings of silver even more pronounced. Her sunset hair had become wild in the twisting air and danced like flames in the wind around her.

Wren slowly lowered to a crouch until the knuckles of her left hand touched the frozen ground. She gave no indication of moving, even when the chimera made the decision to strike first.

It turned in a tight circle easily from its wide wings and caught the wind in order to speed toward her, releasing a loud shriek as it dove.

Wren hung her head and drew in another deep breath.

I have seen monsters. And I see you.

Wren's shoulders lurched forward, and she curled into a ball. A loud scream pulled itself from her lungs when searing pain flooded her nerves. Her skin felt as if the blood was boiling beneath its surface, and her lungs struggled to breathe through whatever they were filling with.

She gasped hoarsely before she let out another shrill scream.

The bones of her spine flared outward and sent a boiling-hot pain throughout her entire body. They cracked and twisted inside of her loudly as they shifted into new positions. Her skin stiffened as it gradually turned to black scales that formed and hardened over one another.

The worst cry soon followed.

Four giant, feathered wings ripped away from her back, each tendril coated with bright red blood and identical to the color of her sunset hair.

Wren threw her head back and cried out while a clawed foot slammed into the ground. Her face had morphed into that of something resembling a dragon, but her new form still retained the expressiveness of her human form. Sharp, backward-pointing teeth gleamed from her blue-black lips that were curled into a furious snarl.

The chimera had stopped mid-swoop as it watched her change.

The spell had grown large enough that the top of the single-floor cottage only reached to her shoulders. She had a mane of red-and-orange plumage surrounding her face that followed the length of her elongated neck. The top half of her body was covered with razor-sharp feathers, while the bottom half was covered with rigid, blue-black scales. Her eyes were a glimmering shade of silver with the same blinding brilliance as light off of water's surface. Four clawed feet planted her firmly on the ground as each pair of wings unfurled. Her long tail flicked behind her and was tipped with a matching set of four miniature sunset wings.

The wind began to pick back up as the pain of her transformation subsided, and she refocused her attention.

Lionel watched on in horror. Each scream that had ripped its way out of her felt like a dagger to his heart. The depth of their relationship made it so that he felt her pain right alongside her. His heart broke when her silver eyes met his and moved on without a sliver of recognition.

She turned to the alchemist and let loose a deep, threatening growl.

His eye was wide with an obvious mixture of terror, confusion, and twisted glee.

Wren didn't even try to hold back the second growl that rumbled in her chest. As soon as the sound reached the top of her throat, it became a wild roar. With sheer disregard for the circling chimera overhead, she rushed at the mutated man.

Curved claws caught her in the shoulder and knocked her back to the ground. Once she was able to collect herself, a cold grip closed on her tail and ripped her backward.

The golem held her firmly while the chimera moved in for a second strike. It was able to land a few lashes of its talons along her belly and side, but to no effect against her thick scales.

Lionel jumped when he felt an inexplicably strong hand close on his bicep. He had been watching Wren and kicked himself for not paying close enough attention to the other man.

"Why don't we go play while my pets keep yours busy?"

The alchemist didn't allow Lionel a chance to protest before he shoved a sweet-smelling cloth into his face.

Lionel's knees buckled, and everything went dark. Though he could not see, the last sounds he heard were the raw, animalistic cries of Wren's fury.

CHAPTER EIGHTEEN

"If you want to see a miracle, be the miracle."

Morgan Freeman

W REN HASN'T BROUGHT UP LEAVING LATELY." Elliot's observation warranted an inquisitive glance from Nik, who walked beside her.

"Oh?"

They passed by stands of flowers with petals still coated with thick, opaque frost. Any flower that had made it through the night was already wilting inside of an icy sarcophagus.

"I imagine that can only mean one of two things," she mused. "Either way, I'd wager that she's made her decision."

"And what do you think that is?"

Elliot stopped in her tracks and turned to face him. "What do *you* think she's decided?"

Nik shrugged one shoulder and paused when she did. "I don't know. She can be hard to read sometimes."

"Sometimes?" Elliot's chortle echoed in the cold air. "Try always. I swear, she keeps more to herself than Lionel does."

"Well, he *did* raise her."

Elliot smirked at him, though it didn't reach her eyes. "I think she's going to bolt."

He watched her closely with a raised brow. "Why do you say that?"

"Because she has *you* now."

"Me?"

She pursed her lips and looked at him blankly. "You're her ticket out of here. Whether she'd admit it or not, she's always intended to get out of Black Rivers. I know that she adores Lionel, Jack, and me, but it's not enough to keep her around anymore. Not when the rest of her life is nothing short of abuse . . . Plus," she added with reserve, "I don't think Lionel would have ever let her go alone."

"I think Lionel underestimates her."

This time it was Elliot's turn to look at him curiously.

"Wren is definitely trouble, that's without question." The corner of Nik's mouth quirked into a small smile as he spoke. "Her temper and wit do her no favors, and her demeanor alienates her in many ways . . . But she doesn't give up. And she's stronger than she knows."

"Hm," Elliot hummed and tapped her chin. "None of what you said is wrong, but it's a big world out there, and she's . . . well, you said it. Trouble."

"You're trouble, too."

She giggled and nodded. "You got me there."

The music throughout the festival was lively, albeit muted by the cold day.

Elliot tugged on Nik's coat sleeve and pointed down an alleyway. "There's a really cool jewelry stand on the next street over that I spotted yesterday. I can point out things I know she'd like. That's a shortcut we can use."

Nik shook his head but allowed himself to be pulled along.

The crowd on the other end of the alley was significantly larger than where they had come from. He extended his arm to guide Elliot closely behind him.

She snorted once and pushed his arm away. "I'm fine, relax. Come on." She turned before Nik had finished surveying the crowd. "It's this way."

They walked for a short while through the dense crowd. Every so often, Elliot would hurry ahead to make sure they were still heading the right way. When she did, she'd smile and wait for Nik to catch up to her.

His large frame made it more challenging to move amongst the people as fluidly as she could. For being so small, the little human was agile.

Her mop of curls bounced as she hastened her pace to look ahead again.

Although Nik did his best to keep up with her, she was persistent.

"Nik, this wa—"

His eyes shot open wide, and he rushed forward, pushing through the crowd carelessly. He could pick up a few of the high-pitched sounds that she made trying to fend off whoever was assailing her, though all of them were heavily muffled.

Nik turned a corner just in time to see Elliot being pulled into the shadows of an alley across the street. He hurried after her, shoving anyone in his way.

Once he was in the alley she'd vanished into, he broke into a sprint. Luckily, the alley had only one way to go.

At the sound of footsteps ahead of him, his pace hastened.

When he rounded the next corner, Nik had to screech to a stop.

Brock stood before him, wearing a large smile on his face and blocking his way.

"Hiya pretty-boy," he hummed. When sober, he was much easier to understand. "Didn't expect ya ta be on babysittin' duty. Figured, with the warden gone, she's fair game."

"What are you talking about?"

"Eh? The girl." He cracked his knuckles loudly. "Birdie didn't show up fer work today. Figured she'd be with the girl. My guys must notta noticed ya out with 'er." The brute of a man stretched his arms across his chest. "I ain't complainin' tho'. Been wantin' ta beat the shit outta ya since I firs' saw ya."

"The feeling is mutual."

Brock glowered and cracked his knuckles purposefully.

Nik lowered himself to a fight-ready stance. His eyes remained set on the hulking man in his way.

Brock didn't wait for Nik to move before he rushed him. He caught Nik's shoulders with a wide swing that vaulted him into the stone wall of the narrow alley. Brock was on top of him instantly with two fistfuls of Nik's jacket and slammed him into the wall a second time.

Brock smashed his skull into the top of Nik's head and dropped him to the ground.

Nik shook his head as he stood. He ignored the sting on his crown and stared the man down.

"I'm warning you now." His voice was calm and level, but his eyes flared. "If you continue, I will not let you live."

"Ooo, scary," Brock feigned. "I'd like ta see ya try."

"So be it."

A heavy aura filled the small space in the blink of an eye and smashed into Brock's chest. The invisible force bent him over, and he coughed violently before lifting his head to glare at Nik.

"Yer like 'er," he sputtered and straightened. "Yer an enchanted."

Nik shook his head.

"No. I'm cursed."

Finished with talking, the reaper extended his right hand out before him, palm down. Flashes and flickers of purple emanated around his hand and gradually started to churn in tight loops beneath it. A black object began to materialize beneath his open palm, the flickers and flashes quickly becoming electric.

The length of his scythe formed in seconds. His skeletal hand grasped it tightly, and Nik spun it to rest at his side. The weapon was taller than him, with a broad and sharp blade curling from its tip.

Without another word, it was Nik's turn to rush Brock.

Brock took two wide swings of the blade to the shoulder and chest before he resigned himself to the ground. He clutched his bleeding limb tightly and begrudgingly met Nik's eyes.

"I ain't tellin' ya where she is." He coughed and pushed himself to a sitting position. "So ya might as well kill me."

Nik approached slowly and slammed the blunt end of his scythe into his gushing shoulder.

"I already told you that I was planning on it. Regardless of what information you provide."

He lifted his blade, watching as the fear of realization flooded into Brock's bloodshot eyes.

The flicker that exists in every set of eyes when they finally face death shone in his; no matter the pride of the host, the eyes *always* begged for mercy.

Before Brock had the chance to take his next breath, Nik swung his scythe and filled the narrow alleyway with absolute silence.

Lionel's vision struggled to focus through hazy waves of confusion and nausea. He tried to touch the throbbing spot behind his eyes but found his arms held fast to his sides. He looked down to see five leather straps that fastened him to a painfully cold and flat surface. He squeezed his eyes shut and tried to even his erratic breathing.

The last thing he remembered was being outside. Wren's scream echoed in the back of his mind, and he winced.

"Wren!"

Lionel tried to move again, his consciousness finally catching up with him.

"Ah, you are already awake. Hm, must have made that last batch too weak." A gangly hand examined the cloth beside Lionel's head on the table. The alchemist made his way around the table in the center of the small room.

As Lionel's eyes followed him, he slowly understood where he was. "Who are you?" His voice was strained, stinging his throat as he spoke.

The single all-black eye pinned Lionel and made the breath freeze in his chest. The alchemist chuckled and shrugged as a sickening smile began to split his cracked lips. "I suppose you at least deserve to know the name of the man who will end your life."

Lionel's eyes widened, and he had yet to recover his breath.

"I was once called Ubel." That grin widened. "Surnames are unimportant. Now, be silent. Can't have you distracting me."

Glimmering silver tools were laid out beside his arm, and a bright light hung above him. The floor of the room was black and hard. And it reeked of blood.

There was a plethora of clear glass jars in every imaginable shape and size that lined each and every wall around them. Most of the jars were organized categorically.

By body parts.

When Lionel's eyes turned back to the alchemist, to Ubel, the looming mutant was directly beside him.

It was now that he realized the leather patch on his face had been removed, revealing the horribly scarred flesh beneath it. The eyeless socket seemed to peer straight through him.

"That potion was supposed to keep you asleep for the procedure," he hummed through rotten teeth. "I wasn't going to kill you right away in case I need both, but I'm not making another batch just for you. Plus"—his large arm reached for one of the gleaming tools—"if the procedure doesn't kill you, the pain after should do the trick. If that happens, I'll just take both."

Lionel could hear muffled cries outside and thought only of Wren. Nothing Ubel said made any sense.

"Now, now." The alchemist grabbed Lionel's chin with sharp nails. "If you move during the procedure, you'll ruin that lovely eye for both of us."

"What?" His question escaped before he was even aware he'd formed it.

The cackle that followed chilled his blood to ice.

"Your eye, boy. I'm going to take it and put it here." He giddily gestured to his deformed face. "Lucky me, they are my favorite shade of blue."

The alchemist pulled a small rope beneath the cold table that forced his head to slam down against the hard surface. The cord was stretched across his forehead and dug roughly into his skin.

Lionel squeezed his eyes shut, but it did nothing to deter the deranged man.

He pulled on the skin above and below Lionel's eye to force the lid open.

Cold metal touched the top of his cheek and grazed along the bridge of his nose. He tried to close his eye, or at least jerk his head away, but the hold on him was too great and his body was still half-numb from whatever was on that cloth.

Lionel felt cold pressure against his face and nose before a sickening *snap* silenced Ubel's maniacal laughter.

Hot pain followed and engulfed his entire body.

The howl that exploded from him shook the glass windows and threw his already-overloaded senses into chaos.

WREN WAS ABLE TO FREE HER TAIL FROM THE GOLEM'S HOLD AND lashed out. Her claw caught hold of a small gap between two large boulders that helped to form its chest. A low growl rippled through her, and she kicked out as hard as she could.

The curved claw successfully dislodged the two boulders. With the enchantment broken, the rest of the rocks fell into a shapeless heap in the snow.

She instantly turned her attention back to the winged chimera.

The creature was wise to keep a distance between them, but with its comrade defeated, there was no evading the spell's silver gaze.

Her wings shuffled against her back, and her claws rustled into the frozen earth. Her knees and muscles relaxed as she readied herself for takeoff.

But she froze when a piercing scream emanated from the cottage.

Lionel!

She looked to where he had been standing, only to find him gone. Her heart lurched in her chest, and she broke into a gallop toward the cottage, disregarding the circling beast overhead. Her four legs hastened against the ground, and her wings flapped instinctively, propelling her faster and farther with every beat.

Before Wren had the chance to get airborne, sharp talons grabbed the base of one of her wings with both claws.

The chimera lifted her into the air briefly before it slammed her back into the ground.

Wren growled and pushed herself to stand. Now that she was much closer to the cottage, she could clearly hear Lionel's broken voice.

Fury boiled over inside of her.

Without another moment's hesitation, she lunged at the chimera. Wren charged forward with her teeth bared and embedded them into the feathered neck of the creature. When she knew that her hold was sufficient, her jaw snapped shut.

Wren rammed the chimera into the ground and spit out a mouthful of the creature's severed flesh.

It cried out as it writhed across the sparce snow, staining a shocking area around it a hot, sickening red.

She narrowed her eyes and turned to run full speed toward the cottage.

Toward Lionel.

Rearing up on her hind legs, Wren was easily taller than the structure. She heaved her weight upward with the aid of her four wings and gauged the distance above the cottage.

With three thoughtful pumps of her wings, she pivoted and dove.

Her scaled body slammed into the stone with such force that even rock submitted to her.

The alchemist stood, frozen in awe, with a cerulean-blue eyeball in his right hand.

Wren's silver gaze shifted to Lionel.

Blood poured out of his eye socket and down his face. It matted in his golden hair and the scruff of his stubble. He was strapped to a metal slab that was smeared with even more blood. His head rocked limply from side to side, lost in a delirium of overwhelming pain.

Wren growled darkly and approached the alchemist. She looked at the eyeball in his hand and took another menacing step forward.

The reverberating rumble seemed to have paralyzed the hideous man.

She closed in and snarled, knocking him away and into a shattered wall that was already littered with broken shards of glass. The severed limbs that had once been in the now-broken jars filled the area around him enough to trap him beneath them.

She turned her attention to Lionel the instant the alchemist's body hit the ground.

He was unresponsive but breathing.

Her sharp claws struggled with the tightly bound leather straps for fear of cutting him unintentionally.

Wren half-registered the sound of movement in the glass as she gathered Lionel into her front legs. Her immense wings flexed behind her in two synchronized pairs and beat once. They ascended quickly as each wing pumped in perfect timing with the other three.

Wren faintly heard the alchemist calling after them as she rushed away.

She pushed as much air as her wings could manage. Panic and fear crept deeper into her mind every time she forced herself to examine Lionel.

With every painful look, she willed herself to fly faster.

Nik sat in the empty apartment with his head in his hands.

He'd searched every building, event booth, and home that he could find. Not one trace of Elliot was to be found, even as night had moved in.

Jack perched himself on the table, facing Nik. He let out a soft meow and hopped to sit beside him. The stark-white cat pressed his face against Nik's arm affectionately and purred.

The door downstairs slammed shut and jostled Nik to his feet.

His large hands held Jack upright while he stared in the direction of the stairs.

The cat wiggled and mewed at the sound, itching to be put down.

"Nik? Nik, are you here?"

Wren's frantic voice rocked him from his stupor.

"*Fuck!* Nik, please, if you're here"—her voice cracked with a sob—"I need help!"

Nik dropped Jack, who landed on all fours with a huff, and hurtled toward the stairs.

Nothing could prepare him for what waited at the bottom.

Lionel was soaked in blood and barely moving. His head hung low at his shoulders, and his face was obscured by matted, blond curls. While he was naturally fair-skinned, the pallid shade of blue he now wore made Nik's chest tighten.

Wren shuffled him off from her shoulder as gently as she could. But she was exhausted under the weight of his limp body as she struggled to ease him down. A burning sensation spurned on her shoulders and back, and she tried not to wince.

They were practically crumpled, bloody heaps on the floor.

Wren wore a rough canvas sack that she'd found in the trash near the outskirts of the city. She was covered in smears of blood, making her bloodstains indistinguishable from Lionel's.

"Please," Wren breathed as she slouched against the floor. "I can't carry him anymore."

Nik wordlessly lifted Lionel and brought him upstairs. After settling him into the couch and checking his vitals, he hurried back to Wren.

She had forced herself to stand, using the short table as an anchor. Her knees trembled beneath her own weight as she tried to take a step.

With a heavy sigh, Nik looped his arms around her and lifted her against his chest. He tried to ignore her hiss of pain when his hand touched the center of her back and adjusted his arm lower. He carried her up the stairs to the mustard-colored chair and eased her into it. Nik cupped her face with his palm and carefully turned it to look at him.

"What happened, Wren? What happened to Lionel?"

She opened her mouth to speak, but no words came out. Her eyes drifted to Lionel, and a sob silenced her. She couldn't hold back a pitiful moan when her heart throbbed painfully.

"I couldn't save him in time," she managed between tears. "I couldn't do it. I failed. I failed *again!*" Wren shook her head violently. "I failed him," she choked out as she wiped salt and blood from her eyes with the crook of her elbow.

Nik knitted his brows together as he frowned. He looked to his friend and felt a similar pang in his chest.

"Let me take a closer look at him." He had to force himself to look away from Lionel's face, away from his eye. "Just stay right here, okay? Try to calm down."

Nik lifted Lionel's head to get a better look at where his eye had been and sighed heavily. With a great deal of reluctance, he lifted his free hand to hover just above Lionel's eye socket.

A soft purple glow emanated from his palm with a gentle hum.

The silence in the room was unbreakable until Nik shifted his friend into a more comfortable resting position.

Lionel groaned loudly and winced. His head rolled against the couch, and he let out two quiet whimpers.

Another knot welled in Wren's chest. She let out a whimper of her own when it twisted around her heart.

"The good news is that he isn't going to die from this . . ." Nik pressed his fingers into his eyes for a brief moment before he was able to look to Wren. "He's in rough shape, but medicine and rest will help. What *happened?*"

"An alchemist." Her voice was still gruff and raw. "The aura that we felt was an alchemist's deception sorcery. He lives i-in the woods. In a cabin. He took Lionel's eye." Tears welled again, and she shook her head. "I couldn't stop him in time, Nik. I couldn't do *anything.*"

Nik stood with his hands clenched into tight fists at his sides. He looked her over, taking in her full appearance for the first time.

She was haggard and bleeding. Bleeding from everywhere. Spots on her shoulders and legs seemed to be bleeding for no apparent reason. In fact, the only physical wounds he saw were a decently sized slice around one shoulder, and something peculiar on her back.

The sack she wore fit her poorly, but the dip in the back allowed him to see the tips of four wide wounds that were just beginning to scab over. The sack was so saturated with blood that parts of it clung to her body.

"Why are you wearing a potato sack? Where are your clothes?"

"Gone." Wren dropped her head to her hands. "Same with my armor. And my green coat."

"*Why?*"

She hesitantly met his eyes.

For the first time since her return, he noticed her irises.

There was no trace of hazel. In their place were two bright silver circles that nearly vanished against the whites of her eyes.

"I shifted. *All* of the way." Wren slammed her clenched fists into the mustard-colored chair. "I couldn't control myself, and I became that monster again. I was too busy fighting off his creatures. I didn't even see Lionel get taken."

"Is that where you got this?" He gestured to her shoulder.

Wren sighed. "Yeah, I took a talon to the shoulder. It grabbed for my wings, but it just clipped me."

"It?"

"Another chimera. This one was a birdlike drake thing," she murmured.

Nik was silent.

They both listened to the sound of Lionel's shallow breathing.

"I need to take a look at your wounds."

Wren shook her head and refused to meet his eyes. "No, Elliot should do it." She looked up from the floor and scanned the room. "Where is Elliot?"

CHAPTER NINETEEN

WHERE IS ELLIOT?"

The question hung in the air, unanswered.

Wren's eyes narrowed, and her hands dropped to her lap.

"Nik?"

He looked away from her with a deep frown darkening his face.

"She disappeared at the festival. One second, she was right in front of me, the next she was gone."

Wren leapt from the chair at him. Fresh, hot tears burned her eyes and cheeks as they streamed down her blood-covered face. The burning pain along her shoulders and back were overshadowed by the new rage that stewed inside of her stomach.

"You said you would protect her! Nik, where did she go? What happened?"

Nik held her by her uninjured shoulder but kept her at an arm's length. "Brock's goons took her," he replied evenly. "I looked for her everywhere. I only got back minutes before you." His thumb rubbed into her shoulder. "We are going to find her, Wren. Don't think that they'll get away with this."

She pushed his hand away roughly. Her silver eyes were narrowed dangerously as she stepped away from him.

He followed her retreat.

"Get away from me," she hissed. "I'm going back to look for her." Her furious eyes followed Nik as he slowly moved closer. She continued to step away from him, each one only compounding her anger.

Nik's hand caught her elbow and brought her against his chest. He wrapped his arms around her and held her close.

She instinctually responded by breaking free from him and smashing her palms against his chest.

Her enraged strength managed to put a considerable space between them. Wren's hands trembled at her sides as she stared at him silently, the coldness of her gaze radiating. She breathed heavily as she tried to rein in her emotions.

If Elliot was here, she would tell me to calm down and regain control.

Wren's back went rigid. She shook her head and turned away from Nik.

The sound of Elliot's voice reverberated in her mind with encouraging words and unexpected wisdom that the curly-haired human could somehow always come up with.

That did it.

Wren collapsed to the floor in tears. Her unrestrained sobs shook her body viciously. She cupped her hands around her elbows and rocked forward.

Strong arms collected her from the floor and cradled her against a warm chest.

"We will find her, Wren," Nik soothed, rubbing the crown of her head with his thumb. "We need to clean you up so that you can rest first."

"I can't rest," she protested weakly. "I have to find her *now*."

"Stop it. You have to take care of yourself." He moved her away, still holding her by the shoulder to level his stare into hers. "If you don't, you'll be in no shape to help her."

She looked at her bare feet with a choked whimper.

Nik lifted her head with a gentle finger under chin and frowned. "Let me take a look at your back."

"No!" She withdrew from him so fast that she stumbled to the floor. "I'm fine!"

"You are *not* fine!" He raised his voice above hers. "You are bleeding from everywhere, and I have to see what condition you are in!" Nik clenched his hands at his sides. He took a long, deep breath and returned his voice to its normal volume. "Wren, please. For *once*, listen to me."

Although Wren glared at him, hot tears still ran down her cheeks. She tightened her lips and turned away from him. From her sitting position, she drew the sack up toward her shoulders. She was mindful to keep the front of her body covered and dropped her head in shame.

Nik crouched behind her and stared in bewilderment.

The four wounds were each as long as his hand. They were staggered with the two closest to her shoulders relatively close together, whereas the lower two were wider apart and near the bottom of her ribs.

A few tiny feathers poked out of the clotting blood and pointed in every direction.

Nik reached to pull one out of a part of the wound that hadn't quite stopped bleeding yet.

"Ah!" He withdrew his hand to examine his thumb and forefinger. A small bubble of blood seeped up between the papercut-like wounds. "It's sharp," he murmured, mostly to himself.

He couldn't help but notice a wide scar just below her left shoulder blade. It had fully healed, but the pale-pinkish color gave him the impression that it wasn't that old.

"Does it look as bad as it feels?"

"Um." Nik hesitated and carefully touched her skin.

She shivered violently and cast a dark look at him from over her shoulder.

"Sorry." He tried to smile. "But yes. They look bad."

"Great."

Nik gathered a small handful of the sack and re-covered Wren's back. "Let me see your shoulder."

"Oh, please."

"Wren."

She glared at his hands, not daring to meet his eyes.

"Show me."

"Fine! Gods," she mumbled and tugged her right arm out of the makeshift sleeve of the beaten sack.

Nik gently grabbed her arm and lifted it to be parallel with the ground. As he examined it closely, he noticed that the curve of the wound was more than just getting *clipped*.

"This one is still bleeding."

"It doesn't feel great when you hold it like that, either."

"Don't be shitty. I'm just trying to help."

Wren sighed and closed her eyes. "I know. I'm sorry." She relaxed her arm in his hold so that he could move it around more comfortably.

"This one is pretty deep." Her lack of response made him growl, and he stood abruptly. "Stay here. I'm getting stuff to clean those out."

"Don't bother." She slowly worked her way back onto her feet and took an unsteady step away from him. "I'm going to take a shower. I'll clean them out then."

He pursed his lips and rolled his eyes. "Fine. Don't cut yourself on your stupid feathers." With that said, he turned away from her and attended to Lionel instead.

No matter how hot she made the water, her body felt frozen. She had long since washed the blood from her hair and skin, but she still felt unclean.

Numb hands turned the spigot off, and the faucet gurgled to a stop.

Wren stood still in the steam until the last of the heat it retained vanished. She listlessly dried and dressed into a pair of insulated pants and a long-sleeved tunic. She winced when the tunic brushed over the cleaned and half-heartedly wrapped wounds on her shoulder and back. Wren dried her hair and groaned aloud. She dropped to the edge of her bed while she rubbed her towel against her scalp. Her hand suddenly stilled, and her silver eyes went wide.

The sound of Lionel's panicked voice still rang in her mind as though she was locked inside of an echo chamber. It sent a shiver up her spine, followed closely by a jolt of pain.

Wren covered her face with a pillow and let out a single sob. She remained in a slouched position with the pillow against her face and unwillingly began to weep.

Flashes of memories from her other form appeared in waves. The pain of her transformation was at the forefront of her mind and made it difficult for her to find her composure as the last few hours replayed behind her eyelids.

She could still feel the acidic burn of boiling blood beneath her skin and tried to ignore the persisting tremor of her hands.

While most of the scales sloughed from her body as her size disintegrated, many made the painful return to human flesh with an agonizing, lingering sensation. Her back hurt; the four spots that her wings had ripped open twinged with pain and recollection each time she moved.

The sight of Lionel strapped to the metal slab smacked her across the face, and the pillow slipped from her hands.

He didn't deserve that . . .

His golden hair had become matted with red-black blood staining the curls. His delirious mumbles reverberated in her mind and made her chest ache.

Wren took a deep breath and forced herself to sit upright. Her hands clutched the edge of the bed, and she glowered at the closed door. Her next thought was the sickening grin of the alchemist. His repulsive laughter as he held what wasn't his.

I'll kill him.

With another heavy sigh, she forced herself to stand and finally faced the mirror in the bathroom. She looked about as bad as she expected to and shook her head. She turned to exit her room but paused at the door, her hand hovering over the knob. Wren steeled herself with a scowl and clicked it open.

There was no sound in the common area.

She pushed her door the rest of the way open and walked out of her room. She caught sight of the vacant couch, now stained with Lionel's blood, and frowned. Wren sighed and instinctually made a pot of coffee while trying to avoid looking at anything that would remind her of Elliot's absence or of Lionel's weakened state.

Jack mewed from the table, drawing Wren's silver eyes from her hands.

She started a kettle and laid out paper and loose-leaf tobacco on the counter.

The stark-white cat made a soft sound as he hopped up to sit in front of her on the surface. His slate eyes stared at her, full of love. A loud purr emanated from his chest when she reached to pet him. His head rolled affectionately in her palm in response to the scratches she gave his chin.

"Don't worry, Jack," Wren whispered. "We *will* find her. And I'll kill each and every person involved."

He peeked at her before he let out a meow of approval.

While the kettle boiled, Wren rolled herself a cigarette and found her place against the glass door. Her eyes were locked on the dark outside as though Elliot would appear by sheer force of will. Her arms wrapped tightly around her chest, which painfully tugged at the scabbing wounds on her back and shoulder. She ignored it as best she could and rolled the cigarette between her thumb and fingers.

The chill from the glass pressed against her skin, but she couldn't be bothered to notice it.

The sound of a wooden door opening and closing broke her from her trance.

Nik walked from Lionel's room and silently regarded Wren with a small nod. He was also dressed in fresh, comfortable clothes with slicked back, still-wet hair.

"He's resting now. The bleeding has stopped, and there's no sign of infection."

Wren pursed her lips and turned to the glass.

"This is all so messed up," she muttered darkly and lifted the rolled tobacco to her lips.

"I know." As Nik walked by the kitchen, he noticed the kettle. "*Coffee?* You really should get some sleep."

"How can I sleep?" She kept her back to him. "I need to be out there. I need to be looking for her." Her voice lowered to below a whisper. "Every minute I'm here is another one that she's scared and alone."

Nik gently grasped her hands and turned her away from the glass to face him. He tried to offer an understanding smile.

The motion caused the roll of paper to fall from her lips and tumble to the floor.

"I know, Wren. I know." His golden-green eyes took her in. He looked to the floor and glared at the cigarette. "I don't expect you to forgive me for this. I still haven't."

He flinched when something cool touched his cheek, and he lifted his gaze to see her silver eyes watching him.

Her cold thumb brushed across his face once. After a brief pause, Wren shook her head slowly.

"I understand." Her voice cut short from a welt of emotion balling in her chest. "It isn't your fault. I know that you did your best." She lifted her hand so that she could brush her knuckles gently along the hint of new growth across his cheeks.

He watched her in bewilderment as she caressed his face. Nik couldn't help but notice the redness around her eyes, as well as the shadows that darkened the space beneath them.

"Your stubble is already coming back," Wren unconsciously whispered in the quiet.

Nik lifted a hand and cupped the side of her face with his palm. He turned it over to trace the scab along her cheekbone with the tip of his fingernail. With a sigh, he brushed a stray lock of hair behind her ear and touched the nearly healed scab that curved around its helix.

"You keep looking at that." She turned to face the other way and pulled his hand back. "I know that it's hideous, but you're making me self-conscious about it."

Nik gently took her chin with his thumb and forefinger and brought her eyes back to his. "There is nothing about you that is hideous, Wren. Not even your temper." Nik looked away briefly and recaptured her gaze with a small smirk. "Okay, maybe *sometimes* your temper."

She couldn't stop her own small smirk that twitched at the corner of her mouth. However, it did not linger for long before her face slipped back into an unfeeling mask. "Okay, so then why do you keep looking?"

Nik's eyebrows knitted together in uncertainty. He pursed his lips and wordlessly pulled Wren against him in a careful embrace. He was mindful of the state of her back as he squeezed her. "I regret looking every time I see it." His baritone voice rumbled in his chest against her ear.

"What do you mean? That's not really better than thinking it's ugly."

"What I mean is"—he paused and sighed—"that every time I look at it, I regret not killing Honorah and Brock in the middle of the street. Then and there."

Wren chuckled once and shook her head. "Let me go so I can get some coffee."

Nik's arms tightened. "No."

"Nik, stop playing and let go."

Instead of listening, he buried his nose in her damp hair. The floral scent of her soap was overwhelming. "I'm not letting you go, Wren." His voice was so close to her ear that it made a jolt shoot down her spine. "At least not until you are asleep."

"I already told you. I won't sleep even if I try to."

Without another word, Nik lifted her into his arms and made his way to her open bedroom door.

"Come on, Nik. Put me down."

Nik finally obliged when he reached her bed. Instead of setting her down, he propped one knee onto the mattress and heaved them both onto the bed.

With an easy twist of his waist, they fell into the folds of her blankets and landed in the same position that he carried her in. He glanced down his chest at her with a sad expression.

"Try to sleep, Wren. If I have to stay with you the entire night, I will. You *need* to rest," his low voice whispered. He cupped the back of her neck and pressed a soft kiss against her forehead.

She shook her head and pushed her hands against his chest to move away.

"No, Nik. We need to come up with a plan to get Elliot back. I'll sleep when she's home safe."

He tightened his lips and closed his hands around her wrists. With a gentle tug, he brought her crashing down on top of him.

Wren stared at him with wide eyes. She had fallen so far up his torso that she'd landed with her face only a few inches from his. A wild blush erupted across her cheeks, and she hurriedly pushed back against the mattress.

His hands released her wrists and drifted to her waist. Nik eased her back down for a final time and brought her face to his.

Wren stared at him, a deep confliction battling behind her eyes while they were fixed on his.

"I'm sorry that I got mad," he murmured softly. "I'm thankful that you're safe." Nik glanced to her lips for just a moment before he consumed them.

Morning light broke into Wren's room like a search light. She stirred and blinked herself awake, wondering when she'd fallen asleep.

Wren rubbed her eyes, still sore and crusted from crying. She moved to sit up but was stopped by something heavy. Confused, she looked down at her waist to see an arm wrapped securely around it. She followed it to see the sleeping form behind her.

Nik's eyes were closed lightly. His breathing was slow and even through parted lips.

She felt a blush flood her face as flashes of last night returned to her.

They had kissed until her until exhaustion finally overtook her; the ghost of his lips still lingered on her mouth and neck. Her blush burned the tips of her ears as her waking haze wore off. Wren was able to wriggle herself loose enough to shift into a sitting position with her back against the headboard.

She was half surprised when the pressure didn't hurt the wounds on her back. Her shoulder, however, was a different story. She was at least grateful that her body healed *those* wounds quickly.

Her movement drew a semiconscious murmur from Nik. He adjusted his hold on her to encircle her hips completely and pulled her closer.

Wren watched him for any sign of waking. When he showed none, she touched his face with delicate fingertips. She brushed away whisps of ebony hair from the corners of his eyes, then folded her hand over to trace up his cheekbone and down his jawline. She reached his chin and paused.

Wren took a moment to gather the courage, but once she had, she hesitantly brushed her index finger across his lower lip. She took a quiet, heavy breath and drew a straight line down the center of his chin. She paused at the crest of his Adam's apple before she ventured toward the hollow of his throat.

Wren chewed on the inside of her cheek and looked away from him. She shook her head, yet reluctantly glanced back from the corner of her eye.

He looks so peaceful, she mused as she turned to face him again. Unable to resist, and despite her better judgment, her hand found its way back to the curve of his jaw.

She had been so fixated on his features that she didn't notice the emerald eyes slowly open.

Wren jumped when Nik's hand wrapped around hers.

Her yelp of surprise stirred something in his chest, and his lips quirked with a smirk. He brought her hand from his jaw to his lips and turned it over to place resolute kisses against her wrist. He advanced up her arm and drew her closer to him the farther up he got.

"Nik," she said softly in a gruff morning rasp. Wren coughed to clear her throat and pulled away from him. "We need to get up. It's morning."

"Just give me a moment," Nik murmured in a drowsy voice.

"*Why?*"

His hands quickly re-collected hers and pulled her back into a lounging position against him. He shifted his weight so that his face was nestled into her hair.

"You're always so cryptic. Are you trying for mysterious? Because it's just annoying when you don't answer." Wren felt him laugh against her back. "We need to get up so that we can put a plan together to find Elliot, and we need to check on Lionel."

"I'm well aware, and we will. I checked on Lionel a few hours ago." Nik shifted so that Wren's back was flat against the mattress underneath him. His hands, planted firmly on either side of her head, propped him up over her. He smiled at the look of surprise in her eyes. "Who knows if I'll ever get to have you in this position again."

Wren's face went red so quickly that she couldn't hide it in time.

"Cut it out, Nik." She turned her face to the side with her eyes shut tight. "You're being ridiculous."

"Ridiculous?"

"Yes."

"How do you figure?"

"Because you're doing that thing where you try to distract me from something. It's ridiculous and childish. This is important, Nik. We need to leave before we give the kidnappers any more of a head start than we already have."

"Me? Distract you? That doesn't sound like me," he murmured as he leaned in to kiss her neck.

"Really?" She pushed him back and shook her head. "*That's* your takeaway? Ugh, fine. It doesn't matter." She lifted herself onto her elbows. "I'm getting up. *You* can stay in bed as long as you like."

"Fine, we'll get up. Just one more, before we do."

"One more wha—"

Nik's arm curled around her while his other hand knotted into her hair. He slowly sat back, drawing her along with him, and cradled the curve of her head to hold her as close to him as possible. His lips moved easily against hers and twitched with a smirk when her breath hitched softly.

It only took half a heartbeat for her to return the kiss.

THE ROOM WAS STALE AND COLD. SMALL SLIVERS OF LIGHT FROM above cast rocking shadows that made the space even more difficult to take in.

Elliot hazily noticed that not only were the shadows moving, they were making noise as well. Lots of it.

Voices.

A sharp pain shot from the side of her head. Her hand shakily reached for the source to find a smear of dried blood across her temple, and she reached up into her hairline. The combination of the cacophony above her and the realization of her head wound made her stomach lurch.

Elliot heaved over the edge of where she was lying and retched a number of times. When the sick feeling in her stomach faded somewhat, she gasped in gulps of air. She covered her eyes with the crook of her elbow and rolled onto her back with a groan.

The room felt like it was moving.

Her head was spinning. She turned over just in time to gag again. Elliot's hands grasped desperately at the rough surface she was on. She couldn't make sense of anything around her. The rocking of the room paired with the sharp ringing in her ears made it nearly impossible to find her bearings.

The sounds and rancid smells around her overwhelmed her

senses. Heavy thuds from above and metallic clangs assaulted her worsening headache.

It was the cry of the birds that snapped her back to awareness.

Seagulls.

A creaking, rocking room.

. . . Boots?

Elliot's eyes widened in realization.

She was locked in the bowels of a ship.

Now in her right mind, she squared her shoulders and sat upright. She glanced around the cramped space slowly, trying to avoid aggravating her headache. She focused on easing the turbulent feeling in the pit of her stomach and wrapped her hands around the edge of her seat.

Light in the small room was sparce. There were only three tiny portholes along the walls that allowed any sunlight in aside from the thin slivers of light that were able to beam through the gaps of the top deck.

Even squinting, Elliot struggled to make out the far end of the room. She turned her attention to the lock that held her iron cage shut tight. She grasped it to turn it over in her hand as she examined it through blurry, salt-stained eyes.

It was a relatively simple albeit rusty padlock. Her eyes widened when she noticed the small pinhole on the bottom of the lock.

A quick release.

She dropped it and immediately started to look for anything small enough to fit inside of it.

The small iron brig was squalid and caked in filth and grime. A combination of barnacles and rust covered nearly every square inch of the wide bars. The corners were occupied by dark heaps of what could only be described as something no one would put their hand into. Two chain links held the cantilevered wooden slab she sat upon to the wall.

A *clink* brought her attention to the farthest wall.

Elliot peered as far into the shadows as she could. It took her a few moments to realize the small sound had come from something metallic.

The ship rocked to one side enough for a sliver of light from above to fall directly on where she was looking for a fraction of a second.

A key ring. It dangled from a small hook mounted on the far wall at shoulder level.

She tried to gauge the distance from the brief moment she had to see it. Although her vision was still groggy, Elliot estimated it wasn't more than ten feet away. She looked around the cage in hopes of finding . . . anything.

Her eyes reluctantly drifted back to the heaps in the corners of the brig cell. She took a hesitant step closer to the corner nearest to her and tried to take a deep breath.

As she slowly approached, something shuffled against the wooden floor.

Elliot froze.

"H-hello?" she whispered in the softest way that her racing anxiety would allow. "Is someone t-there?"

The patter sounded again but from a different corner.

Elliot spun to look at the new source as her breath stilled. She withdrew her arms to her chest and stood straight upright.

Suddenly, all of the corners began to emanate sounds. Small shadows moved out of them slowly. They were bulky with fur and had long, trailing tails. The sparce light did well to hide their details.

Elliot looked up to the suspended platform she had awoken on. She reached out to it, trying to keep her feet planted to the floor. Her fingers brushed against it as she strained, but her reach fell short. She lost her balance when the ship rocked in the water, and she hit the floor. She quickly hugged her legs to her chest and looked around.

Elliot was surrounded on all sides by little creatures, near enough for her to see them clearly.

Rats.

Tens of rats had encircled her.

They had stopped their approach about a foot away from her. Black eyes peered at her motionlessly. Quite possibly the largest rat she had ever seen in her entire life stood directly in front of her. It had positioned itself much closer to her than the rest.

It was easily as big as Jack, perhaps even slightly larger.

The rat lifted its front paws off the ground, all the while keeping his black eyes locked on her.

"Are you hurt?"

Elliot was still as stone, staring back at it in silent disbelief.

He took a few, tentative steps closer. "You are still bleeding."

She finally blinked herself out of her stupor and nodded.

"I-I-I'm fine." Elliot struggled to keep the shaking from her voice. "I'm s-sorry. You su-surprised me."

The rat turned his head to inspect her. He drew near enough to reach out and touch her, but he didn't. Instead, he folded his arms behind his back and hummed once.

"Apologies. You had taken quite a hit to your head." His gray arms opened out to her and rotated in place to gesture to the other rats. "Our rattenkin had feared the worst."

Elliot blinked.

"I did? I don't remember getting hit." Her hand unconsciously drifted to her temple. She winced when her middle finger acciden-tally grazed the lump. She stared blankly at the smear of blood on her fingers before she lifted her eyes to meet those of the rattenkin. "Thank you"—Elliot looked around to the others—"for worrying about me. That's an awfully kind thing to do."

The crowd of 'kin shuffled and squeaked in tiny, warm sentiment.

"The captain has been bringing many young women on board, as of late. Though he does have a hard time *keeping* them on board."

"He throws them overboard?"

He chuckled and shook his head. "No. They escape."

Her heart leapt in her chest with the glimmer of hope. "Escape? And you help them to?"

"Aye. Though"—he dropped onto all fours and began walking around her—"it's more difficult to do once we've set sail, obviously. Lookouts and navigators would spot you in the water in no time. Not to mention what waits in the open ocean. So, we will move once we reach port."

"What port?"

"Border Port. We are about a day out now."

An unexpected fear washed over her. "How long have I been out for?"

"Three days."

"*Three days?*" Her breath caught in her throat, and her heart dropped.

"We've been at sea for two," he corrected. "It took a bit longer for them to get to the sea, as they were delayed while still in port. You put up quite a fuss. You had the quartermaster in an arm bar when he tried to restrain you and broke a deck hand's nose when you got free. Quite an impressive hit, too." The 'kin chuckled and nodded, his whiskers twitching. "That's when *that* happened." He tapped his own temple. "The captain knocked you out cold."

"Shit," she whispered.

"If you are wise, pretend you are still asleep whenever you're checked on. The captain has been acting strange since we set sail. The crew's been on edge, and they have been minding their manners. They've left you alone so far; might as well use it to your advantage."

Elliot smiled. "I agree, thank you." A pain rumbled in her stomach, and it gurgled loudly.

"Bernard." The large 'kin beckoned someone behind him.

A sandy-coated 'kin, just over half the size of the first nodded once and scampered off.

Elliot tilted her head at him curiously. "What is your name?"

"Augustus. Gus, if you don't mind."

"Gus," she repeated. "I'm Elliot."

"We know. The man that brought you here said it a number of times. He seemed to know you pretty well, though he did not speak of you kindly."

Bernard returned with a sizable chunk of bread clutched in his mouth. He made a beeline to Elliot's side and offered it to her with what had to have been a smile.

She hesitantly accepted it and offered a small smile in return. "Thank you very much." She took a modest bite of the bread to gauge how well it would sit in her stomach before committing to the entire piece. "You said that the man that brought me here knows me?"

Gus nodded.

She remembered the festival, Nik, and the busy street. She remembered calling out to Nik when someone had grabbed her. She remembered being blinded by a bag, and two men's rough voices. One of them she recognized, but one she couldn't place.

Elliot had to strain to think of the person that belonged to the voice that she knew. It made her pounding headache worsen, but she had to know.

She *had* to figure it out.

It then occurred to her in a flash.

One of them had belonged to Brock.

"Was he large? Ruddy face and dark hair?"

Gus shook his head. "He had dark hair, but he was a rather gaunt-looking fellow. He dropped you with the captain and ran back in the opposite direction from where he came, like he was running from death."

"One of those voices *has* to have been Brock. Maybe if he wasn't there when I was handed to the pirates, I know he was involved . . . But why would he kidnap *me*?"

As she deliberated aloud, she failed to notice the sea of curious eyes that watched her.

The rattenkin clan looked amongst themselves before turning to Gus for direction.

"There is a bounty out for the acquisition of a woman matching your description. It states that she is to be delivered alive and in good condition, but I know not of who she is to be delivered to, nor of the explicit reason for the bounty itself."

"A bounty? On me?" Her fingers tightened on the remaining hunk of bread. "But why?"

"I know not," Gus repeated gruffly. "What I do know is that you are the spitting image of the woman drawn on the postings. Many of those we have helped escape look similar to you, but none so closely resemble her as you do."

"That's unsettling," she groaned and closed her eyes. "So, if it *is* me in the bounty, the only reasonable conclusion as to why would be because of my relationship to Wren. I haven't done anything to make enemies . . ."

"Wren Gibbs? Of Black Rivers?" Gus tucked his arms behind his back and began to pace. "Very interesting. You make a good point. Brock, being from Black Rivers, would likely have very intimate knowledge as to why the bounty was put on you."

Elliot's eyes shot open. "You know Wren?"

"Not had the pleasure, no." The charcoal-gray 'kin gave her a small grin. His eyes seemed to glow against the dingy, barnacle-covered walls of the cage Elliot was trapped in. "But I do have close friends that have been directly affected by the young lass."

"You do?"

"Aye." His dusty whiskers twitched with another smile. "My good friend Heilyn is one. His daughters were rescued from what would have been a fatal encounter with two grifters. The eldest daughter claimed that she witnessed your friend, the . . . *tempest*, rescued by a large man of shadow. It's a rather strange description, but there are stranger things in this world."

"Yes," Elliot admitted quietly. "I am familiar with the event. I'm glad that his daughters are both all right." She couldn't stop her fingers from curling into fists, crushing the remainder of the bread into a tight ball. "I know the man, too. His name is Nik. He's a reaper." She spoke through a set jaw.

"A reaper, eh? Very interesting. You don't happen to know if he is a penitent reaper or not?"

Elliot arched a brow, still bitter at him for getting taken and not yet ready to admit to herself that *he* wasn't at fault for her kidnapping. She chewed on the back of her lip and nodded.

"He is."

Gus gave Bernard another look.

Bernard, in turn, looked to a satin-colored 'kin with a silky gray coat that shone in the sparce light.

"Melony," Bernard squeaked in a quiet voice. "What does the text say?"

Melony propped herself onto her hind legs and faced Gus directly.

"If memory serves correctly, it speaks not of a reaper directly. But I do recall mention of something to do with the balance of death." Her black eyes turned to Elliot briefly, an indiscernible look within them. "I admit, I thought little of it. My interpretation of it was to be a vague characteristic, not literal death."

"What is the line, directly?" Bernard persisted.

Melony pulled a satchel that had been secured across her back to rest atop her chest. Pink fingers flicked through numerous pages of parchment before locating a specific piece. She tugged the page out and unfolded it in order to read it aloud.

"Threat of a great war looms over the coming generations. Evil will spread and cast all that it touches into darkness. Yet the light gifted by the gods shall never be lost, as long as there exists those willing to defend the weak at their own peril; as long as there exists a willingness to accept the responsibilities of freedom; as long as there exists the fight for what is just and good, the people shall be in the favor of the gods and, therefore, be gifted their light and power that will pass unto posterity forever.

"The light of the spell cannot be catalyzed by fire nor sword, by cleverness nor strength, by diligence nor dedication. The Three Elements must first come together in unison for the light to be called upon.

"Only with the Conscience of the Father, the Protection of the Mother, and the Balance of Faith and Death will the true power of the light be revealed and will bring down the might of the gods.

"Should the light fail to overcome the darkness, all that is known will be lost and must once more be found before the light of the spell will return.

"Should the life of the vessel cease, it will be in a flash of light. A new vessel will be made, and the light of the spell will be once again cast into existence.

"The union of the Three Elements is essential for destiny to smile upon the side of the righteous. To stop the great war."

Gus scratched his chin and furrowed his whiskers.

Melony took a few steps to his side and passed the parchment to him.

He clutched the page and made a small sound as he examined it. "Interesting. It seems as though our interpretation may have been incorrect. We may be in the throes of the prophecy's unfolding right now."

Elliot waved her hands and frowned.

"Whoa, whoa. What are you talking about? What is that?" She pointed at the paper and looked between the pair of 'kin.

Gus gave her a curious look and held the page out to her. "It is a prophecy. This was given to us by a traveler, who obtained it from a daemon."

"I have so many questions that I don't know where to begin."

Gus chuckled. "We have some time. Ask away."

"All right." Elliot gave a meek laugh and scratched her arm. "Thank you." Her eyes scanned the ink on the parchment repetitiously before they turned back to Gus and the other rattenkin. "What is this prophecy? Why is it significant, and what does it have to do with Wren?" There was a gnawing feeling in the back of her mind that Gus didn't think that Wren was a tempest.

Gus gave her another curious look, as though he already knew she was withholding.

"The conflict between good and evil is something that will exist forever. Nothing can fully destroy evil, and inversely, nothing can destroy good. That is reality. From our understanding, this prophecy describes the light of the spell as a sort of check to balance out the inevitability of evil wrought from false promises and empty words of the wicked that can spread like summer fire. We saw just that when Tanner went for the crown in Arnica. A four-winged beast rose against him and stopped his slaughter . . . Tales only tell of one four-winged creature to have ever existed. A creature said to be the creation of the gods themselves . . .

"This particular prophecy is one that was gifted by the goddess Yu'e a few decades ago." He accepted the document when Elliot handed it back to him, and he passed it along to Melony.

She silently folded it back up and tucked it into the satchel at her chest.

"Daemon are conduits to the gods," Gus continued. "Although they have colonies scattered throughout the world, there exists only two true clans: one that devoutly serves the gods and one that has embraced dark magics. If it is true that this is a prophecy received from Yu'e herself, it is safe to assume that it is a prophecy from the peaceful sort of daemon.

"Many years ago, I encountered a traveler in Border Port. He'd just come from Smith Town. We only met twice, many years apart. The last time that I saw him was the day that he gave me that prophecy in exchange for a favor. He explained that it was a gift and was to be protected at all costs."

"All right, well that only answered one of my questions . . . sort of."

"Aye." Gus scrunched his nose and motioned at his family to scatter.

They all obliged and vanished as instantly and silently as they had arrived.

"Your other questions are a bit more difficult to answer." He began to pace again and turned his snout to the moonlight through the port hole over their heads. "I am not at liberty to speak of many of the things that will answer them. All that I *can* say is, based on the bounty on you, your mention of a *penitent* reaper now at her side, and your relationship to the . . . tempest . . . You are all very important to existence as we know it."

"That sounds heavy." Elliot winced at how small her voice must have sounded.

Gus gave her an unsure look before he padded closer to her. A paw reached out to pat her hand, and he offered her another smile. "It will be *heavy*, but your allies are strong and many in number. Fret not, and have faith, Elliot."

CHAPTER TWENTY

"Muddy water is best cleared by leaving it alone."

Alan W. Watts

WREN WALKED IN FRONT OF NIK WITH A FOUL EXpression on her face.

"We should split up to cover more ground," she insisted again.

"No," he replied flatly.

She folded her arms and sighed. It really was no use.

They had already combed through Black Rivers, the village within the kingdom, and the northern farmlands throughout Wheatrich in three days.

The only place they had left in Arnica was Bay City.

The maritime city streets were soaked by the steadily falling sleet. They were practically empty, as the vast majority of villagers wisely stayed out of the weather. Lights inside of the buildings shone in orange and gold, helping to slightly distract from the onslaught of frozen, saltwater rain.

Slightly.

Nik's thick hood shielded his head. His leather jacket was latched all of the way to his chin, and he kept his hands stuffed in his pockets. The dip of his hood kept his face dry but not necessarily warm. He kept pace with her easily, consciously matching her speed to walk only a step or two behind her left shoulder.

Wren wore a mostly weatherproof hooded cloak. The bottom of the cloak brushed against the top of her ankles as she walked and was drenched at the hem. Tall boots and warm pants insulated her legs, but the cold that she struggled with came from her bones, not the atmosphere.

Nik's crimson scarf was strung around Wren's neck and covered enough of her face to protect her nose from the sleet. One hand was tightly wrapped around the staff of her spear, the glove that protected it from the weather completely soaked through.

Evening set in quickly, urging any lingering townsfolk home.

Nik and Wren, however, stubbornly pressed on.

"Excuse me," a meek voice called to them.

Wren turned to see a young woman whose voice she recognized, though not immediately.

"Lady Wren." The woman approached quietly. Her hood obscured much of her face, but when she tilted it up to look at the pair, it clicked.

"Hello, Gwen," Wren replied cautiously.

"I need to speak with you." She took another small step closer. "It's about Elliot. Please," she insisted. "Please come with me."

Wren and Nik exchanged a look before her eyes turned back to Gwen, and she nodded once.

They allowed her to lead them to the more populated part of Bay City.

The loose-stone street came to an end, and wooden planks began. The planks formed docks that twisted around impressive structures built into the stone cliffsides. The high spokes of underwater mountains rose hundreds of feet out of the ocean, and nearly every one of them was littered with these pathways and buildings, winding upward in spirals.

Orange lanterns glowed in the bleak evening light. They were spectacularly vibrant against the gray-green sky and shimmered whenever the salty wind would howl through the peaks. The lanterns followed the hundreds of steps and ladders that were constructed to navigate the vertical city.

"This way." Gwen maneuvered them to face a staircase so long that its end wasn't visible in the blinding precipitation.

Wren stopped short and folded her arms. "Where are you taking us?"

Gwen's eyes widened, and she put her hands up in surrender. "To my father's pub," she stammered. "He told me that he saw Elliot a few days ago. The moment I saw you, I knew I had to bring you to him." Her voice dropped, and she stepped close enough to Wren to reach out and touch her, though she knew not to. "We can't talk in this weather, my lady. Please trust me. My home is warm and dry. You *need* to hear what my father has to say."

Wren took a step away from Gwen. Her back hit something hard, and a hand found the side of her waist to steady her.

"Let's go, Wren," Nik said softly through the rain. "It's the first lead we've found. We'd be foolish to decline."

"Fine." Wren looked to the blond woman from the corner of her eye. "Let's go."

They walked for what felt like hours in worsening weather and up endless stairs.

After ascending a steep curve of the mountain, they reached a residential area of the seaside city.

Wren didn't miss the faces peeking out from many of the windows as they passed by. As soon as they'd realized they'd been noticed, people would smile or wave at her. None scowled or turned away in disregard.

A girl, no more than fifteen, was jumping and stomping in puddles along with many other, younger children, all giggling and squealing with glee. The joy in their laughter seemed to brighten the air around them with a gentle haze that juxtaposed the bleakness of the weather.

The youngest of the group noticed the passing trio and spotted Wren. She rushed to the oldest girl and tugged on her arm, pointing into the storm.

The oldest peered at Wren, and upon recognition, her face lit up. She grasped her little brother's shoulder and joined her sister in pointing at the group led by Gwen.

As she whispered into his ear, his eyes widened, and the young boy waved at her emphatically.

The sleet was too heavy to hear what his tiny voice called to them, but his smile shone like a midday sun.

She hesitantly regarded them with a subtle bow of her head and a guarded smile.

The oldest girl bounded toward a woman in the doorway. She clutched the woman's hand in her own and pointed with a wide grin stretched across her face.

The woman looked first to Gwen and waved with a confused look. When her eyes turned to Wren and Nik, her face dropped in shock. Without a thought to the weather, the woman rushed into the storm and to the edge of the fenced-in property.

"My lady!" she called to Wren and braced herself on the fence to come to a stop.

Wren blinked and paused. Her eyes flicked from the woman to the young girl following behind her.

"My lady," she repeated breathlessly and reached out to Wren.

Her sunset eyebrow quirked in skeptical interest, but she did not budge.

"Charlotte," Gwen hissed sternly. "Get back inside, lest you cause a scene. Our lady has business to attend to."

Charlotte kept her eyes locked on Wren, but she nodded. "Yes, apologies," she murmured and took a step back.

The young girl leaned around her mother's hip to get a better look. "Momma," she whispered and tugged on the woman's skirt. "Momma, Sam said that she'd be scary, but she isn't. She's so pretty. Why would he lie? Lying is bad."

"Hush, child."

Wren pretended not to hear their exchange and sighed. She took a small step toward Charlotte and extended her hand.

The woman startled and quickly clasped Wren's hand with both of her own.

"It is nice to meet you, Charlotte."

"You too, my lady." She nibbled her lip as she glanced at her daughter. Charlotte leaned toward Wren and dropped her voice. "Forgive me if I speak too freely, but we hear rumors of how you are treated in Black Rivers . . . and in the kingdom. It's despicable, I think." She clapped her palm on top of Wren's twice. "You are always welcome here, my lady. Please think of us, should you ever need somewhere to go. Anyone here would take you in with open arms."

Wren froze. "Um," she stammered and tried to smile. "Thank you. You are not speaking out of turn. You merely speak the truth."

Charlotte gleamed and bowed her head. "Apologies for holding you up, my lady. Really, the pleasure is all mine."

"Please, get yourself inside. This storm is only worsening."

Charlotte gripped her daughter's hand and nodded. "You're right. Charlie, get your siblings inside and get cleaned up for bed." Her eyes found Wren's for another moment. "Thank you, my lady . . . for everything."

Wren tried to ignore the corners of her lips twitching into a small smile and gave another subtle bow of her head to mask it.

"Here, this way." Gwen urged the pair farther down the road.

A short journey led to a heavy wooden door on a huge stone building covered in years of calcified salt from the constant spray of the surrounding ocean.

Gwen had to put all of her weight into the door just to open it and stepped to the side so they could enter.

Inside was a spacious and warm room. A small handful of townspeople hovered over drinks at their tables, their hushed voices filling the cozy pub with quiet conversations entwined in the soft hum of music.

A pair of minstrels strummed their instruments and sang in unison. The tune that filled the room was one of joy and redemption. They both had lovely voices that did well to add to the sense of hospitality that the open room had.

A large man stood behind the bar with a cold stein of ale clutched in his hand. He noticed the door open and regarded his daughter with a broad smile. He had light hair that was pulled back. Only a few blond whisps escaped the tie and hung around his cheekbones. An unkept beard the color of wet sand covered most of his face and was aged with white and gray.

"Gwenny, ya sister is refusing to leave her room again. Settle in and try to at least feed her something for dinner, would ya?" His dull eyes noticed Nik first, then Wren. "Ah, welcome, my lady!"

Wren shook her head and held up her free hand. "There's no need for formalities. Please, just call me Wren."

He nodded with a friendly smile and turned his attention to the ebony-haired man.

"I'm Nik." His careful eyes surveyed the room before they settled on Gwen's father.

"Heilyn." The man nodded. "Heilyn Michair." He placed his stein on the counter and gestured to the wall of alcohol behind him. "Can I pour ya two a drink?"

"Whiskey sounds perfect." Wren smiled sadly and removed her cloak and gloves.

"Here." Gwen beamed and held out her arms. "I'll put these by the fire to dry off. My lady?"

Wren blinked at Gwen's open hand before she realized she was glancing at her spear. Wren allowed the young woman to take it and looked away.

Gwen turned to Nik with the same hand-out gesture.

"Thank you." Nik nodded and removed his jacket. "Thank you both."

"Think nothing of it." Heilyn retrieved a glass bottle filled with amber liquid. "What can I make ya, lad?"

"Whatever you're drinking looks great."

The barkeep laughed heartily and nodded. "Aye. Go ahead and take a seat. I'll get these to ya. Ya both must be beat from that storm!"

Wren and Nik made their way to an empty table nearest to the fire.

A few patrons looked at them as they walked by, but any that made eye contact offered her a wordless nod before returning to their own matters.

Gwen hung their outerwear on a pair of hooks near the hearth. She balanced Wren's spear beside her cloak and motioned for them to sit. Once their guests settled in, she looked to her father.

"If I tell Laila that Lady Wren is here, I bet she'd come out." Gwen looked to Wren with a smile. "Would it be all right if I invite her down?"

"Sure," Wren replied softly. "But be brief. You are kind, and I'm sure that your sister is too, but I do not have time to linger any longer than necessary."

The blond woman gave her a polite smile and nodded. She ducked behind the bar and hurried up a flight of stairs hidden behind a black curtain.

Wren sat down as close to the fire as she could. Without the warmth of Elliot's radiant energy, she couldn't shake the chill that followed her like a shadow. The thought of her friend in distress made it impossible for her to fully relax, even in the welcoming heat emanating from the fire.

Nik sat across from her with a heavy sigh. His gaze flickered about the room before it turned back to Wren.

Her posture was rigid, arms folded, and she was staring into the fire with a scowl.

"You're still cold?" Nik's quiet question went unanswered as footsteps approached.

"Ah, the whiskey will help with that, lass." Heilyn set two empty glasses down before her, followed by the entire bottle beside it. "Help yaself, em, Wren." He hesitated before saying her name, not yet comfortable with the informality. A large stein filled to its brim was placed before Nik. "Plenty more, son. Don't be shy."

"Thank you for your hospitality." Wren turned to Heilyn. "I apologize if I seem rude. I don't have a lot of time to lose."

Heilyn shook his head fervently and sat beside her. "Think nothing of it. I'm glad Gwenny found ya." He uncorked the bottle and poured a generous amount into both glasses. "I have information that I hope ya could use. It's about Miss Elliot."

Nik watched Heilyn intently as he spoke.

"I was picking up a shipment right on the docks, three days ago." He paused until Nik nodded. "I overheard something. It sounded like a young lady in a bout of trouble. And, well . . ." He sat upright and looked in the direction of the curtain. "As a man with two daughters, I felt it my responsibility to take a look. Gods, I pray that someone would if it had been one of *my* daughters." His eyes turned purposefully to Wren, and he cautiously gathered her hand into his. "And I thank my stars every day that the gods heard my prayers, and yer the proof, my lady." He brought her hands to his bowed forehead. "Anything ya need is on the house. I insist."

Wren offered an awkward smile and averted her eyes. "Yes, well . . . I'm glad I was there. But you praise me too much." She touched the large man's bearded cheek gingerly. "It *is* my duty to protect those like your daughters. Black Rivers is dangerous. Especially at dusk."

Heilyn nodded and kissed the back of her hand. "Duty or not, my daughters are still with me today because of ya."

"Please." Wren urged and clutched her glass as she dropped her eyes. "Continue with what you saw." She took a deep breath before tossing the contents back in one swig. Her eyes slipped shut from the tingling burn that seeped through her chest but did nothing for the throbbing ache.

Heilyn eagerly poured her another serving and continued.

"I see Miss Elliot in the arms of this real seedy-looking fellow. Poor girl had a canvas sack over her head, but she fought like hell. Broke some fellow's nose, I tell ya."

Wren couldn't stop the smirk that cracked her otherwise stoic face.

Atta girl.

"I tried to intervene. I had Sam, Charlotte's oldest, load up the ale while I went to help her." He downed half of his glass and let out a cloudy breath. "They had a whole crew. I got through a few, but they'd already got Miss Elliot on board." Heilyn shook his head. "I'm not sure how I got out of there without getting hurt, but I'm not the sort of man to question my luck."

"I'm glad that you didn't, Daddy." Gwen reappeared with a tray full of food. "Laila is cleaning up, but she is very eager to meet you again, my lady."

Freshly baked bread surrounded tenderly cooked meats and roasted vegetables on the wide silver platter. She placed a plate and silverware in front of Nik and Wren and offered them each a cloth napkin.

"Dig in!"

"Heilyn." Wren loaded her plate with a hearty slab of meat and potatoes. "Did they say anything about where they were going?"

"Aye. Border Port."

"What?" Wren almost dropped her plate and stared at him. "In Dendros? *Shit!* And they have a three-day lead."

Heilyn gave Nik an apologetic look.

Nik shook his head and offered a small smirk. "Wren, we will find her. You heard Heilyn. She's not going to be pushed around."

Wren turned away with a burning look in her eyes. She nodded with stilted motion and pursed her lips. "Yeah."

"I'm sorry, my lady," Heilyn interjected. "I knew the news would upset ya. I didn't know how else to say it."

Wren shook her head and placed her hand on top of his. "No, I'm sorry. You've been wonderful, Heilyn. I truly appreciate your help." She sighed and poked at the roasted potatoes on her plate.

The barkeep smiled softly and leaned back. His aged eyes flickered to her companion.

Nik's attention was locked on Wren, whose smoldering hazel stare had returned to the fire.

"If ya don't mind my sayin', my l— Miss Wren. Ya seem different."

She furrowed her brow and turned to blink at him. "Pardon? How do you mean?"

Heilyn looked between them again and grew a knowing look. "The last time I saw ya—" He stopped short and winced when he noticed her expression.

Wren met his eyes with a silent plea to avoid bringing up that night.

The night that Seth died.

"Ya've been such a lonely thing," the barkeep tried again. "It's nice for my old eyes to see someone taking care of *ya* for a change. It isn't an insult, my lady. Good people on ya side can make one helluva difference when it's most important." He patted her shoulder. "Can I get yas a room ready? It's only getting worse out there."

The déjà vu made Wren's stomach lurch.

"Two beds, please."

"Border Port ahead, Cap'n."

"Aye. Begin docking procedures."

"Docking positions, lads! All hands!"

Elliot lay on her side with her back to the door.

The raucous commotion above her shuffled chaotically as the ship neared its destination. The shouting men stomped around so heavily as they rushed through their jobs that streams of dust and silt filtered from between the wooden slats of the deck.

Gus perched himself on the edge of the suspended platform that was cloaked in shadows.

"Almost there, Elliot," his quiet voice whispered. "Melony and I will distract the crew." His hairy nose turned to the side. "Fang? You will get the keys and unlock the door. Silver and Jasper, take the lifeboat off the ship, then lead Elliot to Market Road. If we leave port before you get back, you two will return to the rattenclan in Dendros and remain there until we return. We can't risk another abduction in our absence if we were to wait."

The two brothers nodded and stood upright on their hind feet. The taller of the two, Silver, had pitch-black fur. A long, vivid stripe of gray covered the bridge of his nose and forehead. Jasper's coat was a sandy brown along his back with a light brown belly. They both wore dark tunics that concealed needle-sharp daggers. Small cloaks covered their shoulders and ears and made their bodies nearly indiscernible from the shadows.

Jasper tipped his head to Elliot. "In our care, we will get you back home safely."

Elliot smiled in return. "Thank you. Everyone."

Gus nodded. "Get ready. They'll be in port soon. We wait for Esther's signal." He gave Elliot's forearm a reassuring squeeze before he leapt from his perch and made for the shadows.

The creaking of the ship was the only sound in the dingy room. No one dared to break the silence in fear they'd miss Esther's call.

Elliot listened to the men above her. She closed her eyes and tried to focus on each step.

Items in the room slid across the plank floor as the ship turned sharply.

The table Fang was crouching on toppled over, taking him with it. He scrambled to right it as quietly as he could manage.

Other 'kin in the room soundlessly rushed to help him move it back into position.

The rocking lessened considerably, and the ship slowed. Smaller adjustments were made now, allowing everyone to reposition before it was time.

A single loud chirp broke the silence, and the horde of 'kin moved in an instant.

Fang leapt from the table and snatched the keys off the wall easily.

Melony and Gus had been long gone by the time Esther called out. They rushed up the hidden highway that their forefathers had carved within the walls and shadows of the ship. They hastily made it to the middle deck that housed the crew's living cabins.

Men bustled around, hefting bags and crates to the top deck for unloading. They moved instinctually, unaware of the creatures that scampered between their footfalls.

Melony raced ahead of Gus and turned sharply into a corridor with a sturdy ladder at its end.

Gus was right behind her.

Her steadfast paws carried her up the ladder at lightning speed. She never took her deep black eyes off of their destination: the vacant crow's nest.

They moved in coordinated formations up the braided ropes that secured the sails to the mast.

Luck was on their side with the cloudy, nighttime darkness that made them nearly invisible.

They selected the rope tied into a knot at the top of the crow's nest. Instinctually and in unison, they began nibbling at the rope. Their jaws moved around it methodically to make it appear as though the line had frayed and snapped on its own.

Following Esther's signal, Fang hurried to the door of the brig and nestled the key into the lock. He planted his claws on the curve of the padlock and twisted.

The lock clicked, and the latch popped open.

Silver and Jasper rushed out ahead of Elliot and up the stairs. They waited at the top, peering in every possible direction.

Jasper held his paw out to Elliot to signal for her to wait. He tucked behind a step when four men dashed by the doorway.

Elliot took the opportunity to relock the door to the brig.

Fang gave her a strange look as the lock clicked shut in her palms.

She smiled back and shrugged one shoulder. "Just to mess with them."

He smirked and flashed a quick thumbs-up in response before he hopped into the darkness.

Silver gave the signal for them to follow. He took lead and bounded across the deck.

The shadows were everywhere and deep enough to provide excellent cover. The moon that peered through the veil of gray clouds cast long and creeping shadows for them to weave through undetected.

The pair of 'kin darted through every single hollow of darkness they passed, checking for any lurking men who might've noticed them before moving on.

Elliot followed closely behind, only ducking into shadows that the brothers had. She tried to keep herself from grinning at the sound of the chaotic crew attempting to wrangle a line that had broken.

They clamored frantically as the top of the main sail flailed in the wind.

The brothers were able to lead her to the lifeboats without being spotted.

Silver motioned for her to jump in and quickly followed.

Jasper emitted a soft sound, and a mass of 'kin swarmed the lever.

Their combined weight and teamwork cranked the handle and lowered the boat quietly into the water. They scattered the instant the bottom of the boat touched the water's surface.

The side of the lifeboat scraped against the wooden dock as it landed.

Jasper scurried down the rope and urged Elliot out to the dock beside Silver. Once they were all clear of the boat, he made another sound.

The lifeboat began rising back into its original position against the top deck.

"Wow," Elliot breathed. "You guys are incredible." Her quiet voice held a bright smile.

"Thank you." Jasper smiled back. "Let's hurry. Silver will lead."

The 'kin were on either side of Elliot in single file. Just like aboard the ship, they stuck to the shadows. The trio were out of sight from the boat, but they could still hear flustered shouting.

"We better hurry up," Jasper squeaked to his brother. "It won't be long until they realize she's gone."

Silver picked up his pace as they traced the coastline.

Elliot struggled to keep up. The lethargy of not eating for three days paired with a head-wound left her weary, but the pure adrenaline pumping through her body pushed her onward.

"How far do we have to go before we can rest?"

The pitch-black 'kin glanced at her over his shoulder briefly before he scoffed.

"We are headed toward the mountains. We can find shelter in the valley between them," Silver replied, annoyance clear in his voice.

"You can do it, Elliot," Jasper encouraged her from behind. "Just keep breathing and focus on your home. It'll help keep you going."

They made it through the entirety of Border Port and to the foothills of the southern mountain before the moon had moved very far. Once they made it into the valley, they would be able to use the river as a trailhead to ensure they would be going in the right direction.

They ran until Silver spotted a withering structure. He sped up and vanished into the dark, tall grass, leaving Jasper to keep pace with Elliot while he checked it out.

By the time she and the sandy-coated brother made it to the building, Silver impatiently stood in the doorway. His pink fingers drummed against the rotting wood doorframe.

Jasper gave his brother a dirty look.

The larger 'kin simply turned away and led the way into the barn.

It was rather spacious and had long since been abandoned. Most of the roof had collapsed into the structure, but the remaining portion still offered cover from the elements.

Silver beckoned her inside and guided her to a ladder. "There's a loft up there. It's drafty, but I'm sure it's better than the brig."

"Thank you, Silver."

He nodded curtly. "I'll find you something to eat." Without another word, Silver vanished into the night.

Elliot obediently made her way up the ladder to the loft. It wasn't very big, as the caved roof had crushed most of it. But it had a variety of crates stacked around its space that were all sealed shut.

Jasper appeared beside her with a wide smile.

"I bet if I could get these open, we would find supplies inside. What else would people store in the loft of a barn?"

The tan'kin nodded and hopped over to the nearest one. "They're made of wood, so I could get through them. Only thing is"—he paused and fluffed his cheeks with his paws as he grinned—"it'll take me a while."

"I'll help, Jasper. Together, I'm sure we can figure out a way to get these open."

Elliot spotted an old hammer covered in dust and cobwebs and plucked it from the ground.

The wooden handle was rough and splintered. It easily punctured the flesh of her palm, but she pushed the pain from her mind in order to help Jasper get the box opened.

They painstakingly tore into the first box together. The pair were silent as they worked.

Jasper watched her thoughts overtake her and decided to politely remain quiet.

"Does Silver dislike me?"

He shook his head. "You needn't mind Silver." Jasper picked a small bundle of wood fibers from his teeth. "He seems aloof and unfriendly, but, deep, *deep* down, he's got a big heart."

Elliot gave Jasper a grin and laughed. "I get it. I have a friend just like that." She turned her eyes to the slivers of wood in her palm.

The thought of Wren knotted in her chest painfully, and her weary arm lifted the hammer once more.

Wren turned over under the handmade quilt and sighed. Her eyes were shut tight as she tried to will herself to sleep.

Border Port is a long walk. Maybe . . . seven days on horseback? The kidnappers already have a three-day start, and who knows which way she's gone from there. She groaned and covered her face with a pillow. *Gods,* she thought desperately. *If you're listening . . . if you're real . . . please watch over her . . . Please keep her safe . . .*

Wren couldn't remember the last time she'd prayed. The hopelessness of the situation had finally cornered her. Something deep inside of her decided to exhaust every conceivable method to find and protect Elliot. She pushed aside how ridiculous she felt and tried again.

Help me to be stronger. Help me to find her. Give me something, damnit.

She rolled over again and opened her eyes to peer out the window.

From her bed, she could see the start of the sunrise through the peaks of the underwater mountains. Yellow ribbons of light gradually trickled into the darkness reflected on the steady surface of the water.

Last night's storm seemed like a different world compared to the beauty of the new one beginning to wake.

Wren sat up and sighed. She glanced to the other bed, only a few feet to her right.

Nik's large shoulders were cocooned in his quilt. His breathing was as even as the waves she could hear through the closed window.

She pursed her lips and sighed through her nose.

He'd slept like a rock the entire night.

Wren knew this because she'd hardly slept at all. She stood from the bed and made her way to one of the many bookshelves throughout the room. She ran her fingers along the spines as she tried to read them with her skin, seeking any texture that stood out.

The spines all felt similar, aged and smooth.

But then the tips of her fingers brushed over something rough and intriguing. She wrapped her hand around it and lifted the book to the sparce light.

The front of it was blank, and edges of the leather cover had long since dried out. It was discolored by unidentifiable stains and littered with abrasions in the leather. The spine was worn and pliable, like that of a well-read book would be.

Wren retreated to her bed and nestled under the quilt. She hugged the book to her chest and drew her knees in. Her eyes turned to stare mutely out the window, reluctantly allowing her thoughts to wander. She stayed like this until enough light had made its way into the room for her to manage reading by.

Wren cracked the book open and allowed a loose slip of paper to fall out. She turned it to the light with a furrowed brow.

Hastily written words filled the page, making some of them difficult to read in the dim light.

We risked our lives in order to obtain the information within these pages. Deliver it to the Bookkeeper; I am not able to. He will know what to do.

I regret to beg the same of you . . . To risk your life for a journal. It is a thankless deed that will, with any luck, never be known nor remembered.

My clan's movements have been under surveillance, so I am not able to complete the task that was bestowed on me without compromising the location of my family. I cannot risk them. I will not risk them.

Take this letter and hide it within these pages. The Bookkeeper will not recognize you. Present this page to him, and he will know what to do from there.

For my dear friend, the information in these pages is well worth the risk that we volunteered to take. I pray you feel the same. This young man is a good one. He is clairvoyant and will be of great use to our cause in the months to follow. This meeting must have been fated.

My friends, we may still have a chance to end the Northern War and stop Seth Tanner before he strikes.

Signed,
A.R.

Wren blinked in confusion. She turned the slip of paper over to examine it. Other than the rushed handwriting, the page was blank. She nibbled her lip and tucked it between the last page and back cover. Her curious eyes then turned to scan the first page of the book.

The journaling within this book is to be of the utmost secrecy. If knowledge of it were to reach the ears of the king, we will all be hanged for treason.
This book does not exist.

Wren hesitated before turning to the next page. The same handwriting that was on the slip of paper littered both sides of the page.

Seth Tanner is not alone!
We have records of his correspondence with various pirate lords, and an unknown sponsor of his war that calls themself "R." The intercepted letters are in a presumed order, as we were not able to collect every single one, and none have been dated.
Captain Bale began to grow suspicious of our existence in his world. Once the letters disappeared, he tore his ship apart and threw nearly every crewman overboard for accused mutiny. He made for port with the few men that remained, and we saw our only chance.
We had to disappear. We were able to recover the letters and get them into this book. After this passage, you must use this book to keep record of all that you find.
Both Bale and this "R" are aiding Tanner with obtaining supplies like weapons, horses, and gold. Men that Bale was able to coerce into joining are being smuggled in through the Greater Bay ports as merchants and mercenaries. They

have been planning this war for a very long time. They have been preparing for years.

Use this journal to track your movements and record any prophecies that may present themselves to you, no matter how seemingly insignificant your vision may seem. We cannot make this journey together as intended, lad. Let my words on this page remind you that you are never alone and that you are very important to our cause. Without you, I see no hope for success.

Do not forget to write anything that you see.

I hope to meet you again.

Signed,

A.R.

Wren flipped through the pages of the book but found no letters within them.

The dates on the following pages were from over twenty years ago and written with an entirely different hand. The sheets were yellowed from age and stained with bled ink and moisture exposure.

I made it to Smith Town and found this journal you hid for me. I admit, I'm not entirely sure what I should write for this first entry.

The townspeople here are quiet and private. They keep to themselves and politely say hello and thank you. I'm going to stay here for a little while and hope for a premonition. For now, I'll have to settle for my own thoughts.

When I ran into Captain Bale's crew in the pub back in Dendros, they were all ridden with scurvy and as weightless as ghosts. For whatever reason, they assumed that I was a bar hand. I learned a lot from the short amount of time I spent serving them someone else's food and drink. Dishonest, yes. But I feel that it was a necessary evil, as the men were very forthcoming once they had full bellies.

One told me of a deal I could get in on, if they were able to hire a cluster of ogres for, and I quote, "future use." That still doesn't sit well with me. At least I wasn't lying when I told them I have no money.

I plan to use my time in Smith Town gaining as much intelligence as I can. The people here are friendly, but any mention of Captain Bale, Seth Tanner, or R., and I only ever receive confused faces or knowing ones that claim to know nothing. I can tell they are lying, but I need to lay low for as long as I can to obtain supplies and information for the rest of my journey.

Not to mention, Smith Town is well known for its black-smithing. I hope they will take labor as payment.

I will record my progress.

Signed,

G.

There is a boy here that the villagers call Raven. I'm not sure if that's his real name, but it's what Baldmar, the master blacksmith, refers to him as. Raven isn't unfriendly, but he won't allow me to come very close. I've learned that he likes raw vegetables and bread with butter.

The poor thing is skin and bones. He is so pale and has pure white, ice-colored eyes. He looks and moves like a ghost. I do not believe that he is a human, but I am not sure what he could be.

I've started to notice him around more often. Especially when I'm in town.

When I am working at the smithy, I feel as though I am being watched from every angle. I think that he's following me, so maybe I can gain his trust enough to talk to him. I'm curious what he would be willing to tell me about the alliance between Bale and Tanner . . . if he knows anything about it at all.

The townspeople tell me that he is everywhere and nowhere at the same time. In his own silent way, he seems to know much more than one would expect. I can feel the energy of the people change when Raven is mentioned or seen. I have unintentionally seen him in many people's minds and memories. Enough that I am certain that his presence here can only be purposeful.

I have put on some weight, and I feel my strength returning. Baldmar is a good man that has endless patience for my ineptitude with a hammer. He has provided me with lodging, food, and clothes. He even agreed to teach me to make my own sword.

As payment, I have taken to helping his family with household chores. The children never learned to read, so I have been tutoring them in literature and mathematics. I believe that is the reason he has been so kind to me; his children are sharp. If they have the desire to, there is so much they will be able to accomplish as they grow.

His daughter, Loren, told me, in confidence of course, that she hasn't seen her father this happy in years.

His son, Lance, has shown no interest in learning his father's trade, but he is becoming very passionate about mathematics. I don't know if I have the heart to tell him I only know so much, but the boy is clever enough to likely figure it out if I stay here too long.

I truly believe that this is why Baldmar puts up with me and everything I am unable to do myself.

Lately, his daughter has been hanging around the smithy and asks her father many questions every day. He absolutely adores it.

I suspect he will have a protégé after all. One that isn't as incompetent at this skill as I am.

Baldmar tells me that the topics of Tanner and Bale aren't outwardly forbidden. People's silence seems to stem from fear.

He did tell me some interesting information, though.

An associate of Tanner's appeared in a neighboring village about a month before I did. His reputation is of a terribly vengeful person. According to Baldmar, there was a man in the borough market that refused to sell him an axe. They argued in the street a short while before this individual pulled out a dagger and killed the merchant right there.

The crowd that witnessed the crime feigned ignorance, and he apparently let them live.

Baldmar does not know this associate's name, as it changes with the person asked. He refers to this individual only as a devil.

Baldmar told me of another incident where an entire family disappeared. The family had offered him refuge for the night, and he took it. The next day, everyone was gone but him. When questioned by authorities, I'm told all he did was laugh and say they were still alive when he left.

No one thought they had passed until he made that statement.

The people here know he is allies with Tanner. He boasts about it constantly.

I need to know more. I am inclined to pay this devil a visit, but Baldmar desperately tried to talk me out of it.

I'm still not sure what to do with this information.

I'll continue journaling as I can.

Signed,

G.

I just awoke from a vision. Apologies if my thoughts are unclear or difficult to read. I have only the light from my lantern to see by.

I saw Raven. There were others with him who looked the same as he: white skin, white hair, and ice-cold eyes. He was younger in my vision. His face had a sort of childish roundness to it yet deeply distressed. He was speaking to a young girl who did not seem well.

She couldn't have been older than four and was curled tightly into a ball. And I remember a shocking amount of blood. I am not able to recall more detail than that.

I believe that he was trying to help her.

He turned to me; the lack of pigment in his eyes made them glow in the darkness around us. I was frozen by his stare.

It pierced something in my chest while he vanished in an instant, and the darkness covered me.

At first, I thought Loren was having a nightmare, but . . .

I heard a child crying, and I just knew that it was not Loren.

A light shone before me, some distance away, so I followed it.

No matter how far I walked, it evaded me. Each step forward became one step back.

I then awoke.

It was not much to see, but I felt a strange mixture of emotions all at once.

I felt sadness and fear but also a cautious hopefulness. I have never felt such things at once, and I am not entirely sure what to think of it yet.

The sadness is what has gripped me. The cry from the un-attainable light makes me nervous. I don't know what sense

I can make from this vision. I haven't had a vision like this before.

They are clear. Lucid. I remember every detail and can recall it on a whim . . .

It hasn't been but a few months since my brother was buried. I still see his face in my mind and hear his voice in my dreams.

I pray that my heart aches from the past, and not from something that has yet to unfold.

The sun will rise in a few hours, so I will try to get more sleep while I still have a chance to.

Signed,
G.

I saw a young woman in a vision. She was full of life and joy and had the most angelic presence. The beauty in her smile is far unparalleled by anything I've seen. I heard the sound of her laugh and wished with all my heart that I wouldn't wake.

Those curls had me at my knees. That smile full of pure, unblemished joy . . . Breathtaking.

She reached out for me, and I could have sworn I actually felt her squeeze my hand.

Gods, please make this vision become true.
Please let this woman not be just a dream.
Signed,
G.

There is a spot near the lighthouse in Border Port where the villagers go to fish. The area is difficult to hike to, but I was able to make it up here pretty easily. I'm not here to fish, though.

I don't feel comfortable journaling in public, but I had to take note of my vision.

Baldmar and I were at the main market to purchase groceries, and I overheard two sailors talking. Their previous port had been Greater Bay, and they spoke fondly of a growing unrest that was beginning to overtake the nation of Arnica. One mentioned an organization he had just joined that was forming a resistance against the crown.

By the time Baldmar and I got out of there, this sailor had recruited half the market to this so-called cause.

There is only one person who can be behind this.

On our way out of the market, someone bumped into my shoulder. Before I could even apologize, I was lost in a vision.

Baldmar had to help me to the lighthouse. It was my first time having a vision in public like that. He was confused, but he understands and respects that my being a clairvoyant must be kept secret. He didn't see who had walked into me, but I don't believe that it had been an accident.

I saw a creature of fire.

Its entire body was ablaze and was as tall as a building. Everything that it touched became engulfed, and the sounds of cracking and screaming resonated in my bones.

Baldmar brought me to this place so that I could write in private. He is a wonderful man.

Apologies for the penmanship. My hands won't seem to stop shaking.

More entries to come, I'm sure.

Signed,

G.

I had another vision of the flame creature. I saw fire and shadows, and a sheet of black rain that did nothing to quell the flames. I can still hear screaming and panic as I write this.

There was a moment where a shadow passed through the fires that did not burn. It flew about the creature as though taunting it. The shadow was shapeless aside from its wings, four. It had four wings.

There was a sharp, piercing sound before a flash of light woke me.

I sat up so quickly that I nearly knocked my lantern off the stand.

I have a theory as to what the shadow was, but I would be foolish to admit it aloud. I would be even more foolish to write it down.

I will say that . . . if I'm right . . . I pray it is on our side.

Signed,

G.

Raven stayed near my dwelling all night last night. I'm not sure, but I think that his presence is affecting me. He has been coming closer to me over the past weeks. There was one time that he nearly spoke to me. He even took an apple right from my hand!

I don't think I'll be spending another season here. Four months is more than enough, I feel. There isn't much left to find out here, but I will begin to chart my course to Arnica.

In spring, I will head toward Market Road.

My work with the blacksmith and the love of his family have reenergized me to make sure I deliver these letters. This war must be stopped. It cannot spread to the rest of this world, a world already rife with conflict.

I learned so much about crafting weapons, knowledge I am not sure I will be able to use, but the time spent learning was unbelievably rewarding.

Baldmar made me promise not to see the devil, and I gave him my word that I wouldn't go. He is such a gentle man that has so much love for the living.

I hope to bring this love and kindness with me to the places I intend to go.

Loren wants to follow in her father's footsteps. She announced at breakfast that she wants to be the greatest blacksmith in all of Yu'e. Her proficiency with her father's tools and eagerness for the trade have clearly breathed new life into Baldmar.

His wife, Cyrene, told me if I can find the daemon trails from here, I might be able to keep out of trouble.

Hopefully.

Baldmar recommended that I stick to the road and avoid the trails. He said that powerful spirits patrol the trails, looking for journeymen that stray too far from the road. What happens to them, I do not know. He didn't want to elaborate, so I did not press.

Journaling may become less frequent, but I will do my best not to miss anything important.

Signed,
G.

I only have a few moments, so this entry will be short.

Raven followed me from Dendros. In my search for the trails, I was found by a daemon colony. Raven's family. Exactly like my vision. So much that I recognized many of the faces.

I am in a locked room, waiting to receive judgment . . . Whatever that could mean. When I asked, I was told, again, that I need to "receive judgment" before I am permitted to leave.

I am not sure what will happen next, but I pray this ma—

Wren furrowed her brow and turned the pages, only to find the rest of the journal blank.

Nik groaned softly and shifted beneath his quilt.

Wren jumped at the sound and unintentionally clapped the book shut.

Loudly.

The sudden sound caused his brows to knit together as his eyes opened. Nik groaned again and rolled onto his back to glare at Wren.

"Do you ever sleep until a normal hour?" His voice was rough and annoyed. Nik pressed his hands into the mattress to force himself into a sitting position.

"Of course. I've also heard that too much sleep dulls the senses."

Nik sighed and rolled his shoulders until he found a knot. The muscles of his bare arms and chest flexed as they moved and twisted to stretch out the soreness.

Wren forced herself to look away, purposely ignoring the heat flooding to her ears.

"Listen. Most people allow themselves the occasional indulgence of sleeping in a little bit later than *dawn*. It helps to ease the body and calm the mind. You've hardly slept these past few nights." His eyes turned to her and narrowed. "And it certainly hasn't helped your mood."

"Is every morning your *occasional indulgence*? Because that sounds like bullshit to me." She glared right back. "I can't help it if I don't sleep. It's not like I'm trying to stay up all night."

"Wren." His tired voice was strained. He let his eyes slip shut and rubbed them with the heels of his palms. "I want you to try something from now on."

"Oh?" She folded her arms and tried not to stare.

"Yes." He shifted to sit more comfortably. "When you can't sleep at night, I want you to come and wake me up."

"What? Nik, I'm not a child. I'll be perfectly fine once I have something to eat and we are on our way back to Black Rivers."

Nik turned his shoulders to face her fully. His bare feet dropped to the hardwood floor with a soft *thud* as he kept his eyes locked on her. "Quit being stubborn and hear me out."

Wren snorted and shook her head. "Fine then. I'm *all* ears."

"You don't have to be a little shit about it . . . But thank you." He couldn't hide the small smirk that played on his lips when she stuck her tongue out at him and continued after a short pause. "You said the same thing the night that Elliot disappeared. You slept *then*."

Wren narrowed her eyes. "That doesn't count."

"What?" Nik couldn't keep the disbelief from his reply. "What do you mean? It absolutely counts. You can't call me childish when *that* is your argument."

"You've yet to make yours."

Nik growled softly and leaned forward to scratch between his shoulder blades in a huff. "The night that Elliot disappeared," he began through a tight jaw, "you made a similar excuse to refrain from taking care of yourself."

"Excuse? Losing Elliot is not an *excuse*." Her last word dripped with indignance.

"Wren," Nik said softly.

She pursed her lips and sucked in a breath through flared nostrils.

Nik took advantage of her quiet to bring the conversation back to his original point. "If you don't take proper care of yourself, you won't be in a proper state to be your best."

"Ugh. You sound like Lionel."

He chuckled in response and shook his head. "But you *did* sleep that night. You insisted that you wouldn't be able to. Remember?"

"I remember." She turned to face him fully as well. "Do you really think that's going to work any time I don't sleep? Believe me, you don't want that. I will say, however, you sure think highly of yourself."

Nik's grin widened. "You didn't seem to complain."

A hot blush lit her cheeks and ears. Wren looked away from him and shook her head. "You're missing my point. I appreciate the gesture, but I decline."

It was Nik's turn to shake his head. "You should at least consider it. I'm even willing to compromise and say only wake me *sometimes.* I'd take that."

"How generous."

"Do you hate it when I kiss you?"

The sudden shift in his voice made her eyes shoot to his.

"N—" She clapped her hands over her mouth. With a quick breath, she continued, "I mean, no. I don't *hate* it."

"Then?"

Wren chewed on her lower lip and shook her head. "*Then,* what? There's no question there."

Nik propped his elbows on his thighs and leaned in. His hands dangled between his knees, and his golden-green eyes held her stare intensely. "What *do* you think when I kiss you?"

Her eyebrows went low. Wren's shoulders slouched together as she leaned back. "I-I need to get up. We need to get moving if we want to get back to Lionel today."

"Wren." Nik gently caught her arm and kept her from moving. "Don't pretend like there isn't something here."

"I'm not pretending," she argued. "I know there's something here, but I don't know what to think about it." Wren stared at the large hand around her forearm. "It's too much to take in all at once. I can't focus on anything." A welt of emotion formed in her chest that she struggled to restrain. "Elliot being kidnapped, Lionel's eye and possible loss of his foresight, the alchemist, the king's *proposition,* this." She waved her free hand in the air between them. "I can't process it all at once. And it isn't fair."

"What isn't?"

"You," she blurted. Wren averted her eyes and tried to tug her arm free. "Never mi—"

"I'm not letting you go until you talk to me. Even if it isn't about *this*." He mimicked her hand waving between them. "You at least need to trust me to help with everything else."

"You don't understand, Nik." She rubbed between her eyes with her free hand. "I can't focus on anything else. At least, not for long without *you* invading my mind." Wren sighed. "I feel guilty. Elliot's been taken to who-knows-where at this point, and Lionel nearly died. That pervy king wants me locked away. People are still disappearing." Her eyes looked defeated as she ranted, and they refused to meet his. "All of these things I should be thinking about, yet I struggle to *not* think about you. It's distracting and entirely unfair."

Nik watched her with an unintentional smile. He stayed quiet, as though he knew there was more that she wanted to say.

Wren turned and slid her legs off of the bed. She mirrored his sitting position across from him and pursed her lips.

"I *do* like when you kiss me," she finally admitted softly. She was at least wise enough to keep her eyes away from his. "But we can't do this. Not *now*."

Nik was silent. He released her arm and held up both palms in surrender.

Wren's eyes were locked on the warm spot his hand left on her arm before she allowed them to find his.

The way he watched her would have made her uncomfortable had it been anyone else. The golden flecks of light that were laced in with his emerald irises seemed to snare every particle of light. There was something within them that called to her. Something terrifying and chaotic yet irresistible.

Before she realized it, her body leaned toward him. She reached out to place her palm on his bare chest as she moved. Wren felt a glint of satisfaction at the stunned look on his face as she slowly closed the distance between them.

The hand on his chest gradually pushed him back while she followed. She registered the feeling of his hand against her cheek before it knotted into her hair. His other hand ghosted over her waist before another sensation overtook her.

Nik's lips encased hers, and he wrapped his arm around her tightly. His hand in her hair kept her mouth against his. He allowed himself to fall flat against the bed, but kept his arms locked around her.

Wren jammed her hands against the mattress to sit up and gasped, eyes wide.

"This was a mistake," she started and tried to get free. "Sorry, it was my fault. I shouldn't have done tha—"

Nik's lips cut her short. The hand in her hair refused to let go as the other looped all of the way around her back. With a soft growl, he flipped them over, laying her beneath him.

"*I* don't think it was a mistake," he said in a low voice. His eyes were fixed on her, and his breathing was heavy. "Do you really think that it was a mistake? Or are you trying to convince yourself that it's a bad idea?"

Wren's head swirled, and instead of answering his question, she felt herself reach for his face. Her fingers grazed across his cheek and eventually to the nape of his neck. With a cautious look, she pulled him in for another kiss.

Nik moved Wren to be beside him with his arms still secured around her waist. Her head was curled into his neck, and her hand was splayed on his chest, just above his racing heart. His hand pulled the neckline of her tunic down slightly on one side to trace lines across her bare shoulder.

Tiny bolts of lightning pricked her skin anywhere he touched.

"You're going to get tired of me," she whispered.

"What?"

"If we were to leave Arnica together. You would be able to deal with me for a little while, but your patience will eventually wear thin enough to make you leave. Gods, I'm not even sure how Lionel did it . . ."

"I couldn't," he hummed into her hair. "Even if I wanted to. I would never be able to stop thinking about you. You really don't see it." He kissed the top of her head as he tucked a lock of hair behind her ear. "Wren, you are one of a kind. Not because of *what* you are, but *who* you are. And I will protect you. No matter what." He paused and flashed a broad smile at her that made the tips of her ears burn. "Not because Lionel asked me to. I will stand at your side because I want to."

Wren smirked and shook her head. "Whatever you say." She deflected in an uncharacteristically soft voice and sat up. "Listen, I found this journal." Wren coughed and changed the subject. She freed herself from his arms and collected the book from atop her quilt. "There are a bunch of entries, then it just stops. It also says something about letters, but there are none. I wonder whose journal it is. Maybe we could ask Heilyn?"

"Hm," he hummed as he took the book that she held out to him. He flipped it open and read a few passages before he chuckled. He patted the quilt beside him for her to sit.

She arched a brow at him but tentatively seated herself beside him.

As soon as she settled in, Nik's arm looped around her waist and tugged her against his chest.

She blushed furiously and forced herself to look at the book instead of the grin she knew would be on his face.

Nik pretended to not notice her avoiding his eyeline and tapped one of the pages with his index finger. "We don't need to ask him who this journal belonged to, Wren."

"What do you mean?"

"You don't recognize the handwriting?" When she gave no response, he angled the book back to reread the pages and nodded. "This is Lionel's journal."

CHAPTER TWENTY-ONE

"The greatest happiness of life is the conviction
that we are loved; loved for ourselves, or rather,
loved in spite of ourselves."

Victor Hugo

S ILVER CROSSED HIS ARMS AND CLICKED HIS TEETH IMPA-
tiently. He leaned against the splintered doorframe of the
barn and sighed loudly through his nose.

"Silver." Jasper let his empty threat trail off yet maintained eye contact with his brother.

"We should start moving now. It's still going to be a few hours
until we are in the valley, and the darkness is our best cover."

"It's been *half an hour*. She hasn't had a chance to breathe since
we got off that damned ship. Give her some time to rest and have
an actual meal."

"She ate last night."

"Silver, rotten bread isn't a meal for a human."

The elder 'kin narrowed his eyes but remained quiet. He glanced
up the ladder, toward Elliot's sleeping form, and clicked his teeth
together again.

"We'll find her something, then we need to go," Silver finally replied flatly. He dropped onto all fours and made a beeline for the tall brush.

Jasper darted off after his brother with a skeptical look behind his eyes.

The pair approached the edge of a small stream that glistened with moonlight. If they followed the stream to its source, it would quickly become the tumultuous current of a fast-moving river.

At least they were going the right way.

Silver's pink paws held the grip of a bow that he'd crafted from supplies Jasper and Elliot had found in the crates. A handmade arrow rested against the bowstring, ready to be drawn back at a moment's notice.

Jasper had crafted himself a three-pronged hook on a braid of strong twine. The inward curves of the hooks balanced their weight enough to be accurately thrown with ease, even with his small size.

The brothers remained silent until Silver spotted a fish. He drew the arrow back and took aim. Once Silver's shot lined up with the fish, the black 'kin released the projectile into the gently flowing water.

Jasper twirled his hook skillfully behind him. He tossed it into the water and pulled until it caught the long side of the fish's body. As soon as he felt resistance at the other end of the twine, he yanked it back as hard as he could.

Silver set his bow on the ground and dashed over. He gripped the twine beside his brother and helped him to pull the struggling fish out of the water.

It wasn't much bigger than them, but it put up enough of a fight to make them pant. The rattenkin brothers drew their concealed daggers, thanking the fish for its sacrifice, and plunged their blades into its flesh. Their synchronized, pinpoint accuracy ended its suffering in half a heartbeat.

They each took a pectoral fin in their tiny arms and hoisted the front end of the fish up to begin their brief return journey.

"Do you think one fish is enough?"

"It'd better be. How do you suggest we carry back another?"

Jasper rolled his eyes and sighed.

They swiftly retreated to the barn where Elliot still slept, with the modest fish bouncing between them.

When she did awaken, it was to the smell of something delicious. She sat up from her makeshift bed and looked over the edge of the loft.

The 'kin had created a circular fire pit just outside of the barn doors that was lined with stones. They had cleverly covered the bottom of the pit with a thick layer of sand and loose stone to prevent the fire from escaping. A modest fish was propped next to the flames, already cooked on the side that she could see.

Her stomach growled, and she hurriedly joined them by the fire.

"Good morning," Jasper's friendly voice greeted her. "Your breakfast is almost done."

"My breakfast?"

"Riverfish. They are common in Aster. For whatever reason, they only live in or around the mountains here. Very high in protein. It'll give you lots of energy."

"You caught that? Just for me?"

"Silver and I did, yes. If he hadn't been there, I might've been swimming."

"Thank you, Jasper. You didn't have to go this far."

The sandy-brown 'kin smiled sheepishly.

Elliot's eyes wandered to the horizon before them. She squinted slightly and rubbed her eyes. "What time is it?"

"It's almost dawn." He pulled the fish away from the fire and handed it to her. "Silver is scouting the trail that we are going to take, so he'll grab what he can find to eat on the way back."

"You didn't go too? Aren't you hungry?"

Jasper shrugged. "I'm a rattenkin. I can eat almost anything as we travel. I'm not worried about going hungry."

Elliot laughed softly and took a bite. It was slightly overcooked, but she wasn't about to say anything about it. It was absolutely delightful, and the gesture alone warmed her heart.

"Will that hold you over until evening?"

Jasper and Elliot turned to see Silver with a bag full of nuts and grains slung over one shoulder. His brother was right; the sack was stuffed with an abundance of things he'd foraged in such a small time.

"It's good, I can make it work." Her bright smile aimed at the black 'kin brother didn't waver. "Thank you for bringing me something to eat. It was too kind of both of you."

"You're welcome, Elliot," Jasper chimed.

"Put the fire out. Let's move."

The trio walked for hours, occasionally breaking into sprints once they entered a clearing as dawn turned to morning. Elliot would crouch as she ran to use the tall grass as cover. Once they'd passed through the area that Silver had scouted, they ran blind.

Elliot nibbled on her lower lip.

When she and Jasper had been digging into the crates last night, he had given her advice for their upcoming journey. He'd been delighted to tell her everything that he knew about the territories and those that lived within them.

There was a strip of cleared, flat land that connected Dendros to Arnica. It was used as a transcontinental trading community that was given the name "Market Road." It was considered a neutral territory without any appointed leader. Instead, it was under the quiet rule of neutral daemon clans that took up residence in the wildlands along the borders to maintain relative order.

Centuries ago, merchants and mercenaries attempted to take ownership of the territory that belonged to the daemon and wildland creatures. War broke out, and most that came into contact with a daemon did not survive the encounter. A few clans of daemon had been lost to the conflict once humans joined forces with other creatures that had a better resistance to their magic. As bloodshed and loss grew too much to continue, a deal was made with the remaining daemon clans to create what is now Market Road. It must remain a neutral territory in order to prevent another bloody conflict.

Disputes in Market Road were to be settled however those within them wished. Many merchants were wise enough to hire private security. Certain districts of Market Road were home to gangs that made their footholds throughout the territory. Each enjoyed their own flavors of crime and sin, and with the lack of policing, grew in boldness along with the generations.

Daemon would only intervene if brawls made it into the wildlands, into *their* territory.

In large part, safety depended on which parts of the road were traveled.

Those who didn't know any better were frequently never heard from again.

Tens of thousands of shops and vagrant merchants cropped up throughout the entire length of the territory that lined each side of the miles-wide road. Market Road bordered the northern portions of Clove and Red Clove, with the entirety of Aster to its north. All of the neighboring nations used it for commerce and travel.

Needless to say, wandering through the most populated area in the north wasn't a wise idea with Elliot's face plastered on wanted posters undoubtedly littering the city.

Seams of railroad were scattered across Market Road, making a two- to three week-long journey on foot into only a few days. It was the better choice for traveling families, as the trains were privately owned and, therefore, under private security.

The trio kept in relatively close proximity to the edge of Market Road. Close enough to occasionally see bodies moving from behind tree limbs and through bright green foliage on the other side of the tracks.

Elliot paid special care to stay low and keep to the darker shadows to camouflage her from sight.

They moved silently. If they could hear voices from the market, it was a sure bet that the market would be able to hear their own murmurs in the early hour.

Large billows of gray clouds loomed overhead, threatening the three travelers with the chance of a downpour. Cold gusts of wind cut through the worn holes on Elliot's clothes. The same ones she had been in when she was taken, sans cloak. The damned pirates took that.

The small human couldn't restrain a shiver that shook her shoulders.

Walking behind her, Silver's careful eye noticed her discomfort and halted. He lifted his nose into the air and sniffed repeatedly. With a shake of his head, his small paws reached for a loose fold of Elliot's pants. The black 'kin gestured for her to follow before he sprinted away from Market Road and toward the white-water river that ran parallel to the road.

She looked to Jasper in confusion.

He shared the sentiment but knew his brother well. With a silent nod, he led Elliot a good distance away from the road. They dodged through increasingly dense brush and trunks with relative ease.

Elliot could only see where she was headed from the brief flashes of light-brown that guided her.

They spotted Silver under the cover of a rock formation. It was large enough to shelter at least four fully grown humans.

"A storm is coming. It would be foolish to continue in our current state if we were to get caught in it." His black eyes looked over Elliot's shivering body. "You need warmer clothing. The only place we will find that is within the market." He approached Elliot to encourage her under the shelter of the massive stone. "It would be best if you remained out of sight. If there are posters of you in Dendros, you can be certain they're in Market Road, too."

Her brows furrowed angrily. "Fantastic. This whole situation is complete bullshit." She sat in a huff and crossed her arms. "Why would someone do this? What's the point?"

"Isn't it obvious?" Jasper's question caught Elliot off guard. He and Silver exchanged a look before the tan 'kin sat beside her. "Gus said something about it while we were still at sea. It's because of your connection to your friend."

"But why Wren? She's just a common tempest."

"Is that its name? Strange." Silver dropped his tiny rucksack on the ground and began collecting sticks. "There is a rumor from Arnica that it's *not* a common tempest."

"What?" Elliot asked, suddenly breathless.

"The bounty specified that you must be alive upon delivery, so that's probably why the pirates left you alone once you were captive."

"And where am I supposed to be *delivered* to?"

"Somewhere in southern Dendros. I'm not sure of the exact location." Silver folded his furry arms and closed his eyes. "The collectors have been shockingly plentiful, though. So many poor girls that fit your description have been trafficked through Border Port since the reward was posted."

"Gods," she uttered in a whisper.

"Nearly every collector ship has creatures like us on board, so many of those girls escaped." Jasper's cheek perked up in a prideful grin. "Gus even made a deal with a family of sirens that live outside of Echinacea Islands to help girls escape by sea. Not only that, but we belong to an alliance of seafarers with one goal: help the helpless. I've never understood how humans could behave in such ways. Sure, there are gruesome members of any species, mythic or mortal. But humans . . . They have their own breed of evil."

"I guess it kind of explains why you don't like me, Silver."

He peeked one eye open at her and stayed quiet for a few moments. "I don't dislike you. I don't *know* you, but you've been able to keep up with us for the most part. That's something. You seem different from most of the ones I've met."

"I guess that's fair," she said, half-sarcastically. "But that doesn't explain why there's a bounty on me."

"I've no proof, but I have a theory." Silver's tone was flat.

"I've got the same theory," Jasper added quietly with a nod.

"What's that?"

The brothers looked to each other before they answered in unison.

"You're the bait to draw your friend out of hiding. Someone is hunting *her*."

"Border Port?"

Wren nodded mutely. She sat painfully upright in a chair beside Lionel's bed.

Lionel, propped into a sitting position, gripped a steaming mug with a gloved hand. A single cerulean orb watched her.

There was a broad bandage stretched over his right eye and around his face that was ever so slightly soiled with red. His drooped shoulders were covered with blankets, and his skin still had a subtle hue of blue to it.

Lionel looked so small.

Wren's face was devoid of any expression. She tried instead to focus on the rich smell of tobacco still staining her fingertips as she brushed her hair away from her face.

Lionel frowned and placed his mug on the table beside him. He reached out to touch her knee softly, wearing a gentle smile.

"Wren?"

She hesitantly met his eyeline and said nothing when his other hand caressed her cheek.

"You can't blame yourself for what happened. We can only move forward now. The important thing is finding Elliot and making sure she is safe."

Wren turned her head away from his touch and stood. "You're bleeding again. I'll see if Kora was able to find more bandages." As she neared the door, she sidestepped Nik so that she could leave.

Lionel sighed and watched her form vanish.

"She has been like this since Elliot was taken." Nik folded his arms and took Wren's abandoned seat.

"Does she eat?"

"Not really," Nik admitted with a shake of his head. "Kora was able to talk her into dinner. I think I saw her take five bites of breakfast before we left this morning. Heilyn's daughters made a feast for us, but she barely touched her plate."

"Ah." Lionel nodded and sighed. "Elliot would want us to hide the tobacco."

Nik smirked and let out a small laugh. "That's not a bad idea. And the coffee."

A silence drifted between them.

They could faintly hear Wren's muffled voice and the shuffle of Kora's long tail along the floor through the walls.

The diminishing daylight made shadows lengthen as the sun continued to set, intensifying the quiet.

After a long pause, Lionel broke the silence. "What is your plan?"

Nik looked to his friend with bewilderment. "*My* plan? Aren't you supposed to be the all-knowing one?"

Lionel chuckled and shook his head. "If only. Had I been, I would have seen the alchemist. I would have been able to connect a few more dots before I lost an eye."

"Actually"—Nik shifted in his seat to watch Lionel as he spoke—"I have some questions about that."

"Be my guest."

"Why did the alchemist take your eye?"

"Ubel," Lionel murmured softly. He felt Nik's questioning gaze and sighed without looking away from his tea. "He said that his name was once Ubel. I have a few theories as to why he would take my eye. The prevailing one is that he intends to use my ability of foresight and influence for his own benefit."

"He can do that by taking your eye?"

"I'm not sure. I hypothesize he knew that our paths would cross. Traces aren't rare, but they are certainly not common. It isn't exactly a secret that there is at least one here in Arnica. He'd only need to know that to know where to set up shop . . . If that is his intention."

"So, am I correct in assuming you think *you're* why he's here?"

". . . Possibly," Lionel muttered, and despite his word choice, he unconsciously shook his head. "I believe it is more likely that he is here for more nefarious reasons. We just happened to cross paths while he had the upper hand." He paused and glanced at his open doorway. "He has been here for a long time . . . That place was well lived in, and he had an abundant supply at his disposal."

"You think he has something to do with the disappearances, don't you?"

"Most assuredly." Lionel nodded without hesitation. "Alchemy is outlawed because it requires sacrifices. All of the people who have disappeared have yet to be found." He swallowed hard before leveling Nik with a serious look. "The room was full of body parts in jars . . . I believe that the kidnappings are happening because he has been building things."

"All right, so he was looking for you? For your abilities?"

"Maybe." Lionel drew in a deep breath that made his chest tighten. "He wouldn't be able to see to the extent that I can, well . . . could." The corner of his mouth twitched with a frown. "And he wouldn't be able to use my ability to influence. But he would at least be able to see his own immediate future. I'd wager he'd only be able to foresee a few hours ahead."

"So, what do you think he wants to foresee?"

"Wr—"

"Knock knock," Kora called from the doorway.

Both men turned to greet her.

She made her way to Lionel's side and began changing the dressing over his face.

Nik had to look away when the bandage was removed.

The nuwa hummed while she worked, politely ignoring the ebony-haired reaper's discomfort.

Cleaning his wound and changing the dressing didn't take very long, but it did feel like ages.

The seamstress's hands worked nimbly and carefully. And shockingly efficiently. Kora gave Lionel's shoulder a friendly pat and smiled at both of them.

"Do you need anything else, yes?"

Lionel shook his head with a smile. "No thank you, Kora. You have already done so much."

"Think nothing of it, yes?" Her three-fingered hand massaged a knot in Lionel's shoulder. "When your family needs help, you help. I will do anything I can to help find Miss Joy, yes. Her mum wasn't just my best customer. I loved her like a sister, yes."

"I know, Kora. We will find her."

She nodded with a gentle smile and turned her attention to Nik. "Did you find anything else out, yes? Pardon my intrusion on the conversation, but she will not discuss anything. She is like a ghost, yes. Blank eyes."

Nik sighed and shook his head. "We met the Michairs. Heilyn told us that Elliot was taken to Border Port."

"So"—Kora shifted to sit on the foot of Lionel's bed—"what is the next move, yes? If we know she's there, we can go after her."

"But what of the alchemist?"

Kora and Lionel both turned to Nik.

He wore a deep frown. His eyes were locked on the window, staring into the empty night.

"If you're right, Lionel, he might be able to foresee us leaving to go after Elliot. He knows what you and Wren look like now, too." He sighed heavily and leaned forward in his seat. His elbows propped him up by balancing on his knees. "You said he'd probably only be able to see *his* future. What if *this* is his future?"

"What do you mean, yes?" Kora's forked tongue hissed her *s* unintentionally.

Nik's eyes slipped shut. He sighed and rubbed at them roughly. "I don't believe this is a coincidence. You said that you think it was a right-time-and-place scenario, but I'm not convinced. What if this was his plan all along? Separate Wren from the kingdom by stealing the thing that means the most to her."

"Miss Joy?"

Nik met Kora's stare, and he nodded once.

"Her sister."

"Interesting, Nikolas." Lionel touched his chin and nodded to himself. "It would make sense that removing my ability to foresee would make us more vulnerable. The timing of Elliot's kidnapping is rather suspect, as well."

"So, the bigger questions are why is someone trying to handicap us, and why was Elliot taken? If we can figure out why, it should make finding out where easier."

Lionel nodded and collected his mug. He wrapped his fingers around it tightly, allowing the heat to radiate through his gloves. "If Elliot is on the eastern side of the continent, it would be reasonable to assume that whoever is behind this does not want Wren here at this time."

"Why, though?"

"Another attempt at the throne, maybe, yes?"

Nik's eyes flickered to Kora for a moment. "That is a possibility we shouldn't rule out."

"Nikolas." Lionel's voice dropped to a whisper. "It is imperative that Wren be kept safe. If something is going to happen, it will be soon. You and Wren returned here only a few hours ago. Were you seen?"

Nik shrugged and crossed one leg over the other. "Probably. It isn't like we were sneaking about. Did something happen while we were gone?"

"No," he replied quietly and dipped his chin. "I haven't *seen* anything, either."

"There was no talk in the market, yes. When I got your bandages and tea, I heard nothing of Miss Wren, nor Miss Joy. Just like always, people look away from a nuwa, yes."

Lionel gave her a soft smile and patted her three-fingered hand. "All we can do is keep an ear to the ground and an eye out for each other."

"Lionel, was that your attempt at a one-eyed joke?"

"What? Not funny?"

Nik smirked and looked back to Lionel's doorway. He could hear Wren moving about in the other room, and he could hear her murmuring to Jack.

"Oh." Nik remembered and turned to Lionel. "Wren found something while we were in Bay City."

"What's that?"

"She found your journal. At least, a journal with handwriting that looks identical to yours."

Lionel's eye widened, and he lowered the mug to the sheets over his lap. It took a long time for him to meet Nik's eyeline.

"Did you now," he mused quietly. "I am surprised that Heilyn did not destroy it."

"What is the journal about? I read it too, and there didn't seem to be a lot of information. It talked about letters, but there were none."

"Ah, yes. Those letters were the true purpose of the journal. Heilyn and his father were integral to getting into Arnica. When his father was alive, he was part of the resistance that was preparing to take on Seth's legion. They allowed me to live there while I tried to find my own place to settle into. It was Heilyn's father that was able to get me into royal commerce by being his bookkeeper. In doing so, I was able to find and afford this building."

"Why did it end so abruptly?"

Lionel's expression faltered for a moment before he caught himself. "That, I cannot divulge, my friend. It is not for me to discuss."

"Lionel," Nik warned. "This isn't the time to be mysterious."

"Believe me, I wish I could. If so, I would have told Wren years ago. I made an unbreakable agreement that prevents me from speaking of it. Even now, I cannot bring myself to share what happened after my last entry. I am sorry," he said softly to Nik's glower.

"Can't or won't, Lionel?"

All eyes turned to Wren, who stood in the doorway.

He gave her a sad smile and shook his head.

"*Can't.* I am prevented by a higher power to be able to speak of what happened after that entry. What I can say is that I heard you, Wren. All those years ago, in one of my visions, I heard the cry of a small child. That vision is why I needed to arrive in Arnica when I did. Even in those days, I knew that there was something much greater at play. It wasn't until I found you that I realized *you* were the crying child."

"Hmph."

Lionel's expression softened, and he shook his head once. "I understand if you would like to be angry with me for this."

Wren folded her arms and ground her teeth together. "I'm not

angry with you, Lionel. I think that it's foolish that you know something clearly important to all of this and can't say anything. But . . ."
She hesitated and finally met his eyeline. "You have always had your
reasons. There are plenty of other things that I can be angry about
instead of you."

CHAPTER TWENTY-TWO

WREN SAT WITH HER LEGS PULLED CLOSELY TO HER chest. She was perched on the roof of the apartment with a cigarette clutched between two trembling fingers. The tall stack of ash that had yet to break away indicated that it had barely moved in quite some time . . . Aside from the slight shivering.

She stared into the horizon, restless eyes fixed on the lands east of Arnica.

Market Road provides a direct connection from Arnica to Dendros. She pursed her lips as she tried to remember all the little things Lionel had taught her of the world when she had been a child.

Without realizing it, his voice began to resonate amongst her thoughts.

'Although Market Road is direct line between the two nations, the journey would be long and beset with hazards.' Lionel's bright

blue eyes shone in the darkness of her mind and made her chest tighten. *'It is seldom taken on foot, as thugs patrol openly and don't take too well to those who linger. Courier services that will transport travelers are abundant and help brave sightseers find their way through. For a price.'*

If she instead made a route parallel to Market Road, she would need to decide which side to take: follow the river that snaked along southern Aster, or the northern frontier land of the Clove territories.

Aster is a more populated and comfortably settled country than the Clove territories, she deliberated. *Despite the populace, the valleys and forests are still home to plenty of dangers. Fae and other mysterious creatures make the empty lands their home and have plenty of ways to ward off unwanted visitors.*

A sharp gust rushed by her, knocking away the tower of ash while simultaneously snuffing out the ember.

Wren groaned and pulled her cloak closer with her free hand.

If I follow the river in Aster on foot, the whole journey would only take . . . She nibbled at her bottom lip. *Two weeks? If I don't stop to make camp, maybe even one.*

'On the other hand,' Lionel's voice in her memories chimed, *'the two Clove territories are predominantly flat and abundant with vast colonies of broad-leaved trees. The trees house their own variety of threat by way of predatory birds that nest within the branches and big cats that will hunt anything they can catch. In turn, many species of prey developed methods of deterrent that make them nearly as dangerous. Such as the predatory meat-plant. Its diet consists* only *of meat.'*

When Lionel had told her of the meat-plant, it made her stomach turn.

'It's a plant that releases a smoky aroma, which will often lure lost travelers or hungry predators in to find its source. The plant itself is flat and has a web of tentacles that'll shoot out of the ground like cannons to snare whatever poor soul wanders across them.'

Things like *that* made most of the Clove territories difficult to settle. Most who tried were never again seen after they kissed their families goodbye.

Travel by sea is out of the question, Wren thought bitterly. *The trip may only be four days but is no less perilous. There's always the potential to run into pirates by sea* and *by port. Port cities are largely populated by rough sailors, aspiring cheats, and accomplished thieves. These particular citizens often wait until merchant ships arrive and unload their cargo before they strike. That way, they don't have to empty the ships themselves.*

It was common practice for merchants to hire protection, which was successful about half of the time. Mercenaries weren't cheap and weren't always very loyal.

As the saying goes, every man has his price.

There is the train . . . but that'd make me a sitting duck. Anyone could recognize me. It's the most popular choice of travel, which means it's probably the last thing I should do. Wren groaned and dropped her head back.

The snow chilled her to the core, but she didn't consciously register the cold. Everything inside was already frozen. Her long sunset hair drifted around her, free of any bands or braids to hold it together. It was the only thing that kept the biting air off of her shoulders and neck.

Wren glanced to the cigarette and cursed under her breath.

Wasted another one, she thought venomously and flicked it away.

Wren heard the *clink* of approaching steps on the metal ladder and buried her face into her arms to pull her knees closer. She listened to them grow closer to her and stop directly beside her.

There was a quiet shuffle before something warm fell onto her head and back.

Nik sat beside her in the snow and kept his stare fixed in the same direction as hers.

As the long silence filled the cold atmosphere, the warmth over her shoulders was instantly identifiable by its earthy, cedar smell.

The notable weight of Nik's coat retained his body heat so well that it helped to restore some of hers.

Wren gripped the lapels to draw it closer around her.

"What are you going to do?"

She sighed and shook her head. "Does it even matter?"

"What?"

Her eyes tightened, and she exhaled through her nose. "I can't even protect the two people that mean the most to me. In *one day*, I lost Elliot, and Lionel nearly died by the hands of some lunatic. I gave away my cover. The bastard knows what I look like, he even knows my godsdamned *name!*" Wren managed to meet his stare for a fleeting moment before she had to turn away.

In the short time they maintained eye contact, Nik almost missed the quick flash of silver that vanished as soon as it appeared.

"Even fully shifted, I couldn't protect Lionel. Even a *reaper* couldn't protect Elliot." She growled and buried her hands into her hair. "Stay and protect the kingdom only to be sentenced to live with that awful, *awful* man to be at his beck and call? Or leave to find Elliot, pick the wrong way to get to Dendros, and fall into some sort of trouble? Would I *even* find her? It doesn't matter. I'll just fail again. Like I do *every* time!"

"You haven't failed, Wren."

"Bullshit. Nik, the night we met, I was about to lose to those grifters. If you hadn't stepped in, I wouldn't even be here right now." She looked away and glared into the snow.

"Wren," he tried again.

"I don't want to hear it. Call me childish all you like, but I have every right to be furious!"

"I never said you didn't. But lashing out at yourself is counter-productive."

She growled and stood. "Just leave me alone, Nik. Get out of Arnica and go far, far away before it's too late."

Nik remained seated but turned his eyes to her. "I already told you that I'm not going anywhere."

"Stop." She held her hand up. "Lionel may have asked you to come babysit me, but I don't want it. I'm a grown woman that can choose to fend for herself. I don't want to be close to anyone. Ever. Never again."

He snared her wrist easily and tugged her back down.

Wren stumbled and dropped her knee into the snow before she ripped her hand free and pushed him away roughly.

Nik caught himself by his elbows and narrowed his eyes at her. He sat up and quickly took hold of his jacket around her shoulders. His hands tightened into fists in the fabric as he pulled her in closer.

"You need to calm down and take in the elements one at a time. You try to take everything head on, all at once, and are surprised when you get smacked down."

"Let go of me."

"When we fought that first night, you knew you couldn't win. Yet your stubbornness compelled you to try regardless."

"Nik," she warned again.

"You are surprisingly skilled, I admit. I wasn't expecting you to be so fearless and bold." His golden-green eyes leveled her hazel ones, refusing to release them. "You can't focus on one thing at a time, Wren. I saw it in your fight with the grifters, as well is in our bout. Your uncertainty is obvious, and your hesitance handicaps you."

"So, what? You knew I was a loser before you even talked to me?"

His smirk cracked the tension between them. "Quite the opposite, actually. But I'm not talking about that right now." Nik felt her shoulders relax slightly, but her burning expression remained. "I can help you learn how to focus."

Wren snorted and slapped him away. "Pass."

His strong hands quickly re-collected the ends of his jacket around her. "Hear me out, Wren. I already know your style of fighting; you won't hurt me. It wouldn't hurt *you* to learn something new."

Objections piled up in the back of her mind, but she kept her jaw clamped shut.

"If there is a way for me to help you, this is at least one." His right hand loosened and lifted to brush a lock of hair behind her ear.

Her wounds from Honorah had nearly healed. There was only a small pale scab left on her ear. Yet the scratch across her cheekbone seemed resistant to fully heal.

"I know that your heart won't let you walk away from this. No matter how angry you are right now, you couldn't do it. Not with the current stakes."

Wren turned her face away from his touch and squeezed her eyes shut. "Please," she whispered. "Don't . . ."

He tenderly turned her chin back to face him with his finger. "You told me that you don't know how I could help you. I think we just figured out a way that I can." His thumb caressed her cheek idly. "Trust me, Wren."

She watched him with cautious eyes for a long time. "What do you have in mind?"

"CHANGE YOUR STANCE." NIK WALKED AROUND HER AND TAPPED her ankle with his heel. "Bend your knees more and straighten your back." His fingers pushed into her spine as his other hand pulled her shoulders back and flicked her elbow. "Elbows in."

"Quit that." Wren turned and smacked his hands away. "Verbal instruction works perfectly fine."

"No, it doesn't. You're shit at listening. Look." He tapped her ankle with his heel once more. "Stagger your lead foot more. Your center of gravity isn't as balanced as it could be when you stand like that."

"Show me, then."

Nik complied and shifted his feet across the mat and fluidly into the stance. Perfectly. His elbows were tucked near his ribs, and forearms positioned across his chest. He had a light bend to his knees that had that annoying bounce to them that hers apparently didn't.

"Now you."

He held the stance for her to mirror.

"No, Wren. Your lead foot." He lurched forward and swept her leg.

She tumbled to the mat of the boxing ring. A plume of dust billowed around her, causing her to cough.

"You are too rigid. You're as unsteady as a drunk toddler." Nik reached his hand out to her.

To his surprise, she took it.

He pulled her upright and put both hands on her shoulders.

"Relax. Close your eyes and focus on your breathing."

She nodded and tucked her chin to inhale a deep lungful of air. Her eyes slipped shut as she repeated the breathing exercise.

Wren struggled to concentrate on her breathing with all of the other things that were tugging at the back of her mind. However, the warmth of Nik's hands on her shoulders helped her to focus instead on something physical and push out the raging current of thoughts that threatened to sweep her feet out from beneath her like Nik had.

They stayed like this for a short while until Nik could feel her muscles loosen and her breathing even.

"Keep your eyes closed," he started in a soft voice, "and take your stance."

The warmth left her shoulders, and she obeyed.

Wren focused on her feet sliding across the mat as she tried to picture Nik's stance in her mind. She corrected herself a few times before she brought her arms up into the position she was trying to memorize.

"Good," he hummed. "You can open your eyes."

Her eyes opened and looked to her bare feet.

"Now, lift your arms a bit more and curl your shoulders inward. Keep your hands ready to strike, but don't lock your elbows. You'll only shorten your response time marginally, but that could be the upper hand that your opponent will be waiting for." He pushed her hands down and moved her back a few steps by the shoulders. "Now, watch only me and take your stance from muscle memory."

Wren took a deep breath, keeping her eyes trained on him. She bent her knees and shifted her feet without looking. A pang of uncertainty itched at the nape of her neck, and she glanced down.

The moment she took her eyes off of him, he dashed forward and effortlessly knocked her to the mat.

"Damnit, Nik! I wasn't ready."

"I told you not to look away from me. Do it again but actually listen this time. You need to trust your body to do it without thinking. Thinking needs to be spent on your opponent, not your own feet."

Wren growled at him yet heeded his instruction. With a deep breath, she dropped into the stance again without looking away from him.

"Good," he said again. "Get ready this time. I'm going to strike first."

A small welt of apprehension tightened in her chest, and she swallowed hard. Wren felt her shoulders tighten up and struggled to relax them.

Nik noticed her stiffen and took his opportunity. He rushed at her and easily caught her by the arm. He bent down to lift her, but she slipped free at the last moment.

Wren rolled over his back and onto the opposite side of him. She hurried into the stance they were practicing and bounced lightly, keeping her eyes locked on him.

He twisted at the waist and locked his arms around her chest. Nik lifted her from the mat and prepared to throw her back down onto it.

Wren grasped at his arms on either side of her and worked her fingers beneath his hands. When she was able to get an angle, she grabbed his ring fingers at lightning speed and yanked them back.

He had to release her to keep his fingers from dislocating.

Wren's back still hit the mat, but she hurriedly returned to her feet and slid back into her stance.

Nik shook his hands and laughed once.

"Cheap but effective." He balled his fists and cracked his knuckles. "Not all opponents will have fingers, though. But I applaud your creativity." With a smirk, he tapped her ankle with his heel. "Again."

Jasper and Silver darted through bountiful piles of goods, weaving unseen from merchant to merchant in search of their intended target. The brothers made their way through the tangle of feet until they found a clothing shop.

Each 'kin had a pouch tied around their back.

The streets were surprisingly empty for it being late afternoon, but the two rats were determined to use it to their advantage. They ducked into a shop and found the interior to be busier than expected. Many bodies browsed through the selections, chattering boisterously over each other.

"Silver," Jasper whispered. "Over here."

They made a beeline in the direction he had indicated. Their tiny paws carried them to a section of the shop where they found women's clothing. Silver sought out a pair of trousers while Jasper located a warm tunic.

The 'kin snatched the articles and hurriedly stashed them into the pouches they carried. Their black eyes peered in every direction to check if they had been noticed.

When they believed the coast to be clear, they dashed out the back of the shop.

They hadn't noticed the pair of icy-white irises witness them lift the clothes.

Jasper and Silver backtracked through the thinning crowds. They came upon the small clearing that had led to their trail back to Elliot.

Fading evening light began to lessen their visibility, so the brothers picked up their pace to make it back before dark.

In their haste, they failed to cover up the small imprints their bodies left in the grass.

Silver made it to their makeshift shelter first. He skidded to a stop and lay flat onto his belly. The cold stone felt good against his racing heart.

Jasper was only seconds behind his brother and caught himself on Elliot's arm. He took a few deep breaths with one paw over his chest while the other tightly clutched the curly-haired girl's sleeve.

"Welcome back," she greeted with a smile in her voice. "I found dinner."

He cleared his throat and sat upright. His black eyes raked over the bounty she had assembled as he removed the pouch from his back. Jasper stood and handed it to her as he passed by to get a better look at the food.

Elliot had found an abundance of carrots, radishes, and potatoes from an unattended supply crate at the edge of the market. She had cleaned everything until the bright colors came to life. Everything was still whole, as she had nothing to cut with.

They ate in relative silence after she changed clothes, the only sound coming from the small crackling fire.

Jasper suddenly shot upright and went still. His ear twitched toward the trees, and he instinctively reached for his needle-thin blade.

Silver heard it at the same time as Jasper, reacting in precisely the same way. His paws collected his quiver and bow in an instant.

Elliot looked up to see a figure standing before them.

He was a little over average height with long limbs and pure white hair that swept the base of his jaw. His skin was the same color as the full moon, with eyes to match. The shadows around his eyes and the brows above them were a wispy shade of charcoal gray. A large, intricate tattoo covered the right side of his neck and most of his visible chest. His clothes obscured the rest of the ornamentation. Pale pink lips were perked into a sideways smile as his icy eyes looked between the three.

At his hip hung a scabbard with an undoubtedly sharp sword sheathed inside.

"How curious," he drummed in a deep voice. "A pair of rats and a girl all alone in the wildlands?"

No one in the company spoke. Elliot had yet to move, and Jasper and Silver had positioned themselves in front of her.

The man stepped closer and idly placed the palm of his left hand on the hilt of his sword.

Silver drew an arrow back as Jasper crouched into a ready position.

"Now, now." He lifted his black-gloved palms. "No need to get testy."

"Who are you?"

The piercing white eyes turned to Elliot. He said nothing as he stared at her for a long while. His head would tilt every few seconds until his lips broke into a wide smile. "I've seen you before."

"I doubt it," she countered and tried to ignore the jolt of panic at the base of her throat.

"Hmm," he mused. "Perhaps not *you*, but I have seen many young women that look very similar to you." He tapped his chin, that eerie grin still painted on his features. "Are you the one from the rumor? Or just another imposter?"

"An imposter," she answered immediately.

"Hmm."

"What do you want?"

Silver's question drew the man's attention away from Elliot.

"No offense, but I cannot be intimidated by vermin with tiny weapons. I don't answer to you." Without turning his head away from Silver, his white eyes slid back to the curly-haired human. "Then, who *are* you, imposter?"

Elliot's eyes narrowed, and she stood. "You think that you can talk to them like that and just expect me to answer to you?"

The man's grin widened, and he tapped the hilt of his sword playfully. "Well, *you* aren't armed."

"Then I hope you're prepared to kill me. I'm not telling you anything."

His eyes gleamed with amusement. "I don't intend to kill you. At least, not with the given knowledge. How about this." He took another step closer and lifted his weapon.

Silver eyed him suspiciously as the man set the blade on the ground.

"How about we all relax. No reason for the hostility."

"Excuse you? You're the one that showed up out of nowhere, refuses to say who you are, *and* you belittle my friends. The only thing you warrant *is* hostility."

His pale lips smirked again as he sat a short distance away from their campfire. "How is this? Far enough away?"

"No, wherever you came from is far enough away."

"Cheeky." He chuckled. "So be it. If it is a prerequisite to have a civil conversation, my name is Garret."

Elliot folded her arms and looked to the brothers.

They looked just as confused as she.

"What do you want, Garret?"

"Well, originally, I was curious as to why two rattenkin would be stealing women's clothing. So, I followed them," he said with a shrug. "It wasn't difficult. It's pretty easy to track prints in the grass. But that brings us to now."

"All right. But tell me this." She narrowed her eyes at Garret and tried to steady her voice. "What business is it of yours that they were stealing women's clothing?"

"Theft is theft." His eyes shined. "I could have them both arrested by the shop's private security right now and collect a reward. Plus"—his gaze locked with Elliot's—"I'm not convinced you're an imposter."

"Look, we are just passing through." Jasper tentatively approached Garret before he sat down at a respectable distance away. "We would have paid for them, but we don't have money. She's practically freezing to death."

"Hmm."

"You've told us your name, but who *are* you?"

His eyes shifted between the three before finally settling on Elliot, which made her chest clench. "Ah-ah, first tell me your name. It's only fair."

"Silver, Jasper, and Elliot." She glared as she spoke. "Now who are you?"

Garret clicked his tongue in disapproval. "I'm not a person for you to be confrontational with. If I'm being honest, I'm probably the closest thing you're going to find to an ally out here."

"If that's the case, I'm glad I won't be here much longer. What would make you an ally? Your tracking ability?"

"Hmm." Garret folded his arms and smiled wide. "Well, seeing as I'm a daemon, I have a knack for getting things around unseen."

"If you're expecting me to be impressed, save it. I don't know what a daemon is," she half lied. Although Gus had given her an idea, she still didn't fully understand what *kind* of creature a daemon was.

"Ahh." He nodded to himself. "That explains quite a bit. Well"—he stretched his long legs out before him so that they could bask in the heat from the fire—"daemon are conduits of the gods that guide lost souls to their destined paths. Many will refer to us as benevolent spirits."

"Are *you* benevolent?"

"Some are." Garret smirked as he dodged her question. "The bad ones don't really care what happens to you; they just stick around to keep themselves amused. Some even initiate misfortune."

"I bet I can guess which you are," Elliot said dryly.

"I'm the kind that's good at getting things from point A to point B."

"Silver? Jasper?" Elliot spoke without allowing her eyes to look away from Garret. "What do you think we should do?"

Jasper remained silent, but Silver took a step forward. "Tell me about this rumor, if you truly are impartial."

"Hmm." Garret's striking eyes watched the trio with a grin. "Well, what do you want to know? A young woman with curly brown hair, dark eyes. About five and a half feet tall. Thin. Midtwenties. Born in Clove, often visits the town of Black Rivers in Arnica during festival season. Reward is three hundred thousand gold coin, but she has to be delivered alive and uninjured."

"Who's offering the reward?"

"Dunno."

Silver growled at Garret's nonchalant response. "Why is there a bounty on a girl that fits this description? What is happening to them?"

Garret shrugged. "Your guess is as good as mine."

Jasper cleared his throat and watched the daemon with a cautious stare. "So, what are you propositioning? Why are you here still speaking with us if you have no ulterior motive?"

"Propositioning?"

Elliot uncrossed her arms and approached the fire. "Jasper's right. What are you looking for? If you're thinking of trying to collect the reward, you're out of luck. I've already been rejected," she bluffed.

Jasper and Silver looked at each other without moving their heads.

"Hmm." Garret leaned forward and narrowed his eyes. "I'm not saying that I don't believe you . . ." His grin never wavered as he spoke. "But I don't. However, I do know someone who *will* know what to do with you."

The 'kin brothers forced themselves between Elliot and Garret once again with their weapons drawn and ready.

"My arrows are tipped with nightshade, and Jasper's blade is much sharper than it looks. It'd be wise for you to leave now."

"Aah, I don't think so." He lifted a gloved hand into the nighttime sky and snapped his fingers. "You'll all be coming with me."

Before they could gather their wits, they were surrounded by an entire daemon hunting party.

"Let's head back."

"AGAIN!"

A hard *smack* cracked in the room. Nik braced himself behind the makeshift sparring pad in his hands as the front of her shin slammed into him.

Her breathing was haggard, and her lips were parted and painfully dry. Sweat poured from her skin, and her muscles quivered from exhaustion. Her form was on point, but she stumbled slightly when her foot hit the ground.

"Good, but you need to know where your feet are when you land." He coughed softly as he nodded. "Again!"

Wren reeled back and swung her leg with as much strength as she could muster. Her elbows dropped from her sides unconsciously as she struggled to fight away her fatigue. Her focus was fixed on her feet. Before she could make contact with the pad, Nik had caught her by the ankle.

He stood upright and turned her leg between his hands so that she slammed face-first into the mat.

"Your form is improving, but you are too tired to keep it up any longer. I told you that I'd put you on the ground if you dropped your elbows one more time." He patted a cloud of dust from his bare chest and arms and wiped a drop of sweat from his eyes.

Wren coughed and pressed her palms down on either side of her head to lift her face from the mat. Her biceps trembled as she struggled to push herself into a sitting position.

Nik's strong hand gently grabbed her by the arm and brought her to her feet.

She was still breathing heavily, but Wren watched him with detached eyes.

"Pick up the pad. I'm not through yet."

"Yes, you are. Don't be foolish. If you keep pushing yourself like this, you won't be able to move tomorrow."

She jerked her arm away from him and staggered backward. "I'm not through," she repeated. Wren backed up until she felt the ropes that surrounded the ring brush against her fingertips. She took a deep breath and charged at him.

Nik effortlessly caught her by the waist and hefted her over his shoulder. "It's time for bed."

Wren would have fought him on it, but truth be told, she really was exhausted.

Nik ascended the stairs and brought her to her bedroom. He set Wren on the foot of her bed and tucked a sweat-soaked lock of hair behind her ear.

"Take a shower and get some rest. You need both."

"Fine," she mumbled and closed her eyes. Contrary to her words, Wren unfurled on the top of her blanket and attempted to go to sleep.

"Wren," he tried again, "go take a shower. You're disgusting."

"So are you, jackass."

"Well, it's your decision to wake up clean or not. Good night."

Her eyes were still struggling to open when she heard her bedroom door slip shut. She sighed deeply but winced when the action shot a jolt of pain through her ribs. Wren groaned and made her way into her bathroom.

Jack was curled into a ball in the basin of the sink. White tufts of fur poked around the inside perimeter of the porcelain. His vivid eyes were veiled behind tired, pure-white eyelids.

Wren showered and dressed as quietly as she could.

There was no doubt the cat heard her, yet he didn't stir.

She made her way to her bed and nestled herself under the familiar covers. The cold sheets hugged snugly around her as she eventually got comfortable.

Wren hadn't realized she'd fallen asleep until a warm hand fell onto her shoulder. It tugged her from her dreamless, silent sleep.

"Rise and shine," Nik's voice whispered. She could almost hear his smirk. "Get dressed and meet me downstairs."

She glared at him without opening her eyes. "What time is it?"

"Early. We have a lot to cover today."

Wren pursed her lips tightly. "I'll be down in five. At least have the decency to let me make some coffee."

A crooked smile spread across his lips. He folded his arms and sarcastically returned her glare with a broadening smirk.

"I already did. Bring yourself some water as well. You're going to need it."

Without giving her the opportunity to rebut him, he stepped from her room and closed the door behind him.

Wren couldn't decide whether she should be amused or pissed off. She dressed in clothing that hugged her comfortably. As she got ready, she tried to ignore her aching muscles. She poured her coffee into a thick mug without bothering to fix it how she normally would.

Wren's eyes glanced to Lionel's bedroom door as she passed by, pausing slightly. She shook her head and filled a canteen with water before making her way downstairs.

Nik stood in the ring with a wooden staff in his hand. He left the lights off, so making him out was difficult. Though . . . his silhouette had become unmistakable.

"Your staff is on the bench. Come into the ring whenever you finish your coffee."

Wren set the canteen on the bench propped against the bottom of the ring. She watched him as she took a swig of her coffee and set it beside her canteen. She gripped her weapon and climbed into the ring.

"So, we are past drills?"

"For the time being. You'll be practicing your form today. In real combat." He shook his head. "It's the only way to make you remember to keep your damned elbows up."

Wren sneered at him.

"Does that look mean you're ready to start?"

"Shut up and tell me what you're planning."

Nik rolled his eyes at her and shook his head. "You're going to learn how to use your height to your advantage. Instead of running head-first into a fight with someone larger than you and getting your ass kicked, you're going to learn how to get the better of them, and maybe, just maybe, even win."

Wren opened her mouth to fire back but clipped it shut and settled for another glare.

Nik's eyebrow quirked at her, almost as if he could tell she purposely kept her comments to herself.

"Focus on side control and get behind your opponent whenever you can. If you are agile enough, you can use their weight and momentum against them."

"How's that?"

Nik slid his feet apart and bent his knees. He drew the staff to stand vertically beside him like a sheathed sword at his hip. His golden-green eyes somehow shimmered, even in the early morning darkness.

"I'll show you."

Wren shifted into a defensive crouch. She held the staff out behind her and pressed her palm against the mat. Her weary eyes watched him, waiting for him to make the first move.

Nik dashed at her with his staff in the same position. As he neared striking range, he came to an abrupt stop and swung the staff over his head. It sliced the air with a *whoosh* when he brought it down toward Wren.

It plummeted toward her, and she quickly evaded. Her shoulder dropped low, and she threw her weight over it in a sideways somersault. Her bare feet landed against the mat, and she sprung forward. The inertia from her tumble helped her to fluidly stand. Wren's hands tightened on the staff, and she rushed him this time.

Nik had pivoted as she rolled in order to keep his back away from her. He held the staff across his chest with both hands at an angle.

Wren struck three times, each one successfully blocked. She was forced to retreat when the tide shifted, and he took the approach.

Nik lurched back and swept at her from the side.

She hurriedly blocked it and spun in the opposite direction to keep space between them. Wren jumped when she felt one of the ropes graze her back. She caught sight of him closing in again and rolled to the side just in time to evade.

He was able to follow her with his swing. With another wind-up over his head, he unleashed a heavy blow.

She lifted her staff with both hands to block his attacks, trying to make each land in the middle of it. When one hit dead center, she flung her arms to the side while his momentum still propelled him forward.

Wren sidestepped him as he stumbled forward and hooked her staff into the crook of his arm from behind.

Nik lifted his forearms to hug her weapon to his chest and jerked forward. He flung her over his shoulder, and she landed flat on her back.

When she opened her eyes, she saw Nik standing above her with a smirk.

"That was a good first try."

Wren growled and jumped to her feet. She didn't hesitate before speeding at him with her staff at her side. She stopped short as Nik had but instead swept low.

He rushed to leap over it.

Wren dashed toward him, weaving her staff between his knees, and braced it against her chest. She continued rolling while maintaining her hold on his leg and flipped him onto his back. She lifted the center of her body to put him into a leglock and didn't let go until he slapped his hand against the mat.

He shook his head and blinked at her.

"One, one."

"Oh, we are keeping score?"

Wren crossed her arms and smirked at him. "You weren't planning to?"

Nik shifted to a sitting position and arched his brow at her. "I was," he admitted. "Just not out loud."

It was Wren's turn to roll her eyes, yet her lips twitched with a smile.

Nik got to his feet with his staff at his side. "That was better. Again."

CHAPTER TWENTY-THREE

"What lies behind us and what lies before us are
tiny matters compared to what lies within us."

Ralph Waldo Emerson

GARRET'S VILLAGE WAS, ADMITTEDLY, VERY BEAUTIFUL. A massive waterfall was the backdrop to a tower of homes that scaled the rising mountain wall. The top of the waterfall billowed over oversized boulders and down into a cavern at the edge of the village.

Most of the houses were occupied by women homemaking with their young children or teenaged daemon practicing weapon-wielding skills with one another. Although there were clear age distinctions, they all seemed timeless. Most of them had swirling black markings all over their bodies, similar to Garret's. Only the children wore no markings, which allowed the pure-moon color of their skin to glimmer in the sunlight.

The eyes of the villagers watched Elliot, Silver, and Jasper with interest. All kept a polite distance, but their stares were brimming with curiosity.

The trio followed Garret and were encircled by the tall, pale warriors with faces like stone. They all had the same stark-white eyes and hair with skin the color of the moonlight's glow. The clothing they wore was unseasonably thin, as though it was the middle of summer.

Every one of them was also stunningly beautiful.

"Where are we going?" Silver's brusque tone alluded to his wavering patience.

"To see the king."

"Pardon?" Elliot's question brought a curious look from a few of those around her and made her instantly insecure. "T-the king is here?"

"Your king? No." The daemon laughed aloud. "We are going to see Dejan. Our king."

Elliot and Silver exchanged an uneasy look. Jasper crossed his furry arms and sighed heavily enough to make his whiskers tremble.

As Garret led them through the center of the village, they drew the attention of seemingly every daemon. Despite the number of onlookers, the most unsettling thing was the silence. No daemon exchanged words or expressions with one another; their white eyes were focused solely on the group of outsiders.

Elliot tried not to blush, suddenly hyper-aware of her own disheveled state and mis-matched clothes.

They were led to a large stone temple directly beneath the waterfall.

The powerful flow of the water was sliced down the middle by an unseen wedge that guided the currents down either side of the structure. A smoky mist shrouded the temple with an air of magic that made everything feel lighter. There was no sense of warm or cold anymore. Instead, the atmosphere was that of a perfect summer's night.

Even breathing was easier.

Two sets of wide stairs formed a half-circle around the front of the temple, their stones permanently slick from the constant exposure to mist from the waterfall.

A tall man stood at the top of the stairs. His long cloak reached to the ground, obscuring his feet. The garment was an inky-black fabric with thin threads of shimmering gold that twisted into curls similar to those that adorned the other daemons' skin. He had aged gray skin and a sense of unwanted wisdom about him. However, he also seemed somehow ageless. He had shoulder-length hair the color of ash. The tips brushed the collar of his cloak as he tilted his head to take in the visitors before him.

Two golden eyes with no visible pupils watched them stoically. Both of his ears were covered in golden rings that started at the lobe and stopped at the crest. A simple golden crown hooked beneath his high cheekbones and swept up his temples. It curved backward to form a circular halo that seemed to float behind his head.

"Garret." He spoke with a deep, rumbling voice. "What have you brought to me?"

Garret glanced to Elliot with a taunting smirk. "I seem to have stumbled upon the girl from the rumors. The one with a reward for her capture. She claims to be an imposter that has been rejected and set free."

"Hm. Rather unusual." He eyed Elliot. "They aren't set free." His dark gray beard shrouded much of his face, but Elliot could feel his eyes on her.

In the few seconds that he looked her over, Elliot's heart felt as though it could stop at any moment.

"And what do you intend to do with her?"

Elliot locked onto Garret with a severe expression.

He winked at her. "I bequeath her to you."

"And her companions?" The voice of the king carried down the long staircase, despite the distance between them.

"Rats. They insisted on coming along. Personally, I—"

Dejan held up a hand to silence Garret. "What are our guests' names?" His golden eyes turned to the brothers as he tilted his chin to the side. They lingered on Silver, whose paw hovered over his weapon, ready for anything in a split second.

"I am Elliot, sir." She bowed her head slightly and gestured to the pair. "This is Jasper and Silver. They are escorting me home."

"Home?"

"Black Rivers." Her voice wavered from his intense stare. "I-in Arnica. I have f-family there waiting for me."

Dejan set his lips into a firm line and drew in a sharp breath as his eyes turned to Jasper and Silver. "You are rattenkin?"

The brothers begrudgingly nodded in unison.

"Do you have any relation to Augustus Rattenkin?"

"He is our grandfather, sir." Jasper's voice was hushed and uncertain, but its lack of volume did not detract from the clear pride he had in his lineage.

Dejan's lips twitched in a slight smile. "Arnica," he murmured as he returned his scrutinizing eyes to Elliot with a frown. He didn't speak for a few uncomfortable minutes as he took a step forward and began a slow descent of the stairs. The daemon king stopped a few steps away from them and held Elliot's eyes captive in his. "The land that has forsaken justice and order to gain political advantage over territorial disputes with Aster. Internal conflict that has crippled a greedy nation being led by a vain and greedier king. Randon Reed, the man that let his own cities burn."

Elliot nodded mutely.

"The undeserving usurper." Dejan folded his arms and narrowed his eyes.

Her heart skipped a beat, and her breath caught in her chest.

"The heir to a long dynasty of men that draw lines on the map because of a shared false sense of superiority. The son who killed his father for the crown." His hands dropped slowly to his sides. "Tell me, child. Are you a follower of this man?"

"No! I-I—" Elliot swallowed hard and cleared her throat. "I *do not* follow him, not in any way! Black Rivers may be part of his kingdom, but it hasn't belonged to him since the coup. It's practically an annex now. He's left law enforcement to a corrupted King's Guard and the thugs that live there."

"The coup . . . You are referring to the uprising of the mage, Seth."

Elliot's brow furrowed in confusion.

"Tanner? *Seth* Tanner? No, he was human, sir."

"I can assure you"—a dark gray eyebrow quirked—"he was not. He bargained his eternal soul for an attempt at the throne with outlawed magic and *became* a mage. He gained more than enough power and had plenty of support behind him to simply walk in and take the crown."

"But"—Elliot tried to ignore the tremor in her voice—"he didn't. He was stopped."

"Yes, by the spell."

Her eyes shot open wide. She had no way to disguise the shock on her face.

Garret, who stood with his arms crossed and his eyes closed, suddenly looked to Dejan in surprise.

"H-how," Elliot managed.

"I have lived many centuries, child. These old eyes can still see, and these old ears can still hear. When word of the civil war in Arnica reached our domain, it wasn't difficult to deduce the creature that stopped him based on description alone. There is only one creature that has four wings."

"Wr— She—" Frustration knotted sharply in Elliot's chest. "No one can know! One whisper of what she is, and the king would have her thrown in prison."

"More likely put to death." He spoke softly and placed a hand on her shoulder. It weighed virtually nothing. "It is true that humans fear what they do not understand; it is simply their nature. Just as ogres and golems are unfriendly, and fae are immortal. Human fear is an incredibly powerful force." He lifted his other hand and motioned to Garret. "You are dismissed."

Garret furrowed his brow and scoffed before he reluctantly turned and left.

Dejan didn't regard the young daemon as he led Elliot and the 'kin back up the stone stairs.

"Humans tend to allow their fears to overtake them, which then allows them to justify acting in ways they know to be wrong. Something as imposing and fierce as a spell is a terrifying concept to them because of the legacy that Eurynome left behind. That night left a scar in the minds of the humans that was so painful that the mere thought of one tempts them to burn any- and everything associated with it. Fear has a funny way of seeping into new generations."

"I can't necessarily argue with you there." Elliot glanced at Dejan from the corner of her eye. "People back home aren't her biggest fans. But Lionel has done a good job convincing them that she's a tempest, not a spell."

To the trio's shock, Dejan laughed once.

"Is that what the boy used as cover?" He laughed again. "Clever lad." His voice dropped affectionately this time, speaking more to himself than out loud.

"I must admit, sir. I don't know much at all about spells. Can you tell me more about them?"

The daemon king looked taken aback for a moment before he nodded once and smiled. "Of course. I can tell you certain things. Know that you will have some questions that I am not permitted to answer." He waited for Elliot to nod before he continued. "Do you know how they got the name?"

"No, I don't."

Jasper and Silver's toenails clicked quietly against the stone as they walked. The brothers had positioned themselves protectively on either side of Elliot and were only half listening to the conversation.

"They are a creation of the gods. It is said that Yu'e herself brought the first into existence. The name comes from their ability to use lightning, which can only be otherwise done by a master magician who has focused on only that for a lifetime. They are called a spell because they are a living, breathing incarnation of the power of the gods, just as lightning is the ultimate power that any earthbound creature can use. In my lifetime," he mused with a chuckle, "my *long* lifetime, I have only known of three spells.

"The first had no name. It was a chaotic thing. Incredibly volatile and unpredictable. The power that it came into this realm with was too much for it to control for long, and it was inevitably consumed by it." Dejean glanced to her without turning his head. "Tell me, child. How did he find her?"

"Lionel? He found Wren living in the woods. On the southern tip of Abagail."

Dejan nodded. He opened his mouth to answer but paused when something she said registered.

"What did you say her name is?"

"Um, Wren . . . sir. W-R-E-N. Like the bird. I think Lionel used to call her *little bird* when she was younger, but I don't know how she got her name."

His golden eyes softened, and a genuine smile leaked across his face. He was silent for a short while before turning his smile to Elliot directly.

"A beautiful name," he hummed. "The first spell was called many things. Because of this, they have different names depending on where you are in Yu'e. Those in the River Realm call them *tora*, their word for a four-winged drake. The central and southern regions refer to them as *uila* or *druk*, which are often used interchangeably. They both mean lightning."

"Wait . . . did you say that she can use *lightning*?"

Dejan's golden eyes turned to her curiously. "How old is Wren?" There was something in the way that he said her name that seemed to make his eyes glimmer.

Elliot blinked. "Uh, midtwenties? We don't really know how old she was when Lionel found her."

"Hm," he pondered softly. "So, she was alone for a while?"

"I think she was around six or seven when he found her."

"Very interesting."

When they reached the top of the stairs, Elliot was stunned by what she saw.

The walls on the building's exterior were made of dense, dark stone. Yet, from the inside, the walls were as transparent as glass.

She could see the entire village from their vantage point, beneath the peak of the waterfall.

Above them, there was no roof. She could see the point at which the waterfall split into two directions but not what was cutting the water in such a way. Although there was nothing visible to stop the mist and spray from drifting in, an unseen barrier fended it off with pulses of energy like the beat of a heart.

"She was older than the others when found. Eurynome and Acela were both found as infants, taken in by the families that found them . . . I always thought it rather surprising that such a young one was able to fight off an army like Seth's. For her to be able to fully change form so young. Very curious."

"What do you mean?"

"I did not think that her body would be able to withstand the physical strain at such an early age. Creatures that live for a very long time often have an extensive maturation process. For her to be able to change form so young is especially odd."

"Does everyone outside of Arnica know that she is a spell?"

The daemon king glanced to her and waved for her to follow him down a long hallway. They walked in silence until they reached a small room at the end and turned to face a set of wooden double doors.

Dejan motioned for Elliot to enter first.

The moment her foot first stepped across the threshold, the dark room burst with light.

Shelves stuffed to capacity with books lined every inch of the walls. Titles scrawled in characters she'd never seen before littered the spines.

A long wooden table stretched the span of the room, leaving only enough foot space to select a book and sit down; two wouldn't even be able to walk side by side. The table was a bright cherry red that gleamed in the light cast from glass lanterns. A single whisp of yellow fire flickered and burned in each lantern, despite not having any wick or fuel.

"Do you like to read?"

Elliot pulled two chairs out from beneath the table and looked to Jasper and Silver with a soft smile. She tugged a chair for herself out and took a seat beside them.

"I do, but I have so many questions."

"In time, young one. I have many answers, but these books have more." He tucked a gray finger into the spine of a book and pulled it free from the shelf. "This is likely the best to begin with. I have matters I must attend to, but I urge you to read while you wait."

"Yes," she replied with a nod. "But I have a request."

"A request?"

"Yeah, um." She shifted uncomfortably and glanced at Jasper and Silver. "May I bathe and clean my clothes before I begin reading?" She wasn't about to admit to the wound on the side of her head, hidden beneath the curls.

The daemon king laughed aloud once. "Yes, of course you may." His golden eyes followed Elliot's to look to the 'kin. "Please allow my people to provide you with any hospitality you need." He whisked from the room without another word.

Not thirty seconds passed before the trio was greeted by a small mob of daemon. Each beautiful face smiled and beckoned for Elliot, Jasper, and Silver to follow them.

"Are you two going to take a break to eat lunch at least, yes?" Kora stood outside of the ring with two fresh canteens of water in her hands. "You hardly ate last night, Miss Wren. You must be hungry, yes?"

"Yeah," she lied. She didn't have an appetite at all. "What did you have in mind?"

Kora's scarlet face lit up with a grin. "Pork and rice, yes, with vegetables." She placed the two containers on the floor of the platform.

"Sounds great," Nik interjected as he wiped his forehead with the sweat-soaked shirt he'd removed a number of rounds prior. "We can run drills until it's time to eat."

The nuwa eyed him with a scowl before nodding once. "I will let you know when it is ready, yes."

"Thank you, Kora." Wren spoke quietly but offered a soft smile.

Kora nodded again, returning the smile with one of her own and made her way up the stairs.

"She doesn't like me," Nik mused as he tossed his shirt behind him.

Wren gave him a sly smirk. "That's not it." She retrieved the canteens and tossed one to him. "She's told me that she finds you attractive. But she's like a mom. They don't usually condone rough-housing. I'd wager that no matter how nice you are to her, she'll always see you as a bad influence on me."

Nik cocked an eyebrow at her as he caught the bottle. He hesitated before he replied. "Now I kind of hope that she *doesn't* like me."

Wren laughed once and shook her head. "It isn't difficult to dislike you."

"You're one to talk, Miss Personality."

She smirked at her hands and shrugged. "Let's get back into it."

Nik nodded as he stretched his arm across his chest and began his advance.

They met in the middle of the ring, stopping with only a foot or so between them.

"Are you ready?"

Wren scoffed. "Are *you* ready?"

No answer came when a shrill cry cut the air.

They looked at each other in confusion then to the front door. The *closed* front door.

A loud commotion began to intensify outside as more voices began to join in. Nik and Wren both rushed out of the ring and barreled toward the entrance.

He beat her to it and swung it open wide.

Masses of people rushed in every direction, clamoring in the panic and disarray. Hands were shoving bodies, and feet kicked around anyone unfortunate enough to fall to the ground.

Wren slid her boots on and pushed by Nik to hurry out into the street. She caught the shoulder of a nearby man and turned him around to face her.

"What's going on?"

His eyes were wild with a mixture of panic and dread. It took a few rapid blinks for him to recognize Wren.

"Th-there's something-g coming t-this way! A t-terrible thing!"

"What is coming this way?"

The man shook his head frantically and shoved her away.

"I need to g-get out of here!" He rushed back into the crowd before she could stop him.

Wren's eyes shot to Nik.

He was speaking to a woman with thin hair and a face creased with wrinkles. Her body was visibly trembling as she struggled to speak. Bony fingers clutched at Nik's arm desperately.

"I-I've never seen anything like it!" Her voice shook terribly as she spoke. "A stitched-together monster with wings and another made of stone!" Her cloudy eyes were fogging with tears.

"Where?" Nik's calm voice seemed to help her maintain what composure she had left.

The woman looked beyond Nik and spotted Wren. She exclaimed with fervor and released Nik's arm to hurry to Wren's side.

"Guardsman, please help us! I beg of you!"

Wren's face contorted through various expressions as she tried to make sense of the chaos around them. She wrapped her hands around the woman's shoulders and leveled their eyes.

"I intend to. Tell me everything that you know so that I can help."

"A stone monster stormed into town from Market Bridge. It smashed through the wall like it was made of straw! Many of the men tried to fight it back, but none of them made a lick of difference!" Her voice hitched, and the woman rubbed her eyes roughly. "The flying beast . . . It's terrifying! Something sinister and twisted!"

It is a chimera, Wren thought darkly.

"Guardsman?"

"Get to safety. Bring anyone that you can find into the kingdom and inform the king of what has happened."

The woman nodded and hurried off as best she could without another word.

Wren rubbed her scalp as she struggled to formulate a plan. She turned to Nik, only to find him gone. Her pulse quickened with dread, and she opened her mouth to call out his name when a warm, heavy hand fell onto her shoulder.

Nik watched the mass of people stumble over one another in sheer panicked terror from behind her. He had slipped into his jacket, holding her cloak out for her, while his eyes remained locked on the direction the crowd was fleeing from.

Wren slid it around her shoulders and knelt down to retighten her boots. Once she stood, a soft crimson fabric dropped onto her, curling around her neck. She glanced to Nik, eyebrows furrowed and low.

"I smell rain. Keep it on." When she didn't protest, he reached out to adjust the scarf around her shoulders. "We can do this, Wren. Remember to focus on your breathing and let *them* come to *you.*" His hands found her shoulders again and gave them a comforting squeeze. "Don't forget. I'm with you this time."

She watched him with conflicted eyes and a deep frown. "What about Lionel? Someone needs to stay with him."

"He's with Kora. I ran inside while you talked with that woman. Told her that we needed to go and for her to stay with Lionel no matter what. She agreed before I even finished speaking."

Wren pursed her lips and looked in the same direction as Nik. She took a deep breath in through her nose and bolted in the opposite direction as the hurried crowd.

She didn't need to look back to know that Nik was a single step behind her.

They made their way into the market, weaving through the narrow streets as they looked and listened for any abnormalities or clues. Before long, the pair stumbled upon a gruesome scene.

The wall.

Blood was smeared across nearly every cobblestone. Broken buildings, broken stones, and broken men filled the area around the shattered wall. Half-lifeless bodies covered most of the ground and rubble. Any who were still alive cried out for death in agonizing, pitiful sounds.

Wren heard the reaper click his tongue against the back of his teeth and sigh. She glanced at him without turning her head for a brief moment before looking back to the men in realization.

Nik put his hands together as his eyes slipped shut and bowed his head so that the tips of his fingers touched his forehead. He slowly parted his palms to reveal a wispy ball of purple smoke. It grew to the size of a large melon that twisted and warped in a tight loop as it pulsed rhythmically.

With a conflicted look on his face, he clapped his hands together, and the ball burst into a cloud of dense smoke that billowed to the ground like a waterfall from his palms. The purple fog curled into tendrils that dispersed like snakes toward the moaning bodies littering the ground. The whisps slithered across the bloody cobblestone and disappeared into their broken noses or busted mouths.

"Guiding light," Nik whispered so softly that Wren barely registered he'd spoken at all, "bring the souls before you back to the creators. Do so with warmth and bring about bodily peace. Free these souls from this realm in your mercy."

A few quickened heartbeats passed before small clouds of green began to drift out from their parted, lifeless lips. One by one, the men became still and silent as the green haze gradually dispersed into the atmosphere.

Wren angled her chin to Nik, and she wore a terse smile.

"That was the right thing to do." She hadn't intended to whisper. "The compassionate thing to do."

"Doesn't make it any easier *to* do. It's done now. Let's keep going."

Wren nodded and took a few steps forward, deeper into the gut-wrenching scene. She circled the demolished market square with her hazel eyes, flitting from the sky to any shadow long enough to be a sufficient hiding place.

The statue that once looked down his nose at the townspeople now stood in chipped, fractured pieces. The town well was gone and the library was in shards; pages and rubble littering anywhere within the wind's reach. The cobbler's stall was nothing more than a pile of broken wood and shattered ambition.

"My, you were easier to find than I thought. It seems the trace's eye did the trick."

Wren reeled around to find the alchemist looming at the end of the street, beside the massive hole in the wall.

Two eyes watched her, one of them being the cerulean orb that didn't belong to him.

Her stomach turned painfully at the sight. She fought to keep any expression from showing.

He walked slowly with a grin stretched across his stitched-together face.

"I admit, I did expect you to look more formidable. I thought rather little of you when we first met. Small and meager, you are as a human. However . . . the strength I saw at my cabin was truly astounding. I'm very curious to examine you more closely."

"That's close enough," Wren cautioned with an even tone. "I won't hold back this time."

A sick grin cracked across the alchemist's face. "Oh, I'm counting on it, dearie." He cackled loudly and thrust his arms high into the air.

A brief silence passed before a piercing shriek shattered the stillness.

Nik didn't miss the shiver that racked Wren's spine at the sound.

The winged chimera rose from behind a building with a tangle of bodies dangling from its talons. It spotted her immediately and dove, men still screaming in its hold.

Wren jumped out of the way at the last second and rolled to

the side. She quickly regained her footing and darted for cover. She nestled herself beneath a slab of fallen stone and tried to take as many deep breaths as she could.

A clawing feeling ripped at her from the core, making every bone in her body cry out at once. She gripped her elbows and squeezed her eyes shut as tightly as she could. Something furious burned at her as her arms and legs violently trembled. The wounds across her shoulders and back ached painfully, and the deeper slice on her shoulder stung like a freshly pressed brand.

The slab shifted over her head, and she hurried away from it before it slapped against the cobblestone and shattered.

Directly above her, the chimera screeched and grabbed at her with its sharp talons.

Wren struggled to evade the creature until a loud crack echoed behind her.

A shadow rushed by her, wielding a long scythe in one hand and a three-pronged dagger in the other. His hands were nothing more than bone, and the skeletal fingers were curled tightly around his weapons.

Nik leapt from a ramp of fallen stone and vaulted from it, aiming upward.

The chimera was low enough to the ground to be caught by the curve of his scythe. It screamed and pumped its wings in retreat. Bright red blood dripped from a deep wound across the bottom of one of its feet.

Nik landed and immediately joined Wren's side.

Her hands were trembling as they clenched against her legs. Her eyes were deadlocked on the alchemist.

He hadn't moved from his spot as his twisted eyes watched the pair curiously. Something gleamed in the cerulean eye nestled into his face. A wide grin spread across his hideous features as he took a slow step forward.

"Get back!"

The twisted man ignored her as he continued to advance, his attention turned to Nik.

"Ah, a penitent reaper. How unexpected." His sickening laugh turned Wren's stomach. "I haven't seen one of you before. My, my. You are full of surprises, little one. Any more friends you want to introduce me to?"

Nik's hand tightened on his scythe, and his eyes narrowed. "Best to listen to her, Ubel. This will only end one way."

The man paused and shook his head. His brow quirked at his own name, but it only seemed to draw a sick, gleeful grin from him. "I'm far too curious to see what *you* can do. Her, I'm not afraid of." He tapped his temple twice and sneered. "You speculate, boy. I know how this ends."

To add insult to injury, the stolen blue eye winked at Wren.

She growled dangerously and dug her nails into her palms.

"That's a rather foolish thing to say," Nik replied flatly.

"Perhaps, but it is still the truth. A spell as young as she." He smirked contemptuously. "She's hardly grown. Eurynome was three times as large when in his full glory." His mismatched eyes narrowed at her, "I know that you will hesitate. The only difference between you and he is that he did not hesitate. Your emotions are your downfall."

Her breath caught in her chest. Wren barely managed to contain herself enough to stay in place.

Don't let him provoke you, she told herself bitterly and glared at him.

"Tell me, boy. Have you seen her in her true form?" He didn't wait for Nik to respond before he continued with a crooked grin. "It's quite something." He began walking toward them again and lifted one hand into the air. "I will have her show you."

When his hand tightened into a fist, a bright light flashed from it for a split second. For a short while, the only sound was his encroaching footsteps. It wasn't long until the space filled with a different sound.

Humming? Wren's eyes shifted around the market square to try to determine where it was coming from.

The answer came when a mob of dark green bodies poured through the hole in the shattered wall. The hum came from buzzing wings that carried long-limbed, large-faced creatures with pitch-black eyes. They were only about two feet tall, but there were tens of them in the market in a matter of seconds. By the sound of the crowd, it was a safe bet that more were coming.

Fae. Wren glowered as she took a deep breath.

They pooled around the point of entry and hovered erratically. Every pair of eyes was locked on Wren, paying no attention to Nik. The mob shuffled restlessly as they watched her but maintained a significant distance.

Wren's breathing quickened as her heart lurched in her chest. She had never fought a fae of this sort before and not knowing what she was up against daunted her.

It *did* look like these were the type that liked to suffocate prey by swarming it.

"Would you like to meet my friends, little one?"

"Not particularly."

Ubel chuckled and rolled his tongue over his gray teeth. He made three soft clicking noises, and they instantly began to flap their wings faster. The buzzing deepened as their excitement intensified.

Nik moved first.

His weightlessness made him impossibly fast as he stripped a weapon from a corpse. The three-pronged dagger in his left hand disappeared in an instant so he could wrap his fingers around a discarded spear.

He paused until his eyes found Wren, and he tossed it in her direction.

She caught it and fluidly broke into a dash toward the middle of the square. Her feet instinctively shifted into a defensive position, and her hands slid along the spear to hold it with both hands in front of her.

Ubel smiled a sickening smile and pointed at her. "Do what you will, my children. Remember, she must be left alive."

With his permission granted, the fae dispersed in all directions before they turned and dove.

Wren's fingers itched along the shaft of the spear as she let out a long breath. She passed a few soft exhales through slightly parted lips before they set into a firm line.

Her eyes shifted to Nik. "Don't intervene until I give the signal."

Nik watched her with a skeptical expression before he reluctantly nodded once.

A handful of the swarm circled her from above, while others charged head on.

Wren sliced through the air with the pointed end of the spear and caught the first one that reached her in the side. She flung the spear around her in a wide circle that sent a strong ripple of air upward. The column of air pushed them away in one, easy sweep.

Wren took a deep breath and turned to face another encroaching mob with a stern look carved onto her face. She shifted the spear to her right hand and dropped into her practiced stance to hold it in the same way she had when sparring with Nik: directly behind her, poised and ready.

She didn't need to look at her feet to know *precisely* where they were planted.

The swarm formed a circle around her, just out of her extended reach. Their wings buzzed with excitement, and most bore their pointed yellow teeth into a sick smile, ones no different from Ubel's.

Wren narrowed her eyes and glanced around her. She twisted her wrist to the side and jumped at the nearest one.

The tip of the spear penetrated its chest, and she instantly thrusted forward, catching two more in the same manor. Wren flung the bodies off the end of her weapon and used the remaining momentum to pick off another.

Their small bodies were protected by thin, delicate skin that ripped open easily. It only took one well-aimed blow to make them bleed to death.

Noted.

A harsh tug on the top of her head brought her attention to three hovering just above her and grabbing at her hair. Their sharp nails occasionally scraped her scalp as they clamored for a handful of hair.

"Shit!" She swung the spear in a circle above her to fend them off.

Another brave fae dove at her, nearly catching the side of her face and neck, if she hadn't noticed and moved at the last second.

Wren felt a familiar growl rumble from somewhere deep in her chest that sent a pang of panic throughout her body. She tried to steady her breathing and shove the feeling far, far away.

A tidal wave of wind charged through the market square and knocked the swarm off-balance. It didn't relent as it swept upward in a perfectly straight line.

The fae were so light that they had no defense against the intense gust. Any that couldn't grab onto something in time were carried into the clouds.

A stillness followed the updraft. It lasted only moments before it was instantly refilled by a pillar of air plummeting downward. The gale-force current slammed the stunned fae into the ground, killing any that were still alive from the force of impact.

Wren turned to face Ubel with fury burning in her eyes. Two silver rings shone in the center of each iris, and they pierced through the growing clouds of kicked-up dirt that cast a haze throughout the market square.

With every passing second, the rings in her eyes grew wider.

"You wanted to see me change again?" Her voice was different. It had a calmness to it that Wren's usually didn't have. It sounded as though an entirely different, deeper voice spoke in tandem with hers. "If you want to die so badly, I will gladly be your deliverance."

A dark smile cracked across his hideous face. "Good."

Wren set her jaw and closed her eyes.

Four fae that had survived her attack hovered behind Ubel and saw this as an opportunity to rush her.

She furrowed her brow and tried to block out everything around her.

"We can beat him," a voice that she somehow recognized echoed in her mind. It almost sounded like her own. Almost. *"We can prevail if you will trust me."*

Her eyes shot open, bright silver and instantaneously alert. They zeroed in on Ubel with a predatory gleam and narrowed with an underlying, unspoken severity.

A twisting column of air formed around her in an instant before it burst outward, sending the approaching fae careening back. The furious wind continued to whip around the square, ripping harshly at loose clothing, hair, and tattered fabric secured to ruined buildings. The current of air carried with it an unseasonable coldness, like that of a subzero night in the dead of winter.

Wren's cloak billowed around her calmly as she watched Ubel from the eye of the storm. A tendril caught the perfect angle to unravel Nik's crimson scarf from her neck, and it was sent sailing into the abyss. The wind was so powerful that even fist-sized stones began to tremble and gravitate into the air and gradually add to the circle of debris around the spell's otherwise still form.

Nik kept his focus trained on Ubel but tried to note the direction his scarf had gone. He perched himself on the roof of a mostly intact building in order to look down to the fight. His jacket sliced in the wind, violently clipping against his face and body. He tightened his lips and shook his head in disapproval.

"Don't do it, Wren. Fight it back," Nik spoke in a whisper.

Wren's eyes narrowed at Ubel as larger stones began to shudder in her gale force, including shards of the fallen slab she'd used for cover. The debris disoriented the few remaining fae as it swirled in the air. The ferocity gradually increased and formed a tight tunnel of wind that soon became a violent cyclone.

Huge masses of gray clouds began rolling in the cold atmosphere, bringing with them an onslaught of icy precipitation. The palm-sized chunks of hail never made it to the ground once they were sucked into Wren's swirling storm.

Trees that still stood in the square bent painfully in the storm. Massive chunks of ice-covered leaves and branches broke free and joined the myriad of potential shrapnel within the angry cyclone. Freezing rain slammed into the stone street and soaked everything within its curtain. It fell in such cold, sharp needles that they audibly shattered upon impact.

"Call your pets," the voice that wasn't Wren's commanded. "I want you to watch me tear each and every one of them apart. I will unravel all of the little parts that you've so carefully stitched together. Then it'll be your turn. I will unravel your stitching, then I will kill you."

Ubel's maniacal cackling filled the spaces between the frozen particles of rain and hail. "You want to meet your doom so badly, little one?" He had to shout to be heard over the heavy rain, but the madness in his stolen eyes glared through the haze. "Gladly!"

CHAPTER TWENTY-FOUR

G LADLY!"

The screech of the chimera was barely audible over a loud clap of thunder. The rumble rolled through the thickening clouds and shook the air as more dull thuds carried outward like ripples.

The winged beast hovered a few hundred feet above the market square, watching the scene unfold. The whipping wind made it difficult for the creature to maintain stability, but its powerful wings kept it mostly upright and out of the storm's reach.

Wren's skin began to darken into black scales that pushed through the cracks between her flesh. She curled into a ball, dead center in the eye of the storm. She let out a terrible sound as four lumps formed over her shoulders and back before her wings broke free one by one. Each wing was coated in bright red blood and feathers that rustled in the heavy wind. Her entire body enlarged as her bones loudly cracked and snapped into new locations.

Ubel commanded the winged chimera to attack, shouting over the weather as best he could.

The creature hesitated before it tucked its wings close to its body and dove.

"Wren!" Nik's voice barely made it through the storm, yet it somehow reached her.

The chimera quickly closed the distance between it and Wren.

Another snap of thunder cracked the atmosphere and startled the chimera enough to give it pause. It glanced around with a hint of panic seeping into its mannerisms as it tried to gauge the distance of the thunder.

This pause was exactly what she was anticipating.

Four clawed feet dug into the cobblestone, unearthing shards of stone effortlessly, and pushed off to propel a large body into the storm at an alarming speed.

The alchemist frantically called to the chimera, but his voice was no longer audible over the unceasing claps of thunder.

Wren's wings pounded against the air and used the tumultuous current of wind that followed her to quicken her advance. Each limb cupped the updraft and pushed to ride it, aimed directly at the chimera.

Her body slammed into the other creature, front claws extended to catch it by the throat and back. The two front wings changed direction while the other two acted like a rudder in the wind for her to turn in an impossibly tight angle as she dug her nails into the chimera's body. She squeezed until she felt warm blood pool around her claws.

It cried out pitifully, but Wren ignored it.

She carried it above the clouds and out of sight from those on the ground.

Thunder growled around them, only allowing a few seconds of relative quiet before the next wave.

Wren reached the peak of her ascent and stopped. The beat of her four wings slowed to allow her to hover, even in the raucous wind. She adjusted her hold on the chimera and turned in an instant. Wren wrapped one of her claws around its face to hold its beak flush against its own neck and tightened her grip on its back.

Its wings struggled violently as it tried to break free, but her nails were sunk in deep.

Wren positioned herself so that the creature was between her and the impending cobblestone. Her wings beat against the air with all of her might in order to keep accelerating. Her shoulders jerked to the side at the last second and aimed directly at Ubel instead.

They slammed into the ground so hard that a ripple of stone, mud, and snow lifted from the point of impact and raged outward. The debris formed a thick cloud of fog that obscured the landing site, even in the downpour of ice.

A huge gust whipped the fog into a tight circle that quickly formed another cyclone. Aside from the angrily twisting air, there was no movement.

Nik rushed toward the storm, signal or no signal. His hands tightened on the snath of his scythe as he neared the twister, unsure of what he'd find.

The wind had taken on a murky reddish-brown hue, and the closer he got, the stronger the scent of blood became. Frozen particles of wind and brown feathers slapped against him violently as he grew close enough to make out a silhouette behind the fog.

A large body lay motionless on the ground, the fur and feathers whipping fiercely within the vortex.

Gradually, another hulking shadow came into view.

This one stood on four firmly planted feet but was still as stone. When Nik followed its line of sight, he was able to make out the figure of a man curled on the ground, struggling to stand.

Nik tried to push through the wall of wind but found it to be impassible. He growled and slammed the blade of his scythe into the current of air. It collided with what felt like stone and sent him flying backward. He landed on the destroyed ground and glared as he righted himself.

He couldn't get in.

Wren wouldn't *let* him in.

Her four wings rose from her back and pumped hard. She lifted from the ground and propelled skyward without taking her eyes off of Ubel. Wren rose into the air, riding the updraft just as she had done before.

He managed to stand and watched her with his own venomous stare.

"Where is your other pet? The stone giant."

Ubel growled darkly. He lifted one arm into the sky with an ashen gray stone clutched in his palm. He squeezed his hand as tightly as he could, and the stone vanished in a puff of black smoke. A sickening grin crept across his lips when a matching flash of black light shimmered against the dark clouds directly above him.

Only a few moments passed before Nik felt the ground tremor beneath his feet.

A massive stone giant stepped through the broken wall. As it wandered into the courtyard, a second followed. Then a third. And finally a fourth.

They were identical to each other: the same perfectly round hole through their bodies with a single floating stone that moved as an eye in a socket would. They were also all double the size of the one that Wren fought before.

Ubel sneered at her. "I brought more this time. Your windstorm can't defeat all four."

"*He is right,*" the voice in her mind chimed. "*Wind won't immobilize all of them.*"

She growled to herself.

"Then what," she muttered aloud.

"*We do have something that will break stone. I told you to trust me,*" the feminine voice reminded her. "*Will you?*"

Wren growled again but gave no reply.

"*Ascend.*"

She obeyed without hesitation and carried herself high into the angry clouds.

"*Take a deep breath and block out everything but my voice.*"

She struggled to ignore the howl of the storm within and around her and tried to comply.

The thunder crackled and rumbled, unleashing unrelenting precipitation, and made her unintentionally wince. A feeling nagged at the back of her mind.

Images of her friends shimmered behind her closed eyes. Lionel's smile, Elliot's laugh. Nik's brooding face. A pain shot through her chest, and the voice pulled her back.

"*Focus.*"

Wren then stilled completely. Her wings slowed until they beat only when necessary to keep her in place.

She pictured the woods. The sound of the falling rain that brought her back to the nights she would listen to it alone, curled into a ball and crying. The loud claps of thunder had always frightened her when she was younger. When she was alone.

Now, they felt like they were a part of her.

A pang of familiarity drummed in the fringes of Wren's consciousness. The combination of remembrance of the forest where she once lived and the voice that echoed in her mind made something click.

For a moment, she remembered the same voice calling to her in the night, only ever calling out a single word. One that she couldn't bring herself to remember fully.

—*iya.*

Wren stayed suspended and still until the only things she could hear were the rush of the wind and the soft pump of her wings.

"Take a deep breath, relax yourself completely, and let me take over."

Doubt made her panic briefly, but she followed the instructions.

A sudden pain shot through her entire body, both red hot and ice cold simultaneously. It rattled through her bones and lit her nerves on fire. A caustic sensation boiled in the back of her throat and blistered inside of her chest.

The clouds around her grew darker, plunging the ground below into the darkness only nighttime brought. Thunder shook the world around her and forced frozen air through each tendril of her half-feathered wings. Needles of pain danced across her skin, originating from beneath the black scales.

She pressed her eyes shut tighter, the burning inside of her chest already unbearable.

"Dive."

Wren folded her wings snugly against her body while tucking her legs to her chest and barrel rolled to change direction, to careen downward.

A current of wind suddenly formed around her and accelerated her descent.

As she drew closer to the ground, the feeling in her throat became somehow more excruciating.

"Let out your rage."

Her pointed teeth gnashed together. Those silver eyes shot open to find herself less than fifty feet from impact, but she didn't veer off. Instead, she did exactly as the voice instructed.

An impossible heat boiled beneath her jaw, and she opened her mouth to scream.

However, a scream was not what came out.

"So, Lionel did the right thing by keeping Wren a secret."

"It is my opinion if I agree." Dejan walked beside the small human with his hands tucked into the long sleeves of his cloak. "He knew that she would have been hunted down by many different sorts. Taken by those who sought to use her as a weapon. Or worse . . ."

"You talk about him like you've met him."

Dejan gave her a curious look before nodding. "Young lad from Heather. Eyes always so full of joy, despite what they see. He is a tall man but fine-featured and slender. Curly, sunlight-colored hair. Infectious laugh and can compel anyone to like him. Though I would often wonder if he wants so badly to be loved because he is unable to love himself."

Elliot couldn't find any sort of response to his statement. She had never heard the painful truth put into such a casual statement.

The pair walked in comfortable silence along a grass pathway that led up the mountain. Behind them, a thundering waterfall echoed in the clear air and grew louder with each step.

"Where are we going?"

Dejan smiled at her. "I am taking you to the temple above the waterfall." He held up one hand, the smile still playing on his face. "Before you ask what that is, you will understand when you see it. For now, conserve your energy for the path to get us there. It is not a short one."

Elliot blushed and turned her eyes to their route.

Even though it was still too early in the season, brightly colored flowers burst from fertile stems in large bunches. Roses in every color dotted the lush green grass. The wind that danced through them all carried a sweet smell and a calming warmth.

"Lionel Gibbs is a well-known name in Heather," Dejean stated without turning around. "His extensive family played a large part in helping the surrounding lands when famine swept through the south. Many are farmers or ranchers, and they contributed all that they could to their neighbors and friends. A very large, very kind family."

"Really? I didn't think he had any siblings."

"He may not directly, but his family name bears great influence in the southern nations to this day. The brothers and sisters of his parents gave him many cousins, and the cousins had many children from their own families."

"So, you *have* met him, then?"

"Yes, for a short time." Dejan gave her a soft smile and continued up the endless steps. "He left Heather by train to reach Lavender Bay. From there, he traveled to Dendros by sea. He stayed in Dendros, in a village called Smith Town, for a few months before leaving for Market Road on foot. We met then."

Elliot followed behind him silently, hanging on his every word.

"He stayed with us for a time, insisting he leave as soon as possible. A very cryptic one, that boy. The rest I've heard through rumors. Such as the spell that he harbors."

"She isn't a criminal," Elliot retorted.

"No, but she *is* dangerous." He glanced at her from over his shoulder with a serious look. "Even more than I anticipated if she is able to turn into her full form so young. That indicates a lack of control over a very large source of power." His eyes grew soft, and he gently placed his hand on the crown of her head. "Fret not, little one. We will speak with Evania and determine what needs to be done."

"Evania?"

Dejan nodded. "Yes, my wife. The queen."

They continued up the path in silence.

Elliot alternated from staring at her feet to staring at the back of Dejan's head. Something about his statement unsettled her. She already knew, from Lionel's memory transference, that Wren was capable of great power, but the way Dejan spoke of her friend bothered her.

But . . . Elliot thought bitterly, *is she really* that *dangerous? More dangerous than that sinister thing Lionel showed me?* She bit her lip. *Lightning . . . She can use lightning, but . . . Can she really control it? Or will* she *be the one being controlled?*

At the last step to the top of the endless stairs, the temple was in full view.

Soft white clouds drifted around the stone pillars that surrounded it. Patterns of stone within the pathway formed pictures and figures in bright colors. The light of the day made them glitter and sparkle in the shine of the sun.

Small streams of water cut through every seam in the stones, flowing through them like highways. The roar of the waterfall bellowed beneath the temple but was muted by the peace that surrounded the clifftop.

Dejan made his way across the stone with Elliot timidly following behind him.

Inside of the temple was otherworldly.

Lush grass covered the floor and worked up the walls, dotted with flowers of every shape and shade. The warm sunlight drifted in and filled the space with the sweet smell of spring. Happy chirps echoed around the empty space as small birds flitted around from perch to perch.

The pair made their way down another short set of stairs that opened into an entirely different biome.

The overhead light had a harder time penetrating the thick canopy of tree limbs that stretched high above, and even the air seemed to have a green hue to it. The chirps that echoed in this room were not only of birds but also the excited chatter of various small animals and reptiles lurking within the bushes.

A tunnel between the trees led to a massive set of golden doors with no handles.

Dejan placed his aged, gray palm against an insignia etched into the doors.

A glowing light emanated from his hand and shot vertically in both directions. A few short seconds later, the two doors creaked open.

A woman stood on the other side.

She was nearly as tall as Dejan and had pure-white hair. It was short enough to graze below her jaw as her golden eyes watched the pair approach. She had gray skin also, but hers held no tattoos or swirling patterns as all of the other daemon did. However, there was a single golden shape in the center of her forehead that blazed in the foggy air.

It was a circular form that had many smaller dots within it. Two short lines bisected the circle and cut them into mirror images of each other.

"Elliot, I presume?"

Her voice was as sweet as the air around them. Its femininity resonated within the walls of the temple and filled Elliot's chest with ease.

"Yes, uh." She hesitated and curtsied politely. "Elliot Joy."

"My," she hummed as Dejan grew nearer to her. "It is no wonder mercenaries had yet to apprehend you. The descriptions on the postings do you no justice, my dear."

The daemon king smiled lovingly and placed a kiss onto the symbol on her forehead.

Elliot blushed and bowed her head again. "Thank you for your hospitality. My friends and I are very grateful for it."

"Yes," she replied and held her hand out to Elliot. "Come with me, child. There is much we must discuss."

Elliot barely had time to give Dejan a worried look before Evania towed her away.

"You must forgive my bluntness, dear, but I must know about your situation. Dejan tells me that the spell has emerged from hiding."

She nodded mutely.

"Peculiar thing, she must be. Tell me, what is she like?"

Elliot sighed, considering her question for a moment before responding. "Difficult. Very difficult. And stubborn. *Very* stubborn."

Evania's laugh filled the space with its music. "I can only imagine. Spells are quite the enigma, but obduracy is something we've seen in all accounts."

"That's an understatement."

Evania laughed once more and gave Elliot a stunning smile. "I understand that my husband began to tell you more about your spell?"

"Yes. Apparently, she can use lightning?"

The daemon queen nodded. "At a great expense."

"What do you mean?"

"Well . . ." Evania brought Elliot over to a stone pedestal with a wide-mouthed bowl perched on top. She touched the surface of the water with a single finger that sent a small set of ripples across its surface. "It takes a significant amount of energy to harness lightning. Even master magicians and spellcasters are seldom able to conjure it, let alone survive its force."

She drew a shape along the water. The tip of her finger left behind a trail of golden flecks that she formed into an image.

"You see, when a spellcaster is strong enough to summon lightning, it can only be summoned to their position. Some may have an array of bolts that can cover a small area, but it is always aimed at the one who called upon it. A spell's lightning comes from within, drawn from the power of the gods. I believe it to be something far more tragic."

"Tragic?"

Evania gave a small smile. "As the only creature on Yu'e born with the capability to create lightning from nothing, I don't know if it behaves the same way as summoning lightning does for a spellcaster. However, I imagine it must not be easy to withstand."

"Well, if anyone is stubborn enough to withstand lightning, it's Wren."

Evania's eyes widened, and she leaned in closer. "What did you say her name is?"

Elliot was taken aback by how similar her reaction to Wren's name was to Dejan's reaction.

Like an inside secret.

"Um, it's Wren. Wren Gibbs. Spelled like the bird."

Evania's beautiful features softened, and she righted herself. "How wonderful to hear." She seemed to sing. "What a lovely boy."

"Who? Lionel?"

The daemon queen nodded. "Yes, dear. He did a wonderful thing."

Elliot blushed and looked away, too reluctant to ask her to elaborate.

CHAPTER TWENTY-FIVE

"One must still have chaos in oneself to be
able to give birth to a dancing star."

Friedrich Nietzsche

*L*ET OUT YOUR RAGE.*"*
The heat that boiled within her left her body suddenly in an excruciating, scorching flood. It burned her mouth and tongue in the same way that acid would as the heat exploded from somewhere deep inside of her.

A jagged pillar of lightning slammed to the ground with so much force that a current of shattered cobblestone rippled outward from the point of impact.

The white-hot force seared into the stone giants' bodies before they burst into smaller tendrils of lightning. Thin fingers of electricity flickered over the entirety of their bodies and left black trails of singed remnants that ate through the stone like a hot blade through butter.

The largest of the giants had taken the blow of lightning full force.

A fissure formed at the very top of its head before it cracked through the length of its body. The boulders and stones that made up its arms and legs tumbled to the ground in a pile of burned rubble.

The remaining giants watched on as the scorched trails of her first strike still simmered on their brown-gray bodies.

Her four wings beat in synchronization to bring her to a hovering stop in order to face Ubel fully. Wren's silver eyes glowed against the darkness of the atmosphere around her. She tilted her head back and let out another scream into the clouds overhead.

This time, a storm of lightning burst from the black clouds and into the empty market within her impenetrable vortex, unrelenting until the remaining giants were all no more than smoldering mounds of wreckage.

Wren lingered above the scene, her tempestuous gaze transfixed on Ubel as she circled overhead.

His mismatched eyes returned her stare, wide with disbelief.

"No! This is not what I foresaw!" His knees trembled beneath him, and the fear that racked his voice was audible even through the torrent of the storm. One knee gave, and the old man fumbled to the ground. He managed to stay in a crouching position without taking his eyes off of Wren.

With a pump of her bottom wings and a pivot of the top pair, she twisted in the air to approach the ground.

A sneering grin etched on Ubel's face as he watched her descend without a word. His aged body struggled to get him out of his crouched position, and the adrenaline coursing through him made him shake too severely to stand.

Her four clawed feet touched down with wings outstretched behind her. A long, blue-black scaled tail waved from side to side as she advanced. The sunset-colored wings that tipped the end of her tail held a metallic gleam when the sparce light touched the drenched feathers at certain angles.

"Who else shall you throw in my way before I kill you? Any more mindless beings who will die for you?" The voice was not Wren's, but it was she who spoke with a growl in the back of her throat. "You must have run out of friends. I don't need any friends to delete you from this world."

"Impossible!" He pointed at her with a knobby finger. "Eurynome could not breathe lightning! How can it be that you are able to do such a thing?"

Wren closed the distance between them with a dark look on her expressive face. She beat her wings once and snarled. Her claw clipped the ruined cobblestone as she came to a stop only a few yards from him.

Another billow of black clouds began to swirl in the sky above them as a hurried wind rustled through her feathers.

Ubel's desperate eyes looked between Wren and the ominous clouds above her, and his reality finally set in.

"Kill me, you will still fail! My duty was to draw you from hiding, and here you are, little one!" A sick smirk crept onto his face. "He already knows of your presence! Knows of your location! I told him all about you. I learned a lot about you from the first time that we met. You will not survive him!"

Her eyes gleamed with a vibrant, piercing white that appeared to intensify in tandem with the furious winds around them. The light was so bright that her pupils were indistinguishable from the irises, but their target easily connected.

"I am *not* Eurynome," she replied plainly. "And I will *not* fail. I may not know who *he* is, but I can assure you that *he* will fall dead at my feet, just as you are about to." Wren lifted her head skyward once more and howled.

A final bolt of lightning towered from the sky, aimed directly onto the twisted man a short distance from her. He was quickly engulfed by the white-hot energy with enough air left for one short scream.

His shriek carried over the maelstrom of wind before it faded into the echoes of thunder.

Smoke billowed from the small pile of ash, but it was quickly snuffed out by the freezing rain and hail that swallowed the ground.

Wren staggered slightly but caught herself as she scanned the area carefully. The gale gradually quelled as no further threats were identified. Her eyes finally fell upon Nik, who stood at the very edge of the vortex she'd created. Her eyes softened, and she let out a short, reassured breath.

A deep crevasse had been carved into the stone in front of his feet, inches from where the impassible barrier of wind had been.

A sudden pain shot through her, and she cried out softly. Wren stumbled to the side as the world around her began to spin.

"Well done, my child."

The voice tugged at the back of her consciousness and made her shiver. In an instant, the voice vanished from her mind. As it did, it uttered the same single word that had called out to her as a child.

"—iya."

Yet it was still a word she could not understand, even as it was spoken.

The burning sensation beneath her scales was fading, but the muscles in her back jerked in every direction, and her bones started to click back into place. She felt the strength in her legs wane and struggled to stay upright.

Wren remained still as the furious winds became the gentle breeze. Once the last pebble fell back into place, her vision went black. Her body finally crumpled to the ground in a single listless motion.

Nik rushed to her side and dropped to his knees. He placed his palm against her cheek and leaned in to cradle her head.

Up close, he could see the bones and muscles moving through her shoulders, back, and legs. He could also see the stream of tears that covered her face and could hear the whimpers that escaped her.

Wren writhed in pain as the four wings on her back began to recede. Small *pops* and *snaps* reverberated in the otherwise silent street. The blue-black scales all over her body began to quiver and slough off along with tufts of sunset feathers, withering away her enormous size. She curled into a tight ball as the bony parts of her wings withdrew into her back, and she gasped loudly.

"It's all right, Wren," she heard Nik whisper through the darkness. "I'm here."

The biting cold of the late-winter air slowly started to chip away at any body heat that she had retained from the layer of scales. She shuddered when a breeze curled around her body.

Nik held her head in his lap and hastily removed his coat to wrap around her.

"Wren, are you with me?"

Wren felt a cold hand touch her cheek and winced. She tried to pry her eyes open, but the attempt resulted in her stomach turning over. She retched and heaved until her stomach was well past empty. Her hands were trembling so badly that Nik had to hold her upright as her body continued to punish her with violent dry heaves.

Once the worst of her bout of sickness passed, he helped her to lie down and dropped her head back onto his lap. Her sobs wrenched his heart so deeply that he found himself relieved Lionel wasn't here to hear them.

The feeling of hands in her hair soothed away some of the swirling nausea. His warm lap and familiar cedar scent gradually began to overpower the sick feeling still in her stomach.

Nik's baritone voice softly hummed a melody somewhere far away, the only proof being the vibrations each note made in the air.

Wren reluctantly tried to open her eyes again. Her vision still badly distorted and seeing double, she clapped her shaking palms over her face.

He allowed her however much time she needed to compose herself and kept himself busy by running his fingers through her knotted, bloody hair.

"I think I got him," Wren finally managed with a hoarse voice.

Nik caught her peeking at him from behind one hand. "Yeah," he said with a smile and pulled her close, "that was pretty awesome."

Wren recoiled with a disgusted face.

"What? You were great out there. Why the look?"

Silver eyes stared at him for a moment. "Huh." Wren turned her attention to securing Nik's jacket around her body. "I've never heard anyone refer to a mass slaughter as *awesome* before. It caught me off guard."

"You see"—he helped her to stand—"when you want to say it like that, it has a negative connotation to it. And that's not what happened here. If you hadn't killed them, they would have kept killing."

Wren fastened his jacket as high up as it would go as she twisted her nose at him.

"What I meant was that *you* were awesome. I don't know if you noticed, but I did next to nothing that whole time. Next time, I'm not going to stay on the sidelines just because you asked nicely. You got to have all of the fun."

Wren gave him a blank look and shook her head.

Next time . . .

Something in her chest thumped, and she staggered forward.

Nik caught her by the elbow and flashed his dazzling smile.

"I don't have the energy to argue with you. I just want to go home."

Nik's arms closed around her and lifted her from the ground, tucking one arm behind her knees. He held her close to his chest, mindful to keep his jacket closed securely around her and his arms away from the wounds on her back.

"You like being carried, don't you?"

"Beats walking."

"DO YOU NEED MORE WATER, YES?"

Kora pressed a cold rag against Wren's forehead to remove the debris that was still embedded in her skin.

"No, thank you. I'm fine, Kora." She gently brushed Kora's clawed hand away and smiled. "Really. I just want to take a shower and sleep."

The nuwa frowned and leaned toward her with the rag once more. "I'm sorry, sorry," Kora muttered, unintentionally hissing her *s*. "You mussn't sleep with rocks stuck in your face, yes."

"There are no *rocks*," came Wren's dry response.

Lionel smiled at them from where he stood in the kitchen. He leaned against the counter with his arms folded across his chest.

Nik was beside him with a bowl full of pork stew that Kora had made with their untouched lunch in his hands. His vigilant eyes had been monitoring Wren's movements and mannerisms since they'd arrived home, but the growl of his stomach was too much to resist the allure of Kora's cooking.

"I'm glad that you both returned safely." Lionel's movements were stilted and tense. Although he spoke to Nik, his attention was locked on Wren.

Nik nodded as he swallowed another mouthful. The warmth of the stew helped to soothe away the chill from the storm that had lingered. It also helped in that the stew was delicious.

"I am too," Nik admitted. His voice dropped to a whisper before he continued. "You foresaw this, didn't you?"

Lionel didn't answer right away. His fingers fidgeted at his elbows, and he glanced to his friend for a long moment. "The day that I called for you, yes. I foresaw destruction of the marketplace.

I saw Wren change . . ." Lionel stared at her from across the room with a sorrowful look etched into his face. "She was alone. She . . ." He hesitated. "I didn't like what I saw, and I had to do something if there was any chance that I could stop it from happening."

A long silence stretched between them.

They watched as Wren and Kora bickered. The nuwa was smiling, despite the fact that Wren was not. The spell, surprisingly, put up very little fuss.

Nik remained quiet. He was sure there was more Lionel wanted to add and patiently allowed his friend time to put his thoughts into words. He had stew to enjoy, anyway.

"I thought immediately of you, Nikolas. Of our promise. I asked a friend to get a message to you in the middle of the night. He was certainly not happy to see me at such an hour, but he is a man of his word. He left immediately after making his preparations for the journey." He sighed and smiled a sad smile. "She and I had a fight the night before I had my vision. Wren was so angry with me that she refused to leave her room for nearly two days."

"That sounds about right," Nik replied with a cautious levity to his voice.

Lionel huffed a soft laugh and winced. His hand drifted to his face and hovered over where his eye once was.

A white bandage had been wrapped around the top of his head and covered his eye. The wound had at least healed enough to stop bleeding.

He took a deep breath before his single cerulean eye finally turned to Nik.

"But my vision had a much different conclusion." Lionel gave him a sad smile. "I am glad that the outcome was . . . not *that*." He lowered his voice, speaking mostly to himself. "I suppose he was right after all." His attention shifted back to Wren with tight lips. "But we are now in uncharted waters."

"Well, that may be a good thing."

Lionel laughed and shook his head. "When did *you* become the optimist?"

Nik responded with a one-shoulder shrug and returned to eating his supper. He lifted his eyes suddenly and pointed his spoon at Lionel. "The alchemist said that her winning was not what *he* foresaw," he said around a mouthful of stew. "It's plausible that he did not gain your ability to foresee, but only what you had already seen."

"Interesting. I hadn't considered that."

"Wren," Kora cautioned loudly. "You need something to eat before you sleep, yes. There is still a full pot of stew."

The tone of the nuwa's voice drew Lionel and Nik's attention instantly.

"Kora, I mean it." Wren's tone wasn't much better. "Just let me go to bed."

"Not without dinner, yes! What would Miss Elliot say?"

The room fell silent.

All eyes turned to Wren, who was, in turn, staring at Kora with an unreadable expression.

Kora regretted her question the moment she spoke it and hastily tried to apologize.

"It's fine," Wren said quietly and raised her hand. "You're right." She made her way into the kitchen and poured herself a modest portion without a word.

No one missed the change in her demeanor the instant Elliot's name was uttered, and all shared a look.

Lionel rounded the table and removed the bowl from Wren's grasp. He set it on the face of the table and collected Wren's hands into his own gloved ones. He knelt down so that their eyes were practically level.

"It will be all right, Wren," Lionel murmured and caressed her hair. "We need to have faith. It would be foolish to think the worst before we know the whole story."

Once the warmth of his touch registered, she careened forward to press her face into his chest and wrapped her arms around him. She clamped her eyes shut and listened to each beat of his heart, trying to ignore the sting of tears at the corners of her eyes.

Lionel wrapped his arms around her and pressed his lips to the top of her head. When he felt her body shudder, he placed his palm on her back and rubbed small circles across it.

"It's okay, little bird," his voice hummed in her ear, for only her to hear. "My world."

Wren struggled to keep her composure.

Lionel's embrace reminded her of times they'd been like this throughout their lives together. Her hands tightened on his clothing and hugged him closer as slivers of memories flashed through her mind.

The first time she saw a Season's Festival fireworks display and cowered in Lionel's arms from the explosions. When she had broken her wrist in a fight but was angrier at herself than she was in pain, he soothed her with his warmth. When a baby bird she tried to save passed away in the night, he held her as she cried.

"I love you, Lionel," she managed in a choked whisper.

An intense warmth blossomed in his chest, and he clutched her closer.

Kora had slithered away and into the kitchen to allow them their privacy. She looked to Nik through the corner of her eye and paused.

"Lionel said you're both old friends, yes?"

Nik nodded as he took a sip of his stew. "Yep, grew up together."

"Fascinating." She turned her shoulders to face him directly. Kora's fangs poked out from her smile as she leaned in to examine him more closely.

Nik gave her an awkward smile in return and looked away.

"It makes an' old nuwa wonder how you two were as young ones, yes."

"Rambunctious."

"Disruptive."

Lionel and Nik both answered at the same time and exchanged a laugh.

Wren dislodged her arms from around Lionel's torso and turned toward her room. Since her back was to the others in the room, she was able to wipe away the stubborn tears that managed to escape. She snatched her bowl of stew from the table and advanced on her room with her eyes locked on the floor.

"I'm going to take a shower and go to bed." She twisted the handle of the door and closed it behind her without turning around.

Wren leaned against her door for a few moments, trying to will away the tears that still drained down her cheeks. She wiped her face with the inside of her arm and sniffed.

Puffy eyes glanced around her bedroom as though they were searching for something. For some*one*.

Without Elliot's presence to lighten the space, her room felt cold.

Wren found a glimmer of relief in her chest when her gaze fell upon the blankets.

Jack was sprawled across her bed like a belly-up starfish. With a tail. He blinked lazily at her as the door had tipped shut. The tip of his tail flicked to the side in recognition, but the cat remained in place as she passed by.

Wren reached her free hand out to caress Jack's head and ears as she rounded the edge of the bed.

He eyed the bowl of stew that she placed on her bedside table yet still refused to move.

Wren started the water in the bathroom and moved to undo the buttons of Nik's coat around her. Her fingers hesitated over the top one, daring herself not to look in the mirror.

The tips of her ears flushed with heat when it registered why Nik had wrapped it around her so hastily. She glanced down her chest and pulled the jacket open slightly.

Yup. Naked.

Wren tried not to revel in the way the fabric felt on her bare skin. She shook her head and rubbed at her ears with frustration. Despite her best efforts, curiosity got the better of her, and she glanced into the mirror.

The inside of his coat was lined with what felt like silk. It was such a deep shade of purple that it appeared black in the shadows yet gleamed a bright violet in the light.

The length of his coat hung on her like a tent. The broad shoulders sagged over her far-narrower ones and the sleeves were too long. Laughably too long. The hem of his jacket brushed her legs, just above her knees.

Her face went hot, and she quickly undressed and showered.

"Rise and shine, girly."

Elliot grumbled and turned over, tugging the thick blanket tighter around herself. "Go away, Garret."

He knocked on the door again, harder this time. "Evania is waiting for you, you know."

"Fine!" She flung her pillow at the closed door and sat up. Her curly hair was an untamable mop that bounced around her face with every motion. "I'm up, okay? I'll be down in ten minutes."

"Breakfast ends in five."

"Shit," Elliot muttered darkly.

"It isn't a great idea to skip breakfast on your first day of training."

She paused as she pulled on her trousers. "Training?"

Garret grumbled loudly from the other side of the hardwood door and sighed. "I'll get you breakfast. Be in the garden in ten minutes."

She knew that it would be polite to say thank you, but she didn't want to. Every fiber of her being wanted to detest him, but her better side was trying to convince her not to hold their first introduction against him.

"Thanks," Elliot said, then immediately cursed herself.

"Mm-hmm." His response was flat. "Ten minutes."

Elliot dressed in three, including the time it took to carefully stuff her mess of curls into a ponytail, being mindful to hide the dressed wound. She spared a quick glance in the mirror above the dresser, and her face dropped. The dark circles under her eyes glared against her olive skin, and she glared right back. She hurriedly shoved her feet into a pair of tall brown boots that had been brought to her last night, along with a full new wardrobe.

Elliot closed the door behind herself before she turned down the hallway and rushed toward the staircase.

The living quarters that she was provided were nearly as spacious as Lionel's entire apartment, constructed above the library. The hallways were well lit despite the fact that the light had no source. The light was warm and sweet-smelling, as though the sunlight of the early morning was inside with her.

Elliot reached the bottom of the staircase and dashed through the library.

The librarian regarded her silently with a raised eyebrow before returning to their book.

Her feet carried her as quickly as they could until they rounded the final corner to face the garden.

Evania stood in the center of a myriad of rocks placed in a careful pattern that formed rings.

They overlapped each other in chaotic formation, but each ring was purposely placed to depict a larger picture.

If seen from above, the rings looked exactly like the rings of a very, very old tree.

A short distance from Evania was a small wooden table with a tray, glass, and silverware. As Elliot grew closer, she realized that it was the breakfast Garret had promised.

Ripe and colorful fruit overflowed from a bowl atop the tray and, beside it, a plate with a generous omelet placed on top. There was also a glass filled to the brim with what looked like orange juice.

"Good morning, my dear. I hope that you slept well." Evania's breathtaking face flashed a smile, and she motioned to the tray. "Please, take a few moments to eat before we begin."

Elliot nodded once and eyed the food again before cutting into the omelet. "Before we begin what?"

"Training, of course. I cannot, in good conscience, allow such a lovely girl to have no way to defend herself once you are out of our protection."

"Protection?" Her question was muffled by a mouthful of cheese, egg, and meat.

"Yes." Evania's voice was warm as she spoke. "You see, this particular daemon clan has remained a mostly well-kept secret. The place that we are in now is enchanted, invisible to those outside the barrier of our magic, so we are able to live freely. A river flows on either side of our domain, and from your world, the two rivers appear to be nothing more than an expansive lake. We must keep ourselves a secret, as even our enchantments can be broken.

"Daemon are one of the few inhabitants of Yu'e that are born with the potential to use powerful magic. Because of this, there are always poachers that seek our utility."

Elliot watched her so attentively that Evania had to remind her to take another bite.

"There was another clan, one founded by my son, which had a stronghold in the forests south of Dendros. When the railroad was built right through his land, he was faced with two choices: move or make a stand."

Elliot gulped and stared.

Evania's voice was like honey, drawing her in deeper with each word. While her words and manner of speech were soft and understated, the powerful look within her golden eyes easily overshadowed her unforgiving sweetness.

"He chose the latter. There was a great conflict between the humans and daemon. In the end, he was forced to move."

"Why?"

"Well, a few humans fled the battleground and made it back to nearby towns. It was only a matter of time before they returned with a battalion of ruffians, now knowing where the daemon clan resided. He had yet to master the art of concealment, so they were unfortunately rather easy for the humans to find."

Elliot cleared her throat and made sure her mouth was empty. "I hope that it's not rude to ask this." She hesitated to gauge Evania's expression. When the daemon queen gave her every indication to continue, she did. "Why are daemons a target for poachers? What did you mean by *utility*?"

"Not rude at all, my dear." She placed her hand on Elliot's shoulder and smiled. Evania helped her to stand and led her by the hand to the center of the rings. "Because we are born with the potential for magic, some have an ability that grants a very peculiar power: we can make someone magical. To an extent. It is not permanent, but depending on the strength of the caster and their choice of incantation, it can last long enough to win a war."

Elliot's eyes went wide as realization washed over her.

". . . That's awful. So, people just want to capture and exploit daemon so they can gain magical powers?" She had to force herself to keep the frustration beneath the surface. "What a terrible thing . . ."

Evania released the young woman's hands but didn't move hers away. "Yes, but the other side of it is that we can enchant our allies. There are plenty of tales of brave warriors standing up for morality, against malevolence, and succeeding. Our allies exist in companies, as every role is as important as the last. Men, women, and creature alike sought out our kind, though it is up to the wisdom of The Mother whose requests would be accepted. Our contribution to tales such as those is a badge we wear with great pride."

Elliot smiled at the daemon queen.

"There was one man, a human, that I truly admired. He had the perfect balance of brutality and mercy to have the makings of a great king."

"Do you remember his name?"

"Of course." She nodded. "I will never forget Dimas. A very tall man, indeed. Probably the tallest human that I have ever seen, yet he was a gentle giant."

"Was? Is he not alive today?"

Evania shrugged and drew a deep breath in through her delicate nose.

"I've yet to hear of his passing. I pray that he is still among us." Evania's pure-white hair drifted in the gentle whisps of wind. Her glittering eyes watched Elliot intently before she smiled. "Dejan and I shared a long conversation last night and came to a decision, should you choose to accept the offer."

Elliot blinked quickly and furrowed her brow in confusion.

"With the current events unfolding as they are, it is obvious that there are integral players destined to be involved in their unfolding. We believe that you and your spell are among them, and I have been happened upon by you. I do not believe it is coincidence that our paths have crossed." Her smile broadened, and something in her golden eyes glimmered. "I will teach you magic if you would like to learn it. If you are granted acceptance."

Before Elliot could reply, Evania lifted her arm into the air, extending her palm directly above her.

The grass beneath their feet began to shimmer in gentle currents of wind, yet the breeze rose no higher than the tips of the tallest blades.

The gray stones surrounding them gradually began emanating a gentle golden light, starting from the center and emanating outward. The small portion of atmosphere around each stone was weightless and unmoving. The glow then turned quickly into a beam of golden light that formed a wall around them. Once they were surrounded, the light softened into a gentle eggshell brown that hurt less to look at.

As Elliot was trying to process Evania's magic, streams of blue and green snaked across the face of the wall. They twisted to where Evania's outstretched hand was still waiting. The two colors dripped onto her like melted wax and spiraled upward until they reached her elbow. The streams of color were a mass of free-floating particles that hovered around her hand and forearm like a halo.

Evania touched the portion of the wall before them and drew the rough outline of the continents in green.

"When the territories were first decided, the Court of Balance did their best to ensure it was divided equitably. The vast majority of realms agreed to the map and built their own communities within their respective lands.

"A few, greedier regions felt they deserved more than they received and threatened to take what they saw as their own. Conflict worsened when Clove split into two new nations hundreds of years ago. Fighting at their boarders persists unto this day, their resentment rooted so deeply that it still plagues them. Once the crack started, it didn't take very much for the rest to fall apart.

"Aster and Arnica have been in similar conflict, especially over the lands between the rivers. *King* Reed has done a poor job of trying to repair the damage left by his predecessors taking Black Rivers as their own. When the Asterians appointed a new leader, it quickly became clear that peace was in order. I am told he even agreed to release any claim *his* predecessors had on the lands between the rivers if it would result a meeting. But the coward King Reed still refuses to meet with him.

"Because of this, the two neighboring nations have been on the brink of war. It is only as of late that things have grown more serious."

Evania drew the two northern countries within her original outline of the main continent in blue.

"Trading between them has trickled down to smuggling. You see, the people of this nation do not hold the resentment that the crown is clinging to. They want to trade with their neighbors. The town of Abagail is a perfect example. It was once the most popular market in the north."

Evania's slender gray finger tapped the drawing, putting a dot over Abagail on her sketch.

"It was once a thriving town that, at the time, rivaled Market Road in terms of varieties of merchants and their available goods. I have heard that it is rather dilapidated now and rife with petty crime since trading with Asterians became outlawed."

Evania wiped the streams of color away with one swipe of her palm. Now that her canvas was clear, she drew another outline.

After a few strokes of Evania's fingers, Elliot's eyes widened as the picture became clear.

It was the same four-winged creature that Lionel had shown her.

It was *Wren*.

Evania's sketch was an identical depiction of Wren's stance when she stood before Seth. The glowing eyes against the silhouette that had been burned into her mind left her stunned. The four wings were outstretched and proudly on display, making her massive form all the more imposing.

"When the spell arose to stop Seth Tanner, everything that had been known changed in one night. All of the reputable clairvoyants and prophetic interpreters foretold of his victory in claiming the Arnican crown. The emergence of your spell . . . Her timing . . . Her *power* . . . She has changed everything."

CHAPTER TWENTY-SIX

"At the center of your being you have the answer; you know who you are and you know what you want."

Lao Tzu

THE NIGHT OF THE ATTEMPTED COUP, THE NIGHT THAT Tanner was killed, was a night all of Yu'e heard of within a matter of weeks. Rumors spread throughout the regions, always ever-so-slightly changing with each retelling." Evania spoke softly and placed one hand on Elliot's shoulder. "The rumors soon became so outrageous that they were dismissed as lore. The general public seemed to have decided on purposeful ignorance instead of admitting what could be true. That a spell lives.

"The scar that Eurynome left on Yu'e runs deeply to this day. Deeply enough that there are a few that are easily tempted to action. Those that know enough of his rampage knew better than to let news like Seth's demise go unheeded."

Elliot furrowed her brow and scrunched her nose. "I don't get it." Her quiet statement was met with another gentle smile. "If the crown never fell, and Seth was stopped, why did it matter so much that a spell had anything to do with it?"

Evania laughed once and shook her head. Her pure-white hair moved around her like the grass in the ankle-high breeze. "Reed twisted the truth of what happened. He made the spell out to be a third-party opportunist making its own attempt at his crown while Seth attacked his gates. There was never proof that he defeated her, so now he's laid root to the fear of thy neighbor. His versions of the story gave new life to the fear of spells. Thanks to Eurynome."

Elliot nodded and dropped her eyes.

Evania lifted her palm from Elliot's shoulder and traced the silhouette of Randon Reed's kingdom gates, the very same that she had seen in Lionel's vision behind Wren. And they were on fire.

"Very few witnessed the encounter, as most of the beings that were present that night were killed by the spell. Those that did survive gave very little descriptions of the event, leading to quick dismissal as a delusion. Randon's skewing of events only fanned the flames of dread. The only knowledge people have of that night are what they've heard in rumors."

Her gray fingertips drew long tendrils of fire in blue. The particles darted from her palm and onto the wall of light, moving as though the fire was alive.

"Dejan was shown something . . . Something terrible once again emerging from Arnica that will come to be soon. The war in the north may very well still be upon us, even with Seth Tanner gone." Evania's eyes locked onto Elliot. "A darkness still festers within Reed's territories, and you must be prepared. My husband's vision changed on that night. The night she rose. This newer vision holds hope, it seems. A light that he hasn't seen for a very long time." She smirked. "A wild card."

Elliot met her stare, but a creeping feeling itched at the forefront of her mind.

"Why must I be involved? I'm just one human."

Evania's expression became confused, and she tilted her head. "You love her, do you not? Her *human* side?" The daemon queen reached for Elliot's hand and laced their fingers together when Elliot nodded. "She will need your strength if she is to stop what is coming, so why not be as powerful as possible when you stand at her side?"

Elliot gripped Evania's hand as an ennobling wash of emotion swept through her.

"So, my dear. Are you ready for your initiation?"

WREN WAS WRAPPED INSIDE OF HER BLANKETS, SILVER EYES burning holes in the ceiling. She didn't need to look out of her window to know that it would still be hours until the sun rose. She groaned loudly and turned over to push her face between two pillows.

A few minutes passed before she heard a soft rap on her bedroom door.

Wren sat up and glared through the darkness but said nothing.

"Wren? May I come in?" Lionel's whisper was nearly inaudible through the thick wood.

There was a short silence, followed by a soft *thump*.

Wren pulled her door open to see Lionel standing before it with two large mugs of steaming coffee.

"I was hoping we could talk. Just us."

She nodded wordlessly and stepped aside for him to enter. A small smile pulled at the corners of her lips as she gladly took the hot drink from him and reveled in the warmth against her palms.

"What do you want to talk about?"

"What do you think?"

Wren opened her mouth with a witty retort on the tip of her tongue but refrained and instead settled with a shrug.

"Nikolas told me much of what happened in the market, but I would like to speak with you about it as well. If that's all right."

Wren shrugged again and blew across the surface of the coffee. "I don't think *I* even know what happened."

"What do you mean?"

She scratched the back of her neck and looked away from him. "When I shifted," she started with a nervousness tinting her words, "it was like I wasn't even there. It's never happened before when I've changed . . . Like something else was in control of me. I was just a conduit."

"Oh? A conduit for what?"

"This voice," Wren answered without thinking.

The expression that blossomed across Lionel's face made her wish she'd said nothing.

"You heard a voice? In your mind?"

Wren shook her head and twisted her nose. "It was in my head at first, but then, after I became . . . *that*, I felt it as though it was my own."

"Hm." Lionel took a tentative sip from his mug. "What did the voice sound like?"

"I don't know," she admitted and turned her eyes to her feet. "But it was familiar."

"Interesting." Lionel sat at the edge of her bed and patted the spot beside him.

She moved instantly, abandoning her mug of coffee directly beside the abandoned bowl of uneaten stew. Wren sat and curled against him, pressing her ear against his chest. Her eyes slipped shut as the rhythmic strum of his heartbeat lulled her own.

Lionel wrapped his free arm around her shoulders and half cradled her.

"I think I've heard it before. When I lived in the woods . . . before I met you," Wren whispered. "I can vividly remember at least one other time. I think it was calling to me, but I don't know what it was saying."

"Hm?" His chest rumbled against her ear, and she wrapped her arms around him.

"During a thunderstorm. It was in a flurry of freezing rain and flashing skies. I hated thunder and lightning." Her shoulders stiffened from the memory. "I wasn't sure if I was dead or dreaming."

Lionel let a comfortable silence filter in as Wren sifted through her thoughts. His gloved palm rubbed small circles along her back, mindful of the places Nik had warned him about. The places he'd seen before.

"I felt a presence, like a warm light. I had found shelter that night, though it was very shallow. The storm raged against the open cave entrance, and I had nothing to fend off the cold. The unbearable cold." The tips of her fingers tightened in his shirt, and Wren pressed her eyes shut. "I was soaked to the bone, about to succumb, when I felt something wrap around me. It was warm and soft, but the light that accompanied it was too bright for me to see anything. I didn't physically feel anything there. It was like it was all in my head, but it . . . wasn't. It just came out of nowhere and kept me alive that night. I was going to die, and then I didn't."

"You said there was a voice, too?"

Wren nodded. "Yeah, it called out to me. It only ever said one word, but I don't remember what it was."

"Really? Fascinating . . ."

Wren sat up slightly and met Lionel's eyeline. "The voice that saved me from the cold was the same one that I heard in the market. It was the same one that I spoke with when I had fully shifted. Without a doubt."

"Fascinating," he said again and reached for her coffee. Lionel handed it off to her with a wide smile.

She returned the gesture and took a careful sip. Her eyes flickered to the large patch of bandage on his face. A pang of guilt knotted in her side, and she quickly looked away.

"How are you feeling?"

He chuckled and dropped his palm on the crown of her head. "I am perfectly well, Wren." When she didn't meet his gaze, he kissed her forehead. "You must forgive yourself, my dear. You got us both home safely. Be proud of *that*."

Despite what he had said, her eyes burned. She struggled to blink away the building tears and buried her face.

"I'm sorry," she whispered. "I'm so sorry."

Lionel untangled the coffee mug from her fingers and placed it on the table. He turned back and embraced her with both arms tightly.

"Hush," he murmured into her hair. "Don't let something that you needn't be sorry for burden you, little bird. That will only hold you back."

They stayed like that for a while, wrapped in each other's arms.

"Lionel," Wren said softly.

"Hm?"

"I have to tell you something."

"Do you?"

Wren sat back and put her hands on his shoulders as she nibbled her lower lip. "We have to leave Arnica. All of us. You see, the king, at the ball, he . . ." Her eyes slammed shut, and she sighed. "If I don't leave, he's going to lock me inside of the kingdom with him. He threatened you and Elliot if I refused. We can't stay here any longer."

Lionel gave her a sad smile, and he nodded. "Yes." He cleared his throat and looked away. "I know that. It has been a very long time since Black Rivers felt like home to me."

Wren nodded slowly and turned her attention to the lump of fur at the foot of her bed. "Do you think Jack will go with us?"

At the sound of his name, a pure-white ear flicked once, and a groggy eye peeked at them. He lifted his head and gave a soft meow.

Lionel chuckled. "I think that was a yes."

Wren sighed. "But where do we go? Heilyn said that they were headed to Border Port in Dendros, but that was days ago. Who knows where she is now."

Lionel gave her a reassuring smile and patted her shoulder. "Well, we must keep something in mind."

She gave him a confused look in response.

"If Elliot has escaped on her own," he continued, "she will return here looking for us. Arnica is the only place she'd think to look if she managed to get away."

"What are you saying? That you're going to stay here? Lionel, the king will come after you if you stay."

He nodded. "I plan to camp out near Market Road and wait for her, hoping that's the route she will take to return."

"So, we can all stick together there."

Lionel stood and turned to face her fully. There was a sadness in the depths of his cerulean eye as he looked her over once. "We cannot remain together, Wren. What if she needs your help? You won't be able to find her if you stay in one place."

"But—" she started.

He shook his head. "You know that I'm right, Wren." Lionel caressed her cheek and tried to smile. "Please don't argue with me on this. It is already hard enough for me to fathom letting you go."

Tears burned at the corners of her eyes, and her brows knitted together.

"I don't want to leave you," Wren managed with a shaking voice.

Lionel pulled her into a tight hug and kissed the top of her head. "I don't want you to leave. But we both knew that this day was inevitable."

"Nik said that he'd travel with me days ago," she murmured against his chest. She didn't need to see his nod to know that he had truly foreseen their parting. Her arms tightened, and her eyes stung. "You really thought of everything."

"I think only of you, little bird. Everything I do." He left his words hanging when his own voice choked up. "Everything is for you."

She pressed her nose into his shoulder and felt the sobs rattle through her.

He rubbed her back and struggled to contain his own tears.

"No matter what happens," Wren whispered into his curly blond hair, "you'll always be my father."

Lionel's heart wrenched, and he pressed his forehead against her neck as he held her closer.

"And you will always be my daughter, Wren. I am so grateful that I was able to watch you grow into such a strong woman. I am so proud to have been your father, even if not by blood."

"You'll always be my father," she repeated and finally allowed herself to cry.

"Is that everything?"

Nik adjusted the rucksack slung over his shoulder and glanced between Kora, Lionel, and Wren.

Lionel had a pack of his own strapped to his back and a grumpy ball of white fur in his arms. He wore a thick coat and snow boots. A pair of lighter shoes dangled from the side of his bag that was stuffed with as many clothes as he may need and supplies to make a campsite.

Kora stood beside him with Elliot's too-large suitcase clutched in front of her and held it with both clawed hands. She was also wrapped up well in warm clothing and had another smaller bag strapped to her waist.

Wren carried two bags, one against her back and the other strung across her chest. She clutched her spear with her right hand and scowled.

"Should be," Nik replied. "If we take anything else, it'll only weigh us down."

"Oh, before I forget." Lionel shifted Jack to one arm and fished something out of his coat pocket. "Someone left this on the doorstep." He grinned and pulled Nik's crimson scarf from his jacket's folds.

Nik chuckled and accepted it with a nod.

Wren said nothing as she glanced around the living room one last time.

Remorse and hesitation petrified her in place as the memories of each room flooded into her mind. Memories of her and Lionel growing together, laughing, arguing . . .

Her chest twisted, and she shut her eyes.

"Let's go," Wren said quietly. "If we stay any longer . . ." She paused and clicked her teeth shut. She couldn't finish the thought.

"Yes," Kora agreed with a hiss and a smile. "I feel much sadness in leaving my shop as well." She slithered to Wren's side and dropped the suitcase. It landed with a soft *thud* at the same time as the nuwa's scaly red arms wrapped around her.

They shared a short hug before parting and making their way to the stairs.

Lionel and Nik followed them closely. The trace paused at the doorway, watching his company descend to the ground level. He cast one last look into the apartment and frowned.

Jack purred in his arms and pressed his cheeks against Lionel's chest.

"You're right, Jack," he said softly. "It's just a house."

The four made their way out of the building and walked together in silence until they reached the ruined statue. The group paused in a half-circle and faced each other.

Kora and Lionel stood to one side, closer to the road that would lead them through the demolished wall and Market Bridge.

Nik and Wren stood to the other side, closer to the road that would bring them to the train station.

Wren's face was muddled with a flurry of emotions as she stared at Lionel.

He smiled at her and moved to give her a hug.

Jack shifted to do the same as he was sandwiched between them. His short legs curled around her neck, and he began to purr loudly.

"We will see each other again, Wren. Don't fret." Lionel kissed the top of her head and ruffled her hair. "Trust in Nikolas and be the brave, headstrong woman that I know you to be." Reluctantly, he let go of her and smiled sadly. Lionel turned to Kora and nodded once. "Let's head out before everyone begins to wake."

The nuwa gave Nik and Wren a parting smile and followed behind him.

Wren watched Lionel's back silently. The expression on her face was unreadable and flat, but her slightly labored breathing gave her broken heart away.

It took every ounce of strength to keep himself from looking back at Wren. Lionel knew that he'd be unable to leave her if he did.

Nik's hand fell onto Wren's shoulder once Lionel and Kora turned a corner and vanished from her sight.

She remained unmoving for a few moments, staring at the corner they had taken.

"Let's go, Wren." Nik leaned closer to her so she would hear his quiet whisper. "We should get out before the town wakes up, too. The first train will be leaving soon."

"Yeah," she muttered and allowed him to lead her away from Black Rivers.

BOOK ONE END

*"Fantasy is hardly an escape from reality.
It's a way of understanding it."*

Lloyd Alexander

Bestiary

Creature | Traits

Alchemist: A human that has embrace the dark arts. They craft tinctures, potions, and spells that allow them to sidestep the laws of natural balance. A penance must always be paid to use any sort of alchemy, often in flesh.

Arion: Muscular, oversized horses in every coat and color imaginable. They are extremely intelligent and can anticipate storms far before most other creatures. The largest known arion was the size of a two-story cottage. Its age was unknown, and there is no way to tell their age - aside from asking.

Boar: Hybrids of man and beast. They can be a variation of the genetic splice, some more fortunate than others. They are grumpy and short-tempered; disagreeable by nature and make excellent salesmen when given the right motivation.

Bulltoad: Bulltoad are amphibious creatures that stand upright and do not engage with haggling. They are well-known to readily resort to violence. Attempts to reason with them logically during an argument will often resort to the same outcome as hitting one's head against a wall and expecting it to turn into a unicorn.

Daemon: As conduits of the gods, they can have an array of abilities that range anywhere from healing magic to offensive magic. They are reclusive and not known for their sense of humor, but will always welcome a friend as a brother and will never turn their back on an ally.

Dragon: Apex predators of their given environment. Flying dragons are able to breathe either fire or ice, with a few exceptions that include poisonous gas or magma, with a long body, four legs, and a set of powerful wings. Water dragons can swim at staggering speeds and grow to even more staggering sizes. Tales of sea monsters are seldom free of water dragons. Ground dragons have no wings but are as fast beneath the surface of the earth as their brethren in the sky or water by using their powerful legs to burrow.

Fae: Always seen in groups and are not known to wander far from their families. They are tricksters by nature, some more malevolent than others, and find joy in causing distress or misery onto others.

Grifter: Grifters are a subspecies of vampire that prefer seasoned meals. And, by seasoned, they will cause their prey to release high amounts of adrenaline from fear before feeding by inflicting terror or torture. Or both.

Human: While humans are seldom gifted with abilities, there are accounts of humans with magical powers. These include mage, trace, tempest, healer, and more.

Imp: Light-footed and nimble-fingered creatures that can move unnoticed by the untrained eye. They do not have a temperament intended for interpersonal interaction, unless they are in the company of others that share the same personality traits. Many consider imp to be a wingless fae.

Kappa: Amphibious, two-legged creatures with webbed fingers and a wide, salamander-like mouth. They can breathe on land as well as underwater. Many opt to live in fully-aquatic communities far from the realm of land-walking creatures.

Mage: Mage are humans born with magical abilities. Abilities will vary on the individual, but offensive magic is the most common kind. Healers are far rarer, but are just as powerful if well-disciplined.

Nuwa: Similar to bore and bulltoad, nuwa are a hybrid of human and serpent. Nuwa are three-fingered crafters that often prefer the wilderness to the company of others. Those that live outside of society can only communicate with nuwa that speak the same languages. Those that live within society have a gift for learning language and often know many different dialects.

Omen: A chimera that is a culmination of three creatures. Omen are specifically made to be creatures of nightmare and will frequently include penance from scorpions, tarantulas, bats, bears, giants, dragons, viper, and more.

Peryton: A stag beast with the physical attributes of a bird. They are seen in a variety of coat-colors and wing shapes, but only the males will have antlers and wings strong enough to fly. A female peryton has wings, but they are more akin to a male peacock's veil of feathers.

Rattenkin: Large rats with black eyes and nimble hands. Families of rattenkin can rival the numbers of heavily-populated civilizations. They are clever by nature and extremely intelligent. Many are also able to communicate with various species of creatures and, like nuwa, have a gift for picking up languages.

Reaper, Common: Common reapers are souls of any species returned to the realm of the living and seek redemption through loyal service to the gods. They do not speak, unless to other reapers or to the gods themselves. They cannot be reasoned with and, should one appear, death is a guarantee. They can teleport and move through shadows without detection and are armed with a scythe and the ability to manipulate the darkness.

Reaper, Penitent: Penitent reapers are souls returned to the realm of the living that are intended for a greater purpose than common reapers. Gods will appoint souls that have passed to specific duties that can range from protection to elimination. They have the same abilities as common reapers, but a penitent reaper will be granted a unique ability that will complement their purpose.

Spell: When not in human form, they are a four-winged, dragon-sized creature with both feathers and scales. Overall size and shades will vary depending on the individual. As adolescents, they only have power over wind; only upon maturation can they breathe fire. Only once a perfect balance between chaos and calm within the beast is found is it able to use lightning.

Tempest: Similarly to a mage, a tempest is a human that is born with the ability to control the wind and create or quell storms. It takes many years to master the ability, but once accomplished, a powerful tempest can break up tornados and create hurricanes.

Trace: Similarly to a tempest, a trace is a human that is born with the ability to read memories upon skin-to-skin contact. They are also able to "read" the memories of objects that have been infused with memories. Many are clairvoyant and, in rare cases, they can also be healers or mages.

Winged Chimera: A chimera that is a culmination of three creatures. The winged chimera that was created by Ubel was done with penance from an eagle, a serpent, and a ground dragon.

www.ingramcontent.com/pod-product-compliance
Lightning Source LLC
Chambersburg PA
CBHW070303310726
48976CB00005B/1556